Praise for *Knock Knock*

"Grens is an immensely compelling character whose sharp intuition and dedication to justice are reminiscent of Harry Bosch. This tense, sophisticated procedural can stand alone, but readers will find themselves drawn to Grens' seven earlier investigations."

—*Booklist* (starred review)

"Roslund's fourth has punchy prose and plot twists that readers expecting another brooding Scandinavian noir won't see coming." —*Kirkus Reviews*

"[A] heart-pounding thriller . . . Roslund's serpentine plot and visceral character development brings each cliffhanging chapter to a staggering revelation on how tasty a dish of cold, karmic revenge can be. From the first *Knock Knock* on the door of a murder scene to discovering the killers behind it, this novel is a breathless, suspenseful read." —*Shelf Awareness*

"Roslund cleverly interlaces two disparate storylines, and readers will marvel at just how much action can take place in a period spanning only three days. *Knock Knock* has handily reaffirmed all my Scandi-noir gushing."

—*BookPage*

KNOCK KNOCK

ANDERS ROSLUND

Translated from the Swedish by Elizabeth Clark Wessel

G. P. PUTNAM'S SONS
NEW YORK

PUTNAM
— EST. 1838 —

G. P. PUTNAM'S SONS
Publishers Since 1838
An imprint of Penguin Random House LLC
penguinrandomhouse.com

Copyright © 2019 by Anders Roslund
Translation copyright © 2021 by Elizabeth Clark Wessel
Published by agreement with Salomonsson Agency

The Library of Congress has catalogued the G. P. Putnam's Sons
hardcover edition as follows:

Names: Roslund, Anders, 1961–, author. |
Wessel, Elizabeth Clark, translator.
Title: Knock knock / Anders Roslund; translated from the Swedish by
Elizabeth Clark Wessel.
Other titles: Jamåhonleva. English
Identifiers: LCCN 2020000054 | ISBN 9780593188217 (hardback) |
ISBN 9780593188224 (ebook)
Subjects: GSAFD: Mystery fiction.
Classification: LCC PT9877.28.O77 J3613 2021 | DDC 839.73/8—dc23
LC record available at https://lccn.loc.gov/2020000054

First published in Swedish as *Jamåhonleva* by
Albert Bonniers Förlag, Stockholm.
First G. P. Putnam's Sons hardcover edition / January 2021
First G. P. Putnam's Sons premium edition / April 2022
G. P. Putnam's Sons premium edition ISBN: 9780593188231

Printed in the United States of America
1   3   5   7   9   10   8   6   4   2

KNOCK KNOCK

EARLIER

'm five years old.

Almost exactly.

I know that. Five years and a few days and a few nights.

It still feels like it just happened. I was sitting at the kitchen table with Mom on one side and Dad on the other and Eliot and Julia were across from me. And I blew out five candles all at once. They were in the middle of my cake and they were red with a little blue, too, but only at the very, very bottom, when you looked really close.

A few days and a few nights.

I clear my throat and try to smile, like I always do when I sing. It's my favorite song. *Happybirthdaytoyooou.* And if I sing it loud enough, my voice bounces off the ceiling and the walls and comes back to my open arms, where I catch it and hold on tight.

Happybirthdaytoyooou. Happybirthdaytoyooou.

When I sing, I don't hear the TV. A kid's show. I've been watching it almost all day. Just like yesterday. And the yesterday before that. I didn't get to do that before. But I do now.

I stop singing, stand up; it's hard to stay on the floor when my legs want to move, which they do a lot. I hop out of our living room, which is so big. I have to be careful here, the sofa is almost brand new, and the table is made of glass. If I touch it, my fingers leave smudges.

I jump all the way to Eliot's room, where he's sitting at his desk chair with his desk lamp on. He's pretending to read with a book open in front of him. But he *can* read, I know it, he's in second grade now. Eliot's gotten nicer the last few days. Probably because I turned five. I'm not four anymore, I'm big now. He doesn't even push me away from his racetrack anymore, the one he keeps high up on a shelf so I can't reach it. And he even let me win twice with the blue car that has a yellow line on its roof. He never did that before.

I always jump on one leg. Just one leg at a time. And if I use two, I go back and do it all over again. I came up with that myself.

Julia has a dollhouse in her room. It's really old. And I'm not allowed to touch it. If I do, Julia runs straight into my room and grabs my dollhouse and shakes it hard. But my big sister is asleep. She's on her tummy and her face is turned away. Julia can't see that I moved the tiny furniture, which is supposed to be on the top floor, down to the bottom floor.

In here I can't hop. Then she'll see me. I have to sneak. If Julia wakes up, if she sees me by the dollhouse she'll scream, and maybe even jerk on my arm.

Mom is sitting on a chair in the kitchen, laughing a little. You can't hear it, but she's smiling while she watches my five-year-old hopping feet. She's been happy for a while now, and it's so nice when Mom laughs, it doesn't matter if it dribbles onto the floor a little when you drink orange juice straight out of the carton, or if you drop a little sugar and flour on the kitchen table because you're baking. I grab onto the edge of the table and pull myself up into Mom's lap. It's always so easy to talk to her. I like to put my ear to her tummy and listen to how her voice sounds deep down inside before it comes out.

After I sit on Mom's lap I like to hop on one leg out to the creaky wicker chair in the hallway, to Dad. He likes to sit there, he reads a lot of newspapers, and it's a little quieter out there with the jackets and the umbrellas. I listen. Yes, it is, it is quieter. And the chair is so big, almost like an armchair. I'm able to squeeze in next to him. I think he likes when I sit there. Then he can still use his arms to flip the pages of his big, rustling newspapers.

Eliot and Julia and Mama and Papa. I think I like them even more than before. I can talk as much as I want. And they listen.

It's fun to turn five.

And then keep celebrating it for a few more days and nights.

I sing it again. *Happybirthdaytoyooou. Happybirthdaytoyooou.* I sing it loud, really loud, trying to sing over the knocking on the door. Then more knocking, harder this time. Finally I stop singing, and hop down from Dad's chair, and run super fast. I stand on my tippy-toes and jump as high as I can. I'm just able to grab on and turn the tiny bar.

Mom taught me how. I am always supposed to lock the door behind me. The shiny bar should be turned to look like a mouth and not a nose.

And that's the one I'm trying to turn right now.

A beautiful door.

Dark, heavy wood, early twentieth century. It somehow belongs with the muted, hollow sound of his knocking that fills the rounded stairwell, echoing off the slightly too steep steps, the high and elegant ceiling, and the flowery wallpaper that grows more lushly realistic on every floor. Ewert Grens, standing in front of an apartment in central Stockholm, knocks again even harder.

"Somebody's in there. I hear them all day long. I hear it through my living room floor, in my hall, even in the bathroom. You wouldn't believe how thin the walls are in this building."

A voice, pinched and irritated, comes from behind him. Grens doesn't turn around, doesn't answer, just rings the bell for a fourth time.

"Someone's singing—probably one of the kids, I'm fairly certain they have three. And I think it might be a TV, too, very loud. It's been on for at least a couple of days. And not during the day—all night, too. I was the one who called, I live in the apartment upstairs."

The detective superintendent finally glances behind

him. A man, just over forty, arms crossed, the kind of guy he dislikes immediately without really knowing why. The type who puts their ear to the door and listens.

"Happy birthday."

"What?"

"That's the song the child sings. *Happy birthday to you*. Over and over."

The neighbor called in about the strange sounds. And called again when strange sounds turned to strange smells.

"I'm going to have to ask you to return to your own apartment now."

"But I'm the one who . . ."

"Yes—and you did the right thing. But now I need you to go back upstairs so I can take care of this."

Grens waits until he's completely alone before knocking a third time, impatiently, urgently, as if the muted and the hollow are calling out decisively. When no one opens the door, he bends down to peek through the mail slot, but before he gets there, someone on the other side tries to turn the lock. They don't manage, but they try again. He can hear a quiet thump on a hardwood floor.

"Police."

Thump, thump, like someone jumping.

"Police. Open the door."

A lock that is slowly being turned. A handle that seems to move on its own.

Ewert Grens doesn't like using a weapon. But still he grabs the gun from his shoulder holster and takes a step back.

Her hair is quite long. Blond. He doesn't know anything about children, but if he had to guess—she's four, maybe five years old.

"Hello."

She's wearing a red dress. Big stains on its chest and stomach. She smiles, her face is also stained, maybe from food.

"Hello. Are your mom or dad at home?"

She nods.

"Good. Can you go get them?"

"No."

"No?"

"They can't walk."

So strange.

How the stench, sharp, intrusive, a stench he's so familiar with, which met him faintly as soon as he entered the beautiful stairwell and assaulted him anew the moment the child with stains on her dress and her face opened the door—how that stench doesn't really become part of his consciousness until he takes a few steps into the hall and is standing in front of a man slumped over in a chair between a coat and a shoe rack.

"This is my dad."

A large hole sits on the right side of his forehead. Shot at close range from the front, probably a handgun and a soft-point bullet, half lead, half titanium.

"I told you."

The other bullet hole is slightly smaller, shot from an angle, just below the left temple.

"See they can't walk."

Ewert Grens doesn't have time to stop her from

jumping into her father's lap, arranging his stiff, unwilling hands so that they're not in her way, squeezing in between his right thigh and the chair's armrest.

"Come here."

"I'm going to talk to Daddy."

"Come to me."

Grens has never held a child of that age, and they're heavier than he imagined. He grabs hold of her shoulders, then lifts her gently.

"Are there more?"

"More?"

"Is it just you and Daddy?"

"Everybody's here."

Her mother is sitting in a chair in the kitchen. She seems to have her eyes shut, lips frozen in a smile. Two bullet holes, just like the father—forehead and temple. There's sugar and flour on the table, her clothes, and the floor. It doesn't want to let go of the soles of his shoes as he walks across it. Mostly Grens stares at the cake, which sits untouched on the large kitchen table, five extinguished candles, green marzipan.

"It's mine. My birthday cake."

"It looks delicious."

"I blew the candles out myself."

The two siblings are exactly where the girl says they've been for a long time. In their rooms, the sister lying on the bed, bullet hole in the back of her head, the brother at his desk, shot straight from above, bullet hole on the crown of his head.

That terrible sound. A TV, at maximum volume, a kid's show. Ewert Grens turns it off.

The quiet living room feels emptier.

Too much space for a stench more intense than any he's experienced before.

He sits down on the black leather sofa, as glossy as it is long, puts the girl in one of the armchairs. He looks at her for a long time. She doesn't seem scared, just hums quietly to herself.

"You have a pretty voice."

"Happybirthdaytoyou."

"Very nice. You just had your birthday?"

"Yes."

"Five? Like the candles on the cake?"

"And a few days."

"A few days?"

"And a few nights."

Ewert Grens looks around, struggling to keep breathing, slow and steady.

A few days and a few nights.

That's how long this little girl has lived with the stench.

NOW

PART

1

He's never liked summer.

Something that chafed at his skin, something he'd fought year after year until finally he stopped fighting it at all. That's the way it is. The heat. The quiet city. People walking around in shorts, laughing too loud.

Detective Superintendent Ewert Grens lay on the brown corduroy sofa, its stripes long since worn away, his head cradled on the low armrest, his back sunk into cushions that had been far too soft for a long time. While that gentle music, his Siw Malmkvist who sang sixties songs just for him, flowed out of an ancient speaker crammed into his bookshelf between overflowing binders and thick investigation reports. Both of his windows stood wide open, but despite the early hour it was already a stiflingly warm twenty-seven degrees inside and out. He'd stopped fighting when he realized he was not alone. He wasn't the only one who was changed by June, July, and August. But they didn't fight the season—they fought people. That terrible heat crept into them, hunted them, played havoc with their boundaries, and it wasn't just in prison corridors that the number of riots increased as the heat became more oppressive; also outside those walls reality shrank as heat pushed down from above. And when heart rates increase, so does violence, so does murder. He'd been a detective for most of his life, and it had been a long time since he could take a break when the sidewalks lacked any snow.

A stubborn knocking at his office door.

They could keep on if they wanted to.

His neck was stiff and tender, his leg aching like usual. The oldest detective on this dusty corridor, second oldest on the entire force. And there it was, less than six months away, that giant black hole that scared him even more than his bed at home, an abyss a man falls into headlong and then never stops falling. The one thing he didn't want to think about, and the only thing he could think about.

That goddamn knocking. They weren't giving up.

More than forty years. My god. He'd been so young when he first set foot in this building, already convinced he belonged here. So young he could never imagine the end arriving. Not because you want it, but because a society you never wanted to be a part of has decided the ending for you.

"Ewert?"

Now it wasn't enough to just knock. Now someone was shouting through the keyhole.

"I know you're in there, Ewert. I'm coming in. No matter what you say."

He was still lying on the worn corduroy sofa when the door opened. She glanced at him, then strode purposefully over to the cassette player and its off button. Siw fell silent. The songs of a much simpler time.

Mariana Hermansson.

Perhaps the only person in the Kronoberg Police Station whom he couldn't bend to his will, who always challenged him, and who had no clue how proud she made her boss when she did.

"Breaking and entering, Ewert."

Her office was at the far end of this hall. She'd started as a temp one summer, and he made sure she got hired full-time despite the bureaucracy and the many applicants who seemed more qualified on paper. And he'd come to treasure her like the daughter he never had, how she'd put a steady hand on his arm when she spoke to him, how she demanded answers to questions he didn't even want to hear, how she laughed at him, made him feel unsure of himself in the only context where he ever felt sure.

"I want you to take a look at it. Now."

He sat up on the edge of the sofa, stretching a little, and pointed to his desk and its mountains of paperwork.

"I don't work break-ins. Too many people dying in this town. And that, as you very well know, takes all of my time."

She wouldn't give up, he knew that.

"Dala Street 74."

"Yes?"

"Third floor."

"And?"

"Apartment 1301."

She held out an envelope to him, and he stared at it but didn't reach for it.

"Is your office this stuffy, too, Hermansson? The AC doesn't seem to be working."

She settled down next to him on the sofa; it was so worn out that they both sank to the floor.

"A break-in, Ewert. But nothing was taken. So I put it aside. Since I, too, don't have *time*."

She nodded at his paperwork. He knew what her desk looked like. The piles even higher. And just as many on her floor.

"I did what I always do, glanced at it, then put it back on top of the pile. Then I did a quick search in RAR to see if any other crimes were reported at nearby addresses in the last few years."

Ewert Grens stretched a second time, but with no yawn. He wasn't completely aware of it, but ever since she'd stormed in here, turned off his music, and started speaking to him in that demanding way she had, he'd been smiling.

RAR. The localized crime report for a specific address or area. He was the one who'd taught her to start there.

"And?"

"Nothing unusual. Just some burglaries. More domestic abuse than those expensive addresses might like us to think. Drug busts. And a few manslaughters."

She leaned forward, the envelope in her hand, poked it into his chest until he took it.

"But nothing I could connect to the break-in. Nothing that would explain why a person breaks into an inner-city apartment in the middle of the day, walks around inside—and chooses to leave without taking anything with them."

"May I open the door to my office again, Officer Hermansson? Would that be okay with you? Maybe someone else has a window open and we can get a little draft flowing in here. It's already twenty-seven degrees. And it's supposed to hit thirty-two!"

"I was about to log out of the system. Put the case aside again, deprioritize down to one of this county's fifty-six thousand open cases. And in a few months, I'd recommend Wilson close it."

Ewert Grens was fanning himself with the envelope now, his eyes closed, trying to herd some air onto his damp forehead—she ripped it out of his hand and pulled out a document, put it down on the rickety coffee table, and pointed impatiently to the first three lines.

"Then I saw this. An annotation at the very bottom of the file. A red flag warning that there's an older case filed away in the restricted archive, available only in paper form. A seventeen-year-old investigation at the same address, same floor, and according to the apartment number, even the same apartment. The kind of investigation you do—when people die in this city."

He was listening now. But still didn't know what she was talking about.

"The note. The red flag."

> *In the case of any report regarding Dala Street 74, regardless of the classification of the crime, please contact Detective Inspector Ewert Grens immediately.*

"You wrote that, Ewert. Signed it."

The document lay on the table between them, her fingers still tapping on the lines she wanted him to look at.

Until he finally did.

"Seventeen years ago?"

"Yes."

"Murder?"

"Yes. Or . . . rather, four murders. A mother. A father. A daughter. A son."

Strange.

How memory works. How it's not there at all until it is, until it comes back and hits you at full force, pushing everything else aside, demanding space.

All the space.

Because he did remember.

Ewert Grens leaned out through the open window into the inner courtyard of the Kronoberg Police Station, where his colleagues sat on park benches, some in the sun with their noses and cheeks red, others lying in the shade of some small tree, drinking coffee from brown plastic mugs.

That suffocating anxiety.

Maybe it was the heat squeezing his body, making him restless. Maybe it was the sweat dripping down his tired back.

Maybe it was a little girl hopping on one foot with food on her face, her little feet kicking up the most horrific stench at the most horrific crime scene he'd ever seen—the rooms that enclosed her dead family.

Ewert Grens liked walking slowly through the streets of Stockholm, always had, all the way back when Anni was at his side, squeezing his hand. Right now the erratic morning traffic honked and jostled forward beside him as he sped down the steep slope of Kronoberg Park, saw his reflection in the water from Sankt Eriks Bridge, exchanged Odenplan's mumbling for the silence of Dala Street.

Sixty-four and a half. Six months to go. Then someone would take his place in his office, make themselves at home there, open his door when someone knocked on it. Just as he'd taken the office from someone nobody remembered anymore. You exist for a time. Then you don't. The police pension is one of the best, they say, and some of his fellow officers planned to walk out that unwieldy iron door the moment they turned sixty-one and never look back again.

To let go of everything.

Become nothing at all.

He'd decided one day that the fears that plagued him were ugly and meaningless, decided he'd had enough of it. He'd wasted enough of his life bent under the weight of what had already happened. And yet despite all that, lately he'd had a hard time sleeping, even on his corduroy sofa, whose overly soft cushions usually made him feel like he was being held, and therefore allowed him to rest.

Because now here it was again. Fear. Because this was all he had. He didn't want anything else, didn't know anything else, didn't even know anyone outside those walls—had never wanted to, never longed for another life.

A few minutes more down the sidewalks of Vasastan where the buildings stood side by side, tightly packed and heavy, their large windows watching him. Until he came to the door marked 74, which he'd left so many years ago, but still remembered.

That round stairwell, the uneven stairs, the elegant ceiling, the continually flowering wallpaper.

And on the third floor, the same heavy front door awaited him. But this time with scratches around the lock, completely fresh, wood chips still hanging loose and not yet darkened.

He paused there, eyes closed, breathing carefully—trying to catch those small thuds in his chest near his heart, the uneven and uneasy rhythm that reminded him of a five-year-old's feet.

"Hello?"

A woman, blond, almost as tall as himself, somewhere between forty and fifty.

"Ewert Grens, detective superintendent at the City Police. I'm here about your break-in."

Her eyes didn't leave his—vigilant, almost hostile.

"Your people already talked to me about this."

"That's correct. But I . . ."

"A woman, a little younger, she sounded younger, asked me questions, which I answered. I don't understand—I've had a burglary before, not here but at my summerhouse, and the police didn't do a damn thing even though the whole place was emptied out, and I called you many times. And now . . . you contact me twice when not a thing has been taken?"

"Detective Mariana Hermansson spoke to you on the phone. But I wanted to take a look for myself."

Those eyes, watching him.

"Well, in that case, I'd like to see your badge."

The inner pocket of his jacket, black leather case.

ID card, metal badge. And just to be sure, he gave her his business card, with his title and telephone number and an email address he barely knew himself.

"It says you're a detective superintendent?"

"Yes."

"Now I'm even more confused. A detective superintendent? Following up on a break-in . . ."

She shrugged her shoulders, stepped back, waved him inside with one of her tan arms.

". . . that wasn't even a burglary, just some damage, and all my belongings, though scattered about, were all still here?"

That memory again.

Demanding space, pushing everything away.

In the hallway an antique chest of drawers and large mirror with a gold frame were replaced in his mind by a chair and a man with a newspaper in his lap and two bullet holes in his head.

The living room with its pine dining table turned into a TV playing cartoons at full blast. And the empty, gleaming kitchen became one that was sticky with food, where a little girl climbed into her dead mother's lap.

Ewert Grens looked at the woman who'd hesitantly let him in, trying to concentrate on her mouth when she answered his questions—lips that turned into red candles on a birthday cake still sitting on a kitchen table, untouched. She told him what he already knew, what Hermansson had written down in her report. Someone broke in on a weekday sometime between eight thirty and eleven. Exterior door with clear scratches made with a hard metal tool, and the contents of the wardrobes and cabinets and drawers thrown onto the floor. But the jewelry box, a wallet with a good amount of cash in it, new computers, and expensive art hanging on the walls all remained untouched—even the thin layer of dust on the frames showed no fingerprints.

Everything was left intact.

Except for a small patch on the floor. She led him into one of the children's bedrooms. Or what had once been one of the children's rooms, long ago.

"We use it as a guest room. When we moved in, it was clear it had belonged to a young person. That was . . . well, sixteen and a half years ago. We'd planned to use it as a child's room someday, too. But . . . well."

Grens sought the woman's eyes and saw a flash of

grief for a child that never was. He knew how that felt, and sometimes he grieved for it, too. Things don't always turn out like you plan.

"And right here, Detective. This is the only place . . . there behind that chair, do you see? They pried up the floor a little bit."

He remembered how a bed used to stand right there, flush with the wall that had a window in it; the older daughter had been lying with her face turned in that direction. Now it was a sofa bed with blue and white stripes, and he was struck by a sudden and overwhelming desire to just lie down there and finish the sleep that had been interrupted.

"You can see for yourself."

The woman pushed away the sofa and a small side table and threw up a corner of the rug.

Ewert Grens's leg ached as he kneeled down on the wood floor. Hurt even more when he lay his heavy body down to get a closer look.

A pried-up plank, split at three places, sharp splinters.

Underneath sat a four-sided hole, almost a perfect square, cut into the concrete that formed someone else's roof.

He measured it with his fingers, guessing four by four centimeters.

A void with no contents.

Something had been lying here. For seventeen years. Something that was gone now.

That damned heat.

Ewert Grens exited a beautiful building out of a beautiful door, trying his best to make room for his ungainly body in the dense and slippery air. Twenty-seven degrees had just risen to twenty-eight and had its eye on twenty-nine. He took off his jacket, unbuttoned his shirt, and kept his stride short.

He'd walked this way last time, too, carrying a child in his arms.

Grens remembered and swallowed hard. It felt like that empty hole—four centimeters by four, missed by him and all of the crime scene technicians—was in his throat, pressing down on his stomach, a cavity, an empty box, a container that no longer contained what had been there for so long.

The weather had been cooler then. Late autumn. He'd been wearing a different gray jacket, and she, after just a few steps, leaned her head against his shoulder, closed her eyes, and let days and nights of waiting for the dead to answer dissolve into sleep. A young police officer who'd been called to the crime scene followed him—this limping man with a child in his arms—in a patrol car, pulled up close, rolled down the side window, and asked Grens to stop, open the door to the back seat, and get in. Grens had mumbled something and kept walking. Oden Street, Sankt Eriks Street, Fleming Street. The child's head rested heavier on his shoulder, her eyes still closed. So trusting, he'd thought, the kind of trust he could never feel, maybe that's how it felt.

Today he took the same path, walking toward the entrance to the Kronoberg Police Station, where a security guard in the glass cage nodded to the detective who always stayed late, long past when evening had turned to night, and the glow of most of the computer screens had been extinguished. The detective who usually slept in his office under a thin blanket on a brown corduroy sofa rather than going to the apartment where loneliness lived. Grens grabbed a cup of black coffee from the machine in the hall, squeezed in between the new copier and an old-fashioned fax. Then just seven steps to his office. He started the music just like always, his own mix tape. Siw Malmkvist began to sing for him again: "Everybody's Somebody's Fool." He sat down at his desk, twisting and turning his leg and upper body and still not finding a comfortable position, lay down on the sofa and kept spinning round and round.

Maybe it was the heat chafing at him again.

Maybe it was an empty box four centimeters long and four centimeters wide.

He rose quickly and left his office.

The dust was even more visible than usual in the hallway, and he pressed out another plastic mug of coffee, black, headed for the elevator and passed by her office, the woman who demanded answers, who saw straight through him.

"Ewert?"

He didn't stop.

"I don't have time right now."

Mariana hurried into the hall, shouting after him while he pushed the elevator button.

"Neither do I."

She walked closer.

"But I want to know."

"You will. Later. Both you and Sven."

"A burglary? And nothing was stolen? And yet I can see on your face that . . ."

"Mariana Hermansson?"

"Yes?"

"Later."

He turned around, the elevator had just arrived.

"Four murders, Ewert?"

She wasn't giving up. The door opened, and he stepped in.

"And now the same apartment? Same investigator? And after he visits the scene he seems visibly . . . yes, visibly, there's no better word—upset?"

They stared at each other.

"Ewert? Talk to me."

He stood in the elevator and she stood outside.

"I thought I'd only made one mistake. But clearly I made another."

"Mistake?"

"I let the man who killed them go—I've always been

convinced of that. But turns out I also missed a hole in the floor."

"Now you've lost me completely."

"And I don't like it, Hermansson—I don't like loose ends."

"What are you saying?"

"That right now this only concerns me."

Three floors down. Cooler. Darker. Just as dusty. Grens stepped out of the elevator and headed toward a gray door that was wider than all the others. The archive. Shelves and boxes and folders. And inside of them somewhere were his four decades among the criminals of Stockholm, investigations of perpetrators and victims, who transform each other's lives forever. There was one shelf he used to avoid—turned his eyes away when he passed by it, made sure to look anywhere but there. An investigation concerning the woman who had been his whole world and who disappeared into herself after her head was crushed under the wheels of the police van he'd been driving. Nowadays he did look, sometimes even stopped there. Just as he dared to visit her grave now, the white cross with her name engraved on it; he even grabbed a watering can hanging from a nearby rusty faucet and watered a tall flowering bush he'd planted because he liked the name—love's ear. She lay in that grave just as she lay in those brown archival boxes. *Anni Grens* written on a label on the cardboard. He ran his fingers gently over the black ink, wrote her name in the air. Then he kept going, deeper into the archives, past other shelves and other Annis.

All the way to the back and the glass wall that stood there.

He waited in front of a small hatch, which was raised just a centimeter by a man of his own age, staring at him through small round glasses.

"I need to see a record from the witness protection program."

It was a file that only a few had the authority to see, which he had to apply for, get a receipt, and be registered in order to handle. The records were kept in a room with all the other sensitive documents stored on behalf of SÄPO, Interpol, and the witness protection program.

"Ewert Grens? It's been a while."

The archivist didn't seem particularly happy to see him. They didn't like each other. Never had.

"The witness protection registry, like I said. An old investigation that was never closed. I'd like to check it out."

Grens fished a used envelope out of a trash can, grabbed the pen hanging from the counter on a string, jotted down the archive number on the back, and pushed it in through the gap.

"Hmm."

"Is there a problem?"

"Your handwriting. Not exactly easy to read."

"It says . . ."

"I can see what it says, Grens."

The archivist typed something on his keyboard and peered at his computer screen.

"Yes . . ."

A few more clicks.

". . . it seems to be here."

"Good. Well then . . ."

"But I'll need your ID. You know the rules."

Grens knew. Same thing every time.

Usually around this time Grens would start to raise his voice, his neck and face would flush an angry red, a vein would start to pulsate near his temple. But not today. Ewert Grens took a deep breath and pushed his ID up to the glass for the eyes of the archivist who'd known him for thirty-five years. And it seemed as if the man on the other side of the glass lingered a moment too long—disappointed by this break in routine and this lack of conflict. Then he readjusted his glasses and with an electric beep he opened a secure door and disappeared into the windowless room behind him, then returned quickly with a blue and a green folder that he pushed through the gap.

"You know the rules, Grens."

"I know the rules."

"Then you know . . ."

"I know that, just like the last time I checked out classified documents—I can only take them if I promise to copy everything and send it straight to the tabloids."

He started to leave.

"I won't disappoint you, I promise."

Hallway, elevator, hallway.

And with every step that he took the blue and the

green folders in his hands grew heavier, almost like a tiny head resting against his shoulder.

The coffee machine. A third cup. Then his office and a Siw Malmkvist song and the folders on his desk.

He stared at them for a long time, first from the vantage of his open window, then the closet, then his corduroy sofa, and finally from the door of his office.

There they lay.

Returning his stare.

He took a step closer.

Put a trembling hand on the top folder. He'd never wanted to return to those tiny hopping feet and that stench unlike any other.

He opened it and met the first page.

A blue folder. Fairly thick. The archive number written in pencil. Rubber-stamped in the top right corner in faded black:

WITNESS PROTECTION PROGRAM

Ewert Grens leaned back on his sagging sofa, took a swig from his plastic coffee mug, then grabbed four stapled stacks of paper.

REPORT:

Seven pages from the Stockholm Police Commission.

INVESTIGATION PROTOCOLS:

Four pages from the Tech Squad.

AUTOPSY FINDINGS:

Twenty-two pages from Solna Forensic Medicine.

PRELIMINARY INVESTIGATION:

Fifty-four pages of his own investigation.

He looked around the room. She'd slept right here. On the very sofa where he was sitting now.

Back then the corduroy was in much better shape, stripes still basically intact, and the little girl slept with his balled-up jacket as a pillow. Deep sleep. Snoring even. Probably for the first time in days.

On Monday, October 23, at 16:51, Det. Grens proceeded to Dala Street 74.

He'd sat beside her, trying to make out what she was saying in her sleep. Several times he almost patted her cheek, but always stopped himself, and readjusted the raincoat draped over her. He knew what he had to do, what he'd learned to do when he trained at FLETC, a U.S. military base in southern Georgia. He and Erik Wilson went there to learn everything there was to know about the FBI witness protection program. Basically it was the opposite of how the Swedish police operated, their clumsy attempts at hiding former gang members from Stockholm's concrete suburbs in isolated and deserted summer camps deep in the Swedish forests. Two days. That's how long these potential witnesses usually lasted. Out there they had nothing to do with their time besides panic. The darkness and silence combined with their fear of death at the hands of their former gang broke them down.

The sign on the apartment door indicated that it belongs to the Lilaj family. The apartment, which consists of five rooms and a kitchen, was searched. The lights were turned on in every room.

The American Witness Protection Program. Grens had copied it. Even before the crime scene investigation was completed, he moved the girl from his office to a safe house that was actually worthy of the name.

The man was found in the hall, in a sitting position in a chair located between the hat and shoe racks. The woman was in a chair in the kitchen, near the kitchen table. The older sister was found lying on her side on a bed in bedroom A. The brother was sitting in a desk chair in bedroom B.

A girl who couldn't yet understand that her family was gone and would never come back, and she wasn't even allowed to bring a single personal item from her former life, the life that had been her entire universe. Nothing. He decided she was going to keep living.

Survive.

So her past would never become her future.

Mirza Lilaj, Diellza Lilaj, Eliot Lilaj, and Julia Lilaj were taken to Söder Hospital. Resuscitation attempts yielded no results. Declared dead at 18:23.

The child in his arms again, he headed out to go shopping in the neighborhood he lived in but never had visited. Children's clothing stores. Toy shops. The homicide department suddenly approved the expenses though they had neither been budgeted nor given formal cost centers. New dresses. New shoes. New hairband. And it made her so happy. Especially the two new dolls and the red baby carriage. As if they were presents.

The victims were placed in cold storage awaiting transport to Forensic Medicine in Solna.

Leave nothing that can be traced back.

The very last thing he pulled out of the suitcase, which a young police officer had thoughtfully packed in her apartment, was a photograph, taken in a studio.

A light blue background.

A mother and a father and their three children smiling at the camera.

Mirza Lilaj, Diellza Lilaj, Eliot Lilaj, and Julia Lilaj have been assigned storage numbers 2003-369380, 2003-369381, 2003-369382, 2003-369383. Only those numbers exist for identification.

A bunker. That's probably the best description of the basement in Östermalm. During the years he'd been in charge of the witness protection program, they'd allowed him to build the very first American-style safe house. It ended up being the only one, when the funds were re-directed to other, trendier activities. A bunker furnished like a small hotel with kitchenette, beds, TV, and well-stocked bookshelves. He'd never imagined its first guest would be someone too young to have learned to ride a bike, a child with no family.

A SUMMARY OF OUR FINDINGS:

A. The bodies of Mirza Lilaj, Diellza Lilaj, Eliot Lilaj, and Julia Lilaj, shortly before death occurred, received gunshot wounds on the head that correspond to entrance 1, entrance 2, entrance 3, entrance 4, entrance 5, entrance 6, entrance 7, entrance 8 on our diagram.

That's why his carefully designed program didn't at first work out as he'd planned. He'd imagined a place for adult witnesses where they would be hidden and guarded until giving testimony at a trial, after which they'd be escorted to a new town and given a new name, new social security number, new background.

B. These entrance wounds most likely occurred two days before the examination date.

He'd also developed procedures with the help of various bureaucratic agencies to produce new school transcripts and new work references and set up a cash allowance to be paid every fourteen days—never leave a trail, every transaction is seen by someone and information can be bought anytime, anywhere. These routines had to be urgently adjusted to create new birth records, issue certificates for swimming lessons, and credibly document attendance at a preschool.

C. The combined number of wounds strongly
   indicates homicide.

Ewert Grens closed the blue folder and pushed it to the side. Information that belonged to one living girl. He grabbed the next folder, a green one—which contained what happened to her afterward. After the crime. After ballistic wound paths and cold storage.

After their deaths.

He stood up, held the folder tightly while he paced back and forth across his office.

A five-year-old who was alive. Who survived. Because someone let her? Or because someone hid her? Or because she hid on her own? Did she curl up somewhere and listen as the only people she trusted were executed one by one, holding her breath without even knowing why. She must have understood that discovery meant death?

He'd asked her, but she had no capacity to tell him how or why.

And now, so many years later, he knew even less.

Grens looked out onto Kronoberg's courtyard as he often did. The sun had moved—some of the sidewalk and a few park benches now lay in the shadows—but the heat lingered. He popped his head out through the wide-open window, leaning forward with his elbows against the frame. Thirty degrees. No air-conditioning. He didn't look forward to trying to sleep tonight with a low of twenty-two degrees, a so-called tropical night.

The green folder, her life, what happened afterward.

He held it. It wasn't very thick, it wouldn't be.

Registry extract with her new name. Her new social security number. Her new personal history. Photo documentation of her adjusted appearance. Her new town, address, contact person, guardians. Her new life.

Ewert Grens left the window, where no cool could be found, and returned to his corduroy sofa. On the front of the green folder there it stood in black, with a black rectangle around it.

WITNESS PROTECTION PROGRAM

He opened it. And then froze.

A blank piece of paper.

And then another.

And another.

An entire stack of blank paper.

A folder from the most restricted archive in the police station that was as thick as it was supposed to be.

But whatever was once inside was gone. Replaced. By nothing.

Her new life.

Someone had taken it.

Blank.

Just like parts of his memory.

Ewert Grens remembered the stench, the weight of her body, what she looked like as she slept in a newly purchased bed in the safe house—a beautiful little flower with tangled hair. But he couldn't recall her name.

His memories now were as blank as her memories were then.

> "Who else came?"
> "Came where?"
> "To your birthday party."

He had interrogated her cautiously. Trying to get a little closer to the truth every day. She never mentioned the assault, the shooting, the murder. She didn't even understand that her family was gone. She'd repressed it all. She'd handled extreme trauma by pretending her way forward.

"It was your birthday. You turned five. And you had a very nice cake. So who sang for you?"

"Mom. Dad. Julia. And Eliot."

"And after that?"

"No one."

"I think somebody else came."

"No."

"One or two or three people who weren't invited?"

"No one else."

"But if you . . ."

"The dolly. With shiny red jacket and white shoes. Give it to me, Ewert. You can take the one with the blue boots. Let's go sit by the dollhouse. You can have the upstairs this time, and I'll take the downstairs."

She turned off. Closed down. Her calendar had started over. When she disappeared from his world a month later, she hugged him and whispered that now she was thirty-two days and five years old. As if those five years were something completely different.

Grens also remembered his fury.

One of the few cases he'd been forced to abandon, even though he was sure he'd found the murderer.

A piece of shit he'd picked up and thrown into a prison cell at Kronoberg. He kept him there for seventy-two hours, as long as he could legally. And that guilty piece of shit alternated between laughing scornfully or lying or staring down at the floor or hissing no comment during his interrogation, while Grens and his colleagues turned over every investigatory stone they could find. In the end, they lost the race against the ticking clock. A guilty fucking piece of shit, feared by everyone, who called himself King Zoltan. When his three days were up he laughed even harder at their lack of witnesses and technical evidence. The moment he was released he headed straight for the airport, took a flight out of the country, and never came back again.

The little girl, whose name Grens forgot, had seen the killer. He was sure of it. A witness in shock who one day just might understand what she had witnessed. The forensic technicians had found traces of hair and urine in one of the wardrobes at the apartment—traces that matched her DNA. That's where she hid. Pissing herself. And from that angle, with the wardrobe door open just a crack, she would have had a good overview of at least two of the murders.

Ewert Grens went over to the window.

He leaned out.

And screamed in fury.

He knew what this meant.

Someone had taken those documents out of the guarded archive, read through the first folder of the preliminary investigation, and realized that there was a witness, then read the second folder and found out what happened to the little girl after she left the safe house and Grens. Someone knew what she looked like, what her new name was, which new town she ended up in, what new family she was placed with. Someone had taken the documents and replaced them with blank paper so nobody else would ever know. And now they could complete their murder of an entire family and erase all of their tracks.

Grens screamed again, straight into the heat of the courtyard.

The life of that now-grown girl was in danger.

In fact she might already be dead.

PART

2

t was the perfect location. A cul-de-sac in a southern suburb of Stockholm, lined by sleepy three-story apartment buildings whose tenants had average incomes, average life expectancies, average educations, a good mix of young and old, those born in Sweden and those who arrived later. This afternoon Piet Hoffmann was walking counter-clockwise in a two-hundred-meter radius, which constituted the outer rim of their defenses. He checked the eighteen surveillance cameras along that route, which were placed in stairwells and garages, on lampposts and rooftops—each one activated by motion sensors. He checked the license plate numbers on vehicles he'd never seen before to see if their owners lived in the area or if they had any police records. He compared yesterday's mental map—which no one else had access to, his memorized map of formal roads and informal escape routes, who was moving where and why—with how things looked today. Nothing seemed suspicious, no warning of any oncoming threat. On his way into the front door of the only high-rise, he stopped by the camera labeled number 14, turning it slightly to the left to bring a dead angle back to life. His base was just an elevator ride up to the eighth floor, a studio apartment with a kitchenette, but it was enough.

"I'm headed out for the day. Everything okay?"

He stood in the tiny hallway, looking at a security officer surrounded by a sea of screens, glancing back and forth from one live stream to another, sometimes rewinding one to make sure nothing was out of the ordinary.

"Everything's good, boss."

Piet Hoffmann went over to the window and lifted the blinds a little, made one last inspection of the cul-de-sac. First he checked the apartment on the second floor, white curtains and a bulky table lamp sitting between two potted plants on the windowsill. The temporary home of a woman in her forties who needed a level-two safe house, who had been given a new social security number, which is the only name he had for her. If he pushed the blinds up just a little more he saw the third-floor apartment with red curtains and exuberant decorative lights. Refuge for a man in his thirties, level three, shot once, and his life threatened by his own brothers. And two doors down—now he pushed the blinds up completely—behind white curtains that were just a little too lacy, an older couple who had been hiding out for the last few months as witnesses in a trial against an incredibly violent gang of loosely associated teenagers. They were all here waiting for new identities and a more permanent housing solution, and he was paid sixteen thousand kronor each and every day he offered them his professional protection. Of course experienced security guards, advanced technical equipment, and weapons weren't cheap, but by choosing to place them together so that just one guard was able to keep watch over them all, and by renting and equipping their homes himself, he'd figured out a very profitable business structure for Hoffmann Security Inc.

"Hello, my darling wife."

He wasn't far from home, but as soon as he stepped out of the elevator and headed toward his car, almost without thinking about it, he'd called her.

"Hello, my beloved husband."

Things were going so well. Maybe better than ever. He didn't even remember it feeling like this when they were newly in love. Back in Sweden, back to something like the life they'd once had. With one big exception— he no longer lied to Zofia, no longer infiltrated organized crime on behalf of the Swedish police, didn't risk his life or his family's every day, every hour for the sake of others. He was even working with his old security firm—but now it was no longer just a facade for his infiltration. Now it was a real company, and he used the skills he'd acquired in his old life to make a good and honest living.

"Zofia?"

"Yes?"

"I'm . . . a little worried."

"You don't need to be."

"I know—but I just can't stop. It's gnawing at me. What if she . . ."

"Piet? Listen to me. She. Is. Completely. Healthy."

He used to find worrying futile, counterproductive.

He'd survived by planning more meticulously, by doing his homework better, by being more prepared than whomever he was observing, chasing, fighting. And then—Zofia had her six-month postnatal checkup. That was all it took for irrationally intense worry for his child to take over.

"She's supposed to be able to turn from back to stomach and stomach to back. Be able to get up into a sitting position by either holding me or the doctor. She's supposed to babble, find a lost toy, pass an object back and forth between her hands. And Piet—*she can.*"

A little sister. At any moment his mind could return him to his place beside the hospital bed, holding Zofia's hand while contractions racked her body.

Normal life, Piet. You promised never to infiltrate another criminal organization, no more death, no chaos, no running.

He remembered so well exactly how she looked when she said it.

My body had decided. One more child. After trying for so long, and believing it would never happen again. My age, that's what I thought . . . but it wasn't that. Calm. Never having to live like that again. I relaxed, Piet. Another child, I don't know, it sounds almost corny, but it feels like this baby is . . . a symbol of all that. Of your promise. Of our new life.

"You never worried like this about Hugo and Rasmus."

"I know, Zofia."

"And she's much more advanced and tougher than they were."

"I know that as well."

The crushing anxiety that the doctor might discover something else. Something they hadn't seen. And it wasn't because she was the first girl or the baby of the family. It was him. Realizing that nothing can be taken for granted. Everything is finite. It would have been much easier to keep living with the lies, living with them until he could no longer remember where lies end and truth begins. Until he no longer knew who he was.

"Piet—we'll see you tonight."

"Give her a kiss from me."

"She's sending one right back."

A ten-minute drive. That was it. Then he was in Enskede with its suburban houses with yards and two cars in the garage. Their home. This was where they'd moved when Zofia was pregnant the first time.

It was hot in the car even with the windows rolled down. Unusual in this country, high temps, high humidity, and only the first week of June. No use wiping your forehead with your sleeve because it was already wet. He parked in front of the rusty gate and lingered for a moment. This was the best part of his day.

If he stretched up a bit, he could see Hugo on the other side of the straggly hedge, playing football with the neighbor's kids, grassy knees and flushed cheeks. And through the kitchen window he could just make out the outlines of a curly head, Rasmus playing with his action figures at the kitchen table.

Piet Hoffmann took a deep breath of the warm and humid air.

Of course he had his doubts now and then.

He'd slammed the door to another life.

Sometimes he wanted to open it up again.

Feel. How he used to feel. Adrenaline rushing through him, impossible to turn it off, his heart pounding with aggression.

Now and then the past sought him out and tempted him with its rewards. Sometimes after the boys went to bed, he'd sit on the sofa with Zofia and admit just how much he longed for one more round. Just once more. Not for the cash. For the adrenaline, the high. To feel a little more, live a little more. An intermediary, that's what they wanted when his past came looking for him. A guarantor for two parties. Most recently, brokering a deal between an amphetamine manufacturer in southern Slovenia and a major criminal network in central Sweden. His sole task would have been to vouch for both sides, be there during the agreement, and act as a bodyguard during the first trip. It was difficult to make Zofia understand how frustrating it was to see these jobs go to small-time dealers who weren't nearly as good as he was, see them rake in the easy money for simple jobs.

But every time he got home, like now, right before he had to look Hugo and Rasmus in the eye, he knew for certain that he'd made the right choice.

And Luiza. Her eyes were just as steady and intense.

Luiza, who would soon have to prove that she could both babble and find a toy.

Besides, he knew if they ever caught him breaking the law again, they'd throw the book at him. He'd have to watch his sons and his daughter grow up from be-hind bars.

No missions, no weapons, no deaths.

Only this.

A house, a home, a family.

This was his life now.

"Hello?"

Piet Hoffmann shouted as he opened the front door. A few years ago, Rasmus would have come running with arms open wide. Now his youngest son was so immersed in his game that he didn't even answer.

"Rasmus buddy? Hello? I'm home."

"In the kitchen, Dad."

The hall mirror seemed to stare at him. He had to turn away. And there it was. Wedged in between the wooden frame and the mirrored glass. A note with no words on it, just a big red heart in the middle. It moved him still, after all these years. Zofia liked to leave small notes for him here and there, sometimes on his pillow when he pulled back the covers, or in his suitcase when he was unpacking in a hotel room somewhere, alone again. Or in the fridge when he picked up a tub of butter. At one time those unassuming messages of love had felt like a demand, and he'd wanted to escape them. Now he longed for those little notes. Felt disappointed when they weren't around.

He liked them so damn much. He liked *her* so damn much.

Rasmus was sitting at the far end of the short side of the kitchen, that was always his spot no matter where in the world they lived, no matter what house Dad dragged them to. The eight-year-old looked up as the sound of steps made their way from the hall to the kitchen, but he didn't stop playing with his action figures, especially the one with a very round stomach and a red hat and blue legs and yellow arms.

"Hi, buddy."

"Hi, Dad."

"What are you up to?"

"Playing."

"I see that—but *what* are you playing?"

"With my new action figure."

"Yeah, and . . ."

"Dad—you don't get it."

Hoffmann looked at the plastic figure with a red hat and blue legs as it jumped away from all the others lying on the kitchen table, watched it do somersaults and mumble something. He realized his son was right. He didn't get it at all.

"Mr. Potato Head."

"Huh?"

"That's another action figure I have, Dad. Up in my room. This isn't one of those—but it's like a Mr. Potato Head. I've never had one of these before. Cool, right?"

"Very cool."

The flour was in one of the cupboards on the wall, the salt on the kitchen counter, eggs, milk, and butter in the fridge. Pancakes. The safest bet.

"You hungry, Rasmus?"

"If you make them in the waffle iron. I want checkered pancakes."

The waffle iron. Checkered pancakes. That started last year. Hoffmann still didn't understand why, or where it came from, but if that's what he needed to do to keep them fed, then that's how the pancakes would be made. He found the iron in one of the bottom cupboards and opened the window, shouted loudly.

"Hugo?"

The dull sound of a foot kicking a ball on the other side of the hedge and then a ten-year-old celebrating when it landed in a homemade goal.

"Yeah, Dad?"

"Are you hungry? Pancakes?"

"Checkered?"

"Yes."

"Then I'm hungry."

Piet Hoffmann was just about to shut the window when he changed his mind, leaned out, and shouted again.

"What about the rest of you? Are you hungry, too?"

The two other players in the improvised football match wanted checkered pancakes, too, so Hoffmann made enough batter for five people.

"Can you set the table, Rasmus?"

"Mmm."

His youngest wasn't listening. The new plastic figure jumped around the kitchen table in his hand. Always some new character from some new cartoon. Over the two years that Piet Hoffmann spent working in West Africa, he took trips home every three months, and every time he did he made sure to bring the most popular action figure home with him.

"Okay, Rasmus. Then I'll set the table. If you clear your stuff."

"Just a minute."

"Now, buddy."

"Just gotta go to the bathroom first. Then I'll pick up."

Rasmus started out walking, but it turned into a run, that's how it was with him: if he left his games and visited this world, he did so in a hurry. Hoffmann smiled. There was something so vulnerable, almost beautiful about being able to leave this reality so completely in the hands of someone else. He took five plates and drinking glasses out of the cupboard, got tired of waiting for Rasmus to come back, and started to move the toys off the table to a bench near the stove. But when he got to the new toy, the one who looked like Mr. Potato Head, who in Rasmus's imaginary world jumped so high, Piet Hoffmann felt a stab in his chest. One he hadn't felt in a long time. A stab in the region of his heart, which meant trouble was on the way.

The plastic figure lay in his hand.

And he felt its weight.

It wasn't all plastic.

He lifted it a few times, weighing it in the air, guessing it was around three hectograms.

Then he inspected it more carefully.

He took off its little red hat. He pulled off the blue legs and yellow arms.

It couldn't be. And yet—it was.

He felt furious, terrified.

This wasn't the way he wanted to get that adrenaline rush back.

He was holding a hand grenade.

Built with a core of TNT and steel balls so as to end all life in its vicinity.

His youngest son had been playing with death dressed up like a toy, here, at their kitchen table.

e was furious.

He was terrified.

Fury.

Terror.

His son, who trusted him with his safety, who trusted him with his whole world, had sat there playing with death.

A hand grenade. Transformed into a toy.

Piet Hoffmann held it in his hand. Let his thumb slide over the hard surface, over the rise on the top. A small oblong ball with a metal casing, with explosives pressed inside, and a spark plug connected to a striking pin, which, the moment it was pulled, would run down toward a fuse and everyone who happened to be in its vicinity would have five, or four, or sometimes only three seconds to live.

Fury. Terror.

Two sides of the same emotion.

It used to be so much easier.

Back then when he chose rage and anger, any fear that pushed its way inside could be used, transformed into more aggression. Psychologists at his school and then at his juvenile correction institute and finally in prison all called it *a lack of impulse control.* They said that's why he preferred violence. But that wasn't true at all. Violence was just a good tool. If you used it correctly. And so he did—he mastered the violence that came so naturally. Until finally Zofia and his kids were forced to pay for it. Until love and truth and trust made life so much more complicated and opened the doors to fear.

The fear that he might lose the people who meant more to him than himself.

He heard Rasmus flush the toilet, heard him washing his hands.

Piet Hoffmann weighed the hand grenade again, almost unconsciously, bobbing it up and down in his open palm. He'd come across more than his share of these in recent years, received offers for them from his black market contacts; the market in grenades had grown in recent years. He had eyes and ears out there—paid for quality information, because it was his greatest asset in the security industry, and quickly went out of date. It was crucial to keep informed about the life he no longer led, though sometimes wanted to.

The bathroom sink whined when you turned it on full blast, which Rasmus always did even though he wasn't supposed to. The water rushed out like a howling rain, and that's why it was so noticeable when he turned it off.

The kind of grenade Hoffmann held would have been smuggled over the border in a box of ten. It was intended for use in combat, but it was also an obvious

choice for a Swedish gang intent on arming itself to the
teeth. Ideal for an army of boys with little money, no
weapons training, whose goal was to seem dangerous
without having to pay for the consequences. Unlike
guns, hand grenades demand no prior knowledge, cost
a measly five hundred kronor, and the fourteen-year-
olds whose job it was to throw them didn't have to be
there when they exploded. They'd drive up to a window
their gang leader pointed out, throw the hand grenade
against the glass as hard as they could, and drive off on
their moped, hearing it explode in the distance. Never
having to see what they've done, never having the sight
of arms and legs torn apart in their mind.

There was a click as Rasmus closed the bathroom
door. The patter of small feet on a short walk back to the
kitchen. Back to what Rasmus thought was just a toy.

"Dad . . . what . . ."

"Come here, Rasmus. Sit next to me."

". . . what did you do! Dad! You ruined my new toy!"

Piet Hoffmann pulled out the kitchen chair closest
to himself.

"Rasmus, sweetheart, please do as I say."

Rasmus did not. He ran over to the table. Everything had been scattered about.

The new toy's hat. Its arms. Its legs.

And Rasmus started to cry.

Big wet tears rolled down his cheeks, as they sometimes do.

"Mine . . . *it's mine*! I don't understand, Dad. Why
did you . . ."

Hoffmann had never hit one of his children, had

promised himself he never would. So his children never tried to hit him. But now Rasmus did.

With eight-year-old fists.

Straight to his father's chest.

Piet Hoffmann waited for the next blow and grabbed him by the arm, pulled him close, and forced his son against the chest he'd just hit. Holding him in his arms, hard but not too hard, until finally the little boy relaxed.

"I'm sorry."

"It doesn't matter."

"No. I'm sorry, Dad. But I don't get it . . . I don't understand. Why did you do it? Why did you ruin . . ."

Then he cried again. A new kind of tears. These were neither angry nor disappointed. Just sad.

"I'm sorry, Rasmus, but you can't play with that ever again."

"But I want to. And it's mine."

"From now on it's not. It's mine. I'll be taking care of it. But first you have to help me, Rasmus. You have to tell me exactly how you got it. Where it came from. Who gave it to you."

Rasmus pushed away from Piet's chest a little. So he could look straight into his father's eyes.

"You're angry."

"No, I'm not angry."

"I can see it. And hear it. You have that voice, Dad. Even though I didn't do anything."

Fear.

That's what his son heard.

And confused it with the rage.

"Maybe I'm . . . a little angry. But not at you. I'm angry with someone else."

"Who?"

"That's what you're gonna help me figure out."

Rasmus pushed away a little more, now he was loose. And Hoffmann let him go.

"Okay. I'll help you. But you're wrong, Dad."

"Wrong?"

"The toy was *mine*. My name was on the envelope."

"Rasmus—what are you talking about? What envelope?"

"The one in the mailbox."

"Which mailbox?"

"Our mailbox. Out front."

Piet Hoffmann's son went to the kitchen window and pointed toward the gate and driveway and a black mailbox with white, spindly letters on it. Painted by Hugo on the day he learned to write the family's last names.

KOSLOW HOFFMA
NN

"I always check it first thing when I get home. And it's always just stuff for you and Mom. Always, always, always. But today it wasn't. Because that's where I found it. My new action figure. With my name on it. To Rasmus and Hugo. That's what it said. And Hugo hardly even plays with them anymore. So it *is* mine. It *was* to me."

"Was it . . ."

Now Piet Hoffmann also went over to the window, both stared at the mailbox.

". . . in an envelope?"

"Yes."

"How?"

"What do you mean how?"

"Rasmus, you're supposed to help me. *How* was it laying there?"

"I told you. In the mailbox. In an envelope. Like when you get something in the mail. Don't you know anything, Dad?"

Piet Hoffmann stroked his son's cheek, chin, grabbed his little head with both hands, and held gently as one holds the dearest thing in the world.

"I'm gonna go out to the mailbox. Take a look for myself. Tell me once more, Rasmus, exactly what it looked like when you came home and opened the mailbox. Before you took out what you thought was for you."

"I didn't just think that. It *was* for me."

"Rasmus?"

Rasmus sighed. A little too loudly and dramatic. The way he thought you were supposed to sigh when something obvious had to be explained. Hoffmann loved that sigh. His youngest son had already started to recover.

"It looked just like it always does. Letters. Junk mail, I guess."

"And?"

"I was looking through it. Everything else was for you. Or Mom. And then I saw it, kind of over to the side. An open envelope. It was brown. And . . ."

"Open, Rasmus?"

"As if someone peeked into it. Or didn't close it up very well? I saw the action figure right away. But I read the envelope first. My name and Hugo's name. That's all. So I was *allowed* to take it out."

"Was there anything else? Next to it?"

"Aren't you listening to me, Dad? You get lots of stuff, like letters, catalogs, all the time, and I want that, too, someday when I get my own mailbox, and . . ."

"That's not what I meant. Was there anything else *in the envelope*?"

"Other than my action figure?"

"Yes."

Rasmus fell silent, thinking hard, staring at the mailbox and trying to remember something he didn't know he was going to have to remember. He was really trying. While Hoffmann fought everything tearing him up inside, trying not to show his son how fucking scared or angry or whatever else it felt like all at the same time.

"I don't know."

"A note? A letter? A message? Next to the toy?"

"Don't know."

"Are you sure, Rasmus?"

"I just took the action figure. That's what I wanted. Okay?"

Piet Hoffmann carried the hand grenade with him as he walked the garden path of square flagstones toward the rusty gate and black mailbox with white text. Away from his little boy. Even though he didn't need to. He knew that now. He'd examined it more closely and realized it lacked its explosive heart. The person who'd transformed this into a toy and put it into their mailbox did so to scare them. The fuse and pin had been unscrewed and the explosives removed. Without them it wasn't a hand grenade. Just a little pile of pressed TNT.

Scare them. That was its purpose.

Remove the heart before delivering—he'd done that himself in another life. A warning to someone who was supposed to pay, or who better not testify, or who better consider getting out of the drug business.

Hoffmann squeezed the oval metal ball in his hand.

A warning.

Why?

The gate creaked like usual, then just a few long strides to the fence. The mailbox hung there. In the very place he'd nailed it to with the help of a then four-year-old Hugo, who had proudly sounded out their last name over and over again to anyone who might listen.

He should maybe secure the area.

But scaring someone by sending them a warning has a purpose. It's supposed to make the recipient start to think, weighing the message, becoming willing to do whatever's needed.

He lifted the top of the mailbox and peered inside.

It looked just as Rasmus had described. Four letters. A free newspaper. A bunch of junk mail.

And at the very back an open brown envelope.

Hoffmann took out the flyers, the paper, the four letters from the city, the tax agency, their electricity bill, and something from Ikea. Then it was only the brown

envelope. He'd grabbed his winter gloves from the hall
shelf on the way out, and he pulled them on now. A bit
too thick, clumsy, but just in case he wanted to dust for
prints later.

```
To Rasmus and Hugo
```

That's what it said on the envelope. Just as Rasmus
told him.

No stamp or postage, and nothing on the back.

He widened the gap with his gloved fingers.

There was something inside. A piece of white paper.
Typed in the same style as on the outside of the envelope.

He fished it out, carefully, and read the sentence,
which contained only five short words.

```
We know who you are.
```

He'd slept a bit between two and three o'clock. Slept some more around half past four. A long night. The kind he thought he was done with. Tense. Completely prepared. His humanity reduced to instinct. Wait, watch, protect. While making sure that the people he was protecting neither noticed nor understood.

After finding the grenade on the kitchen table and the typed note in the mailbox, Piet Hoffmann had used the rest of the afternoon and evening to inspect the house, the garden, and its immediate surroundings. But he didn't find anything else out of the ordinary. Meanwhile he'd gotten in touch with every contact he had left from a life spent in the criminal underworld, questioning the ones who always knew, those that made the threats and those who received them, but still he'd gotten no closer to an answer. He'd held Zofia like he always did when she came home, played with Luiza, who'd passed all the tests at her six-month checkup, quizzed Hugo on his English test, and listened to Rasmus practice the first part of a play that he was in. And then he lay down next to both his boys and read to them until they fell asleep. Not a word about his fury or his fear. Zofia, of course, had noticed what she wasn't supposed to, and asked him what was wrong, but he avoided answering her. Later when it was just the two of them on the sofa, a glass of wine in hand, she'd looked at him as only she could, and he'd hidden behind the excuse that he and Rasmus had an argument about a toy, and that's probably what she noticed, and they were both sorry, as always after that kind of conflict. He'd promised never to lie to her again, but he met her eyes anyway, and she's seen through him, he was sure of it.

"I don't want to, Dad."

Hugo was only ten, but he already seemed like a teenager. Big, small. Clear, unclear. Sure, unsure. Right now he was lying in bed with his blanket over his head, and he didn't want to get up.

"Hugo, you have to."

"No I don't. I stay home by myself all the time. We have a half-day off today. That means I get to sleep in as long as I want."

"Not today. You and Rasmus are coming to work with me, and then I'll drive you to school after lunch."

"Why?"

"I can't explain. But that's just the way it is."

"Does Mom know?"

"Mom already left. With Luiza. Headed to some parenting group—they won't be back until tonight. And today you can't stay home alone. Ten minutes. Then I better see you dressed and downstairs next to Rasmus."

He pulled the blanket down until he caught a

glimpse of Hugo's forehead. He kissed it, then headed down two flights to the basement.

He wanted to scream it.

No.

Mom doesn't know.

Because I won't force her to have to deal with my past ever again.

Zofia was on maternity leave right now but usually spent her weekdays at the same school as the boys teaching Spanish, French, and—when it was needed—Polish. Zofia, who had wedged a new note with a big red heart into the doorframe of his workroom, just a little bit of love that slowly drifted to the floor as he opened and stepped in. He picked it up, kissed it as he kissed Hugo's forehead, and put it in the chest pocket of his shirt. Close to his own heart.

The workroom consisted of a desk, a chair, and a small closet in one corner—which is where he headed now. It was there among the winter coats and dress shirts he never used that he stretched up to a shelf with some storage boxes. And when he reached a little to the right behind one of the drawers, he felt it. A lever. He pressed down and a faint hiss was audible as the back of the closet slid away to reveal another room. A hidden room. Daylight seeped in from a small crack near the ceiling, illuminating a space big enough for a weapon cabinet, a safe, a clothing rack with bulletproof vests hanging on it, and a row of filing cabinets.

A secret room left over from his days as an infiltrator and a liar. Which he should get rid of to prove it was truly over.

He'd hidden the hand grenade on the lower shelf of his weapon cabinet next to his Polish Radom gun. He closed his hand around it, just like Rasmus. A weapon designed to spread death. He opened one of the brief-cases and slid it into an inner pocket. It wasn't going to stay in this house.

Back to the ground floor and the hall. And only one son. Rasmus. Dressed, just like he should be.

"Where's Hugo?"

"Don't know."

"Wait here."

"I'm tired of waiting. The keys, Dad. I'll go wait in the car."

"You stay where you are! Do you understand? You don't go anywhere alone!"

Hoffmann regretted it immediately when he saw the fear in his son's eyes. He shouldn't have raised his voice, let his own worry affect someone else. He kissed Ras-mus's forehead and hurried upstairs.

"Hugo? Come down now."

"Not until you tell me why."

"I don't need to explain."

"Yes. Because it doesn't feel right. And every time it doesn't feel right, it's because of you, not us."

Two little boys who lived on the run for so long. A life they never asked for—the consequences of their fa-ther's life. They handled it so differently. Rasmus, so secure in himself, had just accepted their living condi-tions in another part of the world, and just as quickly adjusted when they came back here. But Hugo needed routines and transparency in order to handle his thoughts, and he never really got used to South America. And then when they returned to Sweden and the house he grew up in, it took him a long time to start trusting the fact that they were there to stay.

"That's not what's happening now, Hugo. This isn't about me."

"Then what's it about? Why can't we stay home like we usually do?"

Piet Hoffmann understood. This was a boy who'd been forced to have a bodyguard because his father told him to, a boy who'd listened to his parents talking about the threat of life in prison when they didn't know he was there, a boy who knew very well that an infiltrator risked his life every day, so it wasn't strange that this boy would sense when something was off and draw his own conclusions.

Not strange that such a boy would be afraid. Just like his father was.

"It's . . . a surprise."

"What kind of surprise?"

"Something for Mom. Which I have to take care of. And Hugo—you can't say anything to her."

Lying to his children was easier. As long as he didn't meet their eyes.

"What exactly, Dad?"

"If you don't know, you're less likely to give it away. Like Rasmus did. Do you remember?"

Silence.

The lie was being judged.

Then he heard the floor next to his son's bed creak. Then Hugo's shuffling feet. His reluctant steps coming down the stairs.

"This is so *boring*."

Hugo managed to look deeply annoyed as he laced up his old sneakers, which he refused to replace, irritated as he put on his backpack and headed out the front door.

"So we just have to sit there while you work. And wait."

Hoffmann remembered back when his boys were curious about their parents' jobs—those magical places they disappeared to while their children were at preschool. Back then a visit to his office meant vanilla ice cream, two big glasses of Coke, and a few episodes of *Winnie the Pooh* in front of the TV. He put his arm around Hugo's thin shoulders, pulled him close, hugged him in the way Hugo would never allow when they were outside.

"Yep. Sometimes, my dear son, you just have to wait. It's a bummer."

On their way to his office in central Stockholm, he tried to liven things up by reintroducing a car game they liked when they were little—counting out loud in Polish, his parents' mother tongue.

"*Jeden, dwa . . .*"

"Jeden, dwa . . ."

A single voice echoed behind him. Hoffmann turned to his eldest son.

"You too, Hugo."

"I don't want to."

"You're gonna make Rasmus do all the counting by himself?"

No answer. Until Rasmus saved them both.

"Don't pay attention to him, Dad. You and me are counting, right? This time I start. And just one at a time. *Trzy.*"

"Trzy."

"*Cztery.*"

"Cztery."

"*Pięć.*"

By the time they parked on Vasa Street, they'd made it to *sto trzydzieści sześć,* one hundred and thirty-six— Rasmus first, then Hoffmann, punctuated by Hugo's sighs—and just a few floors up there stood an apartment with a mail slot labeled *Hoffmann Security Inc.*

He unlocked the security door, then the steel gate, and pressed four digits on a control panel to turn off the alarm. A security firm. That's how the Polish mafia he'd infiltrated on behalf of the Swedish police had worked. A facade for the rest of the world. Hoffmann Security Inc. for many years had been a branch of its parent company, Wojtek Security International. While its owner, Piet Hoffmann, over the span of years worked his way into the upper echelons of power, gaining their trust, and then exposing them, destroying the entire organization from the inside.

"How long do we have to stay here?"

"You know how long, Hugo."

"I thought you might have changed your mind?"

"My big little man—go sit with Rasmus at the conference table. Turn on the TV. Read something. Surf the internet. Play a game. I have *not* changed my mind."

During his years on the run, Erik Wilson, Hoffmann's handler in the Swedish police, paid the rent on this empty apartment every month. Piet Hoffmann hadn't even been sure why he felt it was so important to keep. Using his hidden money to keep the house in Enskede, the heart of his family's life, was an obvious choice—but this expensive office space in the center of the city, whose only function had been to infiltrate the Polish mafia? He understood it later, after they returned to Sweden and after he got out of prison. Through all those years, this had become one of the places where he felt safe—though everything about its history should have meant the opposite, insecurity. But it was a reference point in the chaos. A place to begin finding his way home.

He walked through the rooms—high ceilings, white walls. Windows overlooking Norra Bantorget and Kungs Bridge. An open fireplace like the one Zofia had wanted at home, and which they'd finally recently built. His personal office was next to the kitchen, and a heavy antique desk stood in its middle, two weapons cases along the wall, identical to the one he had at home. This was where he ran the other leg of his business from, his *legal* business, a man who never imagined he could live a life outside the criminal world. The safe houses took up half of the time—and selling and mounting security cameras, installing alarms and bulletproof windows and doors the other half. And now and then, if Zofia approved, he'd do some extra time as a bodyguard, which paid well.

"I'm thirsty."

Rasmus shouted from the conference room.

"Dad! Thirsty."

"Do you see the mini-fridge in the corner?"

"Yeah?"

"Look inside and you'll find something to your liking on the top shelf. It's orange. Starts with an F and ends with A. You can have one each."

When they came inside he'd stepped over a pile of mail on the floor of the hallway, but with his boys settled in now and busy with other things, he returned to the front door and picked it up. He sorted out all the catalogs and the trade magazines for the Security branch, tucked the seven remaining letters under his arm, and carried them to his desk.

"I can't find it."

Rasmus again.

Desperation in his voice.

"Dad? They're not here!"

"I'm coming, Rasmus."

Piet Hoffmann hurried to the conference room, as a soda crisis is a serious thing. He passed by his two boys, sitting at the conference table like the most serious board members imaginable. Hugo, no longer sighing, was deeply engrossed in a game on his iPad, and Rasmus was in front of the TV watching a cartoon, which was paused. Hoffmann opened the mini-fridge and like Rasmus he saw—nothing. At the corner of his eye, his youngest son threw his hands up in a wordless gesture of *I told you so, Dad*, and then Piet continued to the kitchen. There were cans of soda in that refrigerator, and he grabbed two, put them in front of his satisfied boys, then returned to his desk and the pile of letters.

Seven pieces of mail—he flipped through them, searching for information about a shipment of Kevlar vests that should have arrived from a UK retailer awhile ago. The kind of vests his well-to-do clients preferred, and which you couldn't buy in Sweden, even though they were far superior to what the Swedish cops were running around in.

It lay in the middle of the pile.

And it wasn't what he was looking for.

But it was what he'd feared was coming since yesterday, in one way or another.

A padded package, the kind you can buy at the post office. Same font, same typewriter as yesterday. No stamp, no return address.

```
To Piet Koslow Hoffmann
```

You found me here, too. In this place that was once my protective facade.

Who are you? What do you want?

A quick glance at the conference room. There were his beloved boys, each one lost in his own world, so far away from what they didn't need to know.

He felt the padding, pushed his thumbs against its rough surface. Thick. Glued shut, unlike the other one. Only paper inside. Much more paper than in the last one.

There was a penknife in his desk drawer, and he used it to slit open the package that marked the beginning of the most awful, the most overwhelming, and the absolutely shittiest days of his family's life, despite having some pretty tough competition.

He knew immediately what it was and what it meant.

Documents that no one should have access to. Papers more dangerous than firearms.

What Piet Hoffmann held in his hand were copies of logbooks and intelligence reports and code names from the Swedish police's unofficial infiltration program. Documentation that existed in only one copy, locked in a safe in the most secure archive in the Kronoberg Police Station.

It was impossible.

But there it was, lying on his desk.

Tightly written pages from a secret black binder. Details of meetings held in temporarily abandoned apartments in properties undergoing renovation that could be accessed from two different addresses. In the first column, the infiltrator's code name. Then date and time. Then a summary of the information exchanged between the infiltrator and his or her handler. He didn't have to read much to see that these pages, the ones he was staring at, were from his handler Erik Wilson, and they were about him, Piet Hoffmann. About his ten years as a secret employee.

Because there was his code name.

Paula.

That's the only name the police—his employers—knew him by. It was how he remained anonymous while exposing the innermost workings of violent organized crime. In that safe, together with the logbook, there stood a white envelope, which stored the infiltrator's real name, written on a single piece of paper—sealed by their handler on the first day of a mission with a red lacquer seal. In that pile of documents sitting on his desk, there was also a copy of that piece of paper. The answer to who Paula was.

Even that.

Piet Hoffmann breathed in, out, like always when he was seeking calm.

If the wrong person read this. If the wrong person had access to the infiltrator's true identity and previous missions, it meant an immediate death sentence. If any criminal network or mafia organization becomes aware of an infiltrator, a snitch, there's no public trial, only ruthless action.

Death.

It was as simple as that.

"What are you doing, Dad?"

Hoffmann jerked. He hadn't noticed Rasmus sneaking in behind him, and now leaning over the desk and this dangerous pile of papers.

"What are *you* doing, Rasmus? In here? Shouldn't you be watching your show?"

"The episode's over. And I'm out of soda."

Hoffmann stood up, carefully pushing his youngest son in front of him across the wooden floor of his office.

"That's not good. Because I have more work to do."

"But I can help you."

"Unfortunately, Rasmus, this is something I have to do on my own. But what do you say about . . . another soda? And another episode?"

"*Another* soda? Does Mom know?"

"If you want one, it'll be our secret."

A new drink, a new episode.

He ruffled Rasmus's hair, brushed Hugo's cheek, left them to their fictional worlds for one that hardly seemed real.

Someone had gotten inside a safe that nobody had access to.

Someone had opened a sealed envelope and copied the information inside, and knew who he was.

Someone had taken the secret logbook of disclosures he made during his time as an infiltrator and made a copy of it.

Piet Hoffmann breathed in, breathed out, in, out.

And was just about to put the whole stack back into the padded envelope when he noticed one more sheet all the way at the back, different from the others This wasn't a copy. No secrets from the past. Just a white piece of paper with two lines typed in its center. A message that contained a few more words this time.

```
We can kill your children at any
time.

We can expose you at any time.
```

He'd stationed himself on a wooden bench at the top of a small hill that rose shyly above the neighborhood, a hill that must have been forgotten when the rest of the area was flattened out to make parking lots or build the concrete foundations of apartment complexes. From here, he had a perfect view over the schoolyard and the windows of Rasmus's and Hugo's classrooms.

Around lunchtime Piet Hoffmann had driven his boys to their elementary school south of the city, where he'd gone many times for parent-teacher conferences over the years, and where Rasmus and Hugo were finishing up their second- and fourth-grade years. It had all gone by so fast. They were so big now. He and Zofia must have grown up quite a bit as well.

He'd dropped them off in front of the school, tried to hug them but had no luck in the chaos of every student arriving simultaneously, and watched them run toward their friends without looking back once. But he didn't leave them. Nor was he leaving Zofia and Luiza unguarded. He'd placed a discreet call to Juan and Nic last night—two teenagers he'd gotten out of bad spots, and who were completely loyal to him and good with guns—and now they were following Zofia's every step. Twice in less than a day faceless people had contacted him, threatened him, proved how easy it would be to kill his children.

Just the thought. Like a burning knife. That sliced him open from head to heart, and left nothing but destruction behind.

Someone was watching him, following him.

Who?

Somebody wanted something, a warning.

But why?

He almost screamed it out loud.

Show your face, for fuck's sake!

Four periods. Soon their school day would be over. So far he hadn't noticed anything out of place. But he did see the boys during recess: Rasmus and his friends throwing tennis balls at a board with holes cut into it, each one worth a different number of points, and Hugo on the basketball court playing three-on-three. His boys seemed so happy. A part of a context. Zofia had told him as much, how sometimes she could see them from her classroom, and it struck her how normal their lives had become. While they were living on the run, they had only had each other and lacked any form of socialization. But now they were part of a community that was as real as it was normal.

When the bell rang, he drove the short distance to the entrance. The students were trailing across the schoolyard in clumps, talking and laughing loudly and gesturing to each other before they split up. Hugo and

Rasmus lingered at the basketball court, unaware that he was watching them. They seemed to think they had all the time in the world, the way only children can. And when they noticed him, they weren't pleased.

"Again, Dad?"

"Jump in."

"Seriously? We always *walk* home. This is embarrassing."

"Just do as I say, Hugo. Otherwise, you'll attract even more attention and your friends will notice even more that I'm here."

His ten-year-old son didn't seem satisfied by that. But he accepted the logic. He crawled in next to Rasmus in the back seat, hunching down to avoid being seen.

They were about halfway home when the questions started.

"Why, Dad?"

"I can't tell you that right now."

"First we have to go to your office. Then you drive us to school. And now you pick us up."

"That's just the way it is today, Hugo."

"And I know you're lying. Something happened. Something dangerous."

Last year Hugo had interrupted family breakfast when he understood the danger his father was in, the danger his parents were trying to hide, protect their children from. And it was Hugo who'd refused to even speak to his father after he chose to infiltrate a North African human smuggling ring rather than coming home as he'd promised.

His eldest son. Who knew and felt so much.

Piet Hoffmann pulled over to the side of the road and stopped the car.

"Hugo?"

This time he'd have to look at his sons while he lied to them.

"I promise—there's nothing dangerous. Nothing happened. The only thing you and Rasmus have to do is *not* tell your mother that I'm planning to surprise her. That's the only thing you have to help me with. That's why I dropped you off and picked you up today."

"Tell us then. What is it?"

"What?"

"The surprise."

"I will. When it's ready. Trust me, Hugo."

Zofia had put up a parasol on the brownish grass behind their house. Thirty degrees and still climbing. Two proud big brothers hurried over and took turns lifting their little sister out of her stroller, sat down in the shade, and drank a glass of juice with ice cubes in it, then another.

Hoffmann looked around and couldn't see them. That was good. If he couldn't figure out where Nic and Juan were keeping watch from right now, then neither could Zofia or the people threatening them. He stretched an arm into the air, a sign to them that he'd take over now, and they could go home, get ready for the next call.

He kissed his wife, always twice, then it was his turn.

To pick up his little girl.

Luiza. Hugo had chosen her name and insisted it be spelled with a z, just like Mom's. When Piet held her in his arms. Saw that little mouth yawn. Felt those tiny fingers wrapping around one of his own. It was as if she existed, and yet not. As if she were barely real. As if any minute someone might tap him on the shoulder and tell him, *You imagined her, you're holding nothing but air in your arms.*

He kissed her on the forehead twice, just like her mother.

Kissed her cheeks, so round and soft.

Brushed her little nose, her forehead, her chin.

"Piet, what is it?"

Zofia was staring at him. But he couldn't return her gaze.

"Like I told you yesterday. Nothing."

"Please, Piet. Just stop it. I know you so well—the way you breathe, move. Tell me what's going on. I need to know so I can prepare myself."

He didn't answer. Not there in the garden. Not in the kitchen or in the living room that evening when she tried to catch his eyes without the boys noticing. Not even when they were naked in each other's arms, making love in that intense way they rarely did these days, and she suddenly interrupted their movements and pulled away.

"I can't."

"Zofia, what . . ."

"I can feel there's something going on. You're not present. And if you're not here—then I'm not, either. Talk to me, Piet."

Not even then.

He'd promised her the truth so many times. He'd even told her about the deaths he was responsible for.

But this—he couldn't.

And so that's why they lay on either side of the bed, as far from each other as they could get, doing their best not to let bare skin touch.

And that's why when they ate breakfast they focused too intently on setting the table and clearing it, why they brushed their teeth in silence, got dressed, made sure that Luiza was fed and changed, nodded discreetly to each other as he left to drive the boys to school, and nodded to each other again when he came back.

And through it all they never spoke until they were forced to.

"Piet?"

He heard Zofia open the creaking door of the basement and shout his name.

"You need to come up."

He'd just gone down to his workroom and then to the even smaller room inside it and was opening the safe. But he closed it hastily. He knew that voice— serious and worried.

"What is it?"

He hurried up the basement stairs.

"Zofia, it . . . sounds important."

She was sitting at the kitchen table. A package lay in front of her.

"This came for you."

Not especially big, not conspicuous in any obvious way. Other than what was written on its upper side.

```
To Piet Koslow Hoffmann
```

Just like before.

Typewriter, no return address, contents that could only mean trouble.

That's why they both glowered at it, in their own ways.

"Did it arrive . . . just now?"

"Yes."

"But the mail never comes this . . ."

"A courier company. The messenger knocked on the door just as you were headed downstairs."

She looked at him. Expecting him to tell her, finally. Now that it was so obvious.

That the reason for the uneasiness of the last twenty-four hours was lying there on the table in front of her.

"What's in it?"

"I don't know."

"Piet, I know you know."

"I really *don't.*"

And that was the truth, at last. He had no idea. Who, what, or why.

The package was left on the kitchen table. Unopened. A symbol of everything he couldn't say. And they both avoided it, until Zofia and Luiza left for their morning walk, which Juan would follow her on, since Nic was at the school with his brother watching Hugo and Rasmus.

He waited just long enough to be sure they were out of sight.

Then he pulled out a kitchen chair and sat down.

Next to his fury. Next to his fear.

Running his fingers lightly over the brown paper.

He pressed it gently.

Something hard inside. Roughly the size of a cell phone.

He should be careful. Take the package far, far away. Absolutely not open it here, unprotected, in his own home.

He tore open the brown paper.

Ripped through the padding.

It didn't just feel like a phone, it was one. Wrapped in even more paper with more anonymous lines of text.

```
You all looked so happy together.
Family breakfast.

Your boys seem to like yogurt.
But they want it in glasses
and not in bowls. A double
layer of cheese on their bread.
They've got nice backpacks, too.
Especially Rasmus, that red is so
easy to spot. You can really see
him. You know now that we can
expose you. Kill your family.

And we will, if you don't
immediately do what we ask.

Answer when it rings.
```

Piet Hoffmann ran out to the hall closet where he kept some thin plastic gloves. He pulled on a pair and hurried back to the kitchen table and the phone.

It rang the moment he lifted it up.

"*Good morning.*"

A voice changer.

"*Can you hear me?*"

The voice electronic.

"*I'd like you to answer me.*"

A man's voice.

"*So—one more time. Do you hear . . .*"

At least that's how it sounded.

"*. . . me well enough?*"

It could be anybody, with any voice.

"I hear you."

"*Good. I'll keep it short.*"

Perfect Swedish.

"*We know who you are and what you've done. And we know everything—not just what you were locked up for.*"

No noticeable accent or particular dialect.

"*We also know how resourceful you are.*"

And through it all slow, controlled breathing.

"*So we want you to start a small war.*"

For as long as he could remember, Piet Hoffmann constructed mental images of whatever reality he found himself in. He kept these images in an internal album that nobody else had access to. Observations about himself in relation to other people. His movements and behaviors in relation to others' movements and behaviors. A mirror he held up in order to track, plan, be ready. And he had no idea why or how it had begun. It just worked that way for as long as he could remember. It's who he was, or who he'd been forced to be.

Always, always be one step ahead of anyone else around you, know more than they do, and you'll know what's going to happen.

Never, ever let the bastards get you, if you can get them first.

Didn't matter if he was just a kid on his way to school or a man on his way to a narcotics transaction. *If they do this, I'll do that. If they say this, I say that.* It was about knowing which door would open and what he'd find on the other side. A quality that proved very useful after the Swedish police recruited him to infiltrate the mafia.

He survived, and he was the best there was at keeping a step ahead, anticipating his opponent's next move, and making sure his own move was better.

But now.

Now he knew nothing.

He had no mental images.

No mirror to hold up.

Someone was watching him, studying his family, probably doing so right now, and he had no clue who or why.

Start a small war? What the hell did that even mean?

But he recognized the MO. It reminded him of how he used to threaten people. You drive them toward what you want them to do, but you give them just one piece of information at a time. You keep a tight grip on them while pushing them in the right direction. Until your mark really starts to wonder, starts getting worried and scared, more susceptible. That's when you deliver your message—tell them what they need to do.

He checked the time. A quarter past two. After the first call, he'd stopped by the safe houses and transitioned clients out of one of his three units, the older couple hiding behind tulle curtains, who dared to testify against a gang—in their place, an emergency installation of a young woman who had been forced to flee her family after getting pregnant with a man of the wrong ethnicity. He'd then driven to his office on Vasa Street and had a meeting with someone from a computer company in Kista, a recurring customer looking to upgrade their external security. Mechanical. That was probably the best description of how he functioned.

Sure, he looked like he was smiling and talking and selling, he sounded professional and engaged, but it wasn't him. Inside he was somewhere else. With Zofia and Luiza. With Rasmus and Hugo. With whoever was threatening them in anonymous letters, who spoke in a distorted voice, and who would soon be coming back to push him further in the direction they wanted.

Now.

Now was that time.

He could hear the phone ringing in his inner pocket.

"*Good afternoon.*"

The distorted voice. An unknown number on the display screen.

"*You're going to start a small war for us.*"

Piet Hoffmann had just turned off the lights in his office and turned on the alarm, and he was stepping out into the hall when the phone rang. He glanced around quickly. Finding a camera, a controlling eye just a centimeter wide, which could be placed basically anywhere, was as impossible here as on the streets around his house in Enskede. He hurried to the stairs. Was that fucking voice sitting somewhere studying him on a computer screen? Were they across the street in some window? Were they hiding inside a parked car? Was he being watched this whole time and didn't know it?

"Mmm. You said that yesterday. Start a war? What the hell does that mean?"

"*Exactly what it sounds like. And you're going to do it on your own. With a weapon called a FN BRG-15.*"

An already bizarre conversation was now even more so.

He knew most of what there was to know about

weapons. It was still part of his profession. But this? The FN BRG-15? He'd only ever heard rumors about it. Because it didn't exist. Had never been manufactured.

"War? FN BRG-15? Is this a joke? Has this whole fucking week been a practical joke? All your typewritten letters and your little toys?"

It was supposed to be the most powerful machine gun ever built, designed and manufactured by Fabrique Nationale in Belgium, which already made machine guns for the Swedish defense force and twenty other militaries. So powerful it could knock out an armored vehicle a mile away, slice through steel armor like nothing else. In order to do that, it needed a bigger caliber and a new kind of cartridge. But when it was finally ready to go into production, there were no buyers. Someone had done some pretty rotten market research, or probably none at all. Production stopped before it even started.

"Hand grenades, Hoffmann, are never a joke. A dead child will never laugh again. And what if, maybe, just maybe there's a lovely new toy waiting in a side pocket of that bright red backpack? What if we let your son carry it around for a couple of days? So many books in the main compartment, what difference would the extra weight make to a little boy. So if you believe us, it's time to stop asking questions and start listening a lot more carefully."

He understood what the voice was saying.

What it was really saying.

And all of sudden he felt like he was falling right there in that stairwell.

This was no empty threat.

Rasmus had a new grenade in his backpack. Which he'd carried around with him, into their home, their car, and now into his classroom where he was surrounded by so many other children.

"You fuckers . . ."

"*Shhhh . . . what did I just say? Listen. You're going to initiate a small gang war. You're going to do it with an FN BRG-15. You can decide which criminal organization you find the most suitable to start with. As long as it has . . . how should I put this . . . significant influence in the underworld. You choose. You knock them out. And then, using your contacts, let it be known which weapon was used in the attack. Then make sure people know where they can get one of their own.*"

And then that gruesome distorted voice with its distorted reality hung up, ending the conversation. Piet Hoffmann stood in a stairwell in the center of the city with electronic silence.

Then he started to run.

Down the stairs and out into the traffic and the hysterical honking as he zigzagged across the street toward his car parked on the other side. It had been a long time since he felt this way, an anxiety that was so pitch black. He thought he'd worked through it for good.

Rasmus's backpack.

He should call Juan and Nic who were already in the area.

But this was a hand grenade, and he wanted to disarm it himself to avoid any chance of an accident.

A quick U-turn in front of a taxi as the driver

slammed on the brakes, then he sped down Vasa Street, up onto the Central Bridge, and headed south, all the while forcing his thoughts away from his anguish, away from images he couldn't bear, while trying his best to focus on the second part of their conversation. Had he heard correctly? Understood right? Did the distorted voice really mention that weapon? Of course he'd heard the rumors. Heard that despite the official version of events, it had gone into production. That there was a buyer who ordered ten thousand, but then backed out. The rumors had circulated down many paths. But in every version there was a buyer who didn't follow through, and ten thousand guns that disappeared. Now and then, you'd hear that one popped up in various battles during the Yugoslav wars. Other gossip placed them in South America in the hands of drug lords or in Afghanistan with the Taliban. He'd always dismissed it as just talk. But what if they really did exist? Even the much simpler Ksp 58 machine gun that the Swedish military used went for around five thousand euros the last time he checked. And on the black market it would be even more expensive, probably at least seventy-five hundred—and more advanced models probably as much as a cool ten thousand. He didn't need a calculator to figure out the rest. Ten thousand machine guns with a price of ten thousand euros—one hundred million euros.

At Gullmarsplan, the traffic got heavier, almost slowed to a stop. An accident. Lanes closed. His car was wedged in bumper to bumper with no chance of escape.

He considered getting out of the car and making a run for it. There were only a few kilometers left—it wouldn't take him long. But he had to calm down. *Calm down.* Someone wanted him to do something. If they hurt his sons now, they wouldn't get a goddamn thing out of him. That's just how the game is played. Push your victim but don't remove their motivation, push them until they're bent over and ready to get fucked.

"Hello, this is Rasmus's father—I'm sorry to bother you in the middle of class time but . . . is he with you?"

Rasmus's teacher's name was Marie, and she reminded him a little of Zofia. Same age, same determination, both soft and demanding. She didn't like it when parents called during class time. This was her and the children's workplace. She didn't say it with words exactly as she handed over the phone to his son, but he heard it in there anyway.

"Dad!"

That voice. As far from distorted as you could get. It was sincere, spontaneous, trusting.

"Hey, sweetie pie."

"We're writing, Dad."

Surely Marie and her whole class were listening to his conversation with his son. Or at least to Rasmus's half of it.

"What are you writing?"

"Letters."

"That's great. Letters are a great thing to have in case you need to use them later. Listen . . . Sweetie?"

"Yeah?"

"Where's your backpack?"

"Why?"

"Please, Rasmus, just answer the question."

"On my hook."

"Out in the hallway?"

"You have to hang it there. Otherwise, M . . ."

Hoffmann could see the scene in front of him. How Rasmus looked up, met Marie's eyes, and realized she wouldn't like him wasting the class's time talking about her.

". . . Mom gets angry."

Nicely done. Good save.

Hoffmann smiled, grateful for any emotion other than the pitch-black anxiety in his chest.

"Why, Dad?"

"I was just wondering . . . See you soon. I'll meet you in the parking lot."

"Again?"

"Yes, again."

"Hugo's not gonna like that."

Piet Hoffmann kissed his phone twice before saying goodbye to his son and hanging up.

Take out a criminal organization.

He was trapped in a car with his windows rolled down, in thirty-degree heat, and slowly he was starting to understand.

With a weapon that was far more powerful than anything else on the Swedish market.

What the hell this was about.

Then let other criminal organizations know.

What it was they were forcing him to do. What it would lead to.

And make sure they know where they can get more of the same kind.

This was about a new player trying to take over the weapons trade in the criminal underworld of Stockholm. Of Sweden. And they were doing it in the same way it was always done.

Create a need that doesn't exist.

Change the balance of terror.

Be the only one who's offering a new product.

He knew what things were like out there. Knew gun violence had increased in Sweden's largest cities. Knew five times as many people were shot and four times as many killed in this country compared to all the other Nordic countries combined. He knew that in Europe only southern Italy was comparable to Sweden when it came to the number of shootings per capita, and grenade attacks here were comparable to the rates in Mexico. Back when he was part of that world, gangsters kept their shootings in certain circles, well-planned and for the specific purpose of disrupting a competitor's activities—but these days shootings were more likely to be the work of very young men with very bad impulse control. And these days the number of guns in circulation was constantly rising, and guns were no longer seen as disposable after one use. Once they were smuggled here, they stayed here, no longer dumped after a shooting.

And besides, most organizations worthy of the name *criminal* had long since made arrangements with their gun suppliers. They had their own smuggling channels—there was no urgent need for new actors in an already functioning and saturated market.

So.

That's where he came in.

Piet Hoffmann, for the sake of a still nameless someone, had to create a need that didn't exist, make sure the already well-armed wanted more powerful guns.

Piet Hoffmann would alter, maybe even destroy, the balance of terror by creating a new predator with no natural enemy, therefore forcing everyone else to buy the weapons they believed everyone else was buying.

Who?

What organization was trying to enter the illegal gun trade?

And why didn't they take care of this themselves? Why pull him into it—an outsider who everyone knew had already gone straight?

Two ambulances and a tow truck later and traffic finally started to inch forward. In that slow and confusing way of commuters, ten meters at a time. Until he finally reached an off ramp and could exit the chaos of the highway.

He parked with a wheel up on the sidewalk in the zone intended for school taxis. It wasn't pretty but it would have to do. He started to run across the schoolyard, but soon slowed—*he had to calm down*—and he started to walk with long, firm strides toward the white building where the lower grades had their classrooms. As soon as he stepped inside he realized that he'd never been here during the daytime. The PTO meetings and parent-teacher conferences that he'd been to were all held in the evening when the building was empty of children. As he walked through the hallway, he noticed how absence had been replaced by presence, dullness by energy, silence by all those voices leaking through closed doors. He passed three classrooms and stopped in the corridor near the fourth. He saw a long line of hooks bearing the bags and backpacks of twenty-four pupils who were spending their afternoon learning to write letters that might come in handy some day. And above each hook stood a small rectangular sign, made by the students themselves and then laminated. RASMUS in handwriting that Hoffmann knew well, and it made him smile. And next to the name—a drawing of a blue crocodile with glasses and a top hat. Or at least that's what Hoffmann thought it was. A crocodile with its mouth wide open, showing off sharp green teeth. Hoffmann snuck over to the door and peered through its round window. Marie was walking around the classroom with her back to him while her students sat at their desks writing in a concentrated way. She was able to get her two dozen eight-year-olds to simultaneously and throughout a long lesson do what he found so impossible to do with just one eight-year-old—make them focus for more than two minutes in a row.

The glaring red backpack was hanging exactly where it should be, beneath the crocodile in the top hat. A stab in his chest. Rage. Fear. If that voice really had done what it claimed, there was a deadly weapon lying inside. And if it was triggered in the vicinity of twenty-four children, it would take their lives.

He coaxed up the Velcro straps that kept the opening of the backpack together and folded up the flap. Five books. Some math homework. A pen case, striped in Manchester United's red and yellow colors, with happy footballs on its sides. Then the side pocket. And, just as the voice had told him, there it was. Metal, oval, compact. The hand grenade. Masquerading as a toy, with plastic arms and legs and eyes and a big plastic nose above a bushy plastic mustache. Just like last time. And yet not.

Last time was an indeterminate warning, but this was a death threat.

Because this time the fucking voice had left in that explosive heart.

Piet Hoffmann was holding a live hand grenade.

"Dad?"

He spun around. Hugo. With his hands on his hips and eyes that were anything but happy.

"I thought so! I thought that was you out in the schoolyard! What are you doing here? *Inside* the school? Class isn't over?"

"Hugo, I . . ."

"First you pick us up and now you're coming inside! Here!"

Hoffmann closed his left hand around the grenade, slowly moving it behind his back. If he just stood there normally, then Hugo wouldn't see it.

"And what are *you* doing here? Don't you have class?"

"I saw you through the window. And I said I had to go to the bathroom. Answer me, Dad. I asked first!"

The scene was so absurd that for once he couldn't watch himself from the outside; this was a mental image he had no wish to save. A father. Across from his eldest son. In a school hallway outside his youngest son's classroom. And in that father's hand—a live grenade.

"One of your little brother's schoolbooks. He forgot it at home. You know how Rasmus is, right? Loses everything. So I was bringing it to him. You two got it pretty good, right? Your mom works here, and when she's gone, your dad stops by if you lose something."

Hugo dropped his hands from his hips. And his eyes took on another variation of unhappy. He had accused his dad, scolded his father, for no reason. Piet Hoffmann felt ashamed letting his son stand there feeling embarrassed because of his white lie.

"I'll be outside in the car. My usual spot."

"Dad? Come on!"

"Just a few more days. I promise. See you soon."

Then he bent forward, looked around in such a way that Hugo knew there were no other students in the hallway, and that no one, absolutely no one, could see what was about to happen—then his dad pulled him close and hugged him, even gave him a quick kiss on his worried forehead.

They slept with the window open. He'd protested when Zofia pushed it up, but had trouble explaining to her why she shouldn't let in the cool night air after three days of almost Mediterranean heat. He didn't want to risk any more discussions of what couldn't be discussed. That they weren't just sending threats, they were sending death threats to their children. And somehow it was connected to him—to a past he'd promised they'd never have to deal with again.

He lay twisted in their sheet staring into the dim night sky outside, not quite dark but as close as it came in the summer. In the distance he could hear church bells strike three, and he wondered where the wind had carried the ringing from.

Zofia slept quietly beside him, her hand resting lightly on his shoulder, her legs draped over his knees, her lips just slightly parted like usual. Her sleep was always calm, her breathing regular, no matter where she was or what the circumstances they were in. It was a deep sense of security that he envied and knew he'd never possess. He always slept anxiously, tossing and turning and waking up from the slightest amount of light or sound. Or, quite often, like this night—he didn't sleep at all.

He kept close to Zofia's warm skin until the clock bells were struck again, twice, which meant it was three-thirty. And he gave up. It was impossible to rest. His body screamed for sleep, but lost out every time to a mind spinning with unsorted questions.

He caressed her cheek and gently rolled over the edge of the bed so as not to disturb her any more than necessary. The early-morning birds had already landed in the apple trees, the great tit with its keen chirp, the blackbirds with their beautiful songs.

Life as it should be.

He stopped for a moment by Luiza, whom they'd recently moved into the tiny room closest to theirs. She was asleep on her back in the crib both Hugo and Rasmus had used, the fingers of one small hand wrapped around one of its posts. Rasmus was snoring in his room, lying on his left side taking deep even breaths, so convinced that no danger could touch him here, just like Zofia, a song that was so different from the blackbirds. Hoffmann closed his window—*that* he could explain without lying—and then he closed the big ventilation hatch in Hugo's room. Hugo slept like his father, his sheets wet with sweat, his pillow on the floor, always tossing and turning.

The stairs to the ground floor squeaked a bit less if he kept close to the handrail. He avoided Rasmus's plastic action figures, which were scattered throughout the hall in a pattern that would be impossible to re-create. He turned off the alarm and sat down at the kitchen table with a glass of water. So good when those ice-cold drops found their way.

A newspaper stood open at Zofia's spot. Sunday's crossword. Almost completely filled in. Her way of relaxing, always had been. He pulled the paper close and its rustle seemed loud in the silence. She usually liked it when he'd settle down beside her and try to help her solve whatever was left. Tonight that didn't work. The weave of words didn't seem to fit together or make any sense. The letters must have ended up somewhere in Rasmus's workbook.

He stared out through the kitchen window at their peaceful suburban neighborhood.

The reality that made sense—unlike the one that didn't.

An organization with access to a weapon that didn't exist, whose goal was to take over arms smuggling, who had chosen a retired criminal and former infiltrator named Piet Hoffmann to execute their plan.

He watched the blackbird in the apple tree flying from branch to branch, singing just for him. The great tit had flown away, and in its place was a wagtail strutting around on the lawn, searching for insects or earthworms. More reality that made sense.

He knew most of what there was to know about the underworld of Stockholm. He'd belonged to it for most of his adult life. But he'd never encountered such resourceful criminals. Their reach extended not only to a legendary weapon, but also to a high-ranking police officer. There was no other way to interpret the copies of highly classified documents they'd sent to his office. Documents like that were stored in a safe in the Kronoberg Police Station. Only a police officer would have been able to gain access to it.

It was one thing to fight the police—he'd done it for years.

It was another thing to fight criminals—he'd done that just about as long.

But to fight them both from the very beginning. The combination could lead only to a violent death.

A new glass of ice-cold water. For a moment the stabbing inside him almost ceased.

That goddamned fucking phone—he didn't want anything to do with it, and yet he had to carry it with him constantly—it had even rang when he got home with the boys from school. He picked it up, held it in front of him, and didn't answer. It rang later in the evening. Zofia had looked at him, annoyed by the endless ringing, but she didn't ask questions she knew she wouldn't get answers to.

At half past one, at almost the same moment the church bells struck, when he still hoped he might get some sleep, the first text message had arrived. He'd turned the phone on silent when he went to bed, expecting them to make contact and not wanting to wake Zofia, but the vibration on his bedside table was enough.

> We are watching you. We know where to find
> you. We know where your children sleep. But
> you have no fucking clue where we are.
> Answer when we call.

Just before half past two, the next message had
arrived.

> Trouble sleeping? Tomorrow will be easier.
> Then you'll know where to pick up the
> weapon, and when to use it. Then you'll feel
> calm again. And while you're on your little
> mission, we'll make sure your family is having
> a good time. Make sure nothing happens to
> them. Until you've done what you're
> supposed to do and things go back to
> normal. Don't you agree that blackbirds have
> the most beautiful song?

He sat down at the kitchen table, took out the
phone, and read through the only text messages it had
ever received—maybe he'd see something new this
time, figure out something he'd missed a few hours
ago? No. It meant what it meant. *We see you. We are
with you all the time.* This wasn't about using any of his
skills as an infiltrator, yet. It wasn't about blowing up
his family, yet—they knew as well as he did that grenades came with three fail-safes and each required a
great deal of strength. The ring clip had to be pulled
out, the fuse bar pressed down, and the grip fuse folded
forward. And the probability that Rasmus, if he'd discovered it in the backpack's side pocket, would accidentally have set it off was quite small. What this was about
was pushing him toward a willingness to do whatever
they asked, no matter the consequences.

They were doing what he would have done.

And they were threatening him with the old records his handler Erik Wilson filed after their meetings, which were always kept locked away in the police station.

Erik?

Piet Hoffmann hadn't even wanted to consider the possibility before.

Could Erik be the police officer who had shared papers that were more dangerous than weapons?

No.

Piet Hoffmann didn't even have to take that fleeting thought any further, didn't need to confront him—he just knew it wasn't him. Erik Wilson, after more than ten years of close collaboration, where each day literally separated life from death, was one of only two police officers he trusted. There were thirty thousand people employed by that police authority, and there were twenty-nine thousand nine hundred and ninety-eight of them that he didn't trust.

They were acting and thinking as he would have.

Even the mission they were trying to get him to carry out seemed familiar.

In fact it was almost exactly the same as one he came up with—use a weapon no one in the criminal underworld of Stockholm had access to—several years ago for completely different reasons, when he'd planned to destroy another organization in a single stroke. He'd infiltrated a biker gang that was considered one of Sweden's most dangerous at the time. The members who slowly accepted him, entrusted him with tasks, eventually elevating him to "hanger-on" and then "prospect," had suddenly started showing suspicion. He remembered

one evening, during one of his secret meetings with
Erik Wilson, when he was supposed to share information but was just as likely to share his joy or sorrow or
fear or frustration or whatever feeling filled him at the
moment, he had described to his handler exactly how he
planned to survive if the gang members ever found out
who he was. If they ever decided to kill the snitch.

My God.

That was why. That's where it came from.

With the blackbird singing in the tree outside, and
the unsolved crossword lying in front of him on the
kitchen table, he suddenly saw it all so clearly.

*That's how this all went down, that's why this still
anonymous organization threatening to destroy his family had chosen him.*

They'd read those old classified documents, copied
them, and sent them to him to let him know. His meetings with Wilson—the conversations where they found
the inspiration, which they adapted for their own purposes: taking over the Swedish illegal arms trade.

It was his idea all along.

*The infiltrator Piet Hoffmann, code name Paula, had
realized how simple it would be to knock out a large criminal organization and in a single move completely change
the balance of power in Stockholm's underworld.*

Hoffmann knew he was right. This was exactly how
it went down. But still he rose from the kitchen table
and headed toward the stairs—not to go up to his bed
and Zofia's warm body and deep and even breathing—
but to go to the basement and his hidden room. That's

where he'd stashed those fucking copies they'd sent him two days ago. Hoffmann put in the code and opened the safe door, and on the upper shelf there lay the stack of tightly written and highly classified documents. He hadn't read them closely when he opened the letter, it didn't seem necessary, but he would now.

> *"They're close, Erik. Asking questions. And I'm out of good answers."*
>
> *"How close?"*
>
> *"Days. Maybe hours. You have to extract me."*
>
> *"I need more time."*
>
> *"If they find out—we both know what will happen. They'll kill Rasmus. Then Hugo. Then Zofia. Then me. Always from the bottom up. Always youngest to oldest."*

He sank down onto the floor, his back against the safe, and flipped through those long-forgotten notes.

> *"And if I can't get you out?"*
>
> *"You HAVE TO, Erik."*
>
> *"IF. IF I don't have time. What's your plan?"*
>
> *"Then I'm taking out the whole damn club. Every single one of them. The whole fucking organization. At the same time."*
>
> *"I'm serious—what does your plan look like?"*
>
> *"Listen: that IS my plan."*

It didn't take long to find the pages he sought, they

even had a tiny fold in one corner, as if whoever sent
them didn't want him to miss them.

*"Erik, I've been working late. At night, when my
biker friends are getting beauty sleep, I've been going
to a garage in Alby and working on the biggest mine
this country has ever seen. Two meters wide. It took a
lot of Dynamex B—if you only knew how easy it was
to get it from construction sites. Then ship plate and
fifty boxes of M12 nuts. It's parked outside their club
right now, loaded into a truck with a billboard for a
strip club. Hidden INSIDE the billboard itself. Best
camouflage imaginable. I rented the truck and
parked it fifty meters from the biker gang's
headquarters. The idiots even talk about it, think it's
so fucking funny to see a naked lady on the ad
whenever they step outside. I can trigger the bomb
whenever I want with just a little detcord, an
electric lighter, and a couple of cell phones. It would
tear the fucking clubhouse to shreds—nobody would
survive it."*

"What . . . what the hell are you talking about?"

*"If the police can't protect their employees, then
their employees are gonna have to protect themselves."*

*"Have you . . . have you completely lost your
goddamn . . . JESUS CHRIST, YOU CAN'T while
you're working for us, for THE POLICE, you can't
build a goddamn weapon of mass destruction! You'd
start a fucking gang war! You have to abort this
immediately. RIGHT NOW! Take that shit away!"*

*"I'll take it away. When me and my family are
safe. When you've extracted me."*

Six years ago. And every word from that meeting had
been recorded and subsequently transcribed by his handler, just like always.

*"You're my best infiltrator. You've survived
longer than anyone. And when you've been forced to
break the law, I've cleaned up after you—every time.
Because it's in the interest of the police authorities to
keep you out of there. But this, my friend . . . you've
gone too far!"*

*"I don't intend to kill fifty people, Erik, I just
want them to KNOW I can do it. IF I end up in
that situation."*

*"It's too much, too far—for some incomprehensible
reason, I let you go too far!"*

*"If anything is incomprehensible it's that no one
else has realized how easy it would be to change the
balance of power. Take over somebody's territory.
What a catastrophe it would be for any gang if some
other fucking gang was sitting on a high-precision
weapon of this caliber. Just take, for example, this
fucking biker club I infiltrated—it's common
knowledge that they have a weekly meeting in their
head office on Wednesdays at three. Not behind
bulletproof walls—but in a fucking metal shack that
I could destroy with a homemade bomb in seconds!
Hells Angels have weekly meetings and Southside has*

*one, too. And we're in fucking Sweden! I can pop into
the town hall in any city, look at the drawings and
plans for these clubs' buildings because it's public
information. Everything is available—ceiling, wall
thicknesses—anyone can do it. I've done it time and
time again. You cops should do it, too. Have a little
fun, Erik, go in and take a look at Bandido's new
premises or Evil Crew and one thing is for sure—
none of them have any reinforcements. They're too
lazy. And it's never been a problem. Plus it's
expensive. And where do you even get ahold of it. I'll
say it again—if I wanted to go to war for real with
any of the big criminal organizations, I'd knock them
out in one blow. On my own. Park my homemade
device, watch the clock, knowing that they're having
their little weekly meeting, that they're all sitting
down inside. Light that shit up with nothing more
than an internet camera and a remote control."*

Piet Hoffmann remembered those days, that meeting. Those doubled emotions. Tangible panic, palpable
fear, and adrenaline burning inside him so clear and
clean. But reading it now so long afterward, line by
line, felt like meeting those faded school photos he'd
shown Rasmus and Hugo of himself at their age, which
made them laugh so hard. A stranger, that's what he saw.
The very young man he'd once been, whom he could
barely understand or relate to now. A gaze he didn't
dare meet, because the school-age version of himself
would also see the same stranger.

And the notes, which he placed back onto the safe shelf now, were from that very person. One who wouldn't let him go. Who found his way back in. No matter how many times Piet pushed him away. This Piet Hoffmann had been forced to run for his life over and over again, because of the infiltrator Paula.

He closed the safe door, then the door to his secret room, then the closet and his office, then the basement door. In the kitchen he put a dented and discolored kettle on the stove to boil some water, the one they'd bought the day they moved into this house, which they could never quite give up. He poured hot water into a big glass and mixed in some instant coffee.

Suddenly he felt so dizzy he had to lean against the wall.

He'd been expecting this moment for most of his adult life.

The final death threat.

That someone would get ahold of those secret documents, learn his identity. That it would be made public and his family would become a target.

Time to choose.

Carry out this mission—or refuse and wait for a death sentence, because any former mafia associates of his would lose all credibility if they didn't kill him now.

He looked down again at Zofia's crossword puzzle, picked up her pencil. She'd sensed it, of course—knew him better than he knew himself—and knew this night was approaching. He counted a total of nine empty squares scattered throughout the puzzle. But solving them was still just as impossible. No answer made sense. He couldn't focus his thoughts—they danced around him, laughing at him.

As empty as those crossword squares.

Until, after a while, not yet sure why, he stretched over to the counter between the refrigerator and the stove and pulled some white napkins out of a drawer. He unfolded one over the puzzle and drew some aimless straight lines, which soon turned into squares. The first was in the napkin's upper left corner. The next one right next to it. He continued, scribbling them down one at a time, a long chain from one side to the other.

And suddenly he knew why.

He started writing with that blunt lead pencil. It was a bit cramped, the long row was a little too close to the napkin's edge, but the words fit exactly in the first box.

Survive, eleven letters

He filled it in. He could solve this.

P–H–O–N–E–T–O–G–R–A–M

The next row of penciled-in boxes was not quite as straight, and a little shorter with less room to write.

Survive, eleven letters

He knew that one, too.

G–R–O–U–N–D–F–L–O–O–R

He kept going.

Still dizzy, but his mind was crystal clear.

Now and then he'd hear one of the people he loved snore, or mumble a bit, from upstairs. In the meantime the dawn sky was getting brighter, and his big glass of coffee ran out.

Survive, fourteen letters

N–A–S–O–L–A–B–I–A–L–F–O–L–D

Survive, seven letters

D–E–T–C–O–R–D

Survive, eleven letters

R–A–D–I–O–J–A–M–M–E–R

Survive, eleven letters

P–O–S–I–T–I–O–N–I–N–G

Survive, fourteen letters

E–N–C–R–Y–P–T–I–O–N–C–O–D–E

The seemingly random scribbles—squares linked together like train cars, now filled with letters—were the exact opposite. Intentional coincidences. A clear plan.

The plan he'd been carrying inside him since he found a grenade in his youngest son's backpack, and it had become more elaborate as the threats intensified.

He'd already made up his mind.

No more criminal activity.

No more work for someone else's sake, not organized crime and not the police. He'd learned that lesson from both sides. If he gave in even once, he was stuck, expected to continue. Criminals, cops, it worked the same, squeeze until there was nothing left to squeeze.

He'd been given a choice—and he chose not to choose.

He chose not to carry out the mission.

He chose not to wait around for death.

He kissed Luiza on her belly, and for a moment her little hand let go of the post of her crib. He kissed Rasmus's forehead, and his youngest son paid him no mind. He kissed Hugo's cheek, and his oldest son opened his eyes, a flash of worry, but then he turned over and went back to sleep. Zofia he held gently, put his head in her arms, lay there a moment until his breath against her sleep-warm skin woke her.

"Piet?"

"Sorry, but I had to wake you up."

"What's . . . Are you dressed? What time is it?"

"A quarter to six."

She sat up a bit, balling up the pillow behind her neck.

The dawn light was shining more intensely up here than in the kitchen, the blinds ineffective since the window was open.

"I have to take care of a few things, and I won't be back until tomorrow."

"You're going? Right now?"

"While I'm gone you and the children cannot leave the house."

She looked at him.

She knew.

Not what, but she knew.

"This is about that package you got, isn't it? The phone you wouldn't answer? The toy that Rasmus claims he found in our mailbox, which you took away from him without an explanation?"

She'd told him before that he—once the master of it, since he did it to her every day—had gotten rusty at lying. And she was right. Lying, just like everything else, is about practice, consistency. It had to be second nature to him in order not to be noticed.

"I have two people guarding the house. You won't see them, but they're good at what they do. If anything happens, anything that doesn't feel right, you call me immediately."

"And the kids, what should I tell . . ."

"I love you."

He kissed her, and she asked no more questions. He then managed to avoid the creaking on the staircase and the action figures on the hall floor, but he couldn't escape the buzz of that fucking vibration as a third text message arrived while he was on his way out the door.

> Later today you will receive your orders. The
> weapon you should use on our account. Time
> and place in our next message.

Go take care of a few things.

That's how he described those filled-in boxes in the crossword puzzle stuffed into his pocket, which provided the plan not just for his escape, but for his family's, and a place for them to escape to.

Later today.

Piet Hoffmann knew he didn't have much time.

And now he understood how very little.

He started the car he'd parked at the rusty gate of the house that had been their home since Hugo was born. He could still see Zofia standing there, pregnant, laughing until she made him laugh, until they were both giggling and didn't want to stop, it had felt so enormous—that first time they stepped over the threshold hand in hand into their very own house.

Morning traffic hadn't really gotten going yet, almost no slowdowns at all as he drove in the direction of Stockholm's inner city.

He was always one step ahead, that's how he survived.

But not now.

The timing of his actions was being decided by those who threatened him. And when they contacted him later, he'd do what he could to stall them until this evening, maybe until tonight; with a bit of luck and some lies that were more skillful than the ones he'd give to Zofia, he'd stall them until tomorrow morning. Twenty-four hours. But he wouldn't get more than that. He would just have to be ready by then. One step ahead of a faceless organization with arms so long they reached into the upper echelons of the Stockholm police.

He'd left home dressed as usual, same time as usual, moved like he always did. If someone was sitting in

front of a computer monitoring him through a camera—
as he would be if he was them—they'd see nothing unusual. It was now, in his car and on his way, that he'd
slip away from them so he could transform. He doubted
that whoever was watching him had cameras placed
anywhere besides his home and office, but just to be
sure he wasn't being followed, first he drove to a garage
beneath Globen Stadium, left the cell phone they
wanted him to answer on the passenger seat and
switched to a Volvo he kept parked there for exactly this
type of occasion. He drove it to a garage under Med-
borgar Square and a blue car he kept parked there, then
to a garage under Åsö Street and a black Opel.

He drove the oval onto Söderleden, crossed the Central Bridge, took the tunnel from Tegelbacken to
Kungs Street. The city was waking up now, but still
fairly empty, so it didn't take long to get by Stureplan
and Humlegården and on to Valhalla Road and So-
phiahemmet hospital, christened long ago by a queen.
The doctor, a man in his fifties wearing a slightly too
short lab coat, was waiting as promised at the entrance
to the K-building—as far from the front entrance as
you could get. They shook hands firmly, they'd never
met before, but they were about to spend several hours
together locked in a room with no other eyes. They
walked side by side, almost in sync, up heavy stone steps
to something called the Swedish Phoniatric Clinic. At
this time of day it was as empty as the streets.

The large room Hoffmann was led into was divided

into two sections. The first looked like a normal office with a standard desk and standard chairs and a couple of computer screens. And on the other side of a glass door, the second section contained a small operating room with cold bright lights, a stainless-steel rolling cart, and an operating table that could be raised and lowered like a dental chair. The doctor turned on one of the computers, placed a tripod and a microphone on the desk, and pulled a visitor's chair out of a small closet.

"Here we go. Please sit down. We'll need to get acquainted with each other before continuing."

Anonymous. That's what they were.

A white coat with no name tag, a visitor with no medical records.

"Our shared acquaintance said time was of the essence. And that you could pay for speed and discretion."

Piet Hoffmann took an envelope from the same pocket where he'd kept the fucking phone. It was thick—cash takes up more room than you'd think.

"You can count it."

"No need. I trust you. Trust, it's often lacking when we need it the most. Wouldn't you agree?"

Hoffmann dropped the envelope onto the desk next to the microphone stand. Inside was a stack of bills that added up to twenty thousand dollars. They'd once been part of a much larger stash in a suitcase he'd carried home from his hellish trip to North Africa. Enough for a family to get by on for a while.

When the doctor didn't immediately pick it up,

Hoffmann pushed it across the desk to him and wouldn't let go until the money exchanged hands.

"Now you've got your fee. What *you* came here for. I want you to do what *I* came for."

The doctor was wearing a pair of frameless glasses balanced on his nose, and he held them to keep them from falling off as he leaned over to put the envelope into his briefcase.

"Very well, please begin by speaking into this."

The microphone. That's what Hoffmann was supposed to use.

"What should I say?"

"Whatever you like. I need at least twenty seconds."

Piet Hoffmann leaned closer to the microphone while the doctor clicked open a window on the computer screen to something that looked like a regular chart. The scale on the left read *Volume (dB)* and the scale at the bottom read *Pitch (Hz)*.

"What you say isn't important, it's how it sounds."

Piet Hoffmann sat in silence. It was ridiculous—he had no words left. What should a person say when they have no background and don't want to be identified if anyone ever heard this?

"I'll start recording as soon as you begin. Go ahead."

"Phonetogram."

He looked at the doctor who nodded for him to continue.

"Ground floor. Nasolabial fold. Detcord. Jammers. Positioning. Encryption code. Phonetogram. Ground floor. Nasolabial fold . . ."

Hoffmann interrupted himself.

"Is that enough?"

On the screen, a choppy pattern had appeared. Like a map, points linked together in straight lines that formed the borders of a country, or maybe an island in a checkered sea.

"I've made many a recording here. But what you said, what was it now?—well, that was a first."

"Just what I had in my mind. A crossword I solved this morning."

"I know I said it could be whatever you like. But unfortunately that's not enough. It's important that you speak more . . . normally. Complete sentences. So I can establish your basic vocal range. Maybe you could tell me a story. Or describe what it looks like at home, tell me about your children, if you have any. Anything that sounds normal."

Piet Hoffmann did as he was asked. Let his mind lead them through a house he always longed for as soon as he stepped out of it. But he replaced all names, reversed all the facts.

"Good. Good. So . . . two girls?"

"And a newborn baby boy."

The doctor studied the new image, which looked like the borders of a new country on another map, or another island with a new shape.

"Perfect. *Now* we have something to compare with. Your voice is very deep, much deeper than most, but you probably already know that. I say this because I have some patients who come here quite unaware of how they sound. And therefore they don't realize the difference afterward."

Hoffmann nodded. He knew that his voice was easy to recognize. That's why he was here—he had no other choice. His voice, his appearance, his way of moving. It added up to a personality, what could expose a person.

"The fact that your voice is so deep is a good thing. Because only the bass tones will disappear. I just need to remind you—just to make sure we're on the same page—that the new condition we will create, shifting your voice upward, is irreversible. Once I've stretched out the vocal cords and increased their rigidity they'll vibrate more quickly, and from that moment on, your voice will be changed forever. Still deep, still a man's voice, but more like everyone else."

The operation was usually performed under anesthesia.

Piet Hoffmann didn't have time for that.

The doctor with no name tag, after an intense discussion, agreed to using only local anesthetic—so the patient who lay on the operating table staring into the icy light was aware of how his neck was being opened, how the cartilage in his larynx was being pulled tight. The next time they communicated—the wound just freshly sewn and taped up—Hoffmann carried out his end via paper and pen. Every time the doctor tried to strongly recommend that a patient should stay for observation after this procedure, Hoffmann replied via a notepad with the hospital's logo in one corner that he had to go, and he wouldn't be doing that.

When they sat down at the desk again and Piet Hoffmann spoke into the microphone, they could both see how the map had changed—the points and the lines formed a new voice with another tonal range.

"If you go home now you do so at your own risk. Understood?"

"Understood."

"You can eat normally tonight, but don't forget to keep your head bent a bit forward. And please try to speak as little as possible over the next few days. I'm giving you some antibiotics to prevent any infection in the wound."

The doctor handed him a small round bottle with white tablets inside, and then they both stood up. It was over.

Back at the entrance to the hospital, they were met by heat and sound. It was morning now.

"When the thyroid cartilage and cricoid cartilage are pulled together like this, swallowing usually becomes a little more difficult. It's nothing dangerous, just un-comfortable, but it will pass in a few weeks."

The doctor readjusted the collar of his white coat, smiled slightly.

"And there's also the matter of your singing voice. It won't sound like it did before. You lost a few notes. But maybe it's not singing that's got you in such a hurry?"

The traffic was heavier, but still navigable. A couple of times he had to drive up onto a sidewalk, spent a short stretch headed the wrong way on a one-way street, took the car down a pedestrian-only street, but soon he was back in the tunnel beneath the city, headed south. He exited at the Johanneshov Bridge, made a sharp turn toward Södermalm and Skanstull. A right just before Ring Road, where he knew there were a few good short-term parking spots beneath the Clarion Hotel, maximum thirty minutes.

He turned off his car and took out his phone, opened the browser window. Apartments for sale. That's what he was looking for now. A condo in a southern suburb, at least five but no more than ten kilometers from his family's house in Enskede. The price didn't matter, nor did the number of rooms, nor did he care if it had a balcony or tiled stove. He was looking for a building that was cast in place, where the structure was solid concrete, with walls at least fifteen centimeters thick. Impossible for most weapons to pierce. That was his first priority as he searched through everything that was on the market, hundreds of apartments that looked the same because they'd been home-staged by the same companies.

But he couldn't find what he wanted.

His second choice then was to find apartments located on the ground floor in buildings built in the fifties. Especially in the years 1953, 1955, 1958. This yielded more options. He found a total of seven apartments, and he was pretty sure that at least four of them sat on hollow-core slabs—which was key. He cleared his throat, tried out his new voice. It worked. And the doctor was right, not so uniquely deep anymore, just a normal voice, that's who he was from now on. He made the call. Talked to a very friendly and helpful woman at the

Stockholm city planning office, who confirmed this was such a building, built with exactly that sort of floor slab. So the ceilings, walls, and floors would have a helluva lot of air in them—a thin outer layer of three centimeters of concrete framed from two sides in twenty-two centimeters of sand and sound insulation and nothing more.

He asked her to email him the floor plans for these four addresses.

Waited impatiently for what never seemed to arrive and was about to give up when his inbox pinged.

He opened the attachments one at a time.

Turned and twisted the pictures, enlarged and reduced, juxtaposed the sketches of these large residential buildings constructed over sixty years ago.

Finally he found what he was looking for. One was absolutely perfect.

An apartment that not only lay on the ground floor—it also sat just above an air-raid shelter.

The broker, a man in his fifties with a smile like a stencil, was wearing a black suit with busy pinstripes. The look was an attempt at successful lawyer who just won a big case or board member of some huge bank. As if *that* would induce confidence. He spoke in a broad Skåne accent, sat at the corner desk in an elegantly furnished office, and was by far the oldest broker on their staff.

"It's a great location in a very popular area. Close to schools and grocery stores. A great condo association and lots of period details. Very well preserved. Herringbone parquet floors and kitchen with the original cabinetry. Even the original electric meter, you know the kind, black Bakelite, still hanging on the wall. The first thing you see when you step inside."

"I'm here to buy this apartment."

Piet Hoffmann was sitting in the visitor's armchair, and he waved away the bowl of hard candies wrapped in paper bearing the company's logo when the broker offered it.

"And I want to do it today."

"We're holding an open house this weekend. Seller's wishes. Bidding. These are the times we live in—more buyers than there are apartments."

"How much?"

"But—you haven't even seen it?"

"How much . . ."

Hoffmann browsed through a stack of glossy brochures that lay between them on the broker's desk, held up a page with a close-up of the antique electric meter that he cared about as little as he did the location of the closest grocery store.

". . . to get your seller to sign the contract immediately?"

"Immediately?"

"As in right now."

Something greenish, like a blade of grass, seemed to be stuck to one of the broker's front teeth. Food, probably. It was even more visible when he flashed one of his stenciled-on smiles. Hoffmann considered telling him.

"I'm dead serious. And I'm in a hurry so you better

act fast if you don't want me to walk out of here and lose out on the easiest commission you've ever stumbled across."

The bowl of candies. The broker grabbed a couple for himself, somewhat absentmindedly.

They crunched as he chewed.

"Yes . . . well, the price you see in the ad is of course just a starting point."

He pulled himself together.

A possible business deal was sitting in front of him. Which of course meant a commission but also a negotiation. And that was always so much more fun than instructing the photographer on which angle to use and how best to retouch the photos, or going through the list of visitors you had the day after the open house knowing no one was particularly interested in buying.

"Five million one hundred and ninety-five thousand kronor. That's our starting price. But if I'm going to get the seller to bypass the bidding process, well, I guess probably somewhere in the neighborhood of . . ."

"Six million."

"Six?"

"Half a million more if I can move in tonight."

"Six and a half . . . ?"

"If we can sign the papers before I leave here—and I have the key in hand no later than two PM."

The broker was the kind of guy whose cheeks turned red when he got excited. Even his neck turned bright red.

"The seller lives there. The whole family. They're probably having breakfast right now in the kitchen you see in those pictures. Moving out right now without any warning, it seems . . ."

"Seven million kronor. The last five hundred thousand is for you. If you can get them to leave the kitchen table and the beds behind."

When a half hour later Piet Hoffmann backed out of the narrow parking lot of the real estate office, he did so with the deed to a new apartment in hand. The increasingly elated broker only lost his smile for a moment when he realized the buyer insisted on paying that last half million as cash in two sealed envelopes. But he regained it, his smile perhaps even more wide and fake, when a third envelope with an additional one hundred thousand kronor was added to the other two in appreciation for how professionally the whole matter had been handled. Cash. Always useful. A year ago he left North Africa with a suitcase of dollar bills. Most of it he'd been able to launder through various bank accounts and old contacts who took twenty-five percent for their trouble, but some of it still lay in the safe that Zofia didn't know about.

Hoffmann drove to the garage under Globen Stadium and parked next to the car he'd left there this morning along with the phone. Three missed calls— and one text message. Which he opened.

> Tonight we exchange our most valuable possessions. You get our weapon and we get your family. After you finish your mission, we trade back. If you fail, the exchange never happens. We'll be in touch about the precise time.

Avoid. Lie. Delay.

He had to answer.

Somehow.

But he didn't want to talk, didn't want them to hear his new voice, so he'd have to text.

> Been stuck in a meeting. I will do what
> you ask.

He put the phone back on the passenger seat and headed back toward the inner city and Södermalm. The salon where they dyed his hair and eyebrows dark was on Skåne Street. The optician who helped him try out brown contacts, had a small shop on a corner near Göta Street. And at Hornstull close to where Långholms Street met Högalids Street, there was a small studio that was key to the next step in his plan.

The cast that lay over his face, a membrane covering everything except his nostrils, was a pinkish color and just as cool on his skin as usual. The first time he did this, seven or eight years ago, the process made him feel trapped, even claustrophobic, when darkness concealed both his eyes. But now he trusted this woman, who usually worked with film or theater productions. She knew what she was doing, was the best he'd ever worked with. And she never asked why.

A bit messy, slightly runny, and about one centimeter thick. Alginate, which dentists used for dental imprints, and it solidified in ten minutes. Thinly spread and time-sensitive, so that her nimble fingers danced and danced across his face getting it into every nook and cranny. She had cut the plaster strips in advance—now she dipped them in water and draped them over the alginate mask, letting them be sucked into it. The burn. That's what she called it. And the plaster strips did burn for real, got hot on the outside. She occasionally touched them, knocked them hard with her knuckles to check if it was done. Then she gently lifted off his provisional mask.

Piet Hoffmann could see again. And there it was suspended in front of him in her hands. The first version of his face.

"Do you need . . ."

He'd risen halfway out of his chair, nodding at the small studio's exit.

". . . me anymore?"

She'd a wonderful smile, he'd noticed it before, genuine, the opposite of the broker's, and that's how she answered his question. Not indulgently, but kind and patient.

"You know that."

"Right now, I mean."

The cement that was poured into the mask to make it even harder also needed to burn, for another half hour or so, then the alginate and plaster strips would be torn away and the next version of his face cast in the worktop. He knew that, just like she said. She preferred he stayed until the first cast was absolutely hard, until she was sure she had everything she needed to complete her work without him.

"You seem stressed today, Piet. Even more than usual. I mean, you usually are when you show up here. I guess that's why you come, but today . . . you seem almost hunted."

She worked with people's exteriors, transforming them.

But in order to do that she needed to know their interiors as well.

Because the two were connected.

"Hunted. And hunting. What do you say—can I go?"

She smiled again, a smile you could linger in, lean against, someone who knew him at least a little.

"Go. I'll call if I need you. See you in ten hours."

He hurried over to the door and was just opening it when he heard her voice behind him.

"Two flaps above the eyes?"

He turned around.

"Perfect."

"The nose—a little crooked? With large wings of the nose?"

"Sounds good."

"And I was thinking . . . maybe sort of bloated? It's been a while. Jaw. Cheeks. And a bit of a belly."

"Great. Thanks."

Early afternoon and traffic was still relatively sparse. He crossed the old bridge at Skanstull, headed eastward past South Hammarby Port. Shut down. That's what he was. Because that's all he could stand.

Forward, forward never letting himself feel.

Because if he did, if he lost this tunnel vision, let the other reality in, he'd never make it. If he gave in, took out his phone and called Zofia or Hugo or Rasmus just to hear their voices, if he let his own longing get out of hand, then no one would make it to safety.

Forward, forward.

The apartment was in the neighborhood called Tallbacken. The building itself was on a low hill, a large horseshoe-shaped complex with many different entrances and addresses. Number 37 was his destination. A green balcony behind an equally green hedge sat to the left of the front door. He recognized it from the brochure, the dirty yellow umbrella, the string of Chinese lanterns hanging above it like the branches of a very lean fruit tree. He entered the apartment building, went to the door of his apartment, and took out the keys that were the symbol of a completed home purchase. A security door. Two locks, in class 7 and class 6, as promised in the fine print on the website. He opened the door, stepped into the hall. Just a few hours ago people were walking around in here, drinking their coffee, waiting their turn to use the bathroom, looking out the window at a familiar view. They'd left the beds behind as promised, one double and two twins. Luiza would have to sleep with her mother, as she did for the first few months of her life. Kitchen table, kitchen chairs, even a corner sofa in the living room and a TV that should keep Rasmus and Hugo fairly occupied for a few days. It was relatively clean and there were a few sets of keys on the counter, marked *Basement* and *Attic* and *Laundry Room*. It had a particular smell. Their smell, whoever they were. Not bad, just theirs, just like all families have a particular smell that's obvious to everyone but them. He wondered how his family smelled, how much came from him and how much from Zofia and the children.

The building didn't have the bulletproof concrete he'd sought at first. But it fulfilled his other demands. And since the walls lacked the sufficient thickness, he'd have to re-reinforce them himself. In the trunk and back seat of his car he had a heat gun, a toolbox, and polymer plastics and laminates. He was planning to build an inner security door out of plastic, much lighter than transporting a steel plate that weighed a few tons. A transparent film of bulletproof glass that could withstand gunfire even from some of the most difficult angles. A few years ago, he'd come across a Russian manufacturer who specialized in a plastic that was both hard and tough when vacuum-glued to ordinary glass, and he bought out his whole stock. And even at only a thickness of twenty-five millimeters it could withstand automatic gunfire.

He'd build the inner door first, then reinforce the balcony door, then reinforce all the windows.

He'd place seven tiny, hard-to-spot cameras at strategic points outside—strange how something so threatening in one context felt like protection in another—then put detcord in four spots, ambush-mines that he could easily activate from his cell phone.

And finally the most important improvement of all—the closet in one bedroom.

• • •

He couldn't take it anymore. Couldn't leave it be.

"Hello."

She'd been just the press of a few buttons away.

"Hello? Who . . . ?"

"It's me. Piet."

He could hear Zofia's silence. Her confusion.

"Your voice? Do you have a cold? It sounds like you're having trouble breathing. Is everything all right?"

"I'll explain when I see you."

He tried to make out where she was. Interpret the sounds around her. He would guess she was doing the same.

"Tomorrow. You wrote that on the note."

"Maybe earlier. I hope so. But I don't know."

"Where are you?"

"Not very far away."

"What are you doing?"

She'd long since realized something had happened. And that they were back again to him keeping all the *whats* and *whys* to himself.

"I can't tell you. Yet."

"Your voice Piet—maybe it's the connection? Can you call again?"

Home. That's what it sounded like. He could hear the fridge buzzing, a creak in the stairs.

"Hugo? Rasmus? Luiza?"

"Everyone . . . everything's fine. Hugo's still in

school, he's coming home late today, Rasmus is at the neighbor's playing football and Luiza is asleep."

Then silence again. No fridge, no creaking.

Only her slow breath.

"Zo?"

"Yeah?"

"We can handle . . . anything, right?"

"Piet, what . . ."

"We can, right, Zo? Anything?"

She pulled out a chair, probably in the kitchen—sounded like the sharp scrape of the kitchen chairs.

"I think so."

They didn't say more. After a while he kissed the phone twice, and she kissed twice, and they hung up at the same time. Always an even number.

The well-stocked home improvement store was just a few kilometers away. That was where he went to buy a small jackhammer. And the spade. And the plasterboard. And the glue. And the putty. And the screws. And the white paint. And the brass hinge that looked like it belonged on a piano, and the small doorknob. And finally, after he packed the car and was on his way back, he stopped at another store and bought a piece of wood that would form the false floor of the closet.

Back in Tallbacken, he headed down to the basement of the apartment building, walked through its slightly mildewy hall, and passed by a row of storage spaces his neighbors had stuffed to the brim and a laundry room.

Around the corner he found the air-raid shelter. He grabbed two metal wheels that looked like steering wheels, one at the top and one at the bottom of the heavy steel door, twisted them simultaneously clockwise until, with a deep sigh, the locking mechanism released. An air-raid shelter almost identical to the one in the high-rise apartment building where he grew up, housing projects really, that the politicians called left behind. Outsiders in this society. He'd never looked at it that way. He never put it in those words, never formulated the anxiety, restlessness, hopelessness—to him it was the only life he knew, the only place he had. He learned to fight, survive, be part of something instead of outside it. And the air-raid shelter in his childhood apartment building had been their playground—the kids used to sneak down there and turn off all the lights in that windowless room and play hide-and-seek in the dark. That's where he had his first kiss, his first cigarette, his first beer.

The air-raid shelter he stepped into now was, according to the building drawings, below one of the bedrooms in his newly purchased apartment. He checked the emergency exits, the walls, the ceiling, and everything looked exactly how he'd hoped.

On his way back up, he taped a handwritten note on the bulletin board next to the entrance and on the mirror in the elevator asking his neighbors for their patience for a few hours, he'd just moved in and would be doing some renovations, it might be loud. Then he unloaded all of the building materials into the apartment, spread them across the floor of the bedroom, and opened the closet, which had double doors that ran the length of the wall. It was empty just as it should be, only a rod with a few bare hangers on it, and as he opened the doors, even more of the former family's scent rushed out—the smell of their skin against their clothes.

He sank down onto his knees and drew a large circle on the floor, about the size of a well cap. The small jackhammer looked like a hammer drill with a chisel instead of a drill, relatively easy to handle even in confined spaces. He let it hack along his penciled-in line through the thin upper layer of concrete. Breaking into an intermediate space. Air, sand, and even more air in that twenty-two-centimeter thick nothingness. He dug out the sand and shoved it into a trash bin he'd borrowed from the laundry room. The lower layer of equally thin concrete was exposed and the jackhammer chewed and spat its way around the next hole. Done. He was through. He pushed an arm down into the circle, used the flashlight on his phone to illuminate the cold walls below.

Then hurried down into the basement and the shelter to clean up the edges of the hole. It stared down at him like a giant eye—he glued on the Sheetrock, plastered it, painted it, and cleaned the mess off the concrete floor.

Back up to the closet. He didn't want the hole to be visible from either side.

He cut out the particleboard, fashioned it into a blind bottom for the closet, screwed the piano hinge along its short side, and hid the small doorknob behind the doorframe. The hatch could be lifted up with the knob, then pulled back again without landing wrong. He tried and it worked perfectly, at a right angle to the threshold. The closet now seemed to have a completely normal floor.

Piet Hoffmann paused, momentarily overcome by exhaustion.

A break, it was surely several hours since his last.

Deep, slow breaths with his eyes closed.

Yes.

It would work. If it became necessary.

If they had to escape this place, too.

He picked up a coffee and a cinnamon bun at the gas station near the roundabout on Hammarby Road, took the smaller roads through Björkhagen and Kärrtorp to avoid rush hour, and in Bagarmossen picked up two more cups of coffee at a café that had looked exactly the same for as long as he could remember. He parked in his usual spot and took the elevator to the eighth floor and the studio apartment whose blinds were always drawn.

"Hi, Andy—want a coffee?"

"Sure, thanks."

"Splash of milk, that's how you like it?"

"You got a good memory, boss."

Hoffmann handed him one of the warm cardboard cups. The huge security guard took it in one of his enormous hands, thankful for even a moment's respite from the eighteen screens he'd had his eyes on.

"Easy like yesterday?"

"Some drunk dude pissed in the doorway to number 8 just now, two dogs had a fight outside 10 just an hour ago, and a young woman in 12 punched her boyfriend rather skillfully early in the morning on their way home from what I would guess was a bar. So yes—just as calm."

Piet Hoffmann sank down onto the only thing in the room resembling a free chair—an unpacked moving box, which had never found its place—and slurped down the last drop in his paper cup. He cleared his throat, tried to lower his voice as best he could, felt like the guard had already noticed the difference.

"Allergies. Nothing contagious—just an itch in my throat."

"Got it, boss. Pollen is a motherfucker. And grass is the worst—whenever they mow it, I can't stop sneezing."

Hoffmann nodded and glanced at one of the monitors, saw an older couple washing their windows from the outside, the man in the flower bed balanced on a long metal rod with a squeegee in his hand, and a woman with the living room window half-open pointing and directing him.

Hoffmann and the guard exchanged a smile.

Watching people had its moments.

"It's like this, Andy. I need you to listen to me."

"Okay."

"We're adding another safe house."

"A new one?"

"Seven new surveillance cameras. I need you to connect to them this evening and keep watch to make sure everything's as it should be."

"Which number?"

"Not here—a bit further away. Tallbacken, in the Gamla Sickla area."

"I'm not sure I follow."

"Emergency. As usual."

"But if anything happens . . . I mean, I thought the whole point was to have them all in the same place—I can't get there in time if something happens, and I'd have to leave the other three . . ."

Lie.

Piet Hoffmann was pretty good at it; only Zofia could see straight through him.

"A single woman in her forties. Three children, two boys, ten and eight, and a baby, a girl. Safe house has the highest level of security. Nacka Municipality called me this morning, and I said yes—so it is what it is. But I've gone through everything. Doors secured, windows secured, cameras in place. I'll help them move in some-time tonight. And as far as you and Carlos and Bill are concerned, no change other than a few more cameras to follow, one more family."

He was still hungry, his body leaking energy, so he parked in the bus lane near Hornstull and ran into 7-Eleven to grab a hot dog and a low-alcohol beer. Wolfed the first one down, ordered another, checked the time—almost ten hours had passed since he left the small studio on the corner. This time he entered through the back entrance on Borgar Street, crossed the courtyard, and went into the building on Högalids Street, where she waited for him with the smile he could have drowned in once—and she looked pleased.

"Sit down. Let's try this on."

The makeup artist who had helped him so many times rolled out a long and narrow cart whose metal wheels whined angrily, just like always.

"I think . . . well, we've never transformed you quite this much before? Or am I forgetting something, Piet?"

"You're right. It's never been necessary. Now it is."

Four trays were jammed onto the shelves of the trolley, prepped and full.

"I should have broken it down into more sections, then I could have made the details even better, but I wanted to simplify it for you."

She swept a hand over what was about to turn him into someone else.

"One for the right eye, one for the left, one for the nose. And one for the chin and cheeks and neck. Only four pieces. It's easier to deal with in case they start to peel."

She began with the closest tray, carefully lifted up the skin-like piece that lay on top of it.

"I prefer working in gelatin, you know that, Piet, but right now—the weather's just too hot. I have no clue what you're planning to do, where you're headed, but I do know you're usually physically active and gelatin in this heat would just melt off."

He was aware that knowing the usage of a mask was usually the starting point for her designs. And so she

was doing her best to infer the information she needed
but would never receive.

He smiled.

"You're not married to a cop, are you?"

She smiled back.

"No, my husband lives in the fantasy version of what
seems to be your real life."

"Fantasy—how do you mean?"

"He considers himself a playwright. That was how
we met. You know, work."

"Well, in that case—yes. This disguise is going to be
subjected to a lot . . . physically."

She held a shapeless mass in front of his right eye, as
if taking aim, checking the distances, then pressed
down against his skin. In the past Piet Hoffmann had
stayed for the entire process and knew how skillfully
her hands had shaped new features for a new personality. He knew what it looked like when she built the tiny
walls along the edges of the first cast, walls meant to
hold the mixture she poured over it—plaster and a
splash of regular dishwashing soap and something else
he couldn't remember the name of. A filling that solidified, and when she finally tore off the walls, she had
her next cast, on which she built the pieces of the mask.

"Since I couldn't use gelatin, which worked so well
before, I went for silicone. Not perfect, I know, but the
best I could do under the circumstances. The upside is
that it can withstand heat much better, the downside is
that it's more likely to harden. So I experimented a
little—mixed in a few other components. Now it should

be more elastic and skin-like. We'll just have to cross our fingers, Piet, and hope your skin takes to it."

She asked him to close his eyes while she glued a tired-looking eyelid over his right eye. She poked at it, pulled at it—it stayed put, firmly. Then a hanging eyelid over his left eye, then the enlarged wings of his nose, and finally the much larger piece that stretched from the two bloated cheeks to an equally bloated chin.

"I knew your skin tone already, so I was able to do the color matching in the silicone itself. And now . . ."

She looked happy and relieved.

". . . it's perfect. The seams are barely visible, Piet! Whatever remains I can easily cover up."

He reached for a hand mirror lying on the lower shelf of her cart.

She slapped his hand away, shook her head. He wasn't supposed to see, yet.

"I know you don't like dress shirts. But I managed to make it to H&M before they closed, and I picked up one for you. It's an extra large, so there will be plenty of room for the stomach that matches that face."

There was a plastic bag sitting on the floor, out of which she produced his new belly, which she hung around his neck and stabilized with a belt at his waist, a pair of gray dress pants, and a light-blue, summery, thin dress shirt with long sleeves.

"Sort of like a banker—your new look fits better with that outfit than your usual T-shirt, hunter's vest, and worn jeans. Also, no matter how carefully I place the big piece, there will be seams visible on the back of your neck. And I don't want you to have to think about that while you're running around—that won't work. But a shirt collar, Piet, that will protect you if it comes loose, hide it."

She sat down one last time in front of him, a mustache fashioned from real human hair in her hand, the same shade as the newly dyed hair on his head. She adjusted his head slightly backwards, asked him to hold it just like that, and spread glue between his upper lip and nose and then on the back of the mustache. She pressed it down, walked her fingertips over it until she was sure it stuck.

"And the seam is as usual in the nasolabial fold. It's less visible there, hidden by your natural fold."

Now. It was time.

She coaxed a full-length mirror out from behind the coat rack in the corner, carried it over toward his chair, and held it in front of him.

It was time to meet himself.

"You have to promise me to keep as close an eye on it as you can. In this heat—a single wrong move and a seam might come loose. Around the eyes. Or around your mouth. That's what I'm most worried about. I'm sending some glue with you, just dab it on as needed, works for the mustache, too, which might loosen at the corner of your mouth."

Piet Hoffmann looked at the person in the mirror.

The person stared back at him.

Him.

And yet not.

Dark hair. Dark mustache. Brown eyes. Skin sagging on his face. A person who seemed broken and old.

He put out his hand, as if in a greeting, and the mirror image did the same.

"A couple of days, Piet. Then you have to come back. If you want to be sure it won't show. I have the casts and I'll make a couple extra sets and have them here waiting for you. When you come back, I have a really effective removal agent, then we'll do a re-glue. It'll be just as quick as today."

She looked at him. Really *looked* at him.

Checked every seam.

Pulled a couple of badly dyed strands of hair out of his eyebrows.

Asked him to spin around again, then nodded. He was ready.

She smiled her lovely smile and wished him good luck, and it occurred to him how nice it would feel to just stay here. Become another person with another face living another life. But he was in a hurry. He had to keep moving toward those who threatened him. And now he could—in a new shape. Get closer, close enough to take back Paula.

He'd changed cars again, now back to the one he'd started the day with, and then settled down at a café that stayed open late and put the phone down on the table in front of him. Three cups of coffee and biscottis later. Until the text finally arrived at half past ten.

Latitude 59.279751. Longitude 18.229393.
Northeastern edge of Knipträsket lake.

Between the stone and two anthills.
Dig one half meter down.
Collect it before midnight.

Piet Hoffmann looked up the coordinates on his phone. It showed a spot about twenty kilometers south of Stockholm, not far from Saltsjöbaden and Fisksätra. A short walk into the large natural reserve. That's where they buried it.

He'd play their game. But just a little longer. He had to make them think he was doing what they wanted, so he could get close enough to stab them in the back.

It took twenty minutes by car. From the artificial light of the city to the dense darkness and absolute stillness of the forest.

He held a GPS and a flashlight in one hand and pulled a small cart behind him with the other, zigzagging between thick branches and mossy stones down a narrow forest path. He stumbled a few times over a stray root, but never fell, always forward, forward, he had to keep moving.

Buried in the forest.

That's how a lot of the criminals in Stockholm stored their weapons—within a twenty-kilometer radius of the city there were hundreds of private stockpiles buried beneath the ground. Criminals in the underworld hoarded and guarded their weapons like gold—many groups had shared custody of a stockpile, maybe a couple of Walther P99s, a Kalashnikov, which they dug up as needed.

He stopped, checked his GPS. He was almost to the small lake called Knipträsket. The northeast side, with his flashlight it was easy enough to find a large clearing where a big stone shared space with a couple of huge anthills. He was soon standing in front of a newly cleared piece of ground, and checked again to make sure the hood of his jacket covered his face before unfolding his spade.

He assumed they had him under surveillance here, and they didn't need to see his new face yet.

Powerful thrusts.

Aimed toward a weapon worth one hundred thousand kronor a piece. Much more expensive than anything else circulating in this city.

A Glock, brand new and still in the box, could be had for ten, twelve thousand kronor. An AK-47, which cost about two hundred euros at the beginning of the supply chain in the Balkans, went for twenty-five thousand kronor by the time it reached Stockholm. Maybe some idiot might agree to pay thirty thousand, supply and demand, the more desperate you are, the more expensive it will be. But these were bargains in comparison to what he was about to dig out of the ground.

So many more weapons in circulation now than when he was in the game—and so many more shootings. Still, bystanders rarely ended up with a bullet in their brains; criminals shot at each other, robbed each other, drug dealers trying to take over each other's territories. While the politicians just kept talking about getting tougher on crime. But long sentences didn't make a difference. People got ahold of weapons because they needed them. A matter of life or death. And life in prison was still better than no life at all.

Now.

The tip of the spade hit plastic wrapped around wood.

Piet Hoffmann got down on his knees, cleared the last of the dirt with his hands, and lifted out the box. Oblong, heavy. His gloves still on, he pulled off the lid, looking for the FN BRG-15, a weapon that didn't exist.

Dear God.

There it was. It was real.

The most powerful machine gun ever made and some faceless arms dealer was trying to use Piet Hoffmann to corner the Swedish weapons market with it.

Start a war. Change the balance of terror. Force every gang, every mafia, to arm themselves in the same way as their enemies.

He loaded the wooden box onto his cart and then cleared away the dirt and gravel that covered the next box, the tripod, and then the ammunition. He was just starting to head back down the narrow forest path when the phone rang. So they were watching him, even out here.

"You found it."

That distorted voice. It almost sounded pleased.

"I want you to get started. Immediately. Our agreement is a go. We're near your family to make sure . . . well, nothing happens to them. Until you do what we ask. When you've taken out a criminal organization with the weapon you just dug up, when you've launched our ad

campaign, then we'll leave your family alone and hand over the original documents, which describe your years as a snitch. And you'll never hear from us again."

He had to answer. He had to buy time. Without revealing his new voice.

"Bad connection. Call in fifteen minutes."

Abrupt. Almost whispering. Then he hung up. They called again. And again. Only when he was back up on the highway did he stop, pull over to the side of the road, and get out of the car, where his new voice would be watered down by the ambient sounds.

"What's going on?"

"My phone. I didn't have good reception—now it's working better. But I need time. I can't just go take out anyone. I have to choose the appropriate organization for the job. In the most vulnerable situation. With the most enemies. Most . . ."

"How long?"

"Forty-eight hours."

"Twenty-four."

"I need . . ."

"Twenty-four hours is what you get. It's not negotiable. Act—and you'll get your papers and your family back. Don't act—and we send the documents to every organization you ever snitched on, and we start shooting—youngest first. Luiza, that's her name, right?"

Piet Hoffmann lingered for a while in the darkness next to the highway, watching cars rush by. Everyone was on their way somewhere. Just like him—on his way to where the ones who threatened him didn't want to see him. And they wouldn't.

What do you do when a distorted voice thinks they know what you look like?

You mask yourself.

What do you do if that voice thinks you're working for him?

You go your own way.

And—what do you do when that motherfucking voice is convinced that he's kept you at a distance?

You get close. You go all the way in.

He'd done his final car exchange of the day—jumped into a small Japanese rental car he'd picked up at a gas station in Västertorp, where his own car stood along with the phone back in the passenger seat—and now he was parked on a backstreet not far from the house that meant everything to him. Close enough to be able to see, far enough away not to be seen. Listening to the blackbird's melodic song. Wondering if it was the same bird as before. He decided it was, it must live in their tree.

His whole body ached.

He wanted to be with them, checking Hugo's and Rasmus's homework, bathing Luiza in her little tub, holding Zofia in his arms.

Later.

When this was over.

A neighbor passed by with her dog on a leash, a shiny red Irish setter bouncing along happily, and they nodded to each other. She showed no signs of knowing the person she was greeting. A little later a couple with a daughter in Hugo's class parked next to him on this dead-end street, glanced through his windshield as they passed by, but they, too, didn't seem to recognize him.

When the lights were turned off on the bottom floor of his home, the living room, the hall, and finally the kitchen, he grabbed a bag out of the back seat and took out two finger prostheses. Once they went up, it usually took a half hour until Zofia had the kids in bed and the lights in the upstairs' bathroom and in the boys' bedrooms went dark like the night.

He didn't like using these. They felt clumsy and awkward, because he'd learned to live with just three fingers on his left hand. But he had to hide the most noticeable characteristic he had. His final transformation. He greased the stumps of his fingers with gel until the thin sleeve of the prostheses slid on easily.

And suddenly Piet Hoffmann was there again. In a hotel in central Germany some years ago.

He'd infiltrated the Polish mafia from behind the walls of a Swedish maximum-security prison. Been unmasked, sentenced to death, forced to flee. He'd hidden in a ventilation shaft, and when it was time to go, he left two of his fingertips behind on a metal edge. His bones had been visible. It was in a hotel room in Frankfurt where they'd agreed to meet that Zofia peeled back the skin and flesh, wrapped his fingers in sterilized compresses, gave him a high dose of antibiotics, and waited until she was sure the infection was gone. Then she'd used a regular pair of pruning shears to clip the bone off a bit further in, folded the excess skin over it, and glued it all together.

Medical silicone. That's what the finger prostheses were made of. At the moment he was covered from head to toe in materials he'd only ever used to caulk joints. He waved the prostheses, and they stayed firmly attached to the stumps, then wiggled his healthy fingers without bumping into the shells—his ability to move was intact.

A half hour later and night had rocked the whole neighborhood to sleep. He climbed out of his car. Started walking. Strolling. That's what it should look like—a man out for a nighttime stroll, maybe on his way home, maybe just trying to get a good night's sleep.

According to Juan and Nic, the first vehicle that didn't seem to belong in the area was parked just twenty meters from the Hoffmann's mailbox. It had a clear view of the front of the house. A Toyota, not brand new, mid-price range. Exactly the sort of thing he would have chosen to not attract attention. He memorized the license plate number and walked on.

There was a man sitting in the driver's seat.

Piet Hoffmann knocked on the side window and waited for the window to roll down.

"Got a light?"

Hoffmann recognized the man. He'd even worked with him a couple of times—hired him when he needed extra personnel. But they'd never really gelled. That this guy and his friends were his opponents, sent here on behalf of an anonymous organization, made this all the more difficult.

"Excuse me?"

"A light? The wife won't let me smoke at home anymore."

Hoffmann waved the pack of cigarettes he'd bought on his way here. The man in the car was competent. Trigger-happy and fearless. Employed by a security company known for not being picky about who was paying or why, as long as the money was good. Everything inside Piet Hoffmann was screaming now. He wanted to grab onto the motherfucker watching his house, drag him out of his car, force him to say who was paying him and whom he was reporting to. But he couldn't. Not yet. Once Zofia and his kids were safe, then he could unleash himself.

"And, like an idiot, I left the house with no lighter."

"Go away."

"You got a light or . . . ?"

"Are you deaf? Get the fuck outta here."

Now he'd tried his mask and voice on someone he'd met before. It worked. He'd gotten close. In a way Piet Hoffmann never could have.

Not far away there was another car with a lone man in the front seat, his eyes on the back of Piet's house. And when Hoffmann checked the license plate, it was registered to the same security firm.

They were—just like him—guarding his family. While he was supposed to be somewhere else, preparing for the mission they'd given him.

Instead, he continued strolling through the neighborhood he knew so well.

Made a wide circle until he felt completely sure that the two men could no longer see him.

Then he turned back.

But he didn't take one of the streets—there was an old path that snaked in between the backs of the houses, with the branches of fruit trees hanging above, and sprawling raspberry bushes lining either side. He crouched along until he reached the corner of his backyard, then climbed over the back fence and crept the last few meters to a small tool-shed. And when he opened the shed door and snuck in between lawn mowers and rakes, he thought about all those renovations, seen and unseen, which he'd done before they'd moved in.

Rasmus's action figures were still standing in the same pattern in the hall, which his father had learned not to stumble over, and surprisingly the stairs didn't squeak even once on his way up—maybe this endless heat had sapped the energy to whine out of the wood, too. Piet Hoffmann stopped at the door to Hugo's and Rasmus's rooms, two boys deep asleep. He couldn't see Luiza behind the drapery that separated her room from the upper hall, nor through the pile of teddy bears Rasmus had ordered to stand guard outside her crib. But he could hear her calm and steady breathing. Zofia lay with her back to the doorway, and he gazed at his wife's naked body entangled in a thin sheet. He sank down on his knees at the edge of the bed, shook her shoulder gently, whispered.

"Zo?"

She shifted anxiously.

"Zo? Love?"

Then she woke up and turned around. Piet Hoffmann could see the terror in her eyes. He laid his hand over her mouth to stop her from screaming.

"Zo—it's me. Piet."

She tried to scream again. He pressed harder.

"Listen, Zo. It is me. Me. It's me who's about to kiss you twice on the forehead like I always do. And when I do, I'm gonna take my hand away and kiss you twice on your mouth."

He leaned close, and she tried to push him away. His lips touched her warm forehead, then he removed his hand and kissed her twice on the mouth, then put the hand back again.

Maybe she relaxed a little.

Maybe she just wanted him to think she had.

"Zo?"

He loosened his grip, a little bit at a time.

"I'll explain everything to you when this is over. But right now, Zo, you have to promise to just listen and trust me."

He waited, trying to make eye contact.

She didn't scream.

"My voice. My face. But we have to get out of here, now, tonight. So we don't have time to talk about it yet, Zo. Not you and me. Not with the kids. Okay?"

She looked at him.

Perhaps unsure if she was awake or still dreaming.

Then she nodded.

• • •

Zofia held Hugo and Rasmus by the hand. Drowsy.
Tired. While Luiza slept in his arms. Their boys
didn't trust the man who was leading them down into
the basement. But they trusted Zofia who said this was
what they had to do now. Don't turn on any lights. And
be very quiet. Only when they finally reached the basement and were heading into the office did Hugo protest.

"That's Dad's room. We're not supposed to go in
there. *He's* not supposed to go in there."

Piet Hoffmann wanted to hug his son. Say how
proud he was. But instead he said:

"Your dad asked me to do this. Gave me permission.
Even told me how to get inside."

Piet Hoffmann waved for everyone to follow him
into the closet. Then he pressed the hidden lever and
opened the secret room. A room he knew Hugo and
Rasmus had visited once. They never talked about it,
but a gun lying in the wrong direction had given them
away. Zofia, on the other hand, looked as surprised and
duped as she probably felt. But he gave her no time to
ask. She could do that later. After they were through
the next hidden door. The one that even Hugo and
Rasmus didn't know about. Because behind the weapons cabinet, which he now lifted off the wall, there
stood a small white button. If he pushed it, part of the
wall opened up. Inwards. Another hidden door. High
and wide enough for an adult to easily enter a tunnel,
which led under the backyard all the way to the
toolshed—the same path he'd just used to enter.

• • •

They snuck through the darkness. Past the fruit trees and raspberry bushes. He glanced at Zofia, who was staring straight ahead. He wanted to explain to her that it was long ago, when they'd just bought this house and she was still living in a tiny apartment in the city while he did the renovations, and he was another person back then, living in a parallel reality. The one she'd made him leave. But that time was still always there, maybe in documents that threatened his family, maybe in a secret tunnel that ended up being his family's escape route.

They approached the car, parked in another section of their sleeping suburb, loaded the backpacks he and Zofia had hurriedly packed. As he asked Hugo and Rasmus to climb into the back seat of an unfamiliar vehicle with a stranger in the driver's seat, he had to bite his own cheek as hard as he could to keep from hugging them. When Zofia sank down beside him with Luiza on her lap, biting was no longer enough and he had to turn talk radio up loud to cover his mumbled "it's me— Dad." They sat in silence for the whole of their short trip to the ground-floor apartment at Number 37, which none of his passengers had ever seen before.

Silent until Hugo just couldn't take it anymore.

"Who are you?"

Hoffmann adjusted the rearview mirror to get a good look at his son.

"A friend. Of your . . . father's."

"If you're his friend, how come we've never met you?"

"You have."

Hugo peeked at his mother sitting in front of him, and she nodded, as if to confirm the stranger was speaking the truth.

"When?"

Hoffmann twisted the rearview mirror, looking at his wise and thoughtful son.

"When . . . what?"

"When did we meet?"

"It was . . . The first time was long ago. You were little."

"Why are you here and not my dad?"

"I don't know—all I know is that he wants me to help you and your brother and your sister and your mom. He'll probably explain everything when he gets home again."

Now it was Piet Hoffmann who peeked. And when he was sure Hugo had leaned back, he sought Zofia's hand, squeezed it hard.

The horseshoe-shaped apartment building seemed more awake than their suburban neighborhood had been; there was at least one window lit on every floor. Rasmus and Luiza had both fallen asleep during the short journey, while Hugo anxiously tried to make sense of what he was seeing outside the car window.

"What . . . Why are we here?"

"Your dad said you needed to sleep here tonight."

"Why should we do that?"

"He didn't say. But he wanted me to help you. Drive you here, show you."

"Mom?"

Hugo grabbed hold of the front seat and pulled himself forward until he was almost beside Zofia.

"Is it true, Mom? Are we sleeping here?"

Piet Hoffmann squeezed her hand again, he didn't have to catch her eye, he knew what those eyes would say, how uncomfortable she found all of this.

"Yes, darling. Tonight, and maybe a few more nights."

"If you knew, why didn't you say so when we got to bed?"

Zofia swallowed, and before she could answer, Hoffmann interrupted.

"Your mom didn't know it, either. At that point. It's your dad's fault, he should have said something to her and to you. He told me to tell you he's sorry he forgot."

Zofia carried Luiza, Piet carried Rasmus and the two small bags, and Hugo walked defiantly just a few short steps behind them from the car to the apartment building.

"Here? Seriously?"

Hugo made a quick lap through the three-room apartment while his parents laid his sleeping siblings in beds.

"Are we gonna live here? There's hardly any furniture."

"Just tonight. And like your mother said, maybe a few more nights. But the beds are good, which is the most important thing. There's a kitchen table and food in the fridge. Which is also important. And here . . ."

Hoffmann took Hugo's hand and led him into the living room.

". . . is the *most* important thing of all: a sofa and a TV. And I put your PlayStation in one of the bags. You and your little brother can play as much as you want, whenever you want."

He plucked a console and controls out of a bag and some games he didn't understand and put everything on the coffee table in front of his eldest son, then opened the closet in the bedroom and carefully placed the bags onto a newly laid floor, so no one would hear it was hollow.

It was later, after he'd whispered to Zofia to call the boys in sick tomorrow and tell the school they'd be gone for the rest of the week, which was the last one of the semester, after he'd gone to the bathroom and almost drowned in the mirror wondering who the hell was staring back at him, after he'd closed the apartment door and was on his way out of the building into what looked like rain, that Hugo caught up to him.

"Hey, you?"

Hoffmann stopped, turned around.

"Yeah?"

"I know."

"Excuse me?"

Hugo pushed Piet's arm.

"I know it's you, Dad."

"I think you . . ."

Now he shoved harder, more angry than eager.

"Just stop it. I knew it didn't make sense. I knew something was wrong. Then in the apartment—I saw how you moved. Held yourself. I *know* how you walk, Dad. You walk like me. With your feet and arms like so . . . we walk the same way."

And Piet Hoffmann could no longer hold back his fear. It just came, couldn't be denied.

"It *is* me, Hugo. First, promise me one thing—don't say anything to Rasmus."

His eldest son seemed to be considering it, silent and still.

Then he nodded, just as Zofia did when she was lying in bed with her husband's hand pressed over her mouth.

"Why, Dad? Why do you look like that? Sound like that? And why are we here?"

"I can't tell you."

Hugo sighed deeply, but not because he too was scared. Because he was serious.

"Dangerous, Dad."

"What?"

"It's dangerous. For us. That's why we're here."

Hoffmann grabbed Hugo's hand, pulled him closer.

"Not dangerous, Hugo. But you might say that . . ."

"Dad—just stop."

Piet pulled him close enough to hug him and whisper in his ear.

"Yes. You're right. It *is* dangerous, Hugo. That's why you're here. And that's why you have to help me and go back to the apartment. Until it's not dangerous anymore."

A hug that turned into them staring at each other.

Then Hugo swallowed, lowered his eyes, and looked at the ground for a moment. Finally, he turned around without saying goodbye.

Piet Hoffmann hadn't felt this alone in a very long time.

PART

3

Thump. Thump.

Someone hopping. Onto him.

Thump, thump. Thump, thump.

A little girl. She's jumping on his stomach. Her clothes are dirty, and she's laughing and singing. *Happybirthdaytoyooou. Happybirthdaytoyooou.* Singing loud and clear and off-key. But it's beautiful.

And then the thuds get heavier. Muted, hollow.

The little girl is knocking on a door, hitting it with every ounce of strength she has, knocking that won't stop and intensifies in strength, explosions in the same rhythm, bang, bang.

A gun.

Bang, bang. Bang, bang.

The explosions are like volcanic eruptions, furious, roaring.

So close that he can see them, too.

He can see that little head trying to escape, see the first shot penetrate her forehead, tear a hole in her temple.

Bang, bang, bang, bang.

And now the gun turns to him.

And its cold, hard muzzle tears the skin of his face until drops of blood start to fall.

The finger on the trigger starts to pull.

He woke up. In a cold sweat. His heart pounding in his chest. Until he looked at the familiar ceiling. And the walls that were protecting him. He got up from his corduroy sofa, still in his office at the police station. The first step always meant stabbing pain in his stiff leg and his neck and lower back.

Ewert Grens wasn't sure what exactly it was—but something was different.

He limped over to his window and looked out over the police station's deserted courtyard.

And then he heard them again. The shots. Someone shooting and someone running.

Just like in the dream.

And he realized what had changed. It was easier to breathe. The gnawing, sticky heat had been replaced by heavy gray clouds, and now those clouds had burst with a helluva rainstorm, which beat violently against his window and metal windowsill, clattering, bang bang, bang bang. That's what he heard. The shots. That's why he woke up.

The detective superintendent smiled at his own confusion—thoughts born from his own mind—and listened to the rain until the window was just a blur. All the buildings outside, the core of Swedish police operations, were hazy, now lacked any sharp lines. He opened the window and cupped his hands, brought rainwater to his face, and the stuffiness inside drifted away. He ran his wet hands through his hair and looked at his reflection in the top pane of the half-open window, saw those thin, straggling strands slicked back by rain.

A Stockholm night. Which would soon turn into a Stockholm dawn.

Sometime after two he'd finally lain down to get some rest. Apparently he'd fallen asleep. Now he returned to his desk and one of the two folders that he'd checked out of the guarded archive. He flipped through the case file and the autopsy reports of a nearly twenty-year-old investigation without noticing anything he hadn't seen before.

Nothing.

He found no more now than he did back then.

He had instructed Nils Krantz—the forensic technician who was one of the few who'd been a police officer as long as Grens himself—to comb every centimeter of the apartment on Dala Street 74. Fingerprints, fibers, DNA. *Nothing.* He'd analyzed every visit to the guarded archive in recent months. *Nothing.* He'd even ordered an examination of the blank paper left inside the folder, not just dusting for fingerprints—but finding manufacturers, distribution chains, retailers. *Nothing.*

Ewert Grens was pacing anxiously around his office as he so often did when he wanted to make progress but had no idea how or where. Around and around in a tight circle so as not to crash into the closet or the bookshelf. Until it became too cramped, until he crashed into himself, so he headed out to the corridor and the coffee machine and a plastic mug of lukewarm black coffee. From there it wasn't far to Sven's office, where he opened the window just as wide as his own, then on to Hermansson's office and her window. The air started to move. What an amazing invention a cross draft was. Sven Sundkvist and Mariana Hermansson were the only colleagues he could stand, and who could stand him. But they were at home now, asleep in their own beds. He hoped they could keep living the kind of lives where they didn't need an old worn-out corduroy sofa to be brave enough to close their eyes and face sleep unguarded.

The witness protection program folder was lying on Hermansson's desk, because she'd been working on the analysis of the blank paper. Ewert Grens couldn't stop himself from opening it, even though it only made him quiver with rage. It should have told him the story of one little girl's future, of what happened to her, who she became, and where she ended up.

Unwritten pages whose contents were hidden outside those windows somewhere.

He knew that when the trial was over, when an individual was no longer of interest to the police, they were also no longer the responsibility of the witness protection program. These people, who would always have to live with having once been threatened, were now flushed out into another reality, and had to be traced via the records of their new town's tax agency, which had given them their new identity. After the trial, after the investigation was abandoned, a person who had been threatened would just have to make it on their own. But this girl had only been five years old. She wouldn't have been able to fend for herself. She would have been placed into a foster home, into a new life, maybe eventually she would have been adopted and grown up as someone else's child.

Grens had his own special access to the Swedish Tax Agency. The kind of back door criminals often bought or threatened their way into. His own arrangement was different—he and his contact exchanged their services. Information from the police records was traded for information in the tax records. Not quite legal, but it wasn't always possible to find lawbreakers by following the letter of the law.

Right now he was waiting for his contact to call him back. Why wasn't he? Shouldn't matter how late it was. Grens slammed the useless folder shut again and sank into Mariana Hermansson's desk chair. He'd never sat in it before. He had spent the last ten years in her vicinity just a few doors down, and had barely stepped over her threshold. That how it worked, just a part of their unspoken agreement. She could barge into his office at any time and say anything—while he respected her privacy and integrity, which began at her door. Like a child who needed to maintain boundaries with a demanding and overprotective father. He liked it that way. That was why he had adapted himself to her, a rare occurrence for him. She must know she was the daughter he'd never had, even though they never spoke of it and never would.

A palpable feeling of unease.

Not because he was sitting in Hermansson's chair, that felt fine. An unease that had been with him since the moment he first looked at those blank pages.

The missing documents could only have been re-moved by a police officer and handed over to someone who paid for them—only an active police officer could gain access to that restricted archive. This unease was because he found it inconceivable. Corrupt colleagues? In his forty years on the force, Ewert Grens never inves-tigated the crimes of those who do the investigating. And right now he didn't have time, he was searching for a person who hid while four murders were commit-ted in her vicinity, a little girl who had chosen not to remember, but might remember now. A young woman who could be a dangerous threat to a certain violent criminal who might have gotten ahold of her records.

Grens wandered around the silent and empty hall-ways of his department for another half hour, still wait-ing for a phone call that never came. When his restlessness became too urgent and destructive, and he began crashing into himself again, he took care of it as he often did nowadays, driving up to the Northern Cemetery to sit for a while on a simple park bench in front of plot number 603, a spot he avoided visiting for many years. The white cross looked a little crooked, and the brass plate with her name on it had some green schmutz stuck to it. He used the weight of his body to stand the cross upright again, and cleaned the plaque with water fetched from a tap in a corner next to the rakes and watering cans. He dried the brass off with his sleeve. Anni Grens. That's what stood on the plaque. She'd held his hand tight for just a short time, which ended before their journey together barely even began.

It had taken him thirty years to scrape together the courage and longing to meet anyone else. Laura. The autopsy technician whose eyes seemed so present and whose mouth held the warmest smile he'd ever seen. She had made him feel calm despite the fact that they met in the coldest place there is—a morgue. He never understood how someone who spent their time carving up dead people could seem so full of life. He'd sat here on this park bench, debating with Anni if maybe it might be time to meet someone like Laura—and a half year later decided to go back to spending his days on his own. He didn't miss his meetings with Laura, he was the one who ended it, but it had been nice to have a woman's help in breaking out of this prison of his own making.

He was walking back through the enormous cemetery, about half-way to his car, when the phone rang. A blocked number at five in the morning, not many people were awake yet.

"Yes?"

"Couldn't find much. But I got something that might point you in the right direction."

His contact at the Swedish Tax Agency. They never said each other's names out loud, nor made any other personal references, either. They both behaved as if they were being listened to, because they had so much to lose if they really were.

"It took me a while because so much from that time has yet to be digitized. But the fact that you were able to give me the month and the year helped quite a bit.

And it appears, from the handwritten notes I found, that she was prepped for a new name and a new social security number."

"Tell me something I don't know."

"But, unfortunately, I couldn't find which name, or which social security number."

Grens stopped in the middle of the carefully raked path. Graves all around him. They didn't scare him anymore.

"Are you kidding me? Is that all? What goddamn *direction* are you planning to point me in? Straight into a stone wall?"

"However . . ."

It was clear that his contact was annoyed. Or tired. Or maybe annoyingly tired.

". . . there is some information about placing her in a foster family."

"And I repeat myself: tell me something I don't know."

"Unfortunately nothing about which family."

"Goddamn . . ."

"But—and now here comes your direction—I do have a location for you."

Grens started walking again. He left the graves behind him. It was even more peaceful here at the memorial slope where families spread their loved one's ashes.

"Yes?"

"Söderköping. Not a big town, located near . . ."

"I know where it is. Anything else?"

"I was just about to tell you that. In one of those handwritten notes, I found the name of the department head who made all the arrangements. Probably retired by now. She definitely knows. I'll text you everything I have on her."

The detective superintendent was about to hang up.

"By the way . . ."

But changed his mind.

". . . the girl. What was her name? Originally?"

"Lilaj. Just like the others."

"I figured that much. But I can't remember her first name. No matter how hard I try."

"Zana."

And then it came back.

Zana Lilaj.

She'd looked just like her name. A little flower with tangled hair.

It was still too early for rush hour, and it only took him a few minutes to drive back to the police station and the little café on Bergs Street, which opened earlier than any of the others and baked the most delicious cinnamon buns. At this time of day they were piping hot and straight from the oven. He liked to sit at a table by the window and watch his colleagues streaming by on their way to start their workdays.

He knew her name now. And the name of the department head who gave her a new identity—his contact had even sent him the address in the town of Söderköping. In her role as the head of that city's child welfare office she had, according to the notes, been responsible for authorizing the girl's new placement. She would know the name of the foster family who took on a child with no parents or siblings, would know who had raised her, who had turned her into an ordinary citizen.

He dipped the cinnamon bun into black coffee, a habit that calmed him.

Söderköping. In Östergötland. Not so far from the E4 highway or the sea. Grens had visited that beautiful little town on the Göta Canal, first in connection with a triple homicide perpetrated by a young man who cut the throats of his best friends and didn't have any friends anymore, and then on a later occasion for an interrogation of two elderly women who had been fighting over an even more elderly man, then decided to kill their mutual lover and blame each other instead. So this would be his third visit to that summer idyll.

Another coffee, and this time accompanied by a piece of apple cake with vanilla sauce—it was never too early for some things.

"Ewert?"

Ewert Grens turned around.

He hadn't noticed the tall, athletic man opening the café door and slipping inside, until he got to Grens's table.

"I thought I might find you here."

Short dark hair, square face with a straight nose, and a chin that looked like it belonged to a superhero in a comic book. Erik Wilson. Head of the homicide unit, and therefore Grens's boss. He'd once been a handler for the criminal infiltrators that the police publicly denied, but privately believed were indispensable. Until an operation went to hell and degenerated into a kidnapping in a high-security prison, and the police chief was forced out, and Wilson moved up. Strangely Grens found him easier to get along with now as a superior than when they were both detective superintendents— perhaps Ewert Grens had finally accepted there was a need for several versions of the truth in one police corridor.

"Sit down. There's room."

"Ewert, I didn't come here to have a coffee."

"Well, that's what you do here."

"The officer on duty woke me up forty-five minutes ago. Someone found a dead man in a staircase on Brännkyrka Street."

Grens poured even more vanilla sauce over the small plate where his apple cake already seemed to be drowning.

"I don't have time."

"Ewert—I want *you* to take over."

"Sorry, in the middle of another investigation. You want some apple cake?"

Erik Wilson shook his head. He'd been standing up, but now he pulled out a chair and sat down across from Grens.

"What investigation?"

"Breaking and entering. Landed on my desk yesterday."

"And since when, Ewert, do we prioritize a break-in over a possible murder?"

"Since break-ins started being connected to four murders that might possibly become a fifth. Since crimes started being committed *inside* the police station. I'm headed to Söderköping in a couple hours, and hopefully I can explain more when I get back."

Wilson was searching for napkins and found an

unused one on the table next to them, used it to dry off a stray drop or two of sweat along his hairline and his cheeks. It had been raining earlier, the heat broke somewhat, but it was still unseasonably warm.

"It's not often I give you a command, Ewert. Because we both know you're usually more effective when I don't give you orders. But I'm giving you one now. You're not going anywhere except to Brännkyrka Street 56, immediately, and you're going to take over as lead investigator no matter who's in charge right now."

It didn't make sense.

Ewert Grens had no interest in socializing with his boss, not even eating apple cake with him. But over the last few years he had reassessed Erik Wilson. And he'd learned this his boss was no asshole. Grens was one now and then, because he could be, but Wilson didn't have it in him. Besides, Erik Wilson had learned to trust him. He knew that when Detective Superintendent Ewert Grens said he needed to go to Östergötland, it was better to just let him do it, if you wanted results, which Wilson did.

So this new persistence didn't make sense.

"What are you not telling me?"

Erik Wilson waved his hand dismissively.

"*What*, Wilson?"

"I want you to form your own opinion without any prior knowledge."

"If you want me to put off a trip that might help me solve a homicide investigation that I've been working on for years, then I need to know why."

His boss sighed, leaned forward and lowered his voice even though they were alone in the café, other than the owner behind the counter who couldn't possibly hear them.

"I talked to Hermansson yesterday. Or maybe she talked to me, she seemed to need it. In confidence. She told me about the break-in you were looking into. But also about the crime scene investigation you once were in charge of there—and she doesn't like what she sees in your face. She's worried."

"Oh, really?"

"She also told me about four members of a family who were executed with jacketed bullets, half lead and half titanium. One bullet on the right side of the forehead and one bullet under the left temple. On every single one."

Then Wilson lowered his voice a little more.

As if he hardly wanted to be able to hear himself.

"The corpse on Brännkyrka Street. Where I need you to go right now. The officer who was the first on the scene described the very same thing."

"Same thing?"

"An execution. A bullet to the right side of the forehead. A bullet at the left temple. And according to preliminary reports: jacketed bullets that are half lead, half titanium."

Erik Wilson crumpled up the wet napkin, dropped it onto Grens's plate, which was scraped clean by now.

"First an apartment break-in where nothing is stolen that pulls you into the past. And then a few days later a dead man in a stairwell executed in a familiar way. It might be a coincidence. That happens. But I'm a police officer, so I don't really believe in coincidences—do you, Ewert?"

He was lying on his back. As if relaxing. That was the impression he gave at first. Not dead—but rest with a different ending, an awakening. Maybe it was his mouth. The smile. People who smile seem alive. But as Ewert Grens got closer, the impression changed. The dead man wasn't smiling. He was terrified. Or at least he had been at the moment of his death.

He had known it was the end.

Stretched out on the concrete floor of a stairwell with light switches that sat too high and that were hard to push in. Life can cease in darkness, too.

Grens sank down next to the body, his damned knee cracked and wobbled and his hip protested, but the pain was almost a relief. It meant life. Most of the dead man's face, whatever wasn't taken up by that terrified smile, was broken and bloody, and the detective superintendent's eyes were drawn to the bullet holes on the right side of the forehead and under the left temple. And he knew—this was no coincidence. Suddenly he was seventeen years younger in a third-floor apartment with a hopping girl, counting her dead family members.

He didn't just move back in time—he was thrown there, slung. Those two entrance holes were no coincidence. They were copies of what he saw back then. When the medical examiner measured the distance between the nose and the entrance hole, the cheek and entrance hole, the hairline and entrance hole, he would find—Grens was convinced—the proportions to be exact.

The same shooter. Same signature.

And this was—once again—Ewert Grens's investigation. Years later it continued with a somewhat slower and less agile, but also older, wiser, and more experienced detective superintendent. Once again Grens became lead investigator on site, responsible for the crime scene, making the decisions. But this time there wasn't a chance in hell he'd miss a four-by-four-centimeter hole beneath a hardwood floor.

"His identity, Ewert."

Mariana Hermansson was wearing thin plastic gloves while handing him a thick black leather wallet. Grens wondered how she and Sven Sundkvist could already be at the crime scene when he arrived. Hermansson lived in the inner city, but it was still early and Sven would have had to drive at least twenty minutes. Erik Wilson must have called them immediately after receiving the alarm—already confident he'd be able to convince his unruly detective to take over. Ewert Grens couldn't decide if he thought that was a good or bad thing.

"Well, we can certainly rule out robbery."

Hermansson unfolded the bulky wallet and fished

out a driver's license from a plastic pouch on one side and a hefty stack of bills from the compartment on the other side, five-hundred-kronor banknotes mixed with fifty-euro bills and a few hundred-dollar bills as well.

"Real."

She slid a thumb over the license's plastic surface, over the raised image of Sweden, over the UV.

"His ID is real, anyway. I'm not sure about the cash, the technicians will have to determine that."

She turned the license over so Grens could get a better look at the front. The face on the floor wasn't exactly whole, unlike the one in the photograph, still it was obvious they were the same person. Gray and somewhat unkempt hair, an upper lip that was significantly wider than the lower, a steely, closely clipped mustache, and on one cheek three liver spots, which formed a small triangle and gave the impression of a pair of eyes above a mouth—a face within a face.

"Dejan Pejović. Forty-seven years old. Guessing from his name and appearance, I'd say he was from the Balkans. If he's got a police record we'll be able to get everything to you in an hour."

Grens didn't answer her. Preoccupied. He was trying to figure out what felt so familiar.

"Ewert? What is it?"

"I think . . . the name. I've seen it before."

"You've seen it? Where?"

"In the same red-flagged file you gave me. He was questioned in connection with the original crime, part of the suspect's circle. So, Hermansson—he *is* definitely in our records."

Grens used the dead man's shoulder for support as he stood up and stretched out his knee, waiting for that throbbing pain to lessen. The stairwell had been blocked off with blue-and-white police tape, and Krantz and Errfors, the forensic technician and the medical examiner respectively, had arrived with their black tool bags. One deceased person who gave so many living people their jobs. This was the moment they were all waiting for; without the consequences of violence, none of them would have a purpose. The meaning of death as a condition for the meaninglessness of life.

"Number three hundred and ten."

Ewert Grens looked at the dead man, who recently was as alive as he and Mariana were right now.

"Murder, Hermansson. You know I count them. He's my three hundred and tenth."

Nothing could replace the rush.

Grens wasn't even ashamed of it anymore, though he surely was in the beginning. That's just how it was. How *he* was.

A murder investigation grabbed hold of him, lifted him up and pushed him on, gave him something to look forward to tomorrow. *The meaning of death as a condition for the meaninglessness of life.* Every time someone used violence to declare a person's life less valuable than their own, the rush arrived just as strong, it welled up from deep inside and got him through his hellish nights. Sixty-four years old, stout, balding, and alone, or twenty-three years old, slender, strong, and in love, with his arm around his classmate—three hundred and ten times and still the feeling was the same.

So long ago and yet somehow only a moment had passed. He remembered his first time, as a new recruit at the Uppsala Police Station, called to the scene where a husband had killed his wife. Grens, who had never seen a dead person before, parked his patrol car outside a mansion on Valsätra and followed his commanding officer through an unlocked door. The man was just sitting there at his kitchen table with his wife on the floor at his feet, a bloody ax sticking out of her back. Completely empty. That's how Grens remembered the husband's, the murderer's eyes. A bottomless, wordless pit. The man didn't protest as the officers pulled him away by his upper arm, and it was there, at that moment, the very first step toward the patrol car with his first murderer arrested that Ewert Grens felt it for the first time. The same rush that now filled this forty years' older detective in a dim stairwell, and which meant he was slowly getting closer, closer. So distinctly different from that other emotion, the worst of them all, the one he connected to a hopping girl and being convinced he'd found a murderer and then having to meet that bastard's scornful laugh as Grens was forced to let him go free.

"Ewert—I'd like to introduce you to some folks you should have met a while ago."

Marina Hermansson grabbed his shirtsleeve and pulled him toward two very young people in uniform, who had the kind of clear eyes that only exist in those who've just started their journey.

"Lucas and Amelia. They're in their final semester at the police academy. They've been doing their training here in the homicide unit, under my supervision. Amelia did her first training period at county criminal and Lucas just joined us from the gang task force in Tumba. They were the ones who helped me—or helped you, Ewert—analyze the folder of blank paper. And considering how things look here . . . well, I thought it was good if they saw it, too."

The scene would have seemed bizarre to any outside observer: three people being introduced to each other near the feet of a corpse whose eyes seemed to be on them.

"Lucas? Amelia? This is Ewert Grens, detective superintendent and my boss. Technically speaking, he's your boss, too, while you're here. And he's not half so dangerous as he's trying to look."

Mariana Hermansson smiled at Grens, who shook the two outstretched hands, both a bit too soft, but they'd harden over time.

"You're basically the same age."

"Excuse me?"

They spoke in unison, Lucas and Amelia.

So anxious to do the right thing. Or at least to avoid making any mistakes.

"The same age I was when I saw my first dead body. DB. That's what we called them. Don't think many people use that expression anymore."

"Nobody at the academy. But that's why we're here, Superintendent. For the reality."

He looked at two young people who had no idea that one day their time as a police officer would come to an end.

Reality?

Was that where he spent his time?

And if so—what were those three hundred and ten dead bodies?

"Ewert?"

Sven Sundkvist had left the stairwell when his phone rang and gone outside for a better connection, and through the small round windows Grens had caught glimpses of him pacing, seen the slender back of his most loyal colleague. A back the detective superintendent knew so well, whose hunching over and tightening of the shoulders could only mean bad news.

"Yes?"

"It was the officer in charge."

"We've already got our hands full, Sven."

"That's why he called. He knew we were here and why. So when he got a new alarm about ten minutes ago, he presumed we should take that, too."

Ewert Grens moved aside to make way for the forensic technicians photographing the dead man from various angles. But when that didn't satisfy them, since he was still casting shadows on their object, he took a couple more long steps into the darkness of the stairwell and waved for Sven to follow.

"What are you talking about? There's surely someone else who can investigate whatever needs investigating. Like I said, we're full up here."

"Ewert, the on-duty officer received a call from a tenant in an apartment building on Oden Street near Vasa Park. Early this morning, a middle-aged woman thought she heard 'two loud bangs' from the apartment above hers. When she got out of bed a few hours later, she decided to go upstairs and knock on her neighbor's door and discovered it was open. So she went inside. And in the hall there was a man stretched out on his back with two big holes in his head, one a little to the right on his forehead and one just below his left temple."

ejan Pejović's unkempt hair, thin mustache, and liver spots that formed a face within the face were now more than that. Born in Podgorica at a time when the Montenegrin city was still in Yugoslavia. Convicted twice in his homeland—manslaughter and assault, served time in Pozarevac, Serbia's largest and toughest prison. Immigrated to Sweden twenty-two years ago, became a Swedish citizen eight years later. A search of the police records using his social security number yielded fifty-nine hits under the key term KNOWN DANGEROUS ARMED, then another twenty-four hits listed as a suspect connected to organized crime, but only one single conviction—a few months with an ankle monitor for a minor assault charge: Pejović had spit on the shoe of a police officer. The numbers of investigations and prosecutions, however, were plentiful: charges of third-degree murder and manslaughter and attempted murder and assault and battery, always in connection to notorious arms dealers, and which ended up with a lack of evidence or witnesses who refused to cooperate or who quite simply disappeared.

Ewert Grens stretched out on his uncomfortably comfortable corduroy sofa, grabbed a new stack of papers from his wobbly coffee table, and added them to the pile already lying on his stomach. He, along with Sven, Mariana, and the young cadets, had gotten to know the dead man fairly well throughout the day— but they still had no clue about a perpetrator. No witnesses. No shoe or fingerprints. No traces of a struggle, no blood or fibers on the victim's skin and clothing, no scrap of skin beneath the victim's nails.

Two executions.

The murderer had made sure they knew that's exactly what they were.

Just a few hours and kilometers between them.

The first in a stairwell on Brännkyrka Street 56. The second—Grens stretched for another pile, and sure, he could fit that on his stomach, too—in an apartment at Oden Street 88. That's where they were called to next. Branko Stojanović. That was—had been his name. Another man lying motionless on his back. Stretched over a herringbone floor in a penthouse apartment. Jacketed bullets, half lead and half titanium, just like seventeen years ago, just like an hour ago. The two men had led similar lives as well.

Branko Stojanović was just five months older, had grown up in Danilovgrad just a couple of dozen miles northwest of Dejan Pejović's home in Podgorica. They served their first sentences at the same time in the same prison in Pozarevac, immigrated to Sweden the same week, and received citizenship the same month.

Stojanović's name also stood next to Pejović's in an interrogation in the red-flagged investigation—as one of his many informal and violent collaborators.

Their lives echoed each other as closely as any two possibly could.

And yet there was no way they could have known they'd end up naked and side by side in forensic medicine, autopsied on the very same morning.

Ewert Grens shifted the piles back to the table, got out of his sofa, and gently stretched his arms and stiff back while heading out into the hallway. Dark. Silent. The whole department had transformed in the late hour, other than the coffee machine. It roared just like always, stubborn and unrhythmic, like the heart of a newly operated upon person that was getting to know its pacemaker. One last cup of coffee then he'd head home. Not to sleep, he did that much better here at the station, but now and then even the hardest-working detective needs to change his clothes, water his plants, and check his mail.

A warm and windless summer night. Pleasant to walk through. It would take him twenty-five minutes to go by foot from the station to his empty apartment on Svea Road. Once, long ago, they would have covered this ground in fifteen minutes—Anni holding his hand tight as he adjusted his pace so he could always stay close to her. He took the same path no matter the season. Kungsholms Street, Scheele Street, and then as he crossed over Barnhus Bridge and the train tracks, he started, as he so often did, to sing. An elderly couple holding hands turned in surprise, a cyclist rang his bell at the man singing too loud and off-key. Always something from the sixties, tonight it was "Lucky Lips" and perhaps there was even a dance step or two, like the ones he'd once seen Cliff Richard take. He sang, and he remembered different times, all those days that made up his life as a police officer. Half a year left. And then what? How would he ever find that rush again, find meaning, when he'd never bothered to look for it anywhere else? He let his worries swirl away with the chorus and the dance steps, and his collar was getting a little damp by the time he turned onto Observatorie Street. Just a few hundred meters later he caught sight of his darkened kitchen windows.

Grens used to avoid his building's tiny ancient elevator—the cables creaked and complained and swayed ominously—but his leg was sore, and so the detective pulled open the elevator door with the same anxious feeling as when he entered an airplane—the one that meant losing the control that held his world together.

He saw it as soon as he stepped out onto the fourth floor and took out his keys.

Someone had tried to get into his home.

He froze, trying to make sure he wasn't imagining it. Was he so deep inside the case that he'd started living it? Thrown back to another apartment where a little girl hopped around her murdered parents and siblings?

Some of his colleagues left fluorescent wires between their doors and doorframes whenever they left home, and when they came back they used a UV flashlight to find out if anyone had opened the door and broken the thread. Looking for two pieces curled up like snakes on the floor. That was too advanced for an old detective like him. Besides, he didn't need it. Sometimes the old methods were good enough—for example, always leaving a worn-out door handle perpendicular. Whenever Grens left his home, he would push up the handle slightly and make sure it hung parallel to the floor. And if someone else were to push it down while he was away, well, this is exactly how it would look.

A little off, a little tired, an old handle with an old spring that couldn't quite manage to stay upright on its own.

Someone had tried to enter his home.

Grens took his service weapon out of his shoulder holster and held it in front of him as he stepped into a darkened hall.

One and a half steps. Then he stopped, listened.

Silence.

No movements, no breathing.

He continued walking, one slow step at a time.

Past the bedroom. The bathroom. His office.

Nothing.

Until he got to the kitchen.

He couldn't really see or hear anyone inside, but he sensed it.

Somebody was in there.

He held the gun with both hands. A much longer step, maintaining his balance. Then a rapid swing of his upper body around the corner of the wall.

"Hold your hands . . ."

At the kitchen table. A shape in the darkness.

". . . very fucking still!"

Which suddenly moved.

"I repeat: hands still or I shoot!"

Grens stood at the doorstep of his own kitchen, gun pointed at a shadow sitting on one of his kitchen chairs.

"Grens—it's me."

"Hands on the table, nice and easy where I can see them!"

"Goddamnit, Grens, lower your weapon, it's . . ."

It wasn't easy to make out in the dark, but Ewert Grens was pretty sure that the figure in front of him was slowly rising from the table, maybe even stretching out a hand.

"Don't move, you bastard, or I'll shoot! Last warning!"

Then the ceiling light turned on. The intruder had been trying to reach the switch.

"Grens, calm down, for fuck's sake! It's me. Piet Hoffmann."

Ewert Grens took the very last step into his kitchen.

"I know what Piet Hoffmann looks like. You two couldn't even be cousins."

The detective superintendent stood close to the table now, less than a meter between his gun and the intruder's head, who had dark hair and brown eyes and puffy cheeks and a slightly crooked nose.

"So whoever the hell you are—move again, and I'll shoot your head. You made a big fucking mistake when you broke into a police officer's home."

It was an inviting kitchen. Grand. High ceilings with sturdy, white wooden cabinets, dual ovens and shiny knobs, and in one corner there was a narrow hall whose beautifully carved wooden moldings led into a maid's chamber. But neither visitor was thinking of that—their eyes were only on each other. Ewert Grens was staring angrily at the stranger who'd broken into his home. And the stranger continued to make small gestures to the detective superintendent without wanting to provoke the finger resting lightly on the trigger.

"Grens—listen: *I am Piet Hoffmann.*"

"You don't look like Piet Hoffmann. You don't sound like Piet Hoffmann. But you are guilty of breach of domiciliary peace. *Unlawful intrusion into another person's living quarters.* Criminal law, chapter twenty-four, first paragraph."

"Grens, if you'll just let me show you my hands . . ."

"Keep them where I can see them, goddamnit! Palms on the table!"

Grens hadn't fired his service weapon very many times. He wasn't even sure he was particularly good at it anymore. But right now he was ready to shoot, wouldn't hesitate.

And the man who had broken into his home had no one to blame but himself.

"I have to be able to move my hands, Grens, so I can make you understand."

"Go ahead. And I'll shoot you in the shoulder first. And if that's not enough to stop you, I'll aim for the heart."

The stranger with the crooked nose and puffy cheeks inhaled, slowly, exhaled, as if trying to slow his pulse, stabilize his voice.

"Okay. You see, right? I've got my hands on your kitchen table. Just the way you want. No reason to shoot. And if I can't show you my hands, we'll try another way. Let's talk."

"Oh you'll talk. In court. With a defense lawyer at your side."

"The first time we met, Grens, was during a hostage negotiation in a maximum security prison. And you did exactly what you're doing now—pointed a gun at my head. You even fired it! A shot that took exactly three seconds."

"You—whoever the hell you are—that doesn't tell me anything other than that some fool I don't know broke into my apartment, into my home, and sat himself down at the kitchen table where I drink my morning coffee. In my fucking chair!"

The stranger looked down at his hands. Nodding to them again and then to the detective superintendent, as if asking permission once more to move them. Grens didn't nod, he shook his head.

"Just keep them frozen. If you value your life."

"Okay. Okay. Let's talk some more."

The man's voice seemed distressed, as if it might not hold—as if it caused him pain to keep talking.

"The second time, Grens, we met for real. Bogotá. Gaira Café. I taught you to drink *aguapanela*. Sugar-cane pulp and hot water. And we were no longer two freight trains headed straight for each other. I needed your help, Grens, we didn't fight each other—we fought side by side."

Ewert Grens smiled. A smile that lacked any warmth. He was barely listening. He was too tired for this bullshit.

"I'm calling a patrol car to come pick you up. Until then, you better sit there and wait just like you are now. I've got six months until retirement, and I'm in no mood to deal with a corpse on my kitchen floor."

His right hand still on his gun, pointed straight at the intruder's head, he used his left hand to reach into his jacket's inner pocket and pull out his phone.

"Please calm down, Grens, for fuck's sake."

"I am calm. As long as you're calm."

Then he cocked his gun.

As if to emphasize his point.

"Listen. Listen, Grens! The last time we met it was the other way around! *You* sought *me* out, you needed my help—forced me to infiltrate a human smuggling operation in Libya and . . ."

"Hermansson? Ewert here."

Grens had flipped open his phone and pressed one of its few saved numbers.

"I'm currently standing in my kitchen and with my service weapon aimed at a burglar. I want you to send a car."

The female voice at the other end was unexpectedly loud. Or maybe it was Grens who had the volume turned up. Or maybe he'd just turned the phone in such a way that the other side of the conversation could seep out.

"Ewert, are you okay?"

"I'm fine. And in order to ensure that this fucking intruder also remains fine, I need you to send a car immediately."

"To your home address?"

"To my home address."

Ewert Grens smiled. Still not particularly warmly.

"Ten minutes. Then you'll be in handcuffs in the back seat of a police car. I'm gonna take pleasure in testifying against you."

"There was a bloodstain in my kitchen, Detective, when I came home after our last meeting. It wasn't mentioned in any of the police reports."

"Do yourself a favor and shut up."

"And in the weapon's case in my basement. I kept my gun there, a Radom, and it was pointing in the wrong direction because somebody used it. A bullet was missing. And that, too, wasn't in any of your police reports, Grens."

The bloodstain on the floor. The secret weapon's case.

And maybe now Ewert Grens started to listen.

"And then there's what Rasmus and Hugo like to call *checkered* pancakes. Something you apparently made for them, Grens, that I still haven't really figured out. But who would know that outside my family?"

"Checkered pancakes?"

"Yes."

His gaze.

The stranger stared at him and never looked away. Grens was starting to recognize it.

"You said that. Checkered pancakes."

"Yes. I said that."

Ewert Grens de-cocked his gun, lowered it.

And pulled out the other kitchen chair.

"Hoffmann?"

"The one and only."

The stranger looked at the detective with those steady eyes and now slowly raised his hands from the table. The same movement he'd tried several times before—but now he completed it. With his right hand he began to wiggle two of the fingers on his left hand.

"You see, Grens?"

And both fingers came loose. One at a time.

"Medical-grade silicone and an individualized case design. As easy to coax them off as it is to get them on. Finger prostheses. The vacuum inside them holds them in place. Do you recognize me now? Missing two fingers?"

"Why . . . Why the disguise? And your voice—that's not how you sound?"

Grens placed the gun between them on the kitchen table. Maybe to prove that he trusted his visitor. That they could trust each other.

"This?"

Piet Hoffmann pulled slightly at his puffy cheeks and just as puffy chin, ran a hand through his dyed hair, rolled the finger prostheses across the table until they clunked against the gun.

"Death threats. Somebody means business. And what's worse—Zofia and Hugo and Rasmus and Luiza are in just as much danger."

Grens picked up the finger prostheses. Felt them. Rolled them back over the table.

"Why come here—break in—to the home of someone you said you never wanted to see again?"

"I need your help, Grens."

"Go to the police then. They'll help you."

"Are you kidding me?"

"It works for everyone else. Regular people don't sneak into police officers' homes—they go to the police station and fill out paperwork."

"First of all, which of your colleagues would even help an ex-con? That's *not* how it works—and you know it. You harass us. Persecute us. You just want us locked away again."

"Well then, you report *that*."

"And secondly, the police station is the only place I can't go. Because the organization threatening me has contacts that reach deep inside that station. They're working with someone. So now, Detective, we meet for another reason. Now we exchange our roles again. It's your goddamn turn this time. This time you will help me, Grens. *You're* going to infiltrate on *my* behalf."

Ewert Grens poured coffee into two porcelain cups and sat them down, steaming, on the kitchen table. One black. One with a splash of milk. He found a single roll of Marie biscuits in his pantry, and it fit nicely on the table between the finger prostheses and his gun.

"I baked them myself."

Grens smiled. Much more warmly now.

"And the coffee was brewed by a master. Not many people have been served in my kitchen. Anni, of course, when she lived here. Ågestam, the prosecutor, late one night. And now you, Hoffmann. Sven Sundkvist was here once, but it wasn't a very nice evening, so he got nothing. Three guests in over thirty years, not exactly what you'd call a crowd."

Piet Hoffmann took a sip of coffee that was the strongest he'd ever tasted. It ripped into his chest. And washed his mind clear.

"You've got the world's easiest mission as an infiltrator—you have to infiltrate your own colleagues, Grens. Immerse yourself in the institution you already belong to, and no one will question you for it."

"And I should do this . . . *because*?"

"*Because* the organization that's threatening to kill me, kill my family, started out by working with someone inside that station, and then he gave two of these to my son."

Hoffmann had brought something with him. Grens only saw it now as Hoffmann pulled out his chair and showed him a small bag. He plucked out a toy.

"The first one was left in our mailbox. This one was placed in Rasmus's red backpack while twenty-four grade-school students practiced their letters."

Hoffmann put the toy next to Grens's coffee mug. It was approximately the same height and breadth.

"Do you see what it is?"

"You know I don't have any children. I don't know anything about toys. Now and then I catch a commercial on the television, or pass by the window of a toy store, but not often. Not a particular interest of mine."

Hoffmann pulled off the toy's two plastic arms. And plastic legs. And plastic nose. And plastic eyes. And plastic mouth. Until it was no longer a toy. Until it had changed shape.

"But you understand this, Grens."

The detective jumped out of his chair and took a step back.

"What the hell are you up to? A hand grenade—in my kitchen?"

"Sit down."

"With the fuse plugged in! Are you threatening me, Hoffmann?"

"Grens—please listen. One more time."

As the detective superintendent stood with his eyes glued to a live hand grenade, his visitor began to speak. Told him about a warning that was put into his family's mailbox. About copies of highly classified documents sent to his office. About a cell phone dropped off by courier. About instructions to attack any criminal organization he chose with an unknown weapon. And about the contents of a red backpack, which led to Piet Hoffmann's new appearance and a safe house for Zofia and his children.

Ewert Grens stared at the grenade, which refused to move. He then went over to his sink, waited for the water to turn ice cold, and then filled up a glass. He drank it all, refilled it, drank it all again.

"In your mailbox? And in Rasmus's backpack?"

"Yes."

"Disguised as a toy?"

"Yes."

"And Rasmus—he played with it?"

"With the first one. He cried, even hit me, when I took it away from him."

Rage. That was what Grens felt.

The kind that rose from deep inside, which he didn't feel very often anymore.

"You know I'm fond of your kids. They mean something to me."

"I know, Grens."

"So you think you got a sure thing? You come here and tell me about some threats and show me some hand grenade and tell me about Rasmus and Hugo and Luiza being locked in a fucking war-zone apartment? And you think I'll just come running and help you?"

"I've called you many things, Grens. But *a sure thing* has never been one of them. I'm here because I risked my life for many years for your police force. And now a member of that force thinks my family should die. A dirty cop. Whoever's threatening me never could have done so without a cop. And I think you probably dislike that as much as I do, Grens. In fact, I think you might just dislike it enough to try to help me. Help us. Infiltrate your own colleagues. Let *me* be *your* handler this time."

Ewert Grens filled up another glass of water. Kept the tap running full blast so it would get even colder, colder than ice.

Hugo. Rasmus. Luiza.

Two little boys and a newborn girl, whom he'd gotten close to after just a short time.

Dared to get close to.

The only children he'd . . . well, he probably had ever spoken to. For real.

"Are you kind of like our grandpa now?"

"No, I'm not your grandfather. Not anybody's, actually."

It had happened so fast. Suddenly, the boys were on either side of him, while he made them checkered pancakes, and they'd looked at him with such trust in their eyes.

"Our uncle, then? Are you, Ewert? Like an uncle?"

They put their faith in him. Thought he was the

kind of adult who did the right thing. And it had made Grens feel warm someplace deep in his chest from that very first afternoon when he'd hastily filled in as a babysitter.

"No. I'm not an uncle either. I'm not really anything to you."

"Because you can be, if you want."

What began in the Hoffmanns' kitchen, that conversation, had developed into a friendship. Hugo still sometimes came into town without his parents' knowledge and went to the police station and asked to talk to the detective superintendent who spent his nights there on a sofa. And their little sister—Ewert Grens had accidentally been the first to know that Zofia was pregnant with her. Even before her father.

Is that what I should do with myself? Later? In half a year when the police force doesn't want me anymore?

Pretend to be somebody's grandfather?

No.

They had a nice time. It had done him good. But it was hardly the answer to his future.

Grens drank more water. Emptied a big glass in just a few sips. The rage he felt at some criminals, some gang or mafia, threatening children—those children—wouldn't pass; it stuck in his throat and chest, clumping up.

"We need more cold water. And more hot coffee."

He'd just filled the coffeepot and started brewing when his door rang. At this hour? After midnight? First a masked visitor in his kitchen—and now someone was ringing a doorbell that never gets rung?

The gun still lay on the table next to an unopened

pack of dry biscuits. Ewert Grens grabbed it, cocked it, held it behind his back as he walked toward the front door.

It rang again. Obstinately.

He kept the gun behind him as he gently pushed open the door, just a crack that made it as hard to see out as it was to see in.

"Superintendent Grens?"

Two uniformed police officers. Fairly young. One blond, one brunette. That was all he could make out.

"Yes?"

"You called for backup. A burglar. Hermansson told us it was an emergency."

Ewert Grens de-cocked the gun and put it in his waistband, making sure it was hidden beneath his jacket as he opened the door wide.

"Oh yes, right. Just a misunderstanding."

The dark-haired one was slightly larger, and he was the one who spoke.

"A misunderstanding? According to Hermansson, your weapon was drawn. Aimed at the intruder in question."

"We . . . got our signals crossed."

The two officers looked at Grens. They, too, seemed to know Hermansson. And if they did, they knew she didn't *get her signals crossed*.

"We'd like to come inside. Just make sure everything's okay."

Grens first instinct was to order them to go. But that wasn't a good idea. They were just doing their jobs. According to protocol, when you receive an intruder report, you have to go inside and check the premises, make sure no one's standing behind the person at the door with a gun in their back, forcing them to keep the police at bay. It didn't matter if the person who had called it in was their commanding officer or not.

"I . . . ah, I *thought* for a moment that it was an intruder. But it was just an old friend stopping by. He's in the kitchen, we're having a coffee. Do you want one, too?"

The detective superintendent stepped aside, inviting them in. One of the officers headed for the rest of the apartment, while the other followed Grens to the kitchen.

"Here. My friend. Who I mistook for a burglar."

The officer stopped right about where Grens had a half hour earlier. In the doorway to the kitchen. From there the whole room was visible. The police officer saw a frumpy middle-aged man with a puffy face and a grizzled mustache, newly empty porcelain cups, a pack of biscuits, and a coffeepot just about to finish brewing another pot of coffee.

However, the hand grenade and finger prostheses were gone.

And Hoffmann had one of his hands beneath the table.

"Hello. Name's Haraldsson. I'm afraid I managed to give my friend Grens quite a scare."

"Haraldsson?"

"Peter Haraldsson. Old friend."

The young police officer lingered for a moment. As if waiting for the man at the kitchen table to say more.

"Did you want one? A cup? It's fresh."

The detective superintendent nodded toward the coffeemaker.

"No, thanks. I'll just wait until my colleague is finished. If everything looks good, we'll head out."

A few minutes later, his colleague arrived. Done. And they walked on either side of Grens to the front door.

"I'm sorry, guys, made a mistake this evening. But you did a damn fine job, I want you to know that. I promise to make sure your superior officer knows that, too."

The new batch of freshly brewed coffee was just as strong as the previous one.

Piet Hoffmann swallowed, waiting for the rip in his chest that would make his thoughts clear and clean and tangible.

"This was what I found in my mail at my office. It changed everything."

There had been more than just a grenade in that bag. Grens's nocturnal visitor took out a thick bundle of papers and dropped them on the table.

"This is what I found."

The detective looked at the padded envelope Hoffmann placed on top of the stack.

```
To Piet Koslow Hoffmann
```

"The same typewriter used for the other letters. No return address. I'm sure you'll recognize what I found inside. Copies of logbooks and intelligence reports that are supposed to exist in a single copy, locked inside a safe. Notes from all the meetings I had with Erik Wilson—an infiltrator providing information about organized crime to his handler at the City Police, who then collected and used it."

Grens flipped through the stack, reading bits here and there.

Even the contents of the white envelope. The one that should have been closed with a wax seal. Even that had been copied in its entirety. Pages that revealed the infiltrator's code name, Paula, and his real name, Piet Koslow Hoffmann.

He slowly lifted his gaze—from the documents on the table to the face opposite him, which had been transformed so skillfully. And now Grens understood.

The seriousness. The fear.

Someone had access to the only thing that protected an infiltrator—his anonymity.

If this got into the wrong hands.

If the hardened criminals and violent organizations that Piet Hoffmann had infiltrated got ahold of this, if they knew who he really was, that he'd tricked them, deliberately violated the mafia's most sacred rule— never, ever, ever snitch.

If . . .

He was dead.

Zofia, Hugo, Rasmus, Luiza.

Dead.

"I understand your situation. But I'm not sure what the hell they want you to do for them. What they *think*

you're going to do, but won't do, because you've chosen to change your identity and hid your family in a
secure location. Chose to escape."

"Here, Grens. Listen to this."

Piet Hoffmann pulled a phone out of his pocket,
opened some app, and held it forward so Ewert Grens
could hear.

*". . . you're going to initiate a small gang war // with
an FN BRG-15."*

"I recorded our conversation on my phone. They've
transformed their voice, so it could be anyone. And the
clicks here and there are where I've edited out unim-
portant information."

Grens leaned closer to the voice, which had clearly
been distorted by an electronic soundboard.

*"You can decide which criminal organization. // You
knock them out. And then // let it be known which weapon
was used in the attack // make sure people know where
they can get one of their own."*

"Are you with me, Grens? They want me to start a
gang war and kick off an arms race, by using the very
weapon they want to sell. And they want to do it without ever showing themselves. In case it goes wrong. So
they need someone neutral, who can't be connected to
them. I'm fairly certain we're dealing with international
arms dealers, new to the Swedish market. Who want to
start by selling off some of their stockpile of a machine
gun that wasn't supposed to exist and yet does. And
then, once they've done that, take over the rest of the
arms trade."

"'And yet does' . . . What do you mean by that?"

"I've got one in the trunk of my car. Parked about a block away."

Ewert Grens randomly pulled a couple of copies out of the large stack sitting in the middle of his kitchen table.

"International arms dealers who know who you are, what you've done, and what you're capable of? Who have penetrated my police station?"

"As deep as it goes."

Ewert Grens stood up. No longer thirsty for water or coffee. Just restless. Like always, when he needed to think.

A dirty cop. Someone who got into the safe in the investigative unit and stole the folder and the envelope that described Piet Hoffmann's work as an infiltrator. Just like a dirty cop broke into the archive in the basement and stole Zana Lilaj's life.

Two corrupt colleagues at the same time?

Or the same?

He tried the hall. Long and straight. Paced back and forth several times. It didn't help. He wandered in and out of his bedroom, in and out of his office, in and out of the library. That didn't help either. But on the balcony. Out there he could relax. With his view over the rooftops of Stockholm. Out there he could get ahold for just a moment of that buzzing, spinning.

Dejan Pejović. Branko Stojanović.

Within hours of each other, just a few kilometers apart, they ended up dead on their backs in the dawn light. Executed. Identical wounds and identical ammunition. Both associated with notorious arms dealers.

There had to be a connection.

But were they connected to this?

To Piet Hoffmann?

Threats against the Hoffmann family, which in turn were supposed to create an opening for an international arms dealer?

It might be a coincidence. That happens.

That's what Erik Wilson, Grens's boss and Hoffmann's former handler, had said over a piece of apple cake.

But I'm a police officer, so I don't really believe in coincidences—do you, Ewert?

Ewert Grens breathed in the lukewarm air, leaned far out over the balcony's low railing, and his chest tightened when he realized how easy it would be to fall. Against the asphalt. Forever.

No.

I don't believe in coincidences either. I didn't believe in them this morning when I left a stairwell on Brännkyrka Street 56 for a herringbone floor at Oden Street 88 and saw two identical murders. And I don't believe in them now when the deaths of arms traffickers are happening at almost the same time that Piet Hoffmann is being blackmailed by an international arms dealer looking to establish themselves in the Swedish market.

He closed his eyes, the feeling of falling ceased.

A few deep breaths of summer night.

Then he went back to Hoffmann, who was sitting at the kitchen table on the chair that was actually Grens's spot, but which his guest had claimed as his own.

"Yes."

"Yes?"

"Yes. I'll infiltrate the police station, my own work-place, for your sake. And yes—I'll try to discover who sold you out. Who is threatening children that I'm fond of in order to get their share in a market that is costing this country lives every day. But I have my conditions."

Piet Hoffmann opened his arms wide.

"Excuse me?"

"You heard right."

"And here I was starting to smile a little. Conditions, Grens?"

The detective ripped open the roll of biscuits; they were dry and crumbly and stuck to the top of the mouth and tongue and had to be washed down with coffee. Half a cup.

"I'm investigating two murders that I'm convinced are part of this very power struggle, making money off young Swedes shooting each other. And I think they're connected to what you've landed in the middle of. So here's what we're going to do, Hoffmann. You'll be *my* handler as I infiltrate the police station for *you*. And I'll be *your* handler while you infiltrate these weapons dealers for *me*."

Summer nights in Stockholm were vibrant, effervescent, and full of laughter. But to Ewert Grens, who was driving through it all, not even close to participating or wanting to, it seemed more like an endless stream of faceless bodies on their way somewhere. They didn't make any impression, meant nothing, drew no attention from him.

Five and a half minutes. From the parking lot near his apartment on Svea Road to the northern entrance of the police station on Kungsholms Street. That is if he drove a little too fast and didn't slow for the high-spirited people loping across the various streets of the city.

"Hermansson? Are you there?"

He'd called her while stepping out of his car, and she picked up on the first ring.

"Yes."

Her voice sounded faint, confused.

"Hey—are you awake, Hermansson?"

"Now I am. Again."

Grens greeted the guard on duty who nodded back

in recognition and opened the door without asking for a badge.

"In that case—I need all the information we've got on Pejović and Stojanović."

"Now? In the middle of the night?"

"I'm in the elevator on my way up to the department."

He could hear her rising out of bed, her voice getting a little stronger.

"Ewert, what are you up to?"

"The usual. The same thing I've been up to every day since . . . well, before you were born. And I don't know if that means I'm old or you're young. But what I'm doing is investigating murder. In this case a double homicide."

"What I mean is—what exactly are you up to right now? I've been worried ever since you came back from that apartment where the Lilaj family was executed. You were . . . Well, you seemed different. Like you actually cared. About something. At all. You've been shakier than usual, more difficult and evasive. I even talked to Wilson about it. Because I'm worried, Ewert! Because you . . . And tonight? You call from your home and wake me up. Tell me you've got your service weapon out and ask me to send a car or you'll shoot some intruder. A half hour later I get another call. From the patrol car! Telling me it was all a mistake. Apparently, you weren't burgled at all, but instead were sitting there drinking coffee with an old friend. And now. You wake me up for a third time tonight. For something that could have waited a few hours, until tomorrow morning when we do our morning meeting. So, Ewert, I repeat—*what exactly are you up to?*"

The elevator door jammed a little when he got to the department, it had been doing that for the last week. When it finally opened, he stepped out into a dark corridor lit only by the light of the vending machine.

"Hermansson?"

"Yes?"

"The research. Everything we've gathered today on Pejović and Stojanović. Where did you say I could find it?"

She hesitated a moment.

"Hermansson, where . . ."

"Who visited you?"

"That's none of your business."

"Who, Ewert?"

"An old friend. I told you that."

"Who you mistook for a burglar? Try again."

"That's the version you're getting."

She hesitated again. As if trying to decide whether or not to keep demanding an explanation, or if she was too tired, wanted her bed too much for this, and didn't have it in her to keep confronting a boss who had no intention of telling her what she wanted to know.

"Some of it's in my office. On a chair in the corner by the window, in a plastic folder that's marked 'P and S.'"

Mariana Hermansson's office was two doors down from the vending machine and four doors away from his own. And there, on an elegant and translucent straight-backed chair, which she must have brought in herself because there was no way the force would have sprung for something that nice, there sat the plastic folder. And inside it, on the top of the stack, was a black-and-white picture from the medical examiner—a close-up of the hole in Pejović's temple.

"Got it. And the rest?"

"Sven has one. He might have taken it home with him, he sometimes does, but last I looked it was on his desk behind his phone."

Sven Sundkvist had the office right next to Grens. And behind the phone, just as Hermansson guessed, there lay a folder labeled "Hit man? Arms dealers?" in Sven's spindly handwriting.

"Got that, too. Was there anything else?"

"Yes. In the cadets' office. Lucas and Amelia. You met them this morning. I asked them to look into our victims' pasts. They really are so good, both of them, much better at finding their way through all the various registries and websites than you and Sven and me."

"I didn't know they had their own office."

"Well, they didn't. So I arranged one. The space we used to have as an archive, near the copier. It's been empty since we centralized our records in the basement. They helped me clean it out and track down a couple of desks. It turned out pretty nice, I think. But don't say anything to the union, please—because the office lacks any windows or good ventilation."

A big closet. That's how Grens would have described it.

And two narrow desks that had nothing on them other than two more plastic folders, not yet labeled, but still full of papers. He thought again about how these two young cadets were only just starting out, and the fact that they were content to sit in a tiny closet without much oxygen, felt like a symbol of the long journey they had ahead of them. Someone leaves, someone arrives. I'm out, they're in. He wondered which one would eventually have his office.

The Stockholm night was still alive while he headed back home, unconcerned by the approach of day. Ewert Grens wove between late-night revelers still out on the streets, singing and shrieking with their arms around each other, streaming in and out of bars.

When he opened the front door and stepped into his apartment, Piet Hoffmann was no longer in the kitchen. Grens found him in the library reading a book.

"I don't get it, Grens. I hardly knew places like this existed. It's enormous! I've been wandering around forever. Do you really live here? Is this your home? I mean, on a cop's salary, how can, how did you . . . how the fuck can you afford it? And why? What are you gonna do with all this? My whole family could live here, and we'd never even bump into each other. All my relatives, come to think of it."

"We were two. Back then. About to be more. When we filled these rooms with furniture. It was another time—people were moving out of the inner city, not into it."

"We? Your wife?"

"Anni."

"And more? So she was . . ."

"Yes."

"But that's been . . . well, a pretty long time if I understand correctly?"

"Thirty-five years. Since she was injured and moved into a facility. She died just ten years ago."

Piet Hoffmann leaned back in the comfortably worn reading chair. He could have fallen asleep in it.

"So—what you're saying, Grens, is that for over thirty years you've walked through this world on your own? That seems, sorry to say it—kind of sad. Like the man who owns this place wasn't living, just existing."

Hoffmann observed the detective superintendent. He didn't mean to be cruel. But he realized it came out that way. Grens's wounded expression showed he was trying to make sense of this half-life he'd lived in a place that made him feel like a stranger.

"I don't spend much time here. I prefer my office. Quite a bit more, if I'm being honest."

"Now you're making it even easier to understand why you'd choose to live here. In solitude."

Or—Hoffmann looked at Grens again—maybe that wasn't pain in his expression? Maybe, on the contrary, the detective had something in his face that seemed more like gratitude? Because his guest had interpreted his situation, his state of mind, so precisely? Had the courage to say it?

"It's . . . well, I've thought about it sometimes."

"Yes?"

"Moving, I mean. Somewhere else."

"But . . . ?"

"Well, I'm just not that good at it. I don't know, really."

And suddenly the older man resembled his own apartment.

"How does a person do it?"

Desolate. Empty. Even a little sad.

"How do they leave something?"

The two of them observed each other. Not long, but long enough to note that Piet Hoffmann had taken another step further into Ewert Grens's life, into a space where almost no one was welcome.

"Let's go to the kitchen. It's easier to work there. Besides—if we're gonna spend the rest of the night on this, I'd better brew up something hot for us."

Each sat with their cup of even stronger coffee, though Hoffmann hadn't known that was possible. And the roll of dry biscuits that was still difficult to chew. At a kitchen table covered with pictures of the living and the dead—Dejan Pejović and Branko Stojanović. Older pictures taken of them in action discreetly from a distance by police officers during various investigations. And day-old pictures of the two of them on their backs with two bullet holes in their heads. Grens didn't say a word, gave no explanations, no names, didn't want to interrupt something as important as a first impression—so he sat in silence and drank coffee while he waited for Hoffmann's reaction.

"You'll infiltrate for me, Grens, if I infiltrate for you?"

"Exactly."

"And these two here are *my* mission?"

"Not them. They don't have much of a future as you can see. But it's what they're a part of. The illegal arms trade. I want to know who killed them and why. Before more people die."

Piet Hoffmann grabbed a picture taken with a tele-photo lens by a hunched-over undercover detective from across Sergels Square. Two men were standing at the bottom of a large staircase near the entrance to the subway, obviously discussing something.

"This is the only picture you have of the two of them together?"

"I think so. At least the only one my colleagues have found so far. Do you recognize them?"

Hoffmann examined the photograph. Used to read-ing a room under great stress. Now he was in no hurry, and he turned and twisted the slightly grainy image. Until he pointed to the man on the left, the taller of the two who was wearing a black leather jacket and some kind of hat.

"Dejo P. That's what they called him. His name was Dejan, don't remember the rest. A dangerous mother-fucker. Or more likely, wanted to be. I once saw him walk straight into a fucking drug den with a chain saw in his hand. Seriously. Like in some shitty movie. Not sure what he was after. Respect, maybe. He never got mine."

Piet Hoffmann's index finger wandered over the pic-ture of the other man. Wide-shouldered, slightly bent. White T-shirt, gray trousers, and red sneakers. Fat gold chain around his neck, and a newsboy cap pulled low on his forehead.

"Branko. I'm sure of it. Last name starts with an S. And unlike Dejo P, he was dangerous—for real. Branko didn't need chain saws. You just knew. A guy you'd have a real problem with if you made any trouble."

"How well do you know them? Knew?"

"If you spend twenty years in the underbelly of Stockholm, you meet just about everybody. We didn't know each other, Grens—we knew *of* each other. Saw each other around the pubs. Bought and sold a bit. Made sure others could buy and sell. We were all the type that wasn't supposed to be seen. And it wasn't like Dejo P or Branko or I was very interesting—the interesting ones were those we were being paid to protect."

Ewert Grens lifted two of the documents and placed them on the table, propping them against the wall. Pictures from two crime scenes and two dead men.

"You got the first names right, Hoffmann. Meet former Mr. Dejan Pejović and former Mr. Branko Stojanović. Murdered this morning. And as you can see—both have double bullet holes in their heads."

Hoffmann leaned closer to the pictures, studied them, and after a moment he pointed to the two destroyed heads.

"Ulcinj."

"Excuse me?"

"A city in eastern Montenegro. A few miles from the Albanian border. Not far from either Podgorica or Tirana."

"And?"

"It's an Ulcinj execution. That's what they call it, Grens. Two shots to the head—on the right of the forehead and below the left temple."

They drank strong coffee and shared the last of the

biscuits, three each. The detective gathered the pictures and placed the four plastic folders in front of his guest, patted them.

"Your task in our little infiltration exchange: who killed them and why? This is all the information we were able to gather today. Read it. Memorize it. Because I can't make any copies—and I'll need to take them back to the police station later this morning."

Piet Hoffmann patted the stack of documents in the same way the detective had. Illustratively. Before making a similar point by patting his new puffy cheeks and crooked nose.

"And *your* part, Grens? What are *you* gonna do for *me*?"

Ewert Grens opened a cabinet beneath the sink. When he closed it again, he was holding a bottle of whiskey in his hand. Single malt. Light and not at all smoky.

"As you know Hoffmann, I very rarely drink. But not even I can take another cup of coffee tonight. A glass?"

Grens filled two small drinking glasses. They looked at each other, swallowed, felt that warmth spread through their chests. It was rather nice even if it did share space with so much anxiety. Maybe for that reason.

"Okay—*I* ask you to find out who murdered two hit men with links to Europe's mafia-run weapons trade. *You* ask me to infiltrate my own workplace because an organization is threatening you and your family and trying to take over the illegal arms trade. Let's start there, Hoffmann. I think we're sitting across from each other because this is connected. Connected by the Swedish arms trade."

Piet Hoffmann didn't drink hard liquor very often either—wasn't the type who needed extra courage to meet himself. But right now, at this table, in the home of the detective superintendent—it just tasted good. Hoffmann emptied his glass and waited for Grens to refill it before responding.

"I sold drugs. You know that, Grens. And I did time for it. But drugs are a completely different business— that's all about mass imports. Weapons on the other hand, you don't fill up trucks with those. Micro smuggling. Two or three Kalashnikovs or maybe five handguns at a time. No more. That's how it works. The weapons market in this country isn't controlled by large arms dealers. Not yet. It's driven by self-interest. Every criminal organization ensures that they have enough for their own purposes, and then they're satisfied. They buy abroad and use their own channels to bring that shit in. And they don't resell, that's not the point. So, for example, a few years ago when the Råby Soldiers bought up every fucking piece they could get their hands on so that a rival gang couldn't get any, then things got a bit shaky for a while. But that was the exception, Grens. If a new player, the one threatening me, were to step in with a train car full of very powerful machine guns—well, that would change everything. You'd know it immediately, you'd hear about it in your police station within ten minutes. And if you think you have problems *now* with gang shootings . . . well, all I can say is good luck."

"So who's threatening you? Who wants to corner the Swedish market?"

"Listen, if I knew I wouldn't be sitting here. I have gone through every single contact I have—and I've got quite a few, both inside and outside prison walls. They usually know if anything's up. But not this. The only thing I can say for sure is that one of your fucking colleagues has switched sides and that's key."

Grens picked up the top folder and pointed to a picture of a still living Dejan Pejović.

"And these two? Or rather whomever they worked for? Could they be threatening you? Could they know who you are and what you did?"

"No."

"And you're sure about that because . . . ?"

"I'm not sure of anything. But that these two could get some cop to risk everything for them—nah. I don't believe it."

"Who else? The Polish mafia you infiltrated on our behalf?"

"Unfortunately they found out who I was. As you may remember. But after that—well, they don't exist anymore."

"The Colombian drug cartel you infiltrated on behalf of American DEA?"

"No. They didn't know anything. Still don't."

"The African smugglers you infiltrated on my behalf?"

"No, they . . . I probably never told you that, but they're not around anymore either. Grens, listen: I've already been through all my enemies. Every single one, and it's not a short list. It doesn't make sense. This isn't anyone's MO. How they act. Express themselves. Make contact. I don't recognize it. And I'm completely convinced I have never met whoever is threatening me right now."

They drank whatever was left in their glasses. And it still felt good in their chests. But Grens didn't refill again. He'd learned that chemically induced high spirits have a tendency to change shape when you least expect it.

"It's three o'clock. I'm going back out to the balcony for a while. Take the opportunity to study these papers now, Hoffmann. Tomorrow's getting closer by the minute."

He stared out over the rooftops for a half hour while the sun rose. Golden yellow light and warm air made life seem easier. He was convinced—he should make his bed out here in the summer.

When his accidental guest opened the balcony door and stepped out into another reality, he seemed to make the same discovery. For a moment, life met life. At its most vulnerable and powerful.

"You've got it good, Grens."

"I end up here sometimes. When it's hard to sleep. Pretty often, I'd say."

Piet Hoffmann leaned over the railing, much like the detective often did. As if he, too, had to stare down at where it all might come to an end.

"Two more names pop up in those documents. Your colleagues, Grens, claim in their notes that Pejović and Stojanović were often observed with two others with similar backgrounds. Dusko Zaravic. Ermir Shala. I saw them together, in different constellations, sometimes all four of them. Back when I used to live the life. I'm not claiming they were any kind of gang or entity even. More a network that took whatever assignments popped up, they helped each other out, traded favors. If you fucked with one, you fucked with them all. Zaravic and Shala were just as violent as their dead comrades."

Five motorcycles drove by on an otherwise almost empty Svea Road. A roaring sound that grew louder the higher up it went, without breaking the night's silence, it was more as if it were part of it. Stockholm. Big city, small city.

"So if I'm going to infiltrate them. Get close. That's where we have to start, Detective. With the two names that are still alive."

Hoffmann left the railing and walked the length of the large balcony. When he stopped, it was quiet again, only faint voices coming from some patio.

"Ermir Shala, I've never had much to do with. But Dusko Zaravic. He and I, well . . . you'll see that he's only done time once in Sweden. Plenty of interrogations and arrests and prosecutions, but no other convictions."

"I interrogated both of them seventeen years ago. Just like I interrogated the two who are dead. All four were at the periphery of a large investigation, an entire family was executed—but I never managed to figure out how the family was connected to a bunch of Balkan gangsters. One of the few times I let a murderer get away."

"Then you know, Grens—the sort that always wriggle away. The only time one of them was locked up—Dusko Zaravic for assault, kidnapping, and a whole bunch of drugs, he got nine years and served six and a half. Because *I* put him there. One of my jobs as an infiltrator. I succeeded where your police force never could, Grens. He spent the first few years in the Bunker with full restrictions. No leave, no visits. Then his son got sick. Leukemia, I think. And Zaravic couldn't be with his little boy, while he was sick and dying. I have my own boys now, so I get it. And I'm quite grateful he doesn't know about me. Grateful that Wilson, as he always did, made sure to keep my contribution out of it."

Grens rose and they stood shoulder to shoulder.

Two people who didn't trust anyone, but who would have to trust each other.

"It's like this, Detective. Either Zaravic and Shala are the perps who shot their peers because someone who wants to take over the weapons market gave them enough money to do it. Or they'll be the next ones with two holes in their heads. Either way—I need them far away from me to be able to infiltrate. With Shala and Zaravic out there, I can't move as freely as I need to, can't do what you want me to do. So I suggest you arrest them."

"Arrest them?"

"Seventy-two hours. Three days. As long as you can keep a person locked up without an arrest warrant."

"Arrest them for what?"

"Doesn't make a damn bit of difference. Make something up. It wouldn't be the first time—would it,

Grens? When you call and tell me you've got the cell doors locked, well, right then the clock starts to tick. For my infiltration work and yours. Simultaneously."

Piet Hoffmann breathed in the mild air, watching the beautiful colors of the sun rise in the sky.

"Three days, Grens. When the time comes. That's how long we'll have."

Ewert Grens had never figured out which of the many churches on Kungsholmen rang its bells so beautifully on the hour. A bright, hopeful song. At varying volumes, sometimes almost intrusive, other times more like a cautious whisper, depending on the whims of the wind. This morning five metallic chimes rang out loud and clear as he walked down a corridor that was just as deserted as it was a few hours ago, but now considerably lighter.

It took him a while to make his way to his office—he put the plastic folder back on Hermansson's fancy chair and then grabbed a coffee at the machine, put another folder next to Sven's phone, and then took one to the desks in the cadets' cubbyhole, then one more stop at the coffee machine. This had always been his favorite time of day. Before sound and movement filled up the department, and it still felt possible to think clearly.

Piet Hoffmann had been lying on one of the elegant sofas in his living room when Grens snuck out about a half hour ago. A sofa Grens never sat in, in a room he rarely visited. His guest was snoring quietly with his cheek against a lumpy decorative pillow that Anni bought a long time ago. Hoffmann's sudden appearance had made the detective superintendent's work that much more difficult. His primary mission—finding the little girl who had hopped around her dead family long ago—had expanded to include two more objectives: track down the two Balkan men who needed to be locked up for seventy-two hours so that Hoffmann would have room to maneuver, while simultaneously sussing out which one of his colleagues had switched sides.

He emptied his coffee cup, grabbed one of his Siw Malmkvist cassette tapes from the pile on the bookshelf, and started to dance to the music as he had so many times before, both here alone in his office and long ago with Anni.

The girl.

That's where he had to start. Slowly circle in on her. Before someone with very different intentions did the same.

He looked at a faxed copy of an assessment that had been signed seventeen years ago. Charlotte M. Andersen. She had been head of Söderköping's child welfare department, and she was his next step. She'd once decided the fate of a five-year-old girl, new identity, new family, and now she would know where the trail led. A trail he had once erased, according to his own protocols, after telling a child in a safe house with no parents—no family—that she would soon have to leave a place that represented the last bit of security she possessed. She was separated from the only adult she trusted—a police officer name Ewert Grens, who had carried her in his arms all the way there.

He looked at the alarm clock that stood on his rickety coffee table next to his sofa. Quarter past five. Too early. He waited. For fifteen minutes. Then he called the number he'd found online for one Charlotte M. Andersen who lived on Gamla Skol Street in Söderköping. No answer. He waited five minutes, tried again. Waited five more, called again.

Finally, at 5:55 AM, she answered.

"Seriously? Eight times before six o'clock? Who are you? What do you want?"

Her voice was tired. Angry.

"My name is Ewert Grens. I'm a detective superintendent in Stockholm. I need your help."

"And you need it—this early?"

"I can call in five minutes if that suits you better. Or five minutes after that. And so on . . ."

The woman who, according to Grens's contact at the Tax Agency, was now retired still sounded tired and angry. Now after a long sigh she added defeat.

"Very well . . . what's this about?"

"Zana Lilaj."

Silence. A long one.

"A little girl. You gave her a new name. A new life."

Quiet for so long that Ewert Grens thought the woman might have hung up.

"Hello, are you . . ."

"I'm here."

"And?"

"I don't know what you're talking about."

"I'm sitting here with the document you signed. I'm pretty sure this wasn't the kind of decision you made every day, or even every year. You surely remember it. You know exactly what I'm talking about. Who I'm talking about."

Silence—again. And it occurred to Grens that this former department head was acting professionally. Because if she admitted she'd made the decision, even if she didn't reveal a name, she'd have given this unfamiliar voice somewhere to start looking.

"What did you say your name was?"

"Ewert Grens."

"And you're a superintendent at . . . ?"

"City Police, Stockholm."

"Hang up. And wait. I'll call you back."

Seven minutes. Until the switchboard connected them again.

"Well, at least I know you're a police officer. But . . ."

"Her name? Currently?"

". . . it doesn't matter. You won't get anything from me. You'll just have to . . ."

"I'm investigating a murder."

". . . look elsewhere."

"Her life could be in danger."

A final long silence. And when the former department head spoke again it was in a voice that was neither angry, tired, nor defeated. Cold—that's how she sounded.

"You can call me and say whatever you want. My mission then—helping a five-year-old girl—wasn't just about finding a new name or social security number or home. It included a promise to never, ever under any circumstances reveal her new identity. Retirement hasn't changed that—I consider this promise permanent. Have a very nice morning, Detective, as I intend to do."

She hung up. So Ewert Grens called again. And again. And again. But their conversation had reached a dead end.

That was his assessment.

Because when he finally stopped manically calling her, his own phone started to ring loudly, and he picked it up.

"Good. You changed your mind. If you'll just give me her . . ."

"Grens?"

A man's voice. It wasn't Charlotte M. Andersen, changing her mind and calling him back.

"Yes, that's me."

"Officer on duty here."

"And?"

"Regerings Street 79. We were called there a half hour ago, and I thought you should know."

"Yes?"

"A new corpse. Two bullet holes—forehead, temple."

Ewert Grens jumped up quickly from his desk chair, but he didn't head immediately for the elevator, he turned in the opposite direction, the phone still at his ear, and walked toward Mariana Hermansson's office.

"Anything else?"

"The officers on the scene describe a male, well-built, approximately fifty years old, and one meter and eighty-five centimeters tall. Also noted: there is a gun in a shoulder holster. Also noted: a wallet in the inner pocket of his jacket. The shooter made no attempt to disguise that this was anything other than another execution. Even left the victim's ID behind, untouched."

"Wait."

The plastic folder was where he'd put it an hour earlier, still on Hermansson's transparent chair. Grens flipped through it looking for a document hidden somewhere in the middle of the stack.

"And the name? Let me guess."

There. The picture of two of the four who were still alive. Had been alive when Hoffmann was talking about them last night on Grens's balcony.

". . . Dusko Zaravic? Or Ermir Shala?"

The two who, according to the notes that the police's surveillance team had kept, were part of an unofficial network that included the recently murdered Pejović and Stojanović. Doing security and rough jobs for various weapons dealers.

"Ermir Sh . . . How did you know that, Grens?"

"Shala?"

"Yes. At least according to the driver's license found in his wallet. How . . ."

The officer on duty was never able to finish his question because Grens had already hung up.

He had to make another call immediately.

Only one of the four was still alive.

Dusko Zaravic.

The one who Hoffmann had once informed against and sent to prison.

He might have been paid to carry out three executions on behalf of a new competitor in the arms trade. He might be the one who had an inside man on the police force—who had managed to buy off one of Grens's colleagues and who was now threatening Hoffmann. In that case, there were also personal reasons for carrying out the threat because Zaravic would know that it was Hoffmann who prevented him from visiting his dying son. Piet Hoffmann who now had his own sons to lose.

The story continued to evolve and intertwine and so far the detective had found himself at least one step behind. Now he had to find a way to get one step ahead. And so he pushed one of the few numbers he had saved in his phone.

"Hermansson—are you awake?"

"Now . . ."

She stood up and left her bedroom. He was good at picking up on that sort of thing, how Sven—who he would call next—always rolled over to the side of the bed, barely awake, and whispered so as not to wake up Anita, while Hermansson, who lived alone, slammed her feet onto the floor and spoke loudly to clear her throat after a night's sleep.

". . . I am. Seriously, Ewert . . . again?"

"You have a notebook? Pen?"

The creak of a cupboard door opening. The sound of paper being ripped out of a notepad. He could follow her movements through the phone, was just waiting for the scrape of a chair being pulled out.

"Good, Hermansson. Now write down 'Regerings Street 79.'"

"Why?"

"Dead man. Two bullet holes."

She started writing, the scratch of her pen.

"Another one? A third?"

"Go there as soon as we get off the phone. And remember—I want you to send a picture of the dead man to my phone. Okay? Now on the next line 'Dusko Zaravic.' First name is spelled with a 'k,' and the last name with 'z.'"

She dashed this down quickly. This was serious.

"And you'll understand why when you check the folder in your office. Dusko Zaravic has to be found *today*—and he needs to be arrested and locked up."

"Arrested? Why?"

"Use your imagination. Lock him up for the full seventy-two hours we can hold him without proof."

"Why?"

"Because he's either the executioner or he's the next one to be executed. I want him behind bars. Out of the way. So we can figure out the truth."

A fridge.

That's what she was opening, he knew the sound.

"And you, Ewert? Where do you plan on hiding while we turn ourselves inside and out?"

"I'm planning to take a drive."

She was pouring something into a glass, something that gurgled.

"Driving?"

"I'm leaving Kronoberg Station in an hour. Headed to a small town two hundred kilometers south of here. I need an answer someone doesn't want to give me."

One side of the pillow was covered with tiny plastic beads, in a pattern that looked like some kind of tree with sprawling and swaying branches, and it had left an imprint on his left cheek.

Piet Hoffmann sat up on one of Ewert Grens's elegant sofas. He hadn't slept long, but heavy, which was rare for him. And here—of all places. At the home of the police officer who once gave the command to shoot him in the head. Life seemed so straightforward when he looked into Luiza's eyes, but in its other guises it was quite bizarre.

He'd pressed the number the first time just after three when Grens had disappeared onto the balcony. But changed his mind before anyone answered. He tried again just before five and she managed to answer just before he hung up in confusion. But this time he let the signal go through while opening that place in his heart where only Zofia's voice was allowed.

"Did I wake you up?"

"I don't know. Maybe. I can't relax here. But the kids are asleep, all of them. How . . . Where are you?"

He was there. That's what it felt like.

"Close."

With her, pressed against her warm skin, lying next to each other and listening to Hugo tossing and turning and Rasmus's quiet snoring and Luiza's stable breathing.

"A few more days. Then this will be over. But you have to stay in the apartment. You can't go out. The boys can't go out. Don't even open a window. Promise me. And Zo—please hug Hugo and Rasmus and Luiza extra hard for me."

Piet Hoffmann smoothed the pillows and rugs and the velvety sofa fabric, then wandered out into the rest of the apartment, which seemed never ending—it was still so impossible to imagine that blunt detective in this palace. As he approached the library he started to slow. He remembered something he saw yesterday evening when he was sitting in that armchair, flipping through a newspaper and waiting for Grens to come back. On the wall, which was otherwise floor-to-ceiling books, there hung a tapestry embroidered with the words MERRY CHRISTMAS, yellow letters on a red background, next to a black-and-white photograph—a very young man and a very young woman in crisp new police uniforms. And this crocheted tapestry and those two portraits constituted the center, not just of this room, but also of the whole palatial apartment.

He placed his next call from Grens's enormous kitchen with a cup of coffee, a piece of crispbread he'd found at the back of the pantry, and a hardboiled egg that was lying in the compartment next to the milk in an otherwise empty refrigerator. It was to his employee at Hoffmann Security, who was sitting in a narrow studio apartment in a high-rise building, watching monitors that conveyed images of four guarded apartments.

"Up a little earlier than usual, boss?"

"A sofa that wasn't as comfortable as it looked. How are we today?"

"Easy morning, easy night. The protective target in 8 is still asleep, the protective target in 12 just finished breakfast, and I've seen the protective target in 10 in the living room window several times, he's not crying anymore."

Piet Hoffmann barely heard what the security guard was telling him, and it made him feel a little ashamed, but it wasn't these threatened people—whom he was being paid so well to protect—that he wanted to know more about.

"And . . . the new ones?"

"I still don't like having them a couple kilometers away."

"You're right, Andy, but just now it is what it is."

The security guard was pressing a few buttons on the monitors and pushing a few keys on the keyboard, or that's what it sounded like through the phone.

"I see her, the mother, right now. Camera 7, facing the balcony. She's standing in the kitchen in a yellow bathrobe, I think, and staring at . . . well, nothing. However, and this isn't good, boss, but a while ago . . ."

The guard suddenly fell silent.

"Yes?"

"And this isn't good at all."

"What is it, Andy?"

"She's talking on the phone. I'm absolutely sure. She's not supposed to do that, she must have snuck it in . . ."

"My fault—I forgot to inform her last night. I missed it. I was rushed."

"You want me to go over there now? Talk to her? Take the phone?"

"I'll do it. I'll talk to her."

"Because we need to know who she's communicating with. And she has to know it's dangerous. That . . ."

"I'll talk to her, Andy. Discuss everything."

And Hoffmann just wanted to scream now.

Tell me what she really looks like, what you think she's feeling? For real? More broken than I know? More sad? When you zoom in and look at her eyes, are they . . .

But that was the one thing he couldn't do. Because no one, not even his employees, could know.

"Thank you, Andy. You're on it, as usual. And the others . . . how . . . have you seen the kids?"

"I caught a glimpse of the older boy a while ago. Camera 2, facing the bedroom. Worried. That's how he moved. Sometimes it's so obvious. I've seen many a worried child on these screens—but that was definitely one of the worst. What the hell have they been through, boss?"

Piet Hoffmann stayed where he was, as if frozen in that uncomfortable kitchen chair.

Hugo.

His little boy, who was getting big now, and who slept as restlessly as he did himself, who already knew that the world belonged to the safe ones—he, too, had stared out the window just like his mother, anxiously on the lookout for the unknown.

The terrifying.

That image was still so fresh in Hoffmann's mind—his oldest son's troubled face—when he finally swallowed the last of his coffee and pushed aside his plate of crispbread crumbs to make room for this morning's preparations.

On the far left he put the radio jammer, the timer, and his extra phone, the one he would use first. Then a centimeter-wide microphone, which he'd place strategically to capture any voices likely to be speaking another language. Interpreter. That's what he called it. Because, along with software on his mobile phone, it would translate every word in the room he was going to visit. Next to that he lay his Radom pistol, which he kept in a shoulder holster, and his hunting knife, newly sharpened on both sides, which he kept in the other shoulder holster, and finally a bulletproof vest and the hand grenade that now lacked any plastic arms or legs.

A long line of metallic objects—and he knew exactly how to handle them.

However, his disguise.

As confident as he was about the tools that lay in front of him on the table, he was less sure that the puffy silicone on his cheeks or the mustache of real human hair above his lips would hold up to inspection if they were tested again—this time in the bright light of day.

Patience had never been Ewert Grens's strong suit. But on his fourth trip to the coffee machine to take a look at the closed door of Erik Wilson's office, the homicide unit chief had finally arrived. Grens filled up an extra plastic mug with the same hot black drink and hurried in without knocking.

"Good morning."

He placed a cup on Wilson's desk and settled himself on the visitor's chair.

"Good morning, Ewert. Bit early, isn't it? Or did you sleep here?"

"Depends on how you look at it."

"Oh, really?"

"Let's just say I came and went several times throughout the night."

"Why?"

"Because there's been a burglary here."

"Excuse me?"

"In the station. In the restricted archive in the cellar. And in our department. In fact, right here—in your office."

"What are you talking about?"

Grens went over to the safe that stood in the corner of his boss's office. A blob of metal as tall as the detective and just as bulky. And for now, only a couple hundred kilos heavier.

"In there."

Wilson hadn't touched his coffee. Now he did, emptied the whole mug. As if doubting he was awake.

"I repeat—what are you talking about, Ewert?"

The door to the corridor was still open a crack, you could tell whenever someone walked by. Grens closed it—made sure it was shut—and returned to the safe.

"I'll explain more—later. When the time I need has started to tick. But I'm absolutely sure, Wilson. Someone has opened that safe, which you, the formal head of our infiltration program, are responsible for. And they took out some extremely confidential documents. One of our colleagues in this very building."

"For the third time: *what the hell are you talking about*? No one's gotten into my safe. There's been no visible entry. Not a trace of someone even having *tried* to break into it. Are you bored, Ewert? Isn't it enough to have two, possibly three murders to investigate? A break-in—at the police station?"

"It wouldn't be the first time. Not even in this corridor."

They both remembered that night long ago when Ewert Grens decided to break into Wilson's predecessor's office and take the computer that was the key to what was going on at the time. It had been so much easier than either of them imagined, forcing a locked door and making it hardly visible afterward.

"But no one has ever gotten into one of our safes, Ewert. And back then our office doors weren't as secure as the ones we have now."

"Then open it. And prove me wrong."

Erik Wilson glanced at Grens's coffee mug, still only half drunk on the visitor chair—as if still hoping to wake up from what the detective superintendent was telling him, hopefully in some alternative to this reality. And an involuntary shudder passed through his body. Ewert Grens was often difficult to understand and had a way about him that required practice to endure—but he didn't usually indulge in these kinds of theatrics.

"If you'll just look away for a moment, Ewert."

Grens turned around while Wilson input an eight-digit code.

"Very well—and what is supposed to be missing?"

"You can start with Paula's envelope."

The look that Erik Wilson gave Ewert Grens contained a strange mix of emotions.

Astonishment. Fear. Contempt. Distrust.

All at the same time.

"Paula's envelope?"

"Open it."

Erik Wilson had worked for a decade as Piet Hoffmann's handler, and was therefore Hoffmann's only connection to the security of the police world. Erik Wilson had given Hoffmann the code name Paula, and Erik Wilson had written his real name on a piece of paper and sealed it inside an envelope.

That was the envelope that Grens was now asking him to open.

And as Wilson lifted it from one of the shelves near the bottom of the safe, it was immediately obvious that it was *already* open.

A broken seal. An envelope with no contents.

The involuntary shudder was followed by a few more, Erik Wilson's face blanched, and he had to grab hold of the safe for support.

"I . . . don't understand."

"I can see that."

"Ewert, this . . . I . . ."

"I want you to check one more thing. The black logbooks."

Erik Wilson weaved back and forth for a moment, and for a moment he almost seemed like he might lose his balance.

"Which one of the binders?"

"Paula's."

The head of the homicide unit didn't have to search for very long before he realized that all the notes he'd taken during his years of secret meetings were gone. And leaving the door to the safe wide open, he stumbled back to his desk and sank down in his chair.

"Paula. Piet Hoffmann. How many violent criminals, would you guess, Wilson, did we lock up thanks to his reports? How many drug seizures were made based on his info? How many murders and shootings did we solve because he risked his life every day? And it was your goddamn responsibility to keep the truth hidden in that fucking safe!"

Grens looked at his boss. Who just sat there, empty.

"What do you think is gonna happen when those

papers get out on the streets? Or—are they already? What do you think, Wilson, that he . . ."

"I know exactly what this means!"

Ewert Grens smiled. His boss no longer seemed empty.

"And they've also sold you out."

"What the hell . . ."

"Because as you said. No one can break in here. And if that's so, then I'm sitting across from a dirty cop."

"You know how devoted I was to my infiltrators! You know I built the whole goddamn program from scratch and guarded it like it was my own goddamn child! I created the rules that protected them! I took risks for them every single day! And you know how close I am to the Hoffmann family and all that I've done for them! You know that!"

Grens stared at the man screaming at him, who seemed to be disgusted with him. And he liked that man. Not the screaming or disgust, but he knew that the message was genuine. He knew Erik Wilson well enough to know that. A man that Grens had once considered an enemy. But that had changed. Or did Grens change? Slowly, Grens had begun to respect this man, ever since he left his job as a handler and started a new, much more difficult one—being Grens's boss. It was the way he let his staff follow their own lead when it was needed, and how he used his authority to rein them when it was not. A decent man with decent morals. So what Grens was seeing right now was what he'd hoped.

"You're right—I don't think it was you, Wilson. But I think you might have made a mistake."

"Such as?"

"Well . . . are you still single?"

"Excuse me?"

"I've noticed lately that it seems like you've met someone. You've got that look about you. Not something I'm so familiar with myself . . . but I recognize it on others. Love. And when you meet someone, Wilson, you let someone in. Close. Maybe even so close that you get careless."

Erik Wilson stared, silently.

"Who are you seeing?"

Staring.

"Who?"

Silent.

"Who, Wilson?"

"That's none of your business!"

"Yes it is. Because it has something to do with this."

"Who I have dinner with or wake up next to is none of your damn business!"

Ewert Grens stood up and walked over to the still open safe, pushed on the door and saw it slide closed again. A metallic click as the locking pins hooked.

"Okay. Let's assume that. For now. That it wasn't you, that it wasn't whoever you're seeing who got you to reveal the code. But . . . well, it doesn't look good, what happened. Does it, Wilson? And if it gets out. If I were to start talking about it. First of all, that you're not taking care of your responsibilities. Secondly, that there's verifiable information out there that we have worked with criminal infiltrators, which we have always denied, because as we all know it's illegal."

"I don't like your tone, Ewert. What you're implying. I might even call it a threat."

Grens patted the safe, a muted sound.

"What you like or don't like has never interested me. However, solving crimes is something I find rather important. So if my tone makes that job easier, if it gets me the tools I need, then I don't really care what you think you hear."

"The tools you need? Ewert—what the hell does that mean?"

The detective patted the safe again, as if they were old friends, pushed a few buttons randomly, and pulled on the door again, as if to remind his boss that it was supposed to be locked like this *all* the time.

"Okay, Wilson. With my rather obvious tone: I won't talk about what happened in here while I investigate who broke open that envelope and took the contents of that logbook. In return, you'll get ahold of an authentic police badge for our new employee, who looks like this."

Ewert Grens had asked Piet Hoffmann to take a picture of his new appearance and text it to him. The display of the phone Grens placed on Wilson's desk was filled with the image of a tired and rather puffy-looking man staring straight into the eye of the camera.

"And I say to you—who the hell is that supposed to be?"

Wilson pointed to the image of a transformed Hoffmann. And it occurred to Grens that it was working. The disguise. Of course this was just a crappy phone picture on a tiny screen, and meeting someone in real life was much more than just surface appearance, but Wilson, one of the people who knew Hoffmann best, didn't seem at all suspicious and that felt quite promising.

"That's what I said the first time I saw him."

"Who?"

"I can't tell you. But that's the man who is going to help me find out who broke the seal on that envelope. And he needs our help to do it. For three days, to be exact. And his new credentials have to be ready by tomorrow morning. And you'll need to attach a letter of recommendation addressed To Whom It May Concern, stating how reliable and capable Verner Larsson has been during his years as an employee of the City Police, which you will sign."

"Verner Larsson?"

"As good a name as any."

"So you want me to . . . Ewert, have you completely lost your mind?"

"Not quite."

"I would never give a badge to someone who isn't an officer!"

"Mmm. Such a shame. Because . . . how does that go now? We don't use criminal infiltrators. And no one has broken into your office and stolen any incriminating documents. And if . . ."

"That's enough."

". . . I'm not talking . . ."

"That's enough, Ewert."

Erik Wilson was still sitting at his desk staring at the locked safe when Grens headed back to his own office.

As soon as he stepped through his door, he closed it and called the same number he had an hour ago. Mariana Hermansson. Who had now arrived at Regerings Street 79 and yet another stairwell filled with forensic technicians, medical examiners, and a dead man on his back with a bullet hole in his forehead and his temple.

"A copy, Ewert, of the other two. No doubt about it. The same shooter."

"The victim?"

"The initial observations seem correct. A forty-five-year-old male who, according to the ID in his wallet, is named Ermir Shala. Just a quick search in the police records showed that his appearance and height are a match. Also, identifying marks—tattoo of a sword in a stone on his forearm, a birthmark on his right ear, and a distinct scar from one side of his throat to the other."

"Good. Then you can leave the crime scene. And take care of your other two assignments."

"Two? You told me to track down and arrest someone named Dusko Zaravic for some bullshit and hold him for seventy-two hours. That was what you said."

"That's what I said. And he should be arrested. Before midnight. And later we'll have much more to hold him on than just bullshit. But something else has come up that I want . . . well, I want you to take care of it personally."

"What's that?"

"Erik Wilson."

"What about him?"

"He's hiding something."

"Everyone is hiding something."

"Not everyone is hiding something that's connected to a break-in at the police station."

There was silence on the other end of the phone call. Grens could hear Mariana Hermansson breathing, could hear the forensic technicians shuffling around in the stairwell, and a medical examiner quietly recording his observations into a tape recorder.

"Are you there, Hermansson?"

"What are you saying? Do you think our boss broke into his own workplace?"

"I'm saying that I think he's responsible for the disappearance of highly classified documents. Documents that directly endanger people's lives."

"What documents? What people?"

"I can't tell you any more than that."

"But you can call me claiming that the head of our department has committed a crime that would result in immediate dismissal if it were true! You know Wilson, Ewert—he's not guilty of some break-in. It's as unlikely as you or me."

"Maybe he didn't do it personally. But he's protecting someone. I think Erik Wilson is being manipulated."

"Manipulated?"

"He seems to have begun a fairly new . . . well, relationship. Even admitted it. You've probably noticed it, too. A relationship that happens to coincide with the disappearance of highly classified documents from his office. Nobody got in there without his help, either conscious or unconscious, on that I think we can agree. But he doesn't want to tell me who. No matter how hard I press the matter. I want to know, Hermansson. I want you to ferret out who it could be, start by concentrating on the police station. Put together a list of possible colleagues. Who's newly divorced. Who's single. Who might be unhappy enough in their present relationship to consider cheating."

Silence again. He thought he heard the forensic technicians discussing the best way to dust for prints far off in the background somewhere. But maybe that was just his imagination, a lifetime spent at crime scenes just like that one made it easy to call to mind something he knew by heart.

"Ewert, I will not spy on my colleagues. And let me make one thing very clear to you—you will never again ask me to play some double-dealing game with the people I work with! I don't care if you're my superior officer or not. Is that clear?"

Grens usually liked when Mariana Hermansson stood up to him. She was one of the few who dared to do so. But as he stood there with the phone pressed to his ear, something didn't sit right. There was some note in her voice. He knew her. He knew how she worked. And to refuse to take on a superior who might be hiding the truth, who might even have switched sides, that wasn't at all like her.

He was about to say as much. When she cut him off.

"And one more thing, Ewert: if you want me to make this mysterious arrest, while you drive down to Söderköping for an interrogation you won't discuss with me, then you're going to have to take care of the cadets today. Lucas and Amelia will have to go with you, if I'm going after Zaravic. Okay?"

As Grens hung up the phone and headed toward the cadets' closet office, he realized that each step was accompanied by a new uneasiness. And he couldn't quite pinpoint where it came from or how to get rid of it. Other than that he was sure that someone in this police station had sold out to criminal arms dealers by putting highly classified documents into their hands. And that two of the people he'd come to trust and actually like around here, Erik Wilson and Mariana Hermansson, might have something to do with it.

The enormous garage built deep beneath the Kronoberg Police Station always remained the same temperature—warm and comfortable when winter storms settled in over the capital, and pleasantly cool in the midst of heat waves like this one. Ewert Grens opened his car doors and the two cadets jumped in simultaneously—the one named Lucas, who had shoulders the width of Grens's waist, sat down beside him in the passenger seat, and the one named Amelia, who had short dark hair and intelligent eyes, plopped down in the back. The garage door automatically slid aside, and they headed up a steep incline toward the morning sounds of Kungsholmen, up to a lowered bar that a guard opened for them. The exit toward Essinge route and the E4 highway south came next. He started driving faster, heading into their two-hour trip to Söderköping—two hundred kilometers closer to a little girl.

"DB."

"Excuse me?"

"That's what you said, Superintendent. The first time we met. DB. Dead Body."

Lucas had a high, nasal voice, and an accent that sounded like it came from western Sweden.

"That's what you used to call murdered people. Like when you were our age."

"Yes. That's what I said."

"And I thought—how many? How many dead people do you . . . I mean, if you keep track until your age. I mean, now."

"Your age?"

"Yes. Do you keep track?"

"Yes. I keep track."

"And?"

"As of two days ago, three hundred and nine. Yesterday, three hundred and eleven. This morning three hundred and twelve."

The cadet fell silent. As if he lost his train of thought.

"Oh, that was . . . very precise. You *do* keep track. Three hundred . . . But did you say *this* morning?"

"Mmm. Another one, identical. Like the one where we met each other."

"Identical? So why are we sitting here? Why aren't we already there?"

"Because today, this is more important. This trip."

"Why?"

"We're looking for a someone who might end up a DB if we don't find her. That's part of police work, too. Prevention."

Ewert Grens drove through the suburbs of Stockholm quickly, and after a while he realized he was being observed not only by his interrogator next to him, but also via the rearview mirror. Cadet Amelia. She seemed about to join the conversation a couple of times, but stopped because the two in front kept talking. Now she looked at him with eyes that appeared to apologize for her fellow cadet's forwardness. Grens got the feeling that she understood and agreed with him that police work should save lives first, then hunt down those who took them.

He realized he very much liked that.

She reminded him of Mariana Hermansson. Maybe even a little of Anni. She was going to make a good cop.

"What I said before, Superintendent."

Lucas's silence was over. For now.

"About *your age*. I didn't mean to . . ."

"You didn't mean to—what?"

"Well . . . I mean, my dad's a police officer, too. In a small town where not much happens. And he's—just like you—old now. Retired."

The eyes in the rearview mirror. The detective superintendent would rather be looking into them. The young woman in the back seat knew it was too late to save her comrade—the more her fellow cadet babbled on trying to make it better, the worse it seemed to get.

"I mean, what I meant was that . . . that Dad wasn't at all like you, Superintendent, not at all, he didn't have any plans for his future. It was like his police badge was a computer chip. Do you know what I mean? Dad just kinda stopped functioning when they took it away from him."

They passed Södertälje, Järna, Nyköping, and it was only there, about halfway to their destination, that Grens finally stopped thinking about badges and computer chips and what happened to old cops who didn't plan for the future. Instead, what had been gnawing at him since this morning's meeting with Wilson and then even more after his phone call with Hermansson came back. And soon he slowed down at a rest stop to find a place to make another call without an audience present.

"Sven? It's me. Are you alone?"

"Just heading out of the garage with Hermansson. On my way to the elevator. We just got back from Re-gerings Street. Where are . . ."

"Call me when you're alone in your office."

"Why . . ."

"And don't tell Hermansson. Tell her I was calling about the medical examiner's report. Or whatever you want. I don't want her wondering what this is all about."

"But I don't even know . . ."

Grens hung up.

He took a slow walk through a still nearly deserted rest stop.

Two laps around crumb-covered tables where travelers later in the day could picnic, and hot, smelly trash cans that should have been emptied long ago.

Finally his phone rang.

"Sven here, again. Alone. With the door closed."

"Good."

"And?"

"I need your help."

"With what?"

"With Hermansson."

"With Hermansson?"

"Yes. She . . . something's not right, Sven. She's hiding something. And it's making me worried. I want you to check it out. Maybe follow her."

"What are you talking about? Hermansson? Am I supposed to start following *her*? Investigating *her*?"

"That's exactly what I need you to do."

"You know I'm not one to argue. But if you want me to—this is Hermansson, Ewert, Hermansson we're talking about—if you want me to investigate her you're going to have to tell me why."

"I can't do that."

"If you want my help, you have no choice."

Sven was right. Grens knew it. Detective Inspector Sundkvist was not one to argue, quite the opposite—he was almost conflict averse.

"Some documents have disappeared from Wilson's office. Extremely classified. How it happened I don't know. However, not many have spent much time in the vicinity of that safe. I asked Hermansson to help me investigate it. And got the wrong answer. Wrong feeling. And I don't like those kinds of feelings."

"I don't understand—do you think Hermansson stole the documents?"

"All I know for certain is that we have a corrupt colleague somewhere among us. Someone we trust. Whose actions risk destroying people outside the police station. I know her. I understand her. And I know that something's off right now. Follow her. If nothing else, so that we can rule out her involvement in all this."

They spent the last half hour of the drive in silence. Grens made it clear he didn't want to talk anymore, and

Lucas had finally realized that sometimes the best thing you can do in a situation is nothing at all.

Söderköping was a perfect summer town, a little more inviting, a little more charming than other places on this warm June day. People moved more slowly here, the water in the Göta Canal seemed to shine more brightly, and even the shade seemed to offer another kind of cool. The building on Gamla Skol Street was equally attractive—a wooden house from the early twentieth century, two stories and smack-dab in the middle of town. The detective superintendent hadn't called ahead. He had tried that at dawn without success. Now he parked in front of the entrance, went up the stairs with two cadets at his heels, and rang the doorbell.

"Yes?"

The woman who opened the door was a couple years older than Grens himself. That fit. According to his contact at the Tax Agency, it hadn't been that long since Charlotte M. Andersen had retired.

"Ewert Grens, detective superintendent at the City Police. And this is Lucas and Amelia, cadets at the homicide unit."

"You were the one who woke me up this morning."

"I was the one who woke you up this morning."

The former head of Söderköping's child welfare department had no intention of letting them inside. Despite both Grens and his cadets offering up their badges for her inspection.

"Well, in that case you made the trip for no reason."

Back straight. Eyes that didn't look away.

"Because I already told you: I don't discuss confidential matters when I'm in the midst of them, and I certainly don't talk about them later."

"And yet you're going to have to."

"I don't have to do anything."

"The girl I'm here about is in grave danger. Every second we stand here staring at each other her chances of survival go down. Let us in and I'll explain. Then you can decide if you're going to stay silent or talk."

He looked at her, still straight backed, gaze still steady.

And he knew she felt his seriousness and honesty.

Because suddenly she stepped aside.

"Thirty minutes. Then I want you to leave."

A person who lived alone, and who had done so for a long time. She didn't mention it, but Ewert Grens could tell. The way the furniture was placed, the smells, even the way she moved through the rooms. The sort of things only a person who had lived the same way and for just as long would pick up.

"You weren't invited. So there won't be coffee."

They sat opposite each other in the living room with a small round table between them. She in a green armchair with large flowers on it, he on a sofa with a blanket over it, while the cadets lingered near the doorway.

"Zana Lilaj. She had just turned five. I was the one who found her beside her dead parents and siblings. I was the one who carried her away. I was the rock in her life until she left the safe house and came here, to Söderköping, where she was given a new name and a new life. By you."

The former department head looked at him. Brittle, taut. At the same time.

"Dead parents? And siblings?"

"Yes, that's why . . ."

"I never knew. That's how it worked when I ended up with a person's life in my hands. A few pen strokes away with no insight into their past."

"In that case—can you help me now?"

Charlotte M. Andersen was touched, maybe even moved. That was easy to see. But she hadn't lost her focus. Grens thought she had probably been a much better boss than he was.

"No."

"No?"

"I explained this to you on the phone. I keep my promises. That means I will never reveal her new identity. You can come in here talking about a murder investigation as much as you want. You can't force me. Come back with a warrant—I'm not saying anything. Threaten to lock me up—go ahead, open the cell door, Superintendent."

The envelope was in Ewert's inner pocket. He emptied the contents onto the coffee table that separated them. Six photographs. Taken by forensic technicians at various crime scenes. Four of them he put on the left half of the table, the remaining two on the right.

"I want you take a close look at these four here. That picture there, closest to you—that's Zana's father. Killed with two gunshots. To the forehead and the temple. Do you see?"

The former department head was stronger than she

seemed. Though obviously very affected by what she saw. Still, she never looked away.

"And this—this is Zana's mother. This is her big sister, and this is her big brother. All shot in the same way. Back then."

Grens pushed one photograph after another over to the department head. Let her study them for a long time. Until he pointed to the opposite side.

"But these two, lying here, are quite fresh. The latest as recent as this morning, so you'll have to see that one in another format."

He took out his mobile phone and swiped over to the picture he'd asked Hermansson to send, then put the phone on the table as well.

"Three men who were at the periphery of the investigation into the murders of the Lilaj family. Look carefully exactly at their temples and foreheads, and you'll see the method of execution is very similar to the older pictures. That's why I'm sitting here. Whoever killed her family is killing again. Zana Lilaj's life is in danger."

Charlotte M. Andersen stood up from her flowery green armchair and left the living room. Grens could hear the tap running in the kitchen. When she came back she was carrying a tray of four glasses of yellowish juice, handed the cadets two of them and put down one on each side of the photographs on the table.

"Elderberry. I pick them myself, and it tastes delicious. Try it."

Then she drank, a whole glass at once.

"I think I understand what you're trying to tell me, Superintendent. And the more I weigh it, the heavier the side where I depart from principles gets. This is an emergency, you said?"

"I'm not even sure if she's still alive. Someone has made sure that the murderer or murderers have information that I don't—what her name is and where she lives. But if it is too late, at least I want to know."

Charlotte M. Andersen was still fighting against her promise of confidentiality. That's how she had lived her life for so long, steady and loyal. Never betray.

"I gave her the name Hannah. With an h at the end, I thought it looked nice."

That's why it took such incredible willpower for her to say even that much, though she knew what she was doing was right.

"And the foster family I placed her with had the last name of Ohlsson. So—Hannah Ohlsson. Just as normal as I hoped when she was put into the national registry. Sensible, childless people who had helped with shorter placements in the past. Six months later, they adopted her. I visited regularly back then. She was doing fine. When she turned seven, we said goodbye to each other, my oversight was no longer required by law. I think I've run into her a few times over the years here in town, but it's hard to say, children change so much as they age."

"Ohlsson?"

"Yes."

"Where?"

"A sweet little house about five kilometers outside of town. I'm pretty sure that at least the parents still live there."

Ewert Grens had honestly never been much of a runner. And age and a permanent limp after a bullet shattered his knee hadn't made him any better. But that's what it felt like he was doing now—running. Toward the front door and the parked car. Toward the outskirts of that beautiful summer town. Toward a house where a girl who had once been so alone had grown up and become a young woman.

He hoped he wasn't too late.

He hoped she was still alive.

Birger Jarls Street was asleep. Just like the rest of Stockholm's inner city. Even though it was a weekday and almost time for lunch. The buses were just as empty as the sidewalks, the shop staff moving less than the mannequins, the restaurants without the smell of frying but with butter dishes slowly melting away. Over thirty-three degrees and windless—warm had turned to hot had turned to panic.

Piet Hoffmann didn't even notice it. However, after a couple of hours of peering into a window on the fifth floor of an office building, he was sure the two men who worked there were on site. When he leaned forward toward his windshield, he could just make out one of them through his binoculars, the man who early yesterday evening sat in a parked car watching Hoffmann's house while Zofia, Hugo, Rasmus, and Luiza slept. Piet Hoffmann had asked him for a light and the security guard had told him to go to hell without recognizing him at all. Even though they'd worked together a few times. His disguise had held. At least in the dark, with his hair covered and his face partially obscured by an oversized baseball cap.

The people threatening me think I'm out somewhere preparing to start a gang war. They don't know I'm working on getting closer to the people they hired to follow me.

He climbed out of the car, crossed the street, went over to the entrance to 32B, and rang the buzzer.

"Yeah?"

A loudspeaker that swallowed words.

"Hi, my name is Peter Haraldsson."

He'd used that name before. But he'd used so many, lived so many different lives. Piet Hoffmann at home in Enskede became Piet Koslow to the human smugglers in Libya, Paula to the Swedish police became El Sueco to the South American drug cartels and Peter Haraldsson to his neighbors in the Colombian town of Cali. He didn't need any more variations of himself.

"Yeah?"

"I'm a small business owner. I'm here to look into your services."

"Like what?"

"Am I at the wrong place? Aren't you a security company? Someone recommended you to me. Don't you sell security services?"

The terrible loudspeaker buzzed exhaustedly as the door unlocked. Hoffmann took the stairs and stopped for a moment on the fourth floor. It was there, behind the shade of a wall-mounted light, that he taped his package with the jammer and timer. In a few minutes, as he was admitted to the premises of the security company on the next floor, the transmitter would be activated and the cameras tasked with recording his movements would go black.

"Come in."

The man who had been watching their house opened the door.

Tall. In good shape. Spoke Swedish with a slight accent. He didn't recognize his frumpy, overweight visitor this time either.

"Small business owner, you said?"

"Yes, exactly."

"What do you work with?"

"Consulting."

Hoffmann smiled. In a way he thought an overworked numbers guy might.

"Finance, accounting really, but that sounds so boring."

He had already noticed three surveillance cameras. One in the hall, at ceiling height. Then another one in the room he'd guess was the heart of the security company—the setup wasn't so different from his own office, just a few kilometers west of here as the crow flies. And then, a third camera staring at him from the doorframe to the kitchen. All of them useless from this point on.

"So what's this about?"

Piet Hoffmann turned around; the voice had come from the only room he couldn't see. The other security guard. Just as tall and fit with eyes that looked like they were used to being obeyed.

"What services were you intending in buying from us?"

Blend in. Be normal. Probably the most important concept for an infiltrator. Never stick out, be a person with no smell to them. That was how he'd always worked. When you rent a car get the most common—which in Sweden these days was a silver Volvo V70. Peter Haraldsson's shirts should be blue, his shoes black, and when it was cold outside, his scarves should be tied in a plastron knot—a simple knot that skipped the last step and just hung freely instead of sliding through the final loop.

"I need to hire someone to take care of my company's general security needs."

Normal. Especially when trying to fake a meeting in order to get closer, like now. As the owner of his own security company, he was very familiar with the usual questions. A) I'm feeling threatened—can you look into them? B) Goods are going missing from my company—can you help me find out who's stealing? C) I need to review my company's security setup—can you do that? He had chosen C. Even though he'd learned it was never about external security, always about internal insecurity.

"And I want to know how much it will cost. I need a quote."

He looked back and forth between the two men. They weren't paying much attention. They cared about him as little as he did about them. Stressed. Worried. Hoffmann thought he knew why. This morning no one had turned on the lights in the house they were guarding. No boys had headed off to school with their backpacks, no mother had gone for a walk with a stroller. Probably just a couple of hours ago they snuck out of their cars and into the Hoffmanns' garden, peeping through the windows, listening, maybe they even rang the doorbell, which no one answered. They knew now that the family that made their blackmailing possible had disappeared. That their mission was about to go to hell.

"A quote?"

"Yes."

"Um—where is your office located?"

"Västertorp."

"So in the suburbs. And how big is it? In square meters."

"A hundred, maybe a little more."

"With just one entrance?"

"Yes."

"It's hard to give exact numbers before we . . ."

The security guard fell abruptly silent, started to examine his potential customer. It was as if he were looking past the pasted-on bags beneath his eyes and through his brown contact lenses. Into a person who was someone else.

". . . visit you. But you can expect installations to be . . ."

Then he fell silent again, just as abruptly, and sought out his colleague's eyes. It was clear that they were communicating. Hoffmann could feel the two weapons holstered against his shoulder blades, gun on the left, knife on the right, and prepared to act.

". . . well, I'm guessing somewhere around seventy-five thousand kronor. Plus a monthly service fee of eight hundred."

One stood in front of him, the other behind him and to the side.

Piet Hoffmann waited.

But the attack never came.

His disguise worked.

"Could I use your bathroom? The heat really does me in."

Hoffmann looked around, and the man who seemed to be in charge pointed to a blue door just before the entrance to the kitchen.

"There. Use the small button to flush."

After Piet Hoffmann locked the toilet door behind him, he examined the floor, walls, ceiling until he was sure there were no cameras. Then he opened the brown leather briefcase he'd picked up at a Salvation Army and took out two things. A centimeter-sized microphone, the interpreter that only weighed a few grams, which he attached in the gap between the door and the floor. Then he took out the somewhat heavier hand grenade, which had been left in the Koslow Hoffmann family's mailbox—he'd even put the colorful hands and arms and hat back on again—and he put it on the sink. Then he flushed the toilet and let the tap run long enough to wash his hands. He left the bathroom door cracked open so that one of the men would discover what he'd left behind not long after he was gone.

"Great. Thanks. That felt good. Sometimes it runs straight through you."

The stress, worry he'd perceived when he stepped into this office returned. Just the few minutes he'd been away was enough to bring them back to last night and this morning and the mysteriously absent family that was their responsibility. It was clear they wanted him to leave as much as he did.

"Seventy-five thousand, is that right?"

"Yes. That's our price."

"If so, I'm afraid, well . . . I think that sounds like a bit much for us. My company is quite small. But let me think about it and get back to you. Okay?"

He said goodbye to them and gave them a handshake that was as weak as he looked. He didn't turn around, not in the hall, not when he walked by the elevator, and not when he got to the stairs. At the next floor he stopped by the lamp and pulled out the jammer and timer. Then on to the entrance and the oppressive heat and his car, where he would wait until the interpreter conveyed what he hoped to hear.

White brick wall. A lawn that was a little greener than their neighbors'. Dancing garden gnomes next to colorful mushrooms next to a sneaking little garden troll. Blooming flower beds surrounded perfectly groomed fruit trees and flourishing berry bushes. The people who lived here liked their home so much that Ewert Grens— who found it hard to keep plastic plants alive—didn't even really know where to place his feet in order not to destroy anything on his way from the car to the front door. He'd dropped the cadets off at the small police station downtown to hunt down any information they could about a girl they now knew was named Hannah Ohlsson—they were supposed to chat with their local colleagues and maybe find out anything that might not have made it into the official records. He'd felt they'd do more good there than here for two reasons: local police took in a lot more information about their beats than most might assume, and knocking on the door that now stood in front of him flanked by a whole delegation from Stockholm police headquarters seemed like the worst possible way to begin a conversation that required delicacy and trust.

But no one heard him knocking. So he tried the flower-shaped doorbell with a button surrounded by golden petals. Even that was so cozy and well cared for, and it rang a friendly little tune that reminded him of birdsong late at night.

"Yes?"

A woman in her fifties—her hair a shiny silver, her face with a deep tan, her eyes cautious but friendly. A bit farther down the long hall stood a tall, slender man who was wearing glasses like an old-fashioned schoolteacher.

"Detective Superintendent Ewert Grens. I'm here from the City Police in Stockholm."

"We know—a former social worker from the child welfare department called and warned us you were on your way."

The retired department head had claimed to not have had any contact with this family for years. Apparently that was no longer the case.

"Maybe she also warned about why I'm here?"

"Yes. And neither me nor my husband feel very good about it."

The woman didn't sound unfriendly as she pointed to her husband. A little fragile. A little tired. But her voice was calm and collected.

"So we'd rather that you leave."

"I'm not leaving. Not until you've answered my questions."

"We have no obligation to talk to you about our daughter. Not with you or anyone else."

"Not legally, perhaps. But morally. I was the one who long ago stepped into her former world and literally carried her away from it. I took care of her in a safe house for several weeks. I was a temporary parent, you might say. So I think you owe it to me to do exactly that—tell me about her."

Ewert Grens felt a bit ashamed. He hadn't planned to play that card until it was absolutely necessary. The guilt card. He really hated that one. But it seemed like the only thing that could drown out that little doorbell's song. And it had the intended effect. The woman with the silver hair looked both surprised and curious. And somewhat confused.

"I don't understand—it was *you*? So long ago? What are you . . . Has something happened?"

The surprise, the curiosity, even the confusion was gone.

"Do you know something about Hannah we don't?"

And was immediately replaced by fear.

"After such a long time, after you've stopped hoping, you realize as a parent that the worst has happened. And if the worst has happened, you just want it to stop. Do you understand, Superintendent?"

Then finally she invited him in. Through a hall that was as narrow as it was tidy, past a kitchen that looked like it always smelled of freshly baked buns, then a bedroom with a double bed and another with a twin, which still bore traces of having belonged to a young person.

"Hannah's room. And I see what you're thinking.

That all her girly things are still on the walls and on her desk. Although she should be so much older now. But we haven't changed anything. Since she disappeared."

The girl's adoptive mother showed him into the living room, to a lovely armchair, and her husband came in with a tray carrying three coffee cups. Grens didn't really know how or where to start. They seemed to assume that his knowledge was greater than it was. He had no idea what she was talking about.

"Since she disappeared?"

"Yes?"

"You said that?"

"Yes."

"When did she disappear? Where did she go?"

The woman leaned forward, looked at him. Examining him. As if she thought he might be joking and needed to find the answer on his face.

"Isn't that why you're here? Because you found out something new?"

She was right—without understanding why. Ewert Grens was certainly here in her living room because he knew something new. But he wasn't here to share it with her adoptive parents. Not until he understood how to use it to get close to the girl who had once lived here.

"I'll need you to explain what you mean by *disappeared*. I came here because I need to find her before she *disappears for good*. But if I understand what you're saying, the little girl whose room is still intact, has *already* disappeared?"

The man and woman exchanged a glance. In that

way people who have known each other for a lifetime do. A language without words. And they both seemed to have realized why the superintendent poked his head into every room looking for something that just wasn't there.

"Pictures, right? That's what you're looking for. And you're not finding any?"

The father spoke for the first time. The kind of trustworthy voice Grens wished he had. Pleasant but not submissive, dignified without needing to try. This was a man who probably never needed to raise his voice.

"Not even one photo of her. Alone or with us. Not even here in the room where we usually sit. We had pictures—tons of them. But she destroyed them."

Grens looked around at what he'd already seen. Paintings, tapestries, figurines. But no pictures of the one they loved most.

"Hannah started asking us questions after just a couple of years. We don't know why. Maybe someone said something. On the playground or at the school. Or maybe the memories she couldn't reach started to reach her. 'Who am I?' It popped out at almost any time, and always in just those words. It broke my heart every time. 'You're our little girl. Our daughter.' That's how it felt. To us. 'Who was I before? Whose daughter was I back then?' When she got older, eight or nine, she started asking even more often, we told her what we knew. Nothing was left. That her past had disappeared, which was why she had to come live with us. That was around the time she stopped calling us Mom and Dad. Just Thomas and Anette. It never felt like she was trying to be cruel. It wasn't a punishment. That's just how she saw us."

Grens had lost a baby before it was even born. He remembered how much it hurt, even though he'd never met his child. He could only imagine the pain of these parents, who nurtured and raised someone, and now spent their lives fearing the worst.

"She knew her name hadn't always been Hannah Ohlsson. But it took us a long time to convince her that we didn't know what her name was before. That we didn't know anything at all about her past. Just that she came to us after experiencing a profound trauma. That was why she had no parents. Her old life and any record of it had been erased, and only her new life existed. One night while we were sleeping—after another evening of a thousand questions we couldn't answer—she destroyed every single picture of herself. Cut some of them up and flushed them down the toilet. Others she burned outside in a barrel we use to burn up old leaves. 'Those weren't me,' she told us calmly over breakfast the next morning. She'd even found all of the negatives that we kept in a cupboard in the basement. 'I don't exist. So no pictures should exist either.' Of course we wanted to take new pictures. But she wouldn't allow it. And there's no joy in looking at pictures of someone who you've forced in front of a camera. Only one photograph survived the purge. This one."

The adoptive father grabbed his wallet out of his back pocket. Fished a folded photograph from a compartment. A little girl. Who looked exactly as she did the day Grens waved goodbye to her.

"It was in here. So she missed it. The first picture I took of her on the day she arrived."

A little girl smiling at the camera. With no clue that the front steps she was standing on led to the home where she'd spend the rest of her childhood. Or maybe she did know, understood it even then. Because the smile seemed genuine. Like someone who'd been tense for a long time who suddenly allowed themselves to relax.

"Zana."

"Excuse me?"

"Her name. Before. Zana Lilaj."

The two adoptive parents exchanged a glance in that wordless language of theirs. Grens wondered if their daughter had just become someone else to them. More whole. Or if the opposite was true—if she felt just a little less like theirs. Or maybe that didn't matter. At least they had one answer to give the next time someone asked.

"Zana?"

"Yes."

"That was her name when you met her?"

"Yes. And during those weeks she was in my care."

"And her . . . parents? Lilaj, you said? What was the trauma we weren't allowed to know about?"

"I promise to tell you everything the next time we meet. When I've found her. That's why I'm here. I *have* to know where she is because I'm . . . worried. Something might happen to her."

It wasn't that they didn't trust him. It was more that they were shaken. The adoptive parents stood up—still no words exchanged, their lives synchronized—and headed toward the patio and backyard. Barefoot on the green lawn, a bit apart but still together in some way. Grens looked at the shiny gold clock ticking loudly on the wall, this would take the time it took. By the time they came back, they had walked through the past. Which must be why they looked so exhausted.

"You'll have to excuse us, Superintendent."

The woman, who had been childless for so long and then became someone's mother and then just Anette, spoke quietly now, thoughts without energy.

"But first we found out that she might be in grave danger; that's what you meant even if you didn't say it in so many words. Then we were given a name after so many years."

"No need to apologize. I think I understand."

"We don't even know if she's alive. We haven't known for some years. So why . . . why do you think she's in danger?"

"I'll tell you that, too. When I find her."

"We need . . ."

"I'm sorry. But all you can do now is give me more information. I'm going to do everything I can to find her."

The woman looked at her husband again. It was his turn to bring them back in time.

"Her questions continued, but not as often. For long periods she wouldn't ask any at all. She seemed happier. Until one evening when she was fourteen years old. Then everything changed."

The man looked at his wife. Hesitated.

"We still don't know what happened. Nobody knows. Despite an extensive police investigation."

He sought his life companion's eyes again. And she nodded. He could continue.

"A party. Young people having fun. But one of the guests, a boy who was slightly older than the others, somebody's brother, fell from a third-floor balcony. He died immediately. And no one knew why or how it had happened. Hannah took it very badly. Cried. For months. Didn't want to leave home. We homeschooled her with the school's permission. And her questions came back. More numerous and specific. She started to remember. Fragments, images of her biological parents. Her siblings. And words. *Pesë. Tortë.* We didn't understand them at first, and neither did she. But *mom* and *baba* were easier. A linguist who worked for the city helped us. *Five, cake, mom, dad* were the first four words that just . . . came back. Then another twenty-five followed, maybe thirty. Albanian. The language she probably spoke before she came here."

The man's eyes were full of sorrow. He was reliving it.

"We didn't know it yet. But the balcony and the boy who fell were the beginning of a long goodbye. She was fourteen years old then, and when she turned sixteen she disappeared. One day she was just gone. A few clothes were missing from her closet, her toothbrush, maybe a few other things. But no message, no explanation. She called us a couple of times in that first year. We managed to track one of the calls—it came from a telephone booth in a town called Shkodër in Albania.

She didn't say much, just told us she was doing well. We asked her where she was living, what she was doing, and when she wouldn't answer we asked again. Then she hung up. And we never spoke again."

The adoptive father couldn't go on anymore. He shook his head, stared down at his palms, then leaned back in the sofa. Collapsing into himself.

His wife took over.

"Our biggest mistake was trying to help her with those new words. Bringing a linguist here, buying those Albanian dictionaries, even tracking down university courses and encouraging her to seek them out later. We wanted to help her connect with her roots. But instead she became obsessed with them."

Ewert Grens looked at the parents who seemed so alone even though they were two. That's what happens when you lose a child.

"After that last phone call, there's only been silence. We didn't know anything. We still don't, Superintendent."

But I know.

Grens thought that, but he couldn't tell them yet. That their grown-up little girl had journeyed backward. Back to where those new words carried her. To the memories she couldn't reach. Or maybe she *had* reached them—more than her adoptive parents knew. She could have remembered her family and started asking questions without knowing the violent end they met. Maybe she was closing in on the people who had taken their lives without even knowing it. Maybe that's when the contents of her file, locked inside the police archive, were plucked out. Because her questions awoke other people's memories. Maybe that was when someone hired a dirty cop inside Kronoberg to find out who she really was.

And then got rid of her.

The brute they called Zaravic, who was going to be arrested today, locked up for seventy-two hours on Grens's orders, had become even more important now, had even more questions to answer.

"I'd like to ask your permission to search your daughter's room."

They sat on her bed while the detective pulled out desk drawers and looked through various folders and photo albums, and now and then he asked them about where and how. But her childhood room led him no further. A half hour later they stood at the front door, and he thanked them, and promised again to contact them later about what he knew—which seemed to offer them some relief. They'd feared the worst when he appeared at their home, and now they had been given some hope. So as he headed to his car, he turned back and said, "Everything will turn out fine." And he tried to sound much calmer and more confident than he actually was.

The suffocating heat hounding the people of Stockholm's inner city had turned Piet Hoffmann's rental car into a roaring beast, which let loose the moment he sat down inside it. But starting the car and the air-conditioning was not an option. Blend in. Attract no attention. Don't stick out in any way. He adjusted his earbuds until they sounded right, and put his phone on the burning surface of the passenger seat. The tiny microphone hidden in the narrow opening between the bathroom door and its frame worked perfectly, and he opened the program whose software would translate their words if they spoke in another language. His disguise didn't just get him closer—it got him all the way in.

"Did you see his face when I said seventy-five thousand?"

They spoke Swedish. And were probably in the larger room. But one was walking around, that's how it sounded—hard heels against a hardwood floor.

*"Yep—the bastard looked like he was gonna
swallow his wallet."*

*"His next break-in is gonna cost him a lot more
than that."*

"That's what these idiots never get. They . . ."

Suddenly the voices fell silent. And the footsteps
ceased.

"What the hell . . ."

The leader, the one with the eyes used to being
obeyed. He was the one speaking, and now he stopped.
Right at the half-open bathroom door. It was easy to tell
that the sound was coming straight from above. Now
you could hear the door being pulled wide. The slight
creak of its hinges.

"Shit . . . come in here!"

Now they see it.
The little gift he left for them on the sink basin.

"How the hell did that end up there?"
"No clue."
"I was in here earlier, it wasn't there."

A hand grenade. Loaded. Camouflaged with plastic
arms and plastic legs. Just like the one they put in Rasmus's red backpack.

"That guy. Who was just here. He went to the toilet. He . . ."

"Oh fuck—Hoffmann! Hoffmann sent that asshole!"

Piet Hoffmann's skin glistened with slippery, irritating sweat. The windows were down, but the air stood still while the sun beat down angrily onto the car's metal shell. But he couldn't tell if his racing heart and slight dizziness were related to the temperature inside the car or if they were a consequence of his uncertainty about what was going to happen.

If these men who were being used to threaten his family would react as he'd hoped and planned for.

Or if all of this had been in vain.

"What was that fucker's name?"

"Peter Haraldsson, I think—sounds like something he made up during his elevator ride."

"Contact information?"

"If he left any, it's as fake as the name."

"What . . . I don't even remember what he looked like?"

"No clue. A little fat. Hasn't been to the gym for a while, I thought. Too much alcohol or too much work. Or both."

"The cameras."

It was silent while they logged into the computer and checked the files from the hall camera.

*"What the hell . . . it's black? Something's wrong.
It . . ."*

"I wanna see the others."

The next camera was probably in the same room as
them, and the third was in the kitchen.

"Black! Both of them! That fucker . . ."

One of them slammed a fist against the desk or the
bookshelf or maybe even a wall, a muffled sound that
was hard to place.

". . . took them out!"

So simple. He just had to make sure the jamming
transmitter was sending out a much more powerful signal on the same frequency, disrupting it. The result was
exactly what those two security guards were looking at.
Black images. Nothingness. Or rather—everything.
As in the very last piece of the puzzle.

Because now after the family they were supposed to
be watching had snuck out of their house. After a
dressed-up grenade had been left behind on the sink of
their office. After all of their surveillance cameras had
been knocked out. Their opponent had proven he could
reach them whenever and however he wanted to—and
that gave them the final push.

And they reacted exactly as he hoped.

Piet Hoffmann could tell—he was sure of it even
though the sound quality got worse after a moment—that

after a heated discussion they decided to place the call he was waiting for—the whole point of this operation.

The desperate phone call that would reveal their secret client. The organization threatening Piet Hoffmann and his family.

> *"Hey, it's . . ."*
> *"What the fuck—have you forgotten? I call you. You never call me. Don't you . . ."*
> *"He was here!"*
> *"Who?"*
> *"Hoffmann!"*
> *"Hoffmann? Where?"*
> *"In our office. Not Hoffmann himself—but an intermediary."*

Albanian. According to the information on his phone screen.

> *"Intermediary?"*
> *"Yes. In our office."*
> *"You're certain?"*
> *"Yes. Piet Hoffmann knows who we are and wanted us to know that. We have to step back. Our company can't be involved anymore."*

He sometimes had difficulty hearing the voice on the other end. Someone was deliberately speaking quietly.

> *"What you just said?"*
> *"Just now?"*

"About Piet Hoffmann knowing who you are and
wanting you to know that, that . . ."

But the microphone and interpreter heard and translated.

"Yes?"
"Hang up."
"What?"
"That's exactly what he . . . Hang up, for fuck's
sake! He wanted you to call me!"

Piet Hoffmann took out his earpiece as soon as the
call was disconnected. The Albanian-speaking voice
was right. That was exactly what he wanted.

Now there was only one way.

It's either you or me, and I choose me.

He stepped out into the empty street and walked
toward the door he exited less than an hour ago. This
time, he didn't plan on warning them he was coming.
He tore away the tape he left on the lock and hurried
up five flights of stairs. Checked his mask, adjusted his
holsters. And rang the doorbell.

It didn't take them long to open.

"You . . . ?"

"I had a question about the price. Do you have
time?"

The other security guard stood a few steps farther
down the hall. The way they looked at him. They
thought they knew something he didn't.

"Of course."

But they didn't know he knew they knew.

"We have time. Come in."

The security guard that Piet Hoffmann had heard speaking Albanian invited him inside in perfect Swedish, and couldn't quite stop a small smile from stretching over his tense lips. He thought he was looking at an idiot who had voluntarily rung the doorbell and asked to come inside to his own execution.

"Sit down. We'll figure this out."

Those eyes. The look the Swedish Albanians passed between them. *Get ready. I'll take him from the left, you take him from the right.* Hoffmann understood the glance they exchanged. There was always a particular feeling in being surrounded by professionals who'd attacked together before and would do so again very soon.

"I don't need to sit. Just have a few simple questions."

"*You* have questions?"

"Yes."

At that point the man who was in charge transformed. The aggressiveness that had been lurking behind those cautious eyes came rushing forward, game time was over.

"I think you misunderstood something. *You* are gonna give *us* some answers. Here's my first easy question: Why did Piet Hoffmann send you?"

"Piet Hoffmann?"

"You heard me."

"Who is that?"

His eyes. Their eyes. They were close now. About to attack.

"The man who sent you."

The security guard reached over to make sure the blinds were turned down. While his colleague checked that the front door was locked. Then they both stretched. Made themselves bigger. On either side of Piet Hoffmann.

"And you will only get out of here somewhat intact if you tell us *why*."

"I don't know Hoffmann very well. But I know Rasmus."

"Who the fuck is Rasmus?"

"Hoffmann's youngest son. He wanted to figure something out. Which one of you put the grenade in his backpack. He didn't like that."

The last glance.

There it was. The signal.

To attack.

And it was the security guard on Hoffmann's left side who should make the first move. He was going to start beating information out of their flabby visitor. A blow to the kidney. So he'd collapse onto the floor and they'd drag him up again and ask the same question. Until he answered.

But the attack never happened.

Because the flabby man suddenly pulled out a gun. And fired. Twice, once into each kneecap. The attacker fell forward, headlong. Hoffmann spun around, pointing the gun at his colleague instead.

"Your friend never answered Rasmus's question. Which one of you put that grenade in his backpack."

Surprise.

That was the most salient expression on the security guard's face.

"And who put it on top of the Manchester United pen case. He really didn't like that. Tell me . . . *who*?"

It took a moment. Until the silent security guard could stay silent no longer. He pointed to his suffering friend on the floor.

"Him."

"Him—what?"

"He did it. He dropped off the hand grenade."

The next two shots hit more to the side of the knee-caps. Now the other security guard fell forward, toward Hoffmann, who had taken a step closer to the desk to avoid having the body fall onto him.

Then everything got so quiet. Not in the room. But inside him.

Because there was no choice. That's when it never felt like much to hurt someone.

He had even been prepared to kill.

They'd talked so much about it in recent years, he and Zofia. About being human. Remaining human. Zofia, who feared his ability to feel became less every day he spent with violence. A worry that he himself had pushed away. Where is my limit? When I've pushed it too far—will I still be myself? Mostly they'd talked about this—giving yourself the right to destroy some-one else, maybe even their lives, in order to survive.

And they never arrived at an answer.

He tied their hands and feet together with sharp cable ties, wrapped a scarf around their open mouths, then pulled their cell phones out of their bloody pockets. He grabbed both of their right hands and tried each of their respective index fingers, placing them on the button for Touch ID. And the phones unlocked. Once inside, he deleted all the security codes and replaced them with his own. On one of these phones the last number dialed would give him what he wanted. The location of their client. The organization that was threatening Piet Hoffmann and his family. He did the same with the laptops on the desk—opened them with fingerprints. But he had to use one of their thumbs, almost broke it off unlocking. A quick check of the phones and computers showed what he expected—communication had been encrypted. But he had the most important thing, the telephone number of the person he was trying to find. He could work on the encrypted contents in Grens's apartment later.

The two cadets were sitting on a bench in the shade outside the local police station, each with an ice cream in their hands. When Ewert Grens pulled up, they both jumped into the same seats as before. No one said anything for the first few kilometers; the detective superintendent had made it clear he didn't want to talk, and the cadets were young and inexperienced enough to respect that. Though Grens's body was on its way back to the capital, his mind was still with the foster parents who loved every centimeter of their home. He'd gone there to find a missing girl, or at least something that might lead to finding her. He'd achieved neither. But he knew more now.

He knew Zana Lilaj had become Hannah Ohlsson.

Knew that Hannah Ohlsson had started asking questions about who she was not long after her placement.

He knew that when she was fourteen, an older boy's sudden deadly fall had changed everything for her. Or maybe that was just part of the process, when her search for herself accelerated? Maybe one violent experience had triggered other violent memories?

He knew that one night she'd burned every photograph of herself, tried her best to erase Hannah just like Grens once tried to erase Zana.

And then she left, disappeared, never to return.

"How did it go, Superintendent?"

Grens stared straight ahead at the three-lane highway. The chatty cadet had managed to stay silent for almost an hour, which was an eternity in his world—and maybe he just didn't have any more silence inside him.

"I mean, with the family and all?"

"I'm more interested in how it went for you. Did you find anything?"

"We found something."

"Like what?"

"Something about a balcony incident. And a police report the adoptive parents filed for their missing daughter."

Lucas was proud. Wanted to tell. Be praised. And when Lucas was done, Grens did something quite rare, he praised him. Both of them. Because he realized he'd made a wise decision to let them pass their time with his local colleagues—they'd managed to access information he himself wouldn't have.

First, in the documents from the closed investigation into the boy's death: there'd been no witnesses to the event itself, the same story the adoptive parents had given him, but several partygoers described how a fourteen-year-old girl named Hannah Ohlsson was seen being harassed by the boy who died. Her boyfriend. Harassment that during that evening on at least two occasions resulted in loud arguments. Grens wondered if the adoptive parents deliberately left those details out, the *boyfriend* and *harassment*, or if maybe they never knew.

Then out of the other inadequately prepared documents from another discontinued investigation, the one into the girl's disappearance: they had found another trace of her path after leaving. At least initially. Which led to a café in Malmö. Where she'd worked under the table for a couple of months after leaving her parents' home. Until one day she disappeared from there, too. The phone call from Albania became the last known contact she'd made.

New information on two fronts that left his mind lingering in a house with no photos, while his body was kept moving at one hundred and twenty kilometers per hour. That is until his phone rang in his inner pocket, and he searched for it while the car weaved somewhat worryingly.

"Yes?"

"Hoffmann here."

Ewert Grens pressed the phone closer to his ear. A voice that under no circumstances should be allowed to leak out. Even in a car surrounded by cadets who'd never heard of a Piet Hoffmann. Their informal collaboration, based out of the detective superintendent's own apartment, should only be revealed if it became absolutely necessary.

"I'll call you back in a few minutes."

Grens slowed down five kilometers later and exited the freeway, then drove under it, over to the same rest stop as earlier that day. He left the car and wandered around among the tables and benches and trash cans, while calling Hoffmann back.

"Grens here again."

"I need your help tracking a call."

"From your own phone? Or the recipient's?"

"Neither of the phones are mine. But I want his— because it's a he, I heard him—I want his position, the man who received the call."

A family sat down at a table at the far end of the rest area. Coffee thermos and juice packs and sandwiches wrapped in foil. Grens nodded to them and turned toward the thick spruce forest while he spoke.

"It's hard to get telephone companies to cooperate when it comes to regular crimes. Even official ones. This—well, it won't be easy."

"I'm sure you have your ways."

A large, flat stone. Grens considered sitting on it, letting the sun warm his face, just forgetting this whole investigation for a while, people being executed and others who were at risk of it.

"Yes, I have my ways."

He sat down. The stone was hard and had a surprisingly smooth surface, as if nature had sanded it down and placed it here for people who need to rest. He just had to make a few more calls. Like at the Tax Agency, he'd developed collaborations at all of the major telecommunications companies over the years.

"I need all the info you have. Send them to this phone."

"I knew you could solve this, Grens. So I was prepared. It's all on its way to you . . . now."

Grens heard his phone ding just as Hoffmann said goodbye and hung up. He stayed there on that flat stone making a few bargains with his contacts at the phone companies, an exchange of favors, and arranged the cell phone tracking that would give Hoffmann, and therefore himself, a new and clearer direction. Then he and the cadets headed out, but only managed to make it another ten or twenty kilometers before Lucas, still in the passenger seat, couldn't take it anymore.

"Superintendent?"

The young cadet wasn't content this time to stare straight ahead while he chatted. He turned now until it almost felt like he was sitting between the two front seats staring straight at Grens.

"Yes?"

"I thought of something."

"You don't say."

"You're burning."

"What?"

Lucas crept even closer. Though that hardly seemed possible.

"What we talked about on our way here. You know, which didn't go so well. About your age and about my dad. Well . . . I mean, I had just no idea that after so many years a police officer could still care so much. I can see and hear how you're just burning, and it makes me so happy. The thought that I might still be burning after a whole life as a police officer. But it also makes me . . . worried. I . . . I mean, surely, you know, right, that she could be dead? Superintendent? You know you have to prepare yourself for that?"

Grens never answered. Because he didn't want to, and he couldn't.

He knew deep inside exactly what the cadet was trying to tell him. Her adoptive family's tearful worry was justified, and it was now his own. When he told them it would be fine, that was just a bad attempt to comfort them. Because the longer he searched for the girl named Hannah Ohlsson, who had disappeared without a trace, the clearer it seemed to him that she might very well be dead.

4

t's been so long since I felt like this.

Never.

Never like this.

I'm sure of it.

There's even a stillness there in my chest. Right at the point where my anxiety lives. That solid blackness that's always pecking at me, screaming at me from inside—I can't feel it anymore.

I don't even know how to get where I'm going, now that we've landed. But I don't care! I can see the mountains that encircle Tirana's airport, the heat haze that seems so amicable here, the clouds that hang so low, and the palm trees lined up in rows, and everything, everything watches me, protects me.

Thomas and Anette tried their best. They surrounded me like those mountains, they were kind like that haze. But it never reached inside. Into me. To a place that was only mine and that could never belong to them. I feel a little guilty, maybe I should have sent them some message, but there was no other way.

To disappear.

To where I've always been on my way.

I don't understand much of the language that surrounds me, a few words, no context. It doesn't matter. I recognize it. Mom and Dad spoke like that. And Eliot and Julia. I hear sentences pouring out fast, so fast, and they sound like a song that swells inside me.

The taxi I take from the airport smells like cigarettes, and the fabric of the passenger seat has tiny holes on it. At first I sat down on a bus at the exit to the terminal, right next to a bony old woman. Waited. But it never departed. When I asked the bus driver—who didn't speak English but who eventually understood— he sketched something on a napkin, which meant that the buses follow no particular schedule, he was just waiting for it to fill up, and that could take a while. So I ended up in a taxi to the train station, which costs much more, and I'm trying to be careful with what I managed to save from my job at the café in Malmö. My wages weren't great, but the tips were okay, and hopefully it will last me two, maybe three months. There aren't many train stations in Albania except for the one in Tirana and the one in a city in the north called Shkodër. Three and a half hours to go, just one hundred kilometers. But it's cheap, costs just under a few hundred lek, and from what I've heard it's fairly comfortable, even though it can get crowded. As if any of that mattered. I'm on my way home. That's how it feels.

he landscape reminds me of a film rolling by.
Scenes I could step straight into.
And only then would they become real.

The train moves so slowly that I have time to visit cafés in small villages and climb high mountains and walk over lovingly cultivated fields. When the rails run parallel to the paved road, I'm even able to see what's inside the baskets and boxes of the farmers, see how much the pomegranates and cucumbers and beets cost according to their carefully handwritten cardboard signs.

Not long after the first stop at a tiny station that wasn't much more than a pole with a sign and a bench, a young woman in the seat opposite asks me what my name is. I understand that much even though her English isn't extensive, but she wants to practice. I reply as I usually do—Hannah Ohlsson. When she doesn't hear me at first, I try again, but this time I say Zana Lilaj instead. I've never said the name out loud before—wasn't even sure if that was me.

I don't really remember when the images started arriving.

Maybe I've always had them?

First just flashes, puzzle pieces from different parts of my mind about my early childhood. They started not long after I got my new room and new name and even new family. Now and then, often when I was least prepared, a little fragment would come to me, and I was able to put it together with all the others. The images expanded. Got color. Finally even sound and smell. I understood them.

The young woman asks me more, wants to talk, but I don't. Because I can't. As I sit here staring out through the train window at the Albanian landscape, so different from the forests around Söderköping, these images, fragments of memory, are becoming larger and more stubborn. They're pounding inside my head to get out. Or maybe they want to get in? I remember it so clearly. The voices and smells that belong to this place, what I'm seeing and hearing, even though it happened somewhere else. They were in an apartment. Yes, that was it. Dad suddenly blowing out the candles. On *my* cake. Five candles, red and blue. He blows them out and takes my hand, squeezes it tight. It's hurry, hurry. As if he already knows they're on their way. He hides me in the hall, in a small wardrobe, up high on the wall, more like a cupboard than a regular closet for jackets and pants. He pushes me behind some pillowcases and towels, and just as he's about to close it they arrive. Storm inside. Five of them. Just like the candles on my cake. Men I have never seen before. That's why Dad only had time to hide me. And he couldn't even close the cabinet door all the way, so I can hear, even see. When one of the men turns on the TV and raises the volume. When Eliot crawls under his bed. When Dad won't answer their questions, and they say that in that case it will cost him. When Mom and Dad try to stop one of the men from going into Eliot's room and pulling him out from his hiding place under the bed. When they shoot him in the head. Strange shots. Barely audible. When they sit down with Mom and Dad in the kitchen, and Dad is so hysterical that you can barely hear what he says. But I can hear what *they* say. They want Dad to answer a riddle. "Listen: you're in a boat that's about to sink. Far out to sea. It's just you, your wife, and your daughter—yes, we saw her hiding under her bed." Dad stands up and starts to run toward Julia's room, but they grab hold of him, push him down, drag him back to the chair in the kitchen and to the riddle that they aren't done telling. "Okay. We'll continue. You're in a rubber dinghy and it's going to sink if all three of you stay. But—and now here we get to the riddle itself—if you're only two, you just might make it. And you, my friend, are going to have to answer: Who will you choose to save?" All the men are waiting. For Dad's answer. They wave the gun that shot Eliot. Wave it in front of Dad's face and finally he answers. Quietly. Almost a whisper. "Them. I choose them and jump out myself." The men shake their heads and laugh very loud. "No—that's not how the riddle works. You have to choose. *You* have to be one of two left in the boat." They wave their guns around again, then press one against Mom's forehead so hard that it starts to bleed, and Dad whispers again. "My wife. So that our child,

who has so much more life ahead of her, can live."
"Wrong answer again." Now the man who's telling the
riddle stands up. And runs into Julia's room. I can't see
him shoot her, the cabinet door is in my way, but I can
hear Julia screaming and then it stops. Everything is
silent. He comes back and keeps talking. "Wrong answer. A child is just *one* child. While you and your beautiful wife can have more."

"And where are you going in Shkodër?"

The young woman in the seat opposite me, still
wants to practice her English.

I smile, she's friendly, but I shake my head.

"It's . . . a private matter."

"You look very thoughtful."

"The landscape is beautiful."

I turn back toward the window and the world outside the train, trying to show her I don't want to talk
more.

The images won't stop.

Pounding and pounding to get in or maybe out of
my head.

The image of five men sitting at our kitchen table
with their questions and Dad refusing to respond anymore. Because the riddle is complete, now the questions are the same as before—they want to know where
Dad hid something, and I don't understand what that
is. Dad stays silent, so they say that Eliot is gone and
Julia is gone and soon maybe Mom will be gone, too.
Dad is crying. "Zoltan. For fuck's sake. Why?" I've
never seen Dad cry before. He's given up. And he's

about to answer when Mom throws herself over the table and screams "Quiet!" It goes almost as fast as it did when they shot my big brother and big sister. But this time Mom starts it. She spits at the man who is talking—straight into his face. Saliva runs down from his sweaty hairline to his cheeks. And when he shoots her I see where the shots hit her head. One a little to the side, the other right in her forehead. Then he turns to Dad. "Now you can't have any more kids." They grab hold of Dad's arms, pull him across the floor. "But you can still meet a new woman, think about that." Pull him through the hall, all the way to the front door and force him into the chair there. For a moment, almost like a flash, it feels like Dad looks straight at me. From the chair up to the slightly open cabinet door. As if we look at each other, and speak without words. And he says it: "The computer. Everything is in the computer in the second desk drawer in the master bedroom."

All of it is so crystal clear.

The man who shot Mom goes and gets the computer. Tells Dad to open it, and Dad does so, and they all stare at the screen. Until one of them slams the computer shut and says "good" and someone else is standing in the way so I can't see what happens, and I don't really hear what they're talking about, but I hear the shots. Those strange, muted bangs, two times. Then they go. Take the computer. Close the front door behind them.

That's it.

That's as far as I get as I stare out through the train window.

That's where my memory ends. I don't have any more.

After that there's a long black line. That's what it looks like to me.

Until I'm standing on the steps at Thomas and Anette's.

pull down the window as we slowly roll into Shkodër's train station, then, like so many of my fellow travelers, I lean out, hanging there free to wave or call out someone's name or maybe just feel the wind and cool off a little. The wheels squeal against the rails, and the brakes don't seem to be what they should, we rock back and forth and slowly rumble to a stop. The platform is soon packed and hot and people jostle and crash into each other, but I barely notice any of it. I'm so happy to be here.

I walk along a river called Drin, then another river called Buna, and the two together form a dirty blue string that wraps the inner city tight and then lets it spread out again. I wander along stone streets, which are so lively and chatty, and I stop at a café with two tables and four chairs, where I'm served black tea in a tiny, filthy cup and a double-decker sandwich on a red plastic plate by a very fat, very smiley man who sings out loud behind the counter, something that sounds like opera but slides from key to key. I'm in no rush, I know where I'm going. When I get to the square, which has two restaurants and a wedged-in grocery store at Rruga

Kolë Idromeno, I turn right onto Rruga Kardinal Mikel Koliqi and then almost immediately left onto Rruga Hysej. A street so narrow if a driver turns the wheel too hard or too fast the paint gets scraped off their car. And there, in a building behind a yellow-brown gate covered by the branches of a Mediterranean tree that I don't know the name of, I've rented a room on the second floor with access to a bathroom and a tiny kitchen with an electric kettle and a tabletop dishwasher for four plates and glasses.

Tomorrow I'll start looking.

For myself.

A whole week.

And—nothing.

I've been cautious, disguising my questions inside other questions, wrapping them in excuses and reasons that obscure what I'm really looking for. Lilaj. Letters that finally came to me from someplace deep inside just a few years ago, not long after I found the letters that formed Shkodër. Suddenly it seemed so obvious! They'd been spinning around in there for such a long time, back and forth, I'd seen them, but couldn't understand. L-I-L-A-J. Until one morning on my way to school, there it was—my name and Mom's and Dad's and Eliot's and Julia's.

I've visited the police station and the national register and a couple of bureaucratic offices that lack any counterpart in Sweden. The bureaucracy here is a country of its own. With its own language and rules. Freedom can be tough when you haven't had time to learn how to handle it. My questions, though disguised, raise suspicions that can't be satisfied, not because sixteen-year-old girls who speak English are any more dangerous than anyone else, but because undeveloped freedom is often met with constant vigilance.

I haven't made much progress in the cafés and restaurants and shops either, but at least I can have more straightforward conversations there, my intentional questions can be disguised as unplanned. Women don't seem to like me as much as men. I'm not supposed to be out after dark—alone and young. It's not something anyone said exactly, but it's impossible to mistake what they'd like to yell at me. So I always end up talking to men. If I want to find out anything, anything at all, about the family I once had and whatever traces they may have left behind here, so I can paint a complete picture of myself and not just these puzzle pieces, then I'm going to have to keep spending my afternoons alone at the corner table sipping Turkish coffee with way too much sugar in it. And my evenings in the middle of the bar, waiting for someone who just took off their wedding ring to offer me a glass of raki or a foamy Birra Korça.

I've had the most success with a man who's not much older than me, twenty, twenty-two at the most. He started talking to me at one of the cafés. He was sitting there reading like me, and he became curious about my book, an American thriller that I picked up at the airport. After a while he moved over to my table. Philosophy. In Albanian. That's what *he* was reading. He flipped through its pages, showing me, and I recognized a word here or there without saying so. He has a nice laugh that makes a person feel happy. We met again at the same café the next afternoon. By chance. At least

I pretended it was. When he arrived with the same book under his arm, I had already been sitting there a couple of hours, waiting and hoping. We drank several cups each, and I asked him to tell me about Shkodër. He speaks so vividly, as though leading me by the hand down its streets and through its seasons and centuries. With him it feels like I'm starting to understand this city and its surroundings and even the whole country a little better now. I wonder if I dare ask him to help me search for my family and relatives at those bureaucracies I can't seem to handle.

I'll ask tomorrow night. We're having dinner. His name is Lorik, and I'm so thankful that I met him.

bought a new blouse and a short, though modest skirt today. A seamstress two streets away in a hole-in-the-wall shop, who measures and trims and sews while her customers wait. When I see myself in the mirror of my rented room, I can't help but smile. I look pretty. And I know Lorik, who's only ever seen me in jeans and a T-shirt, will think I look nice, too. Going to a restaurant together for the first time is completely different from flipping through each other's books in a café.

But I still have to wear the same sneakers. The only ones I brought with me. Next time I'll upgrade those, too.

I look at the clock, it's soon time. I comb my hair, even put on a pair of earrings I found in a colorful shop near where the square ends, which sells just about anything. Really anything at all. *Real gold,* it said on the tag, but that's surely the one thing they're not—real metal, perhaps—but it doesn't matter, they glitter and make me feel grown up. And when I'm about . . .

Shhhhh.

I freeze mid-movement.

Stand still. Listen. And there—there they are again. Steps.

Just outside my door.

I don't know why I react so strongly. I have nothing to be afraid of. No one's threatened me, other than some of the women at one of the bars, the ones who get paid and think I'm confusing their prospective customers, and once a bartender who thought I should go home because otherwise things might turn out bad for me, since not all men are good. But that's not why my heart starts racing anxiously, like it wants to help me escape. I just haven't heard anyone else in this building. The owner lives on the ground floor and is gone for a month and the man who takes care of the yard sticks to fetching rakes and hedge trimmers from the garden shed.

The footsteps have stopped.

Now there's a knock. Determined thuds against my door.

I freeze, and there are knocks again.

More of them.

"Hello?"

A woman's voice. In English. With an Albanian accent. I don't respond.

"Hello—in there?"

A voice that I could never, no matter how scared or hunted I might feel, find threatening or aggressive or dangerous. Kind. Pleasant.

"Miss, I would really . . ."

I open the door. We stare at each other. A woman in her forties, maybe forty-five. Eyes as friendly as her voice. Cheeks with deep grooves that I would guess come from more than just age. Tired. That's how I would describe her. Or sad? It's hard to say when you don't know someone, have never even seen them before.

I don't reply. Just stand there. She was the one who knocked.

"Miss—it's like this."

A mix of English and Albanian.

"I've heard you're searching."

Now she even throws some German into the mix of languages she's using to try to make herself understood.

"That you . . . yes, ask questions."

It's not an accusation. More a statement. With a note of seriousness. Worry.

I neither answer nor close the door.

I have a hard time making sense of what she's saying, even though now she's settled on English.

"Can I come in?"

She nods to my messy room—I was late, ran to the shower, and left my clothes spread all over the floor, and then I couldn't find my brush and . . . well, I wasn't expecting visitors.

I open the door a little more, and she steps inside. But she doesn't sit down on the bed I point to, the only seat I have.

"It's not good that you're asking questions."

She stands in the middle of the room, and glances now and then through the window. As if she were looking for someone out on the street.

"People get worried about the kind of questions you're asking. And when they get worried, they start asking questions, too. That was how I found out. And how I knew."

I speak to her for the first time.

"Knew what?"

"Who you are."

Now she moves a pillow and sits down. Next to me. Takes my hand, and it surprises me, but I let her hold it.

"Zana. Your name. Zana Lilaj."

"Ah, now I understand—you know Lorik."

"No."

"Okay—you work at one of the bureaucracies I visited?"

"No."

"But those are the only people I've told, except for a woman on the train, when I just wanted to try out how it sounded. There's nowhere else I've even used it."

Then she lets go of my hand, and caresses my cheek instead.

"It's you. Even after all this time."

"I don't understand at all."

She runs her hand over my face. It's not unpleasant, I don't draw back, it's just unexpected and therefore a bit strange.

"I recognize you. Your mouth, your cheekbones. You're bigger now, little darling, but it's you."

"Who are you?"

"Your aunt. Your father's sister. He was my big brother."

"Excuse me?"

"I used to hold you in my arms. You used to lean your head against my shoulder and rest it just there, so calm. You were a newborn the first time we met, and especially the year you were two and three, I saw you often—I pushed you around in your stroller, over the streets of Shkodër, when you had a hard time going to sleep. You were three the last time I saw you. Or, since we're sitting here now, *second* to last time."

She kisses my forehead. That's not unpleasant either. The opposite. Familiar, without knowing why.

I stand up. Even though my head is spinning. Dad's sister? My aunt? This is what I came here for. But if I don't remember her? How do I know if . . .

"I know what you're thinking, darling. I could be anybody. But don't you see how similar we are."

I nod. Doubtfully. I want it to be true. I want it so much my heart is pounding, but not to make me run, this time it wants to dance. Still, I know it's dangerous to hope. Sometimes people say they're your family and end up not being part of it at all—like your mom and dad become a Thomas and Anette.

"Let's sit down on the bed again. I want you to look at something."

We do so, sit down in the same places as before. And the woman reaches for the purse she brought with her and dropped in my pile of clothes.

"Here."

A photograph. The colors faded. Paper rolling up at the edges, so I have to stretch it out with my index finger and thumb.

"Do you recognize them?"

A child, maybe two years old, is smiling at the camera from a stroller. Ice cream in one hand, in both hands, plus quite a bit on the cheeks and chin. A girl. Standing next to a woman, who is leaning forward, pressing her cheek against the baby's head. They like each other. That much is clear.

"Yes. At least her."

I point to the woman. A much younger version of my visitor. She nods.

"Yes. It's me. And I'm sure you also recognize that little child."

Yes.

I recognize the child.

Myself.

"What's your name?"

I look at the woman who might be my aunt.

"Vesa."

Like a whisper, it runs through me. A name that fills up every corner inside.

"Yes. Your name is Vesa."

The photograph tries to roll up again, and I move my thumb and trade my middle finger for my index.

"Was it taken . . . here?"

"Just a few hundred meters from here. At the center of town. You're two and a half. And I'm twenty-five."

She roots around in her purse again. Lays a new photograph on top of the first. I don't have to ask. It's the same child, the same woman. And the other three are Eliot, Julia, and Dad.

"We're at a restaurant. It still exists, over by the bridge that crosses the Drini. Your mother took it."

I'm holding a piece of paper that means everything to me. Five people. Only two left. The two of us.

"But tonight, Zana, you can't go to dinner."

I'm startled by her request. In just a few minutes, I've been told more information than I ever dreamed possible. But I don't want to miss my meeting with Lorik. That feels right, too, as familiar as this.

"I'm sorry, but I'm going to dinner. Tomorrow, if you like, I'll gladly meet you again. And talk more. About everything."

"You can't."

"Can't?"

"It could be dangerous."

I laugh. It's been a long time. I laugh at an aunt whom I didn't even know existed and who after less than half an hour is just as worried about me as Thomas and Anette always were, though they tried to hide it.

"You don't have to worry about me. I'm sixteen years old, grew up in Sweden. It might be different here, but . . ."

I whisper. Not because I'm ashamed. But because Vesa might think this is something you're not supposed to talk about. I don't know, I don't know her yet.

". . . I'm not exactly a virgin. I had a boyfriend. Older. Turned out to be an idiot. But an idiot I could handle."

She takes my hand.

"That's not really what I'm talking about."

The photos fall to the floor. Rolling up together.

"You can't go to dinner."

"I'm sorry. But you're not responsible for me."

She doesn't raise her voice. She doesn't need to. I can see how upset she is.

"You *can't go*!"

Her kind eyes won't let me go. She's holding me without holding me.

"Do you understand? You have to come with me tonight. When we get there, I'll explain why."

"I don't even . . . have a phone. And I haven't heard him mention one. If I can't go, I have to call him. He can't just sit there waiting for me to show up."

"He'll understand."

"How could he . . ."

"Listen to me, darling. When you don't arrive. He will understand."

And now she's holding me. For real. A hug unlike any other. Or any that I can remember.

My aunt's house stands isolated on the banks of the Buna River, close to where that river empties into the Mediterranean, and not far from a small town called Velipojë, which has about a thousand inhabitants. The full moon shining on the river turns it green, and I feel like jumping in from my aunt's jetty, swimming across to the other side. To another country. Montenegro. That's how close it is. I shout out to the people sitting on the opposite shore, who have built a fire on the beach, and they shout back. An invisible border.

My aunt lives alone here. There are traces of a former husband in old pictures on the bookshelf and on a wooden table in the hall, but I haven't figured out yet if she's widowed or divorced. We need to get to know each other better before I ask her that. She'll tell when she's done asking all of *her* questions, so many of which I cannot answer.

It's a beautiful house. Way too big for just one person. The silence of the water and the lack of any neighbors feels peaceful, the noise that's always inside my head seems to almost stop here, but it soon starts again with a different kind of spinning. And when my aunt pulls a photo album out of a huge escritoire, this new noise gets even worse, spreads into every part of me. Suddenly I realize it's impossible to delete yourself. All the pictures I burned at Thomas and Anette's, and all along sitting in a box in a tiny city in northern Albania there were just as many.

Who is that girl with Zana written beneath her picture?

What is she thinking?

I can see that she's me, we have similar features, but I don't feel close to her, she's a stranger. It was too long ago to connect it with the present.

My favorite is a photo that takes up a whole page of the album. Mom and Dad. Before Eliot and Julia and I even existed. They're so young, like I am now. They hold each other, love each other, trust each other. They could do anything, be anything. They have no idea that in just a few years they'll be dead in an apartment in Stockholm, along with their two oldest children. I wish I could talk to them, warn them. Because there, in that photograph, they're still alive.

"You can't stay here, Zana, do you understand?"

"Here? With you?"

"In Albania. In Shkodër."

"I just got here!"

"And now you have to leave again."

"Not stay . . . I'm home. That's how it feels. Aunt Vesa? I'm home for the very first time."

"You've been going around asking a lot of questions. It's dangerous. Very dangerous."

"What's so dangerous?"

"The wrong people found out. And they don't take risks."

"Risks? Why? I don't understand."

"Because your father was very successful."

We're sitting in her large kitchen, high ceilings and coarse wooden beams above our heads, a modern fireplace next to an old woodstove, and at the far end an extra staircase, which was once used by the servants so as not to disturb their employers when they were headed up to the second floor. But for a moment I forget where I am. Something happens. A wave washes through me. Turns my cheeks warm and red. Pride. That's what I feel. So much pride. The first thing I ever hear about my dad—and it's that he was successful.

"So . . . what did he do? Dad?"

"He helped during the civil war."

My cheeks are pulsating now. With even more pride.

"How?"

"You were born around the time the war began, 1997. That's when your dad made most of his money. He smuggled weapons. Over the river and across the mountains to Kosovo. But later, when everything was over, when peace came, he needed to find a new market. So a year later you all moved to Sweden."

My aunt shows me more pictures. Of my family. What we looked like when we left.

"I remember thinking, this will be the last time I ever see you. I don't know why, I just knew. This is from the airport."

A slightly wrinkled photograph. As if somebody had

balled it up and thrown it away, but regretted it and smoothed it out again. My whole family. The only picture where we're all together. And Mom and Dad and Eliot and Julia and even me, none of those faces feel like strangers.

That's us. That's who we were.

"There's a picture I want you to see."

At the back of the album.

"This."

A portrait, but a small one, about the size of a passport photo. Older than the others, you can tell from the quality of the paper and the style of clothes.

"Your grandfather. My and Mirza's father. You never met him. He was in prison. For a very long time. He did the same thing as your father—used the river to smuggle weapons."

It must be obvious to her that I don't understand.

"Your grandfather was a criminal. They were illegal weapons. Just like the ones your father smuggled and sold. That's what he was successful at."

My red, warm cheeks. The wave that washed through me. The pride. I don't really know what to do with it now.

"We grew up in this house. Me and Mirza. He made up his mind when we were young. Your father wanted to be like your grandfather. But I decided to do the opposite—try to live another life. And I chose right— just look at how it turned out for your father."

She doesn't sound bitter. It's no I-told-you-so. Sad. That's what she is.

"And to make sure the same thing doesn't happen to you, you need to leave this place."

"I know now that Dad was shot. Murdered. Executed. I've known that for the last few years. One day I just remembered. I remembered how all of them were executed. But I still don't understand why I can't stay here. With you. I feel more at home now than ever."

"Because it's all connected. Because there are people who still care. Who had no idea, just like me, that you had survived. But they do now. And unlike me, they're not particularly pleased about it."

She takes my hand again, places it in her own. Like in my rented room just a few hours ago. Or maybe that was an eternity ago.

"You have to get out of here. There's a plane leaving from the Tirana airport for Sweden in four hours. I'll drive you there. They won't see us in the dark."

"Now?"

"Yes, now."

We don't move very quickly through the pitch black. My aunt chooses roads that are off the main highways. We pass through small villages and wind through mountain slopes and scare herds of animals that have settled in for the night. The darkness is like an embrace. It holds us. Hides us.

She's nervous. She tries to hide it, but even though we've only spent a short time together I can read her so well. All through the evening in her house as she showed me pictures, trying to make me understand, and when she backed the car out of the garage—worry is her language right now.

It takes an hour longer to drive this way, but my aunt tells me I'll still have plenty of time to catch my flight. We don't run across many other cars, they know better than to guess their way forward over these dark paths, and perhaps that's why my aunt's worry becomes even more tangible when we reach the base of a mountain and meet a vehicle that neither slows nor pulls to the side. On the contrary, it blocks the road, and its headlights are the brightest I've ever seen. They're pointed straight at us.

We stop and sit very still in our seats. I want to ask what's happening, but my aunt is silent, staring out through the front window. Soon a car door opens, I can't see it, but I hear it, and someone climbs out. As he approaches us—it's a man, I can tell from how he moves—his body is just a silhouette in that aggressive light. He lacks any contours, but he's tall, and something that must be a jacket flutters around him. He's also holding something in his right hand. He walks all the way to our car, to my aunt's window. Knocks on it. I don't want to turn toward him, it doesn't feel good, but I can make out the glow of the cigarette in his mouth, and the smoke twirling upward in the light. When my aunt doesn't open, he knocks again, and I can't help myself, I turn a little so I can see his face. And suddenly I'm so happy! All my discomfort slips away, and I want to hug my aunt and whisper that there's nothing to worry about. I know him. That's Lorik.

"It's him."

She doesn't answer, just stares straight ahead.

She hasn't understood yet.

"Aunt Vesa? Aunt Vesa? That's who I was supposed to have dinner with. Lorik! You can open the window. Do it, roll it down. How could he . . . When I didn't come, he came here, aunt, he likes me, don't you see?"

"Sit still. Don't talk. Look straight ahead, the whole time."

"Aunt Vesa, listen, it . . ."

"It's not a good thing."

Lorik knocks again. Peers into the car. At me. Why would I look away when he's standing there?

"Straight ahead."

"Aunt Vesa, I . . ."

"*Straight ahead!*"

I turn my eyes away, the floodlights swallowing me. Then my aunt rolls down the window.

I hear them talking.

Albanian. Words I don't understand. But the tone. Bitter. I understand that. Lorik sounds different. And my aunt sounds the same.

After a while they fall silent, and my aunt leans toward me.

"He wants to see your passport."

"What?"

"Your passport. Take it out."

I notice it now. My aunt is trembling. It's not just fear, it's more than that. Terror. The word feels so extreme, but I can't think of a better one.

I take out my passport. Hand it to my aunt who hands it to Lorik. He flips through it.

"Hannah Ohlsson?"

His voice is just as sharp as my aunt's was. It cuts. Into me.

"Yes."

I speak English to him, like in the café. And he answers, his English is at least as good as mine.

"Is that your name? That's not what you were calling yourself when we met."

"I have two names, Lorik. Both are me."

"Your questions. About Lilaj."

"Yes?"

"We don't like them."

"We? I don't understand, how . . ."

Now I see what he's holding in his hand. A weapon. A gun. Pointed straight at me.

"Why are you asking questions? Why are you calling yourself Lilaj?"

I want to hide behind my aunt. My aunt, who is shaking. My aunt, who is silent.

And for the first time I wish I really was Hannah Ohlsson.

"Answer me—why!"

I don't know much about guns. Except what you see in the movies.

"Because he . . ."

But I know when a gun makes that sound, it's being cocked, and it's ready.

To shoot.

". . . was my father."

And it's surreal.

How I take it all in.

His index finger squeezes the trigger. His eyes, which seemed so soft when we talked and laughed, now so hard.

I even hear it when the shot is fired.

Of course the asphalt wasn't one whit warmer in Stockholm than in Söderköping—the heat had blanketed the whole of Sweden since the beginning of June—but it felt warmer as he dropped off the cadets, parked on the south side of the Kronoberg station, and stepped out onto the sidewalk of Bergs Street. So Ewert Grens couldn't help himself, he sank down—despite his bad knee begging him not to—and placed his palms against the ground. No. He wasn't imagining it. Everything was pulsating. It was impossible to stand still. There was no greater uneasiness than an unbridled, throbbing inner city, choking at every attempt to breathe.

"I want you to do one more thing. Before you go home for the day."

He couldn't shake her off. The girl who had been renamed Hannah Ohlsson, who no longer seemed to exist. Not in person or in any pictures. She must have known that when she tore them to pieces, burned them. How she would disappear without a trace. Maybe even die. But that it was better than not seeking out her past.

"I want you two to turn the investigation after the

missing person's report filed by her adoptive parents upside down and inside out, find out what was done. Or more importantly—what wasn't done."

Lucas and Amelia were halfway up the steps that led to the entrance of the police station, but they stopped and waited as he struggled to his feet.

"What do you mean, Superintendent?"

"I mean I want you to go through every missing person report in Sweden made the year she disappeared. Every report in every police district. People who were gone a few days or much longer or who never came back again. Then go through every Jane Doe who's been found since then. Include records from Oslo, Copenhagen, and Helsinki. People can disappear in one place and pop up somewhere else."

"But if . . ."

"But what?"

Lucas.

The cadet who spoke without thinking.

But now he was—and his thoughts were troubled.

"*If* a body has been found. If we compare all the registries we have—dental records and fingerprint bases and DNA and . . . well, how many reasonably current unidentified bodies will there be? Would we be able to count them on two hands? If she were . . ."

"That's exactly what I want you to determine. Find out that she's no longer here or in the area."

Lucas looked at Amelia, who looked at Ewert Grens. Neither of them seemed to think what he was saying was very clear.

"Superintendent Grens—*that she's no longer here?*"

"Yes."

"I'm not sure I follow."

"Because we need to do our due diligence if we want Interpol's help. So they can help us with the same thing—just a little farther away. In Albania. So we can go through all the unsolved murders and unidentified women's bodies that have been found there."

He then left the cadets on the stairs; both seemed happy to be assigned a task that might involve Interpol. That's what a training period was for, right? Figuring out the things that were so obvious to an old cop who was just about to retire, the day-to-day of a police officer's life. So while Lucas and Amelia continued into the police station, somewhat symbolically, Grens headed to that little café on Sankt Eriks Street where he traded forensic technician Nils Krantz's time and knowledge for a cup of coffee and a double-sized piece of princess cake. He then took a long slow walk along the deserted streets of Kungsholmen so he could speak with Sven in private about why it was so important that he continue watching Mariana Hermansson, their closest colleague for many years—what he didn't mention was if Mariana passed his test, was ruled out as the leak, Grens would have to find someone to look into Sven instead. And when he finally entered his apartment building on Svea Road, he decided to take the stairs tonight instead. He was panting as he reached his floor, and saw his intruder hadn't broken in this time—he was sitting in front of Grens's locked door.

"Good evening."

"Good evening, Detective."

"Maybe you need your own key?"

"I wasn't planning on living here for very long."

"I've never had an extra set, Hoffmann. There's never been a need. But tonight I stopped by a shoemaker in the subway station at Odenplan and had him make me one—though why shoemakers make keys and change clock batteries is beyond me."

Ewert Grens handed over a blank, unused key to Piet Hoffmann, who smiled as he tried it. Yep, it worked. He opened the door, slipped the key into the front pocket of his accountant's shirt, and for the second evening in a row, stepped into an apartment that never seemed to end. He had already placed his bag next to the sofa with the pearl-encrusted decorative pillows, his temporary home, and exchanged his dress shirt for a T-shirt and his dress pants for a pair of jeans, when the phone rang. *That* phone. Which he'd brought with him, against his usual rules. He let it ring while searching for the apartment's owner, found him in the kitchen in front of the fridge, an open carton of orange juice in his hands.

"Grens—I want you to listen this time. Form your own impression. Maybe you'll hear something I don't."

Then he pushed the answer button and held the phone in such a way that both of them would be able to hear.

"Yes?"

"I've been trying to get ahold of you."

The distorted voice. Same intonation, rhythm, way of breathing.

"Many times."

And Hoffmann again forced himself to do what he'd

learned to do over his many years as an infiltrator—hold the rage inside, wait, master the violence so you can strike back when it hurts them the most.

"I apologize. But I've been in a bad position and judged it better not to answer."

"And the weapon?"

He'd been whispering so far. Didn't want to reveal his new voice. But now he wanted to scream.

I know you watched me dig it up, you bastard!

But he swallowed it, because that's what he had to do.

"I've got it in a safe place."

"Good. Then it's time."

Hoffmann looked at Grens, who nodded. He was taking in everything.

"Not quite yet."

"It's time when I say it's time. Because, as you know, I have documents that mean death sentences for everyone you love."

"I need more time. Three more days."

"Three days?"

"If you want me to succeed at the mission you've given me, I need to prepare. You made me your unwilling accomplice because you think I have the skill set you need. So you should trust that I know what I need, and what I need is three days. If you want this to be as successful as you expect."

You couldn't hear where the voice was. Despite the long silence. No cars passed by, no airplanes in the distance or birds chirping, no other voices.

"Three days. Then I release the documents."

Another silence. Electronic. The voice had hung up.

"You were very calm, Hoffmann. I wasn't expecting that. Considering what's at stake."

"That's why."

"And that voice—it's like talking to a fucking robot."

"You would know if anyone does, Superintendent. Have you ever interrogated a violent criminal who answered like a human being? To do what they do—what I *did*—you have to be able to shut down. Completely. Emotions are a liability."

"You don't have to be a criminal to understand that."

A quick glance at the emptiest, most desolate home Piet Hoffmann had ever visited.

And right there, at that moment, they understood each other and were in complete agreement.

That the ugliest, most dangerous enemy would always be loneliness.

During the call, Grens had kept holding the juice without thinking about it, and now he put it down on the kitchen table next to a half loaf of bread, a block of cheese, a stick of butter, two juice glasses, and two porcelain cups. And while the coffeemaker sputtered and coughed, he went and grabbed a whiteboard and a bag of magnets and markers from the hall and brought them into the kitchen, while Hoffmann looked on curiously.

"What are you up to, Detective?"

"I'll tell you—if you tell me what *you're* up to."

Ewert Grens nodded to a balled-up napkin that Piet Hoffmann had pulled from the bottom of his knife holster and started to smooth out. Some kind of crossword, long rows of squares filled the paper, chains of boxes with letters inside. Which he now ran a finger over, one answer at a time.

Survive, eleven letters

~~P—H—O—N—E—T—O—G—R—A—M~~

Survive, eleven letters

~~G—R—O—U—N—D—F—L—O—O—R~~

Survive, fourteen letters

~~N—A—S—O—L—A—B—I—A—L—F—O—L—D~~

Survive, seven letters

~~D—E—T—C—O—R—D~~

Survive, eleven letters

~~R—A—D—I—O—J—A—M—M—E—R~~

Straight lines crossed out each of these word grids. But the last two he had left untouched.

Survive, eleven letters

P—O—S—I—T—I—O—N—I—N—G

Survive, fourteen letters

E—N—C—R—Y—P—T—I—O—N—C—O—D—E

"What am I up to? Exactly what it says—surviving. Protecting my family."

"Protecting a family who might never be able to be protected again. The robot voice is right about that."

Grens folded the napkin together, handed it back to Hoffmann.

"You're good at making plans. But they won't do you a lick of good if those documents end up on the streets. Do they know that—Hugo and Rasmus and Luiza? That if you fail—they can never live in safety again?"

"If *we* fail. *We*. Because this time we're going to help each other. Unlike all those other times. Right, Grens?"

Ewert Grens didn't need to answer. They both knew that this man with no family of his own to protect or mourn or live with would do anything for two boys who sometimes popped up at the police station, and sometimes called him their pretend grandpa. That only a year ago he'd been lying on a floor ready to die, with a murderer's tool aimed at his heart, because that was the only way to protect those boys, the only way for them to survive.

"I found this in an unused conference room at the police station. I asked them to transport it over—I think it will do more good here right now."

Grens pushed the butter and the bread aside and lifted the whiteboard onto the kitchen table, leaning it against the wall.

"Yesterday we established an informal and provisional headquarters—in my kitchen. Turned my apartment into a new police station with just two employees. For an investigation that cannot be handled from inside the real police station because it happens to be full of police and this concerns the police. Or—*one* police officer who sold out, and who's as dangerous as a loaded weapon."

He also moved his own coffee cup, after taking a drink first. And when there wasn't enough room for the magnets and the markers, the butter ended up on the only empty chair.

"I had a coffee with a forensic technician this afternoon. Someone I trade a favor with now and then. And he has . . . well, how should I put this, offered assistance to our new headquarters on a freelance basis."

Grens's jacket was hanging over the back of the empty chair. From the inside pocket he pulled out a bundle of papers. He attached the first one with a magnet to the center of the whiteboard and wrote FINGER-PRINTS beneath it.

"This is from the forensic engineer's computer. An image of a fingertip. The red circles denote characteristics that can be used for identification. We need eight or ten or preferably twelve to use as comparison with the other fingerprints in our database. He found four here. That was all. You see? Four red circles on these threatening letters that were sent to you, and only two on the hand grenade you gave me—the one put into your mailbox."

Piet Hoffmann wasn't surprised. Organizations big enough to be making millions on trading in illegal weapons, in some cases even hundreds of millions, didn't go around dropping off threats or hand grenades without wearing gloves.

"Then there's this."

A new sheet of paper was stuck onto the board to the right of the other one, and Grens wrote WEAPON below it. Long lines of text in such a tiny font size that Hoffmann couldn't even read them from his place at the table.

"Krantz was pretty surprised when I unloaded that gigantic weapon out of a hockey stick bag and onto the table in his lab. He'd never seen one before—and he's analyzed basically everything. But his technical investigation yielded nothing—no traces on either the weapon or ammunition."

Beneath the third paper, he wrote TYPEWRITER.

"Krantz analyzed the text on both the envelopes and the letters, which yielded a one hundred percent match with the same typewriter. A very old Facit T2. Some keys show a pattern of wear that's basically as unique as a set of fingerprints, so if we run across a typewriter we'll be able to say if the threats were written on it."

When Piet Hoffmann leaned forward to see the enlarged illustrations, he realized that the letters H and R were the ones that formed the unique pattern.

Hugo and Rasmus. What an unfathomable coincidence.

The detective put the next three pieces of paper in a row farther down on the whiteboard. THE DELIVERY FIRM—who rang the bell on Hoffmann's door and left a package with a phone inside—had, according to all of their records and files and even handwritten notes, never made a single delivery to that address. THE TELE-

PHONE CALLS from a distorted voice phone—that despite Grens's hiring a hacker younger than half his age who usually succeeded where others failed in cracking the networks of encrypted phones—couldn't be traced to a who or where. The cadets' search for UNIDENTIFIED BODIES didn't yield any matches in Sweden or the rest of the Nordic countries, but it had, in collaboration with Interpol, shown that a total of eighteen unidentified young women's bodies had been logged by the Albanian police over the last five years, which still could be followed up on.

"Did you say the . . . the *Albanian* police?"

"Yes."

"Why would . . ."

"Another investigation I'm working on. Which I plan to keep to myself a little longer. But it may be that there are links to the organization who is threatening you."

"What the hell, Grens—why won't you tell me! You know as well as I do . . ."

"You're not a police officer. Yet. But you could become one. Then I'll tell you more. And maybe you'll even travel down there. To Albania."

Piet Hoffmann looked at the detective superintendent whom he had gotten to know over the last few years, whom he'd even temporarily moved in with. He could read the older man pretty well. And this, he was sure as he studied Grens's face, was no attempt at a joke.

"Albania."

"Yes."

"And, 'You're not a police officer—yet.'"

"Exactly, Hoffmann. You'll head there tomorrow—if everything goes as I hope this evening. As an official employee of the Stockholm City Police. An extremely temporary position, of course, but no one needs to know that. You were the one who said it. I infiltrate for you, you infiltrate for me."

"And I'm headed to Albania because . . . ?"

"Because of this."

The last paper in Grens's stack. But instead of hanging it on the whiteboard, he handed it to Hoffmann.

"You wanted me to position a phone call. Use my contacts and locate the receiver. And much like forensic technician Krantz, I'm a wise enough man to know when not to ask questions. Such as whose phone had called that number. I imagine I wouldn't like the answer, right? It might even require a police investigation of its own?"

Piet Hoffmann didn't say a word. Grens was right—that the phone belonged quite recently to some now very badly injured security guards on Birger Jarls Street was exactly the kind of thing the detective wouldn't want to hear in the midst of his informal investigation at his informal police station. Instead, Hoffmann started to peruse the paper he'd been handed. Information about the phone call he'd forced them to make by leaving the camouflaged hand grenade on their sink basin. *He was here! Hoffmann!* Which would lead him to the person behind this threatening organization. *That's exactly what he . . . Hang up, for fuck's sake! He wanted you to call me!* A conversation that Grens, with the help of his contact at the telecom company, was able to trace to a city in northern Albania called Shkodër. There was even an address—*Rruga Komanit,* and a picture of a building—a white house, luxurious in comparison to its neighbors, on a small street with a forest of antennas on its roof.

"In the room that looks like a tower, there, to the right on the second floor, that's where a man picked up that call."

"We know with that much precision?"

"We do."

"And this city, Grens, which I can't even pronounce—Shkodër, was it?—apparently has some fucking connection to this other investigation you don't want to tell me about?"

Ewert Grens smiled, not much but enough to look pleased.

"Not yet, Hoffmann. I don't want to tell you about it *yet.* An official investigation based in the real police station, which you don't have anything to do with. But yes—it seems like my instincts as a cop were right, there is no such thing as a coincidence. Because the paper you're holding in your hand shows, even proves, that *both* investigations are really just one."

J ust like some cop movie.

Piet Hoffmann stared at the whiteboard on Ewert Grens's kitchen table. Part of a police investigation that would keep expanding. The six documents hung up a bit randomly—the detective superintendent was probably not usually the one in charge of this task—would be highlighted and annotated and more documents would be hung up. Hoffmann was just about to put up the seventh—the phone company's information about the last number dialed by a not-yet- seriously injured security guard and the person who picked up more than a thousand kilometers to the south—when their temporary and comfortable silence was broken. By a doorbell. Three identical notes.

"Are you expecting a visitor, Grens?"

From the front hall. That's where the sound came from. Again.

"I never have visitors. Nobody rings that doorbell. That's how I like it. And now, *while I already have one visitor*, someone comes to my door for the second night in a row. I'm becoming very popular."

The detective headed in the direction of the fading bells.

But he didn't open the door.

"Yeah?"

Instead he was content to shout through it.

"What's this about?"

"It's me—Mariana."

Grens recoiled, unintentionally.

"You've never been here before."

"Well then, I guess it was about time. Are you going to open the door or should I stay out here shouting at your neighbors?"

He unlocked it, and Mariana Hermansson attempted to step inside. But stopped. Her boss stood in the way.

"You never said what this was about."

"What are you up to, Ewert?"

"I . . ."

"After ten years I finally knock on your front door and you won't let me in?"

"I . . . Of course you can . . . What do you want?"

She pushed him a little. Enough to squeeze by him.

"Ewert—are you hiding something from me?"

He'd asked Sven to look into her and even follow her. Unsure who she really was, now that everyone around him was a suspect, and any one of them could be the person who switched sides.

"Hiding? No . . . or yes. But . . ."

He made a quick decision. Took her by the arm. Led her through the hall, into the kitchen. Toward a man she had never seen.

"Yes. I'm hiding something. Him. Because I have to."

Hermansson stared at the man she estimated to be around forty-five, though it was difficult to say since this pen pusher had really let himself go physically, so he could be younger.

"We're working on an investigation, as you can see. It intersects with the investigation you and I and Sven started yesterday. Which hopefully you're here to talk about."

She stared at the whiteboard, which looked like the beginning of a regular fact gathering in an informal preliminary investigation, then at the pen pusher, then at Grens.

"Ewert—what is this?"

"I'll explain, if you tell me why you're here."

"A private investigation? And a man you need to hide?"

"I understand that it's . . ."

"What kind of fucking collaboration!"

"I'll explain. If you tell me why you're here. First."

She declined the chair he'd pulled out from the kitchen table.

"While your . . . *acquaintance* is listening?"

"While my acquaintance is listening."

She looked at the stranger sitting at the kitchen table, trying to decide if her boss had lost his mind or just his judgment, then she turned to Grens.

"This Dusko Zaravic."

"Yes?"

"I don't buy your theory. That he's involved in something that has to do with that whiteboard or *our real investigation, which is being handled at the police station*. Because, Ewert, if three of your buddies have just been executed, and you were either their killer or the next in line, would you spend your night dancing at some gangster wedding without taking any safety precautions?"

Another glance at the stranger. He didn't seem to react to what she said. She wondered what that meant.

"We've got him surrounded. Twelve men. But I have a problem. I can't just invite myself in and ask for a dance at a gangster wedding. So we have to have our ducks in a row for this arrest."

"You do. You have my order."

"Yes, yours. But not Wilson's. Our chief. Do you know why? Because I—the officer carrying this out— can't argue for it if I don't know your reasons."

"You should arrest him because I tell you so. That's enough. *I* answer to Wilson. And *I* want to know— how Zaravic is acting? Is he completely without protection?"

"Yes. He is. But . . ."

"Well—grab him! Or . . ."

Then it came back. That feeling he'd decided to ignore when he chose to expose her to a disguised Hoffmann and the whiteboard of his secret investigation. The feeling that one of the people he trusted most might have another agenda of their own.

". . . do you not want to arrest him?"

"Excuse me?"

"Do you have some other problem with arresting him, Hermansson, that you can't talk about?"

"Didn't you hear what I just said? *My problem is you're hiding things from me and I don't know why!*"

An answer he didn't like because it was no answer.

"Well then."

Not to his actual question.

"I'll have to do it myself."

"You can't do that Ewert, not this time—Wilson already said no, and he's the one you have to convince. But if you can't even convince me there's a reason for suspicion, then . . ."

"Good. Then here's what we'll do. All three of us are headed to the police station. Now."

Mariana Hermansson nodded at the stranger at the table.

"To Kronoberg? *With* your acquaintance who's taking part in your kitchen investigation?"

"In the car ride, my acquaintance—who you don't recognize, even though you've met him before, several times over various investigations—and I will explain to you what's going on. And when we get to the station, my acquaintance, now your acquaintance, will take off and you and I'll head into the police station. And if Wilson, who still can't know who our acquaintance is, continues to say no, then maybe I'll have to ask him the same question I just asked you: Is there another reason that he can't or won't talk about?"

The stairs at the police station separated them. Piet Hoffmann disappeared into the subway station, while Ewert Grens and Mariana Hermansson opened the front doors with their key cards and proceeded into the corridor. Grens had a hard time deciding what part of their conversation had upset Hermansson the most—her shock when she realized it was Hoffmann sitting in the back seat, the fact that she hadn't been able to see through it, or that a criminal organization had broken that last taboo and was threatening the lives of children for their own gain. Or maybe simply the feeling of having been deceived by her own boss, and finally—when he no longer had any choice—being pulled into it so reluctantly. Probably all three at the same time. And things didn't get any better in the elevator ride up when he asked her what she'd found out about Wilson, since she hadn't reported anything to him despite his request. She stayed silent and tried to hide her anger, then snorted and explained that she still refused to spy on their boss. She had been focusing instead on trying to apprehend a criminal because that's what was in her job description.

Erik Wilson was waiting behind his desk when they stepped into his well-appointed office, and it didn't take much power of observation to see that two of his best detectives weren't very happy with each other right now. So rather than wasting any more energy on meaningless discussions, he asked them to sit down and told them his decision.

"I'm with Mariana. No arrest."

"Excuse me—did I hear you wrong?"

"You heard correctly, Ewert."

"I don't think I did—you need to speak a little more clearly."

"We have no formal reason to arrest Zaravic. Is that clear enough?"

Grens, who was just about to sit down, changed his mind and wandered over to the other corner of the room, where he leaned against the safe.

"Jesus Christ, Wilson—do we really have to play this game again when we know how it ends?"

He turned to the locked door, tapped it with his index finger. It was almost possible to hear the locking mechanisms tightening a little more.

"Because didn't you and I already come to an agreement that it would be so terribly sad and terribly unnecessary if I started running my mouth about safe combinations that mysteriously vanished? About information regarding criminal infiltrators that we really aren't supposed to be working with at all? If . . ."

"Seriously, Ewert? How many times do you intend to use that trick?"

"As many times as necessary. And—if we can agree

on that—then I want you to A) give me permission to make the arrest tonight with Hermansson's help, and B) provide me with a properly signed search warrant."

"Then I say A) an arrest—for what? And B) a search warrant . . . for what?"

"I have no grounds. That's something for you higher-ups to figure out with a prosecutor."

"I'm sorry, but it doesn't work like that."

"Maybe not—but then again, we also don't work with criminal infiltrators and nobody broke into your safe and stole anything, so . . ."

Erik Wilson threw his arms wide. Giving up. For now. The signal for Grens to whisper, "Well, then soon I'll have my seventy-two hours," as he followed Mariana Hermansson out. Then, while she was on her way to Bredäng and a gangster wedding, he went back to his boss's office alone.

"So let's discuss the next investigation."

Ewert Grens closed the door to the corridor. This was between the two of them.

"What investigation?"

"The investigation into the investigators. Who broke into your safe. Who is leaking information and endangering our infiltrators."

His boss had been packing up his briefcase when Grens came through the door. There was no sigh, that wasn't his style.

"You like doing things under the radar, Ewert. And so do I."

"Such as?"

"I brought in the professionals. They combed both

the office we're sitting in and the restricted archive in the basement."

Wilson nodded toward the closed door.

"There's no evidence on my safe. No fingerprints, no other traces. Nothing to say there even was a burglary."

"Well, there was one."

"That's the odd thing. You need an electronic key to get in—first a small green dongle you wave in front of the code reader, which identifies you as a particular individual, and then you input your personal combination. At that moment, you've been registered. Centrally. In a computer that controls everything. A monitoring system that keeps track of who opens what and for how long. Every log for the last six months in this office and the archive has been reviewed. No unauthorized persons. And I'm the only one who has opened my safe, and only the archivist has accessed his archive."

Then the chief of the homicide unit lowered his head again to his briefcase. A not particularly subtle sign that for him, this conversation was over.

"And now?"

"No idea, Ewert. Yet."

"So you've got no problem with Paula's identity becoming public? His death? His family's deaths?"

"You know that's not the case."

Erik Wilson stood up with his briefcase in his hand and waited for Grens to do the same. In vain. The stubborn detective superintendent remained where he was, might even have sank lower in the visitor's chair.

"No, I'm not sure I do know that anymore. And that worries me. *However, what I do know* is that no one besides you has been proven to have opened that safe. *What I also know* is that so far you haven't even been able to give me a single explanation about how this alleged theft took place. And, Wilson—it makes me damn suspicious. Makes you damn suspicious."

he apartment had six bedrooms, or was it seven. Maybe eight? Ewert Grens didn't even have a precise answer to Piet Hoffmann's question, he had barely thought about it. He'd squeezed Anni's hand and moved into their penthouse on Svea Road—ready to start the family he'd always dreamed of—back when prices in the inner city were cheap. He couldn't conceive of the millions that apartments like his were worth these days. So yes, technically he was rich despite never having saved more than a few thousand kronor in the bank, all because he chose to live his life without changing, while everything else around him did.

Lots of rooms to choose from—but still they huddled around his kitchen table and the whiteboard. Because it felt right. Because this was where they met in the confusion of two investigations that intersected with each other. Because *if you infiltrate for me, I infiltrate for you* works better when two people sit side by side drinking coffee out of identical cups.

That's what they were doing when Grens's telephone rang at 10:02 PM. Dipping fresh cinnamon buns into warm liquid in a way that reminded Piet Hoffmann of his grandfather. The detective picked up after two ring signals that vibrated between them on the table. The call they were waiting for.

"Yes?"

"It's done, Ewert. Dusko Zaravic has been arrested."

"Did he resist?"

"As calm as he could be."

Grens nodded toward Hoffmann, who nodded back—he'd understood.

"Thank you, Mariana. Good work. Kronoberg jail?"

"He's on his way to an empty cell. And, Ewert?"

"Yes?"

"I still don't know what you want them for . . . but your three days start right now."

PART

6

Night was here and the cool had finally settled onto the balcony making it easy to breathe again. Luiza was asleep, the boys, too, and under the cover of darkness she'd stepped outside for a moment, even though Piet had asked her not to. But she needed it, liked to stand there and look out over the lit-up windows of this suburb. All those people living their lives side by side, unaware of each other.

She tried not to think. Just be. That's what she'd done after realizing she was in love with a man who led two lives, what she'd done while they were on the run in South America and when Piet was serving his last prison sentence. Just be—that's also what he said you had to do to survive prison. Never think about time, past or future, never think about whose fault, just *be* there with a cup of coffee or a newspaper or a pot that needs washing. Until you'd served your time. Didn't matter if it was the state who had sentenced you or your husband's choices.

"Zofia, it's me."

Her phone had buzzed but didn't ring, and she'd answered knowing who it was—only one person had that number.

"We weren't supposed to talk. Only in case of emergency. That's what you said. Has something happened, Piet, has someone . . . ?"

"I'm leaving Sweden for a couple of days. That changes things a little. I can't keep as close an eye on you. So I'm gonna have to ask you to be even more careful. Neither you nor Rasmus nor Hugo can risk being seen. Nothing will happen as long as no one knows where you are. Do you promise that you'll explain that to them? If they can do this, if they can keep hiding, everything will be just like it was before soon."

She looked around, a last breath of the night air, before going back inside.

"I promise."

"Before we hang up, Zo—the hammer and the acetone and the pan are under the sink. You know what you're supposed to do. Inside the bathroom, behind the plastic cover on the wall, there's a new burner phone. Only use it over the next few days *if* things get serious. If the threats escalate."

"What do you mean?"

"There is an escape route."

"An escape route?"

"I've taken security measures."

The phone lay silent in her hand. She was alone, again. And had to keep doing what she'd decided to do—just be. Right now that meant closing the doors of the kitchen, opening up the telephone, and putting the SIM card on the kitchen counter, cutting it up into tiny, tiny pieces, pouring acetone into a pot and dropping the pieces into it. And as they slowly melted away, wrapping a kitchen towel around the phone and hitting it with a hammer until it was impossible to ever put it back together again. The new one was exactly where Piet told her, hidden behind the ventilation cover on the bathroom wall. She'd had time to check that it worked and settle on the sofa when Hugo appeared out of nowhere and sank down beside her.

"Sweetie, did I wake you?"

"I was awake. The whole time. So I heard."

"What?"

"Everything."

"What did you hear, Hugo?"

"Dad called."

"What makes you think it was him . . ."

"Mom—please? You hammered the phone. It smells like acetone. Dad does that. And I know why. So no one can find us."

She hugged him. Tight.

"Go to bed now, sweetie."

Hugo stayed where he was.

"We have to be ready, Mom."

He turned to her, really looked at her.

"Like Dad always is. Totally prepared. For danger. I know we're in danger."

Hugo sat on the sofa, holding his mother's hand. Because it was nice. And because *she* wanted him to. When she next asked him to go to bed again, he did.

He had a plan. He'd wait her out. Pretend to be sleeping. Until she fell asleep. He had a good trick—every time he felt his eyelids getting heavy he'd pinch his thigh hard, because that was the closest to his hand, and he didn't want Mom to notice.

He knew exactly the moment she fell asleep. She started breathing in a special way. He got up very quietly and started to tiptoe. You have to be good at sneaking. Because not only did he hear the hammer and smell the acetone, he caught parts of Mom and Dad's conversation. Mom's part. He heard "escape route." Dad would never say that if it weren't super important. So the escape route had to be. Hugo snuck out into the dark then over to the cabinet beneath the sink where the hammer and the other stuff was kept, and crawled inside it. When he was sure the door was closed behind him and no sound or light could get out, he turned on the flashlight on his phone. He'd lied when Dad asked. Sometimes you have to lie. *"Hugo—you didn't pack anything but your clothes, right?"* Dad had fished his cell phone out of his eldest son's pocket. *"For example, we can't have this with us."* Dad had put the phone in a drawer. So Hugo insisted he had to go pee and Dad told him to be fast, Hugo filled his mouth with water, spat it in the toilet to make it sound like pee, and the sound of the flush was loud enough to cover him going back to his room again, pulling out the drawer, and grabbing his telephone.

Now that phone's flashlight shone around him.

It was dirty under the sink. Old leftovers and dust balls and disgusting damp spots.

And there, in the ceiling of the cabinet, he found it—taped to the bottom of the sink. A gun. A real one. The Polish brand Dad liked—was *that* what he meant when he said an escape route? Hugo pulled it loose, weighed it in his hand. He held it like that for a while, aimed it at the cabinet wall, but then taped it back again—surely Dad didn't mean Mom was supposed to start shooting people.

He turned off the phone's flashlight and crawled out of the cabinet, snuck back into the dark apartment. There were two closets in the hall and he walked into them one at a time. Empty. He shone the light everywhere—found only the smell of other people. The third closet was in the bedroom and slightly larger. He passed by his sleeping mother and brother and sister and opened the closet door, stepped inside, closed it behind him, searching with the flashlight. Completely empty, just like the others. But this one also had shelves that couldn't be seen from below. He took a deep breath and the shelves became steps that carried him upward. No. Nothing. Nowhere. He climbed back down, and it was when he jumped from the last shelf that he felt the floor buckle beneath his feet. He tried again, jumped, landed, and it rocked. An unsteady floor. He got down on his knees, flashing the light around. There. Behind the doorframe. Something black. Like a little knob sticking up. He touched it. It was like the ones on kitchen cabinets. As if it were a hatch. He tried to pull it, but it was impossible since he was sitting on the floor. *On* the door itself. He would have to leave the closet and pull the knob up from the outside. But he couldn't. Not now. Mom would wake up. Or maybe Luiza, and she would wake up Mom. And everything would be ruined.

Because what if this is what Dad meant.

An escape route.

10:41 PM
(2 days, 23 hours, and 21 minutes remaining)

He was about to call her, again. The only person who could ever make him feel anything close to peace. The woman who was soft and hard at the same time, demanding though she never made demands, and she'd taught him that love was something that could be learned, slowly. But Piet Hoffmann forced himself not to. No matter how tightly it squeezed inside his chest. Every attempt at contact meant leaving a trace, and the only traces that should exist were those he chose to leave. Instead, he did what he hoped Zofia did, too—destroyed his phones. First the one that had carried her voice to him and then the one that carried a completely different kind of voice, a distorted one. So when Ewert Grens entered the kitchen to grab a new cup of coffee—which number was impossible to say—he almost stepped onto a pile of empty acetone bottles, a few of his favorite pans, his steak mallet, a couple of kitchen towels with new holes, all spread across the floor—plus tons of tiny plastic pieces that had once sat together.

"Is that what I think it is?"

"I guess so."

"Quite the pile—I suppose you also destroyed *the* phone? The only line you have to those who threaten you?"

"I thought it was time."

"You realize what this means, the next time they try to contact you? All hell will break loose."

"They don't know where my family is. Where I am."

"Yet, Hoffmann. *Yet!*"

"And if we figure out what we need to, it will stay that way."

Grens grabbed a trash bag out of the cleaning closet, held it while Hoffmann filled it up.

"Since this was obviously more than *one* phone, I guess you changed your number. I'll need it. If we're going to keep working together."

"I'll be changing it two times a day. Six different numbers. You'll get a list of all of them."

Ewert Grens's coffee cup was joined by another on the kitchen table, one for himself and one for his guest.

"I want you to sit down."

"Time for an investigation meeting, Detective Superintendent?"

"You could call it that. At the world's smallest police station."

Grens smiled as he put two envelopes in front of Hoffmann.

"Congratulations on your new job."

"What, Grens?"

"Open it."

Piet Hoffmann ripped the first envelope open with his index finger and took out the contents. A black leather case. He opened it. In the plastic pocket on the left was an ID card. *POLICE* stood in red letters and *Police Department of Stockholm* in smaller text beneath a photograph of himself in his current disguised state, a social security number he'd never seen before, and a name he'd never used. In the plastic case to the right was a real police badge, *STOCKHOLM 4514* on a brass plate and the coat of arms with the golden crown.

"Verner Larsson?"

"Just as good as any of your other undercover names."

"Pretty strange, right, Grens? All these years as an infiltrator on behalf of the City Police—with no rights despite contributing to your formal and very real investigations. And now, when the investigation is at your kitchen table, you turn me into a real police officer."

"Yes. And you need a police badge for that. And this."

The next envelope contained a flight ticket and the kind of letter of introduction that usually begins *To Whom It May Concern*, but which was now addressed to one Gezim Latifi and explained that Verner Larsson had been educated at the police academy and, during his years as an officer at the Swedish police authority, had been considered both reliable and capable, a model officer.

"Latifi?"

"A police officer working in the city where that call was picked up—Shkodër, Albania. That's where you're headed."

"And why him?"

"I needed someone I could trust. So I contacted a German colleague I've worked with. He has an extensive network and better judgment than my own. He gave me Latifi. One of the very few in that area that can't be bribed—which is usually a requirement to be on the force down there. Besides, he's nice. We spoke on the phone for almost an hour, and I'm sure he can help you with what you need."

"And what exactly is that?"

"You're looking for two individuals. The perp we're informally investigating from this kitchen table, who is threatening you and your family, whose goal is to take over the Swedish illegal arms trade by selling the world's most powerful machine gun. And a perp who recently ordered the murders of three hit men, which we are officially investigating from the police station. These two individuals I am quite convinced are one and the same—and it will connect both of these investigations to the tower room of a white house. I want to know who it is. And who he's working with in Sweden. Who's running around on his behalf shooting people on my watch."

Piet Hoffmann closed the black leather case, his temporary identity, put it in a pocket on his shoulder holster, and stood up—ready to go.

"Wait a second. That's only half of your mission."

"Okay. What's the other half?"

"I want you to find a young woman who went by the name Hannah Ohlsson, but these days she could be calling herself anything—if she's still alive."

"Who is she?"

"Someone I'm worried about."

"From the other investigation—the one you won't talk about?"

"Yes."

Ewert Grens produced a third envelope.

"It's essential you find the man responsible for those murders. That's your top priority. But for me, personally, it would mean even more if you could take a look at the Jane Does contained in this envelope. If you could gather information and compare that with what I'm sending with you—characteristics of appearance that don't change. Her height, eye color, shoe size, dental records, scar from an appendix surgery, and a few other things."

Hoffmann started to stand up again. But Grens stopped him, again.

"One more thing."

"Yes?"

"Zofia. Your kids. I want to know where you're hiding them."

"Why?"

"So I can protect them. While you're gone."

Always alone. Trust only yourself. That's what Hoffmann believed for a very long time, thought it was the only way to survive. Until one day he learned he could *choose* to rely on a detective superintendent named Ewert Grens, and a few years later he was *forced* to trust him.

That wasn't enough right now.

"No."

"No?"

"I know I should trust you, Grens. Unconditionally. But it's impossible."

"We *have* to trust each other. Even though neither of us trusts a goddamn thing."

"On everything else. But not this."

"That's the only way this collaboration is going to work."

"Sorry—not until you find out who that dirty cop is."

Hoffmann looked at the detective, and it was clear from his face that he had no intention of discussing it any further. An experienced interrogator knew when a question tore down more than the expected answer built up. So while Ewert Grens finished his last coffee of the evening, Piet Hoffmann hurried out of the apartment, down the stairs, and out to hail a taxi. Twelve minutes later he was in western Södermalm, stepping into the studio of a makeup artist who was waiting for him with a smile he could have got lost in.

"Thank you. For seeing me on such short notice."

"You're in a hurry. As usual."

"As usual."

The full-length mirror was rolled out into the middle of the studio. It was easier to meet himself this time—the pudgy accountant was more familiar.

"Where are you going, Piet? Or, let me rephrase that, what kind of weather are you headed for. Temperature, humidity, etc."

"Same as here. Hot. But the heat is more normal there, I guess."

"And we're sticking with this look? Flaps above your eyes, crooked nose with largish wings, slightly puffy cheeks and chin and stomach?"

"That's me. For a little longer."

He sat down in the chair, and thought how nice it was that this time he wasn't going to have any goop smeared over his face or the cement that held the plaster strips while they hardened. With the help of the cast from his last visit, there were more pieces of this disguise waiting for him. The makeup remover released the old pieces so new ones could be glued on, and then she tested the hanging eyelids and the cheeks and chin to make sure they were all firmly attached.

"This will last a while longer. There are two new shirts in the plastic bag, which fit your larger stomach—and an extra bottle of glue, just in case. Check as often as you can. Shouldn't be a problem, but you never know with the heat and physical exertion, it *could* loosen."

The next taxi ride took him to the all-night gas station in Hammarby Sjöstad. That was where he asked the driver to drop him off. One and a half kilometers left. He walked the last bit, approaching slowly to make sure he wasn't being followed. As he stood in the darkness, twenty-five meters away from the apartment that hid everything he cared about, he felt that same poisonous cocktail of fear and rage that he'd felt holding the hand grenade his youngest son had played with—and it made his whole body tremble. That's why he picked up the phone. He *had* to call. But not Zofia, who he could run to in just seconds and hold tight, which would take away his longing for a moment, but afterward would just make it worse. So it would have to be second best. A call to someone who could see her.

"Boss—so late? Did something happen?"

"I'm leaving in a couple of hours, taking a short trip. And I wanted to make sure things were working with the new family? The mother and her three children."

Hoffmann took a few steps back to avoid being caught by the cameras, so Andy wouldn't accidentally detect him on any of his monitors.

"No lights on. They seem to be sleeping."

"And . . . well, have you . . . has anything else happened? I mean if you've been able to see them. How do they seem to be doing that is. The worry you mentioned last time, about the boy—said you could see it on him."

"He seems calmer. The few times I've caught a glimpse of him—the boys stay away from the windows. But the mother? You were going to talk to her? About the phone?"

"Yes?"

"She got another call! I could see it through the window. Boss, how the hell can we assure their safety if they won't follow instructions, I mean . . ."

"It's my fault, Andy. Sorry. I forgot—but I promise *again* to contact her. She'll understand. She seems to be a wise woman."

"And you still don't know why they're there? What happened?"

"Nothing, only that it has to do with her husband."

Piet Hoffmann stood there a long time staring at the windows and the wall that separated them.

Soon.

5:01 AM
(2 days, 17 hours, and 1 minute remaining)

A successful interrogation was based on surprise, and for a man who was locked up drunk, late at night, wearing a fancy tuxedo, it was quite a surprise to be awoken by Ewert Grens's unnecessarily loud and irritating *Gooood morning* being shouted through a small hatch in the door. And it wasn't much more fun when the keys to the jail cell rattled and shook into his head and the sound of the metallic whine of the bolt became a sword piercing his every attempt to think. Or when the cell door was opened and the detective superintendent stormed in, followed by the female police officer who'd brought him in on this groundless arrest. Which was why Dusko Zaravic turned over on his cell bunk and met every question Grens asked with the silence of his back.

"You and I last saw each other seventeen years ago. I questioned you about the murder of a family—I know you remember it, you bastard. And I interrogated your friends Dejan and Branko and Ermir—I bet you remember that, too. Then I questioned your employer, but I was forced to let him go after seventy-two hours and watch him flee the country—I'm sure you remember that particularly well. And, Zaravic, since you do remember all of that, you might also recall that I promised I'd never allow a killer to go free again after I found him? So if you . . ."

"Are you done?"

Zaravic still had his back to his visitors. Ewert Grens leaned closer, hissing.

"I'm done when you and I look at each other and I can ask my questions."

Then they waited in his narrow prison cell—a sink and a floor-mounted stool were the only furniture besides the bunk.

Silent minutes.

Until Zaravic made a point of turning over slowly.

"Say whatever the hell you came to say. And then leave."

"Yes, I could do that, if I wanted to. Leave, that is. Unlike you. But first, an observation: you don't seem particularly upset that your colleagues are being executed, one by one."

"Upset? Why would I be?"

"Because they seem to be dying off rather quickly. Two one morning, a third the next."

"From bullets—not age. So why should I worry? You, on the other hand, Superintendent or whatever the hell you are, how old are you?"

"Three dead. Within twenty-four hours. And the fourth shows up at a wedding without a care in the world wearing that—a white tuxedo, not very careful behavior for a man whose friends just left him."

"I don't walk around on the streets being scared."

"Or maybe you know you don't have to be—because you shot them?"

He laughed. Dusko Zaravic really laughed. Not as a challenge, or with scorn. More heartily. If gangsters were capable of that these days.

"Is that . . . for fuck's sake, is that why you took me in on this bullshit charge? Because you think I'm running around and knocking off my unfortunate brothers?"

Ewert Grens beheld an expression that could mean many things.

I could be sitting in a detention cell with a triple murderer, who has turned one of my colleagues and is in control of classified documents.

Or the man stretching out on that bunk was the next one in line and should be grateful we're keeping him here for a while.

Or he has nothing to do with this at all, not as a victim or a perp.

Doesn't matter, let him sit there.

"We believe that an organization is trying to take over the Swedish arms trade. And that you murdered your potential competitors. On behalf of someone who is currently in Albania."

"Seriously—what the hell are you talking about?"

"We both know you were mixed up in that line of work many years ago. You might even have been in that apartment, employed by the man who likes to call himself King Zoltan. And now there are ten thousand weapons out there worth a billion kronor that Zoltan, or someone who's using you as a hired gun, thinks it's fine to kill people for."

That laugh again. It was real.

"For fuck's sake—you know as well as I do that's as imaginary as the charges you're holding me on. And even if it *were* true, why the hell would I tell you? Look at my hands. I have nails, okay? Do you know how long it takes them to grow out again? I've broken interrogators you can't even touch."

Then he turned around again. The back of his white tuxedo toward Grens and his silent face against the cell wall. The detective superintendent nodded to Hermansson, who was waiting by the cell door—their first interrogation was over.

They'd reached the cell closest to the entrance—which was the liveliest as usual, with yapping inmates and a fan on high and jail guards shouting to each other—when Hermansson began to speak.

"You put on a good show."

"A show?"

"You really made it sound like you suspect him of something. When all you want is to keep him locked up as long as the law will allow."

"He *could* be involved. If he is, I'll know once we find our dirty cop."

He looked at her. Searchingly.

"And that—the dirty cop—still isn't a problem for you?"

She didn't answer this time either.

"Because we're gonna find our colleague who has switched sides, and we're gonna find whoever is shooting people twice in the head. I'll soon have a man in place in Albania who will figure out who's in charge, and who's doing their grunt work."

"A man in place?"

"Yes. A man who thought it would be easier to do what he needed to do with that psycho off the streets."

"The man I met in your kitchen?"

"Could be, yes."

The ride down in the elevator from the Kronoberg jail became uncomfortable in the way such elevator rides can be, when every look and word feels like too much. But this was more than that—Ewert Grens had openly accused one of his closest colleagues of selling them out, betraying them, for a second time. They stepped out of the first elevator on their way to the next, and now they had to pass through five doors that required access cards. Just before the third, Grens couldn't take it anymore.

"I . . . well, I apologize."

She swiped her card, opened the door, and they walked on.

"I . . . never should have accused you. But this whole fucking story, someone breaking into Wilson's safe, and you not wanting to help me and look into him . . . It feels better now, Hermansson. You arrested Zaravic. I no longer doubt you."

She stopped abruptly.

"No, Ewert. You should never have accused me. And you will never do it again. Because I will apply for a transfer. Do you understand what I'm saying?"

She looked at him, *through* him. As only she could.

"Yes, Hermansson. I understand."

The fourth door, the fifth door, and finally the last elevator, now on their way to the homicide unit. But just as they were about to reach their floor, Grens pushed the red stop button, then a button that made them head back down.

"One more thing."

He might as well. Now that the ice was broken. She was the only one who talked to him about these things, who again and again demanded answers, and who could look straight at him and say *you don't know how to separate intimacy from integrity, just like the people we investigate, and that, Ewert, makes you terrified* and still he wouldn't cut her out of his life. That's why she was the one he could talk to about a problem with no solution.

"I used to have a colleague I liked quite a bit. Looked up to. A mentor, you might say. But when he was about to retire . . . He changed. He couldn't handle that big black hole. The emptiness. There was nothing because he had nothing else. One night, with just a couple of weeks left at the police station, he called a squad car, asked them to come to his home. Then he shot himself. A bullet in the mouth. He knew the right way to do it to leave the least amount of trouble for everyone involved."

The elevator stopped again. Now it was Mariana Hermansson who pressed the button in the opposite direction.

"Shot himself?"

"Yes."

"Because he couldn't stand it?"

"His whole life was about being a police officer. He had nothing outside this station. Just a big apartment he shared with no one else."

The elevator stopped again. She pressed down. It stopped. She pressed up.

"What was this mentor's name?"

"Name?"

"Yes."

"He . . . yes, I . . ."

"Okay, Ewert. You don't need to say more."

The next time the elevator stopped, they actually got out, headed into the homicide unit. Hermansson's office was closest, and just as she was about to enter it the detective superintendent put a gentle hand on her shoulder; he'd never done that before.

"I'm not old. I've just lived a long time. Do you understand?"

They stared at each other for a while, she nodded slightly. Grens's next stop was the coffee machine, halfway to his office. Two cups, black.

"Ewert?"

Sven's office was almost next door, and Sven, sitting behind his desk, waved Ewert in eagerly.

"Come in."

"Soon, I'm just going to . . ."

"Now, Ewert."

Grens sank into the visitor's chair, Sven closed the door before settling down opposite his boss and pointing to his coffee cups.

"Can I have one?"

"There's no milk, the way you like it."

Sven had already grabbed one of them, was drinking it.

"You asked me to look into Hermansson."

"You don't need to do that anymore."

"You even asked me to follow her."

"I've talked to her, Sven, and you . . ."

"I did it. Followed her. Even though it felt shitty. A close colleague? Would you allow someone to follow me—or maybe someone already is?"

"I told you . . ."

"Maybe you were right, Ewert."

The detective superintendent had just emptied everything inside him in an elevator. He felt good again. As if he weren't alone with his thoughts. He wasn't entirely sure he wanted to hear the rest of what Sven had to say.

"Mariana and I had lunch yesterday. Here, in the station. She was her usual self. And yet—not at all. I just couldn't quite place it. But when you know someone well, you know when something is wrong."

Sven leaned forward, and it was clear he took no joy in what he was about to say.

"We parted, and she headed off to the prosecutor's office for a meeting. So I did it. Followed her. I'm normally good at it. And yet somehow she managed to lose me several times. Extremely vigilant. Turning around constantly, changing direction. Worried, that's how I would describe her."

Now he lowered his voice, as if he thought what he had to say could be heard several doors away.

"Roslags Street. All the way to Vanadislunden Park. Quite far from the prosecutor's office. That's where she went. A normal apartment building, five stories. She looked around repeatedly before punching in the code and going inside. There was a café across the street, from there I had a perfect view. One and a half hours.

Until she came out. When we met here in the corridor later, I asked how it went, and I felt it again. She seemed off. And she lied. Started telling me about the prosecutor's new ideas. And you know as well as I do, Ewert—the Mariana Hermansson we know never lies. Or, maybe we thought we knew. I checked the building, every apartment owner. No name that was associated with any ongoing investigations—nothing that could be connected to Hermansson, either, not at work or privately."

Ewert Grens sank down even farther into the visitor's chair. Sven Sundkvist was the least dramatic man he'd ever met. Sven never over-interpreted, never let his feelings take the lead. If common sense had a face, it would have looked like the man Grens was across from.

And yet. He had to protest. Because that was only reasonable response.

"There could be so many explanations for why she wouldn't tell you about the company she keeps, or the addresses she prefers to take her walks to."

"Yes. That's true. But I did a little more digging. Our calendars. Went through my notes on meetings we conducted separately in recent investigations. And several of Mariana's own meetings—*listen now, Ewert*—never took place. Nothing so big that it affected the final result. But several of the people she stated she had met, logged meetings outside the station for, confirmed that she never met with them."

And again Sven's expression was anything but happy. "And since both you and I have felt the same thing, and *one* of the explanations is the only thing that it absolutely cannot be, I would recommend that we continue to monitor her. And that you're careful about what you share with her. I'm not so stupid that I haven't realized there's someone else working on this with you, with this investigation, whose name I don't know, and *if* Hermansson isn't the person we think she is, *if* she's leaking information—then more people could end up hurt."

12:12 PM
(2 days, 9 hours, and 50 minutes remaining)

Piet Hoffmann walked through a small but surprisingly modern airport. Large glass partitions and glossy floors and stressed-out travelers staring at departure screens. *Aeroporti Ndërkombëtar i Tiranës Nënë Tereza.* The rental car was prebooked, and within a half hour he was driving north on newly laid asphalt, a highway that hadn't existed the first and only other time he'd visited this country, many years ago and on a very different mission. And for just a moment—the kind that cuts into chest and gut, which transports a person back in time—he missed it. Being on his own. In his own reality with no right and wrong. No consequences. Back then when the bus left from Belgrade or Tirana, and he bought ten automatic rifles at a time. Just a little hustle—fifteen hundred kronor for the guns, plus five hundred to the bus driver for a bag that sat among other bags—no risk involved, all profit. The few times the bus got stopped, the driver, of course, didn't have a clue whose bag that was. Transports twice a week, and the shit made it through every time.

He sighed. Life looked different now.

Because he wanted it to—being with Zofia and the children won out every time against those small highs.

And it wasn't just him. Weapons smuggling had changed, too. Piet Hoffmann might not indulge anymore, but he knew because he got regular offers of *just this once* and *easy money*. The principle was of course the same—most illegal weapons started out legal. It was the Swedish customers who had changed. Now every teenager in every shitty neighborhood wanted to carry a piece. So to keep prices up the people who import weapons have to hold on to them for a while, sometimes even choose who gets to buy it. While more established groups, like Hells Angels and Bandidos, never turned to the open market, but instead structured their supply around hangers-on who were trying to prove their worth. And from the Balkans to Denmark, it was easy. On the other hand, the last bit could be a little dicey, crossing the bridge into Sweden. So now it was all about these small delivery services that seemed to multiply daily. Delivery companies with two cars, two employees, an office in Warsaw and one in Sofia, apartments where people dropped off what they wanted transported to Sweden, companies that were run like normal shipping firms and, just like the bus drivers he'd used, never exposed themselves to risk. The delivery firms that drove the goods from point A to B weren't responsible for the customs paperwork, so if they got pulled over it was never their fault—their task was just to pick up and drop off. The declaration of contents was created outside Sweden's borders, somewhere in the EU where signatures could be bought, then were never checked again.

Piet Hoffmann slowed down as he passed by the city of Lezhë, stopped at a gas station for a coffee and a sandwich at a yellow plastic table under the hot sun. Halfway. A dry but pleasant landscape. Rolling hills, white houses scattered here and there. A blue, cloudless sky, and a wind that meant he wasn't far from the sea.

He'd come here because someone was trying to take over the Swedish arms trade, and that operation might be based in this region, which was quite familiar with military equipment going astray. A couple of dozen kilometers away, on the other side of the northeastern border, there were nine hundred thousand illegal Serbian weapons just waiting for new owners, and at the next border seven hundred and fifty thousand Bosnian weapons. And here and in Kosovo and in Montenegro and in Macedonia, many more were hidden—the weapons that, after the end of the Yugoslav wars, often followed soldiers back to their homes and then into Europe's black market.

A cloyingly sweet coffee, and then he bought a couple of bottles of lukewarm water, and continued on the SH1. Soon the mountains appeared, and the dry landscape beyond his rolled-up windows became greener, louder. He was almost to Shkodër.

9:34 PM
(2 days and 28 minutes remaining)

He had visited Ulcinj once, the coastal city of Montenegro, which was about a half hour away over crappy roads and across a border. That was where he learned that an Ulcinj execution meant one shot in the right side of the forehead and one in the left temple. Though it lacked the sea, the city of Shkodër was more beautiful, its streets in better condition, its restaurants served better food. People seemed happier, more relaxed. He'd checked into a simple hotel on the outskirts of the city, which looked a bit like the apartment complexes in the southern suburbs of Stockholm that he grew up in. He walked around in the inner city, drank coffee, got a bite to eat. Waiting. For the dusk. The darkness. Which was blacker here, fewer splashes of artificial light.

Now he was in the rental car. Where Rruga Komanit crossed Rruga Dasho Shkreli. Narrow roads, still paved, but grass sprang up along the edges and formed its own lane. Stone walls or high iron fences stood around every plot, enclosing it and keeping others out. Most were two-story houses, and telephone lines and power lines crisscrossed above him like a safety net for the sky.

The house he was looking for was painted white and had a dozen antennas sticking up from its tile roof. It was the house Grens had showed him in his kitchen. That's where the phone call placed by the now badly injured security guards had been traced to, specifically to its tower-like structure. According to the land registry that the detective superintendent had tracked down—with the assistance of the Albanian policeman Hoffmann would meet in the morning in his role as a Swedish police officer equipped with a real badge—the house belonged to a middle-aged woman. That was often the case. The kind of man who belonged to an organization like this never owned anything, officially. The lights were on in a few of the rooms, downstairs in what might be the kitchen, and upstairs in a room next to the tower. He'd identified two guards, both armed and each responsible for one of the floors. No other people were visible, yet. But he had time. If he sat here until two o'clock, maybe three, he could still catch a little sleep.

7:06 AM
(1 day, 14 hours, and 56 minutes remaining)

Shkodër's police station looked like most of the other buildings set off a little from the center of the city—the flat roof, the unassuming facade, the AC units hanging like giant square beehives, buzzing under each window. Inside, on the simple wooden chairs of the waiting room, there sat an elderly man waiting to report a break-in, a slightly younger man there to present documents about his two stolen cars, and a family who was there to proudly apply for a passport, *our first, we're going to Spain*. And in the far corner—a Swede named Verner Larsson, whose mission was quite different from theirs.

Gezim Latifi was tall, quite a bit taller than Hoffmann, his broad shoulders filled out his Albanian police uniform, and his eyes were as soft as his steps. A little too handsome, a little fictitious, a little bit Hollywood. He looked like the image of an image—as if he'd stepped straight out of a recruitment ad for the next generation of police officers. He even wore his police hat despite the heat and the fact that they were indoors—it sat low on his forehead.

"Mr. Larsson?"

Hoffmann nodded. The movie police officer in front of him had a very firm handshake.

"After me."

He spoke English with what the Stockholm underworld called a Yugo accent. Though this was the Albanian variation. And this man worked on the other side of the law.

A cubbyhole. His office was no bigger than that. Simple furniture, bare walls. A room without any personality. Hoffmann put the letter of recommendation and his fresh police ID on the equally anonymous desk. Latifi skimmed the text about what an exemplary police officer Verner Larsson was, opened the leather case, and ran his index finger over the coat of arms while he compared the photo to the face.

"Okay. What can I do for you, Officer Larsson?"

Here Piet Hoffmann sat, in an Albanian city, under extreme time constraints, his family in hiding from death threats a thousand kilometers away. But he couldn't help but laugh, a little. He was an actual police officer. Being treated like a police officer, judged as a police officer. Quite a journey for a man who was once Sweden's most wanted criminal.

He started to describe in his version of English—which probably sounded as Swedish as Latifi's sounded Albanian—the assignment that Grens stressed was not a normal investigation, and therefore couldn't be conducted in a normal way. A list of eighteen Albanian cases that involved unidentified female bodies. That needed to be compared to the appearance and special characteristics of a missing Swedish citizen. A document now transported by secure messenger, rather than by electronic means, less danger of falling into the wrong hands.

"Hannah Ohlsson?"

"That was her name at the time of her disappearance."

"Who is she?"

"I don't know more than that, yet. Just a name for me. But my . . . well, my boss, would be very grateful if I was allowed to look over those investigations. As for me, I'm mainly here on behalf of another case. Someone who over the last few days killed at least three men who emigrated from this region. Detective Superintendent Grens talked to you about it over the phone. And mentioned, among other things, a man he arrested many years ago in connection with a multiple homicide of a family, and who had once employed the men who were recently murdered. Arrested—but they couldn't hold him. The suspect left Sweden as soon as he was released, and according to sources the superintendent had at that time, he moved back here. And now, since we've tracked a phone call here, he's a suspect again. Possibly the one who has ordered the hits."

The impersonal room had an impersonal bookcase with long rows of impersonal binders. Latifi pulled one out, opened it with a click, and pulled out the contents, every document, facedown on the desk.

"Was this the man your boss was talking about?"

Hoffmann studied the black-and-white passport photo that Latifi held—a very young man who would later become a major player in Stockholm's underworld. He'd met him at the bar and in jail. King Zoltan. A ridiculous name. But it fit somehow. The type that took up a lot of space.

"Yes. That's him."

"In that case, I know much more now."

"And?"

The Albanian policeman seemed to be searching for the words in English. Not because he was worried, he just wasn't familiar with the investigative terms in a foreign language.

"When I go through our various criminal records I find page after page of misdemeanors—but all very long ago. He was in and out of juvenile facilities. Then everything stops. Not a word all through the nineties. Suddenly his name pops up again. Many years later— October 2001. Just as suddenly as it disappeared. In the General Surveillance Registry with several notes, *KZ was observed in connection with a presumed illegal weapons transaction*, and the same in the suspect registry, *KZ interrogated in connection with an armed robbery and kidnapping*, a total of about twenty hits. Soon the image emerges of an individual in our part of Albania who has taken over the micro-smuggling of weapons along what we call the Balkan route. Deliveries to the whole of northern Europe, but with a focus on the country where demand and thus profitability are greatest. Where you come from—Sweden."

Piet Hoffmann looked at King Zoltan's passport. A

young boy who was now a middle-aged man. There should be more current photos at a police station responsible for watching him.

"Suspicions. Interrogation. We never got further. Or, my colleagues never got further, I was serving in Tirana at the time."

"And what does that mean? That they didn't *get further*?"

"Frankly? In this room?"

"Yes."

"Corrupt cops make more money if the weapons dealers make more money."

"Your colleagues?"

Latifi shrugged his broad shoulders wearily.

"Many of them. It has always worked that way."

"And you?"

Now he smiled.

"Your boss wouldn't have received a recommendation from Germany if I had been one of them. And you would not be sitting here."

A man you couldn't bribe. That's how Grens described him. Hoffmann wondered why. Why not do what all of his other colleagues do? Why settle for less when others have more? Why fight a system that fights back?

"I see you were looking at the photo."

Hoffmann nodded.

"Yes. Surprised there wasn't a more recent one."

"There is. A couple of them."

Latifi gathered the documents that lay with their white backs upward on his desk. Turned over the top one. Photographs from a crime scene.

"Taken just over five years ago. When Zoltan had climbed to the very top of the criminal food chain. Really was King. About to expand, take over the whole of Albania, all the weapons routes from here."

Piet Hoffmann's eyes were drawn to it, and he realized what he was looking at.

One trail had ended.

He had seen this kind of image before, just a few days earlier, at Grens's kitchen table.

A dead man lying on a floor.

Two shots to the head.

One through the forehead, one through the temple.

8:14 AM
(1 day, 13 hours, and 48 minutes remaining)

Ewert Grens was sitting in the back seat. That had become his spot in recent years. Mariana Hermansson took the driver's seat because she was a much better driver than him, and Sven Sundkvist got the passenger seat because he was much better at reading the maps. An aging detective is like a soccer player over thirty—he got moved successively back on the field, from the forward position at the front, making the goals, to midfielder, where his job was to wear down the other team, and then when his career was coming to an end, they moved him to fullback, where it was all about toughness and playing dirty until your opponents gave up.

Dusko Zaravic's large condo was on Valhalla Road, and Grens's search warrant for it was justified by only the vaguest reasons, which in some way confirmed the extremely vague justifications for his arrest. Two lies always added up to a better truth. On the first floor in the stairwell they found the on-call locksmith waiting for them, and he was putting down his toolbox just as the detective superintendent's telephone started to ring. Hoffmann's new number. His first report.

"Can you talk?"

"A moment."

Grens climbed one floor up, lowered his voice.

"I'm listening."

"Your investigation, Grens, is the result of something that began here."

"What do you mean?"

"Seventeen years ago your suspect did come here. And he became the leading arms dealer in the region with his headquarters in Shkodër. And—five years ago he was killed in exactly the same way, same MO, as your three victims in Stockholm this last week."

"Well . . . damnit."

"Yes. It's never as simple as you think it's gonna be. Not even for a detective superintendent who's hoping to lock up the same individual again. Except this time for good."

"An Ulcinj execution?"

"Yep."

Sven had come up the stairs and had been waiting at a bit of a distance for a break in the conversation. Now he interrupted to say that the locksmith was ready, they could go in.

"Soon, Sven."

Grens continued once he was on his own again.

"And now?"

"The house you positioned the call in. I've been watching it, and I know what to do. Nothing has changed other than the name of the man sitting in the tower room, the person in charge. The current king of smuggling. Because that's how this fucking world works. *The Smuggling King Is Dead, Grens, Long Live the King of Smuggling*. But I'll need some more help. More information."

"Yes?"

"Latifi? You're sure about him?"

"I'm absolutely sure."

"Because these are no nice guys. And I'm alone. How can we be certain he's not on the payroll of this weapons dealer? No matter how many German contacts you talked to."

"Trust, Hoffmann. It doesn't come easy to you and me."

"I have to know that he's reliable."

"Listen: this guy *is* solid. Loyal. Keeps his mouth shut no matter what. I can't tell you how I know. But I do."

Ewert Grens had, as he hung up, caught every cautious inhalation, every shift in Hoffmann's voice. Perfect sound reproduction. It had occurred to him before, most recently during the investigation that led him to West Africa last year—how the expansion of the mobile network sometimes worked unexpectedly. Because the richest countries already had good networks, the telecom companies prioritized the poorer regions that lacked good infrastructure. That's where they put their most modern equipment. So when he received a call in a stairwell in Sweden from someone who was in one of Europe's poorest countries, it was via the most advanced mobile network—the kind a police officer could use to track a call that ended up sending an infiltrator to Albania. Which seemed to have turned out to be the right place.

The door to Dusko Zaravic's apartment was open. The locksmith had hurried on to another door for another search, while Mariana and Sven were waiting outside for their boss.

"Important call?"

Sven gave him the same look as when he asked Grens to step into his office, when he made sure no one was listening and warned him about their closest colleague.

A strange, unwelcome feeling.

If Hermansson isn't the person we think she is, if she's leaking information—then more people could end up hurt.

"Yes, Sven. An important call."

They both avoided looking at Mariana. It was simpler that way. For now.

"Plastic gloves on. We're searching for anything that can help a prosecutor extend Zaravic's stay in Kronoberg jail—he just got more interesting."

"Oh, really—how?"

"Such as a weapon. Most preferably a paper weapon."

"Paper?"

"The folder that was stolen from Wilson's safe. Highly classified documents linked to our infiltrator program. As dangerous as any other weapon for those who were involved."

Five rooms. High ceilings. Glass and steel furniture, illuminated by bulging crystal chandeliers. Interior design magazine elegance, blatantly expensive. All immaculate. As if the cleaning lady had just folded up her dustcloths and mopped her last hardwood floor. They opened cupboards, drawers, closets. Turned Anders Zorn paintings, rolled up Persian rugs. Knocked on walls, lit up floor joints, poked at drains and ventilation slots. Until Sven came out of the kitchen and put his hand on Grens's arm.

"Come with me."

Warm air. That was the detective superintendent's first thought as he stepped into the kitchen. Wind from the open window on the wall next to the refrigerator.

"Someone was here for a visit, Ewert. Just now."

"Just now?"

"Look here."

Sven pointed a blue plastic gloved finger.

"Double glazing. You don't want to break it or cut a hole in it because you think it might make too much noise. So you cut the putty instead, pull out the small pins that are behind it, and loosen the entire pane with two large suction plugs. Climb in. When you're done, you clean up any evidence the cops might look for, climb out again. And because it's supposed to seem like no one was here, you put the glass back and put new putty on the outside."

He ran his finger up and down the window's wooden frame.

"This is synthetic putty. Still a little damp. It usually takes two days to dry. Almost as long as Zaravic has been locked up. Someone was here—someone who knew we were coming."

They both heard Mariana dismantling the washbasin in the toilet in the hall.

"The police leak, Sven."

"Whoever switched sides is still delivering information to whomever we're investigating."

"Don't say that, Sven. Don't think it."

"I don't need to."

He pointed to the wooden frame again. This time not to the putty, but to some stains next to it.

"It's solidified. But you see what it is?"

"Blood."

"It's easy to do. When you hold the glass pane, put it back, balancing it to prevent it from breaking. You can cut yourself. Fresh putty and fresh blood. Fresh DNA. If it's from someone we're investigating, there's a good chance it might be in our database. And if it's from a police employee in the homicide unit it would *also* be in our database—we've all provided comparative tests so we can be excluded from the evidence. Do you understand what I'm saying, Ewert? Coming here and not finding a goddamn thing because we were too late, it's not a bad thing—it's the best thing that could have happened."

10:01 AM
(1 day, 12 hours, and 1 minute remaining)

This time Piet Hoffmann didn't have to wait with the crime victims who had come to the station to report

Shkodër's latest perpetrators. Latifi met him at the entrance, and Hoffmann followed his wide back through the employee entrance and into the tiny office that lacked any personality.

"We meet again."

"Thank you—for seeing me."

"We're colleagues. Colleagues help each other."

The black leather case with his badge and its coat of arms lay in his jacket pocket and Hoffmann wrestled down an impulse to pull it out, hold it. It still amazed him. Police officer. On paper. After all these years as an outlaw.

"Coffee?"

Two cups on the table. Very small. Very black contents.

"Turkish. I prefer it. Several times a day."

Latifi took it in one gulp.

"Talk. Then we'll see if I can do something for you."

Hoffmann suddenly hesitated. Not long, but long enough for Latifi to notice it.

"If you want me to help you."

"I do. But what I'm planning to do isn't exactly without its dangers. And I honestly don't know if I can trust you."

"Don't you want that?"

Latifi nodded to the untouched coffee and Hoffmann held up a hand to say no thank you. A couple of seconds later and Latifi had drained that one, too.

"My boss, Ewert Grens, who you talked to on the phone, thinks I should trust you—and he never trusts anyone."

"There you go."

"So convince me, too."

"You're the one who needs help—not me."

They stared at each other for a long time, silent.

Until Hoffmann stood up and walked over to the closed door.

When he turned to say goodbye, Latifi had taken off the police cap he was wearing on his last visit. And Hoffmann realized why. The entire upper part of his forehead was covered by a huge and ugly scar.

"Knife?"

"Bayonet. And then a bullet, from the side, that was supposed to blow away the rest."

"And your eyes?"

"I only see out of one of them."

Piet Hoffmann sat down again.

"You kept your mouth shut?"

"Yes."

"And you're not going to tell me if I ask about what?"

"Exactly."

Grens, on the other hand, did know about what. That's what his trust was based on.

That was good enough. That counted.

Hoffmann put his hand on the sweaty police cap.

"Thank you. For this."

"You've traveled a long way. When you could have sent an email. This is no ordinary investigation. It means more. Maybe it's even personal?"

"Maybe."

"So?"

"A house. Approximately where Rruga Komanit crosses Rruga Dasho Shkreli. Our investigation has led us there. To a tower room on the second floor. Superintendent Grens had guessed it was his kingly friend Zoltan sitting there making calls to some of his old friends. Now we know that wasn't the case. And we need to know who was."

Latifi had a kind smile.

And with the scar visible, he seemed even more human and less like an ideal.

"This, whatever it is you want to do, *my* boss is not going to like. And that is a damn good thing, Officer Larsson."

10:42 AM
(1 day, 11 hours, and 20 minutes remaining)

"Now, you goddamn better answer me!"

Erik Wilson—who had just left the meeting from hell with the police union, which in its turn had succeeded a never-ending negotiation with the personnel department—had been looking forward to ten minutes of solitude in his office before the next meeting he also wanted to avoid, one with the auditors. But now Ewert Grens stormed in.

"You hear that, Wilson! And don't you even think about leaving here until you give me a satisfactory answer!"

It wasn't often the chief superintendent of the homicide unit found himself longing for one of those bureaucratic meetings. But now he did. A furious, spitting, hissing Detective Superintendent Grens was worse than all the budget deficit talks combined.

"Hello to you, too, Ewert."

"This morning I went to carry out a search, which you granted me a warrant for only under protest! And which very few people knew about! And I'll be damned if someone didn't get there before us and clear away every trace of evidence!"

"We have already been through this once. I'm not doing it again."

"Either you're the leak, Wilson, or someone very close to you is. Who are you seeing? Who are you so in love with that you can't see clearly?"

"Okay. Then we will do it again. Go through it one more time. So listen carefully now: this has nothing to do with whom I'm seeing or not seeing. That is only in your head, Ewert. You're going to have to find the leak elsewhere. Maybe with someone *you* trust in *your* proximity? And perhaps like too much to see clearly?"

"I know you understand what I'm saying—you've been an inadvertent accomplice, Wilson. There is no other reasonable answer! The safe is here, in your room! The search warrant came from here!"

"Sit down."

"When you tell me!"

"Sit down, Ewert."

Reluctantly, Ewert Grens dropped into the visitor's chair.

Once the detective really got himself going like that it took a bit for him to wind down.

"I continued to investigate my office and the archive in the basement. Quietly. I requested a new group of analysts—and got some new answers."

Grens really tried to sit still. But he couldn't.

"And?"

Wilson bent over and tapped a hand against the heavy steel plate of the safe.

"In order to get into this, you need a PIN code, which in my case has never been written down, and a preprogrammed card, much like an access keycard for our doors. The new analysts made a total of four discoveries that proved how someone could get ahold of exactly that. Two discoveries up here, and two down in the basement."

"Discoveries?"

"The first, how they got the PIN, we knew before: a very small webcam hidden in a crack in the wall. One in here, directed at my safe. One over the archive counter in the basement, directed through the protective glass at the archive cabinet. When I entered the eight digits of my code, they showed up on the electronic display, and at the same time they were caught by the web camera. The person we're looking for was able to receive my code on their computer or phone—via live broadcast."

Then something started to happen in that office.

"At the very moment, Ewert, while I was here, doing my job!"

Their energies started to shift.

"*Our* job. Our *mutual* job!"

As Grens calmed down, Wilson became increasingly upset—as if only now was he starting to feel the impact of the crime he'd been subjected to. The chief of Sweden's largest homicide unit had been surveilled and used. The victim of an advanced coup in the very place such coups were supposed to be thwarted.

"The other finds were two directional antennas. One out in the corridor, one outside the archive. Not much bigger than the webcams, and just as easy to hide. They can catch frequencies up to ten meters away and pass them on to a card scanner and a card programmer. Whoever set up those directional antennas could then put a blank card into a programmer, push enter, and fill it with the same information that was found on my card."

When people like Wilson, who rarely got worked up, finally did so, it was different from when a person like Grens, who got worked up almost every day, raged around. It was more notable.

"So we have a double lock, Ewert! A PIN code that's only in my mind! A frequency only available on my square plastic card! And then somebody here—*in our unit, Ewert*—someone we trust, mounted that fucking special equipment in the corridor we pass down every day. To hurt us and our work!"

The reversal continued. Something that had never happened before.

For once, Ewert Grens was calm, and Erik Wilson had to be calmed down.

"I know exactly how it feels."

The detective superintendent was holding on to his boss's trembling shoulders, trying to push the suppressed anger that had started to ooze out back inside.

"Realizing you have to be suspicious of those we're

closest to. Because how big is the pool we're talking about? Twenty? Ten? Five?"

Wilson's face flamed red, just like his neck.

And when he tried to answer, he couldn't. Everything was stuck in that red flame.

So Grens continued.

"I asked Hermansson to spy on you, Wilson. Because you continued to withhold information that I believe is central. But she refused, and I didn't understand why. So I asked Sven to spy on her instead. Of course, he refused. It's the way we are, *we don't want, don't want, don't want* to see what we sometimes have to see. But Sven changed his mind. Started watching her. And no one, you should be clear on that, is sadder or more disappointed than I am—but it doesn't look good at all. Mariana Hermansson is behaving in a way she never has before. She's lying. Skipping meetings. Popping up in places where there's no reasonable explanation for her to be. Wilson—look at me—she might be the one we're both looking for. And I want you to investigate her from now on—because I'm too close."

4:33 PM
(1 day, 5 hours, and 29 minutes remaining)

"There. Black Audi. In front of the big gate. You see— he's stretching out his arm, turning his head a little, inputting the pass code. His face, soon, if he just . . ."

"I have him."

Piet Hoffmann and Gezim Latifi had been sitting on

the roof of a run-down warehouse, spying on the two-story house, which was guarded by the same two guards that Hoffmann registered on his last visit. After almost five hours, the man they believed they were waiting for finally arrived. The telephoto lens that Latifi used was much more advanced than the Albanian police equipment Hoffmann had seen so far, and he was pretty sure it had to be Latifi's own. The image of the driver was crystal clear. The sharp eyes, like an attacking hawk. The high forehead, the pale skin, the grizzled side-burns. After the gate opened and closed, and he drove into the yard and disappeared from sight, it wasn't long before the lights turned on in the downstairs hall, then in the stairwell that led upstairs.

"I suspected it was him—now I know."

"Know what, Latifi?"

"Who he is. The man you're looking for."

Latifi twisted one of the camera's buttons and the photographed face went up another magnification.

"Kosovo Albanian. From Pristina. But he's been popping up around here, in the Shkodër area, for the past few years."

Hoffmann guessed he was around fifty. And as each part of the snapshot became easier to see, like small photographs turning into a large photograph, it was possible to discern thin rings of gold in his earlobes and a winding birthmark on his neck that a dermatologist might recommend sampling.

"Hamid Cana. Reminds me a bit of your King Zoltan. Except he's alive. The kind you'll find dozens of hits in our registries for, but never any prosecutions."

Now the lights also turned on in the tower room, and through the window they caught a glimpse of him—or rather a dark suit that sat down next to what seemed to be a desk and switched on a computer screen.

"That house, actually the whole block of houses running due north, were once the home and work-places for political instructors back in the communist days. Our version of the Russian political commissar, party officials with great power."

Latifi grabbed a thin folder from his bag, took out a real estate map that he unfolded onto the sunny tiles of the roof. He circled the two-story house they were watching and pointed to one of its squares.

"That's the room he's sitting in. We know exactly what it looks like."

Latifi smiled.

"Government bureaucracy can be handy sometimes. Everything needs an application and everything has to be approved, a good way to provide jobs and keep peo-ple under control. So—in the national archive I found both the map and these."

In the folder was a bundle of loose paper. The archi-tectural drawings. For the very house they were look-ing at.

"The tower room, according to these very officially stamped drawings in my hand, was the political com-missar's office. Here you can see it in detail, Larsson."

Some people don't need explanations. They just know.

"In case you were ever planning to visit, that is."

Latifi folded the drawings and handed them to Hoffmann.

"Because if you came all the way here to find out who's sitting in that house and running the gun smuggling route to northern Europe—I don't think you have to look any further."

They both studied the images on the camera's display. The man with hawk eyes, gold earrings, and a cancerous-looking birthmark.

"How sure?"

"I'm not just sure, Larsson. I'm positive. He might not lead operations, but he's deeply involved. And I know because I was the one who wrote several of those reports of suspicion about him—and my immediate boss has continually thwarted my attempts to proceed any further. For the very same reason King Zoltan was never charged, too many of my colleagues on the payroll of the arms smugglers."

"Jesus, Latifi, I don't get how you can take it."

The Albanian policeman shrugged his wide shoulders.

"I, too, have a family to support."

Then the smile came back again—or, when Hoffmann thought about it, it had probably been there the whole time, ever since they pulled up to this old warehouse, forced their way in past a locked door, and made their way up to the roof.

"And now and then, Larsson, someone like you shows up—who needs my help spying on a two-story house and it gives me the chance to fuck with the system a little. It's easy to go back to work the next day when I know my boss will lose one of his sources of income very soon."

9:03 PM
(1 day and 59 minutes remaining)

"Grens?"

"Yes, it's me."

"Hoffmann here. Are you alone?"

"Go ahead. I'm in a good spot."

"I just sent a picture to your phone."

"Opening it now. I'm putting you on speakerphone. So I can look at it."

"Do you recognize him?"

"No."

"Are you sure?"

"The eyes, the birthmark—I would have remembered them."

"And the name—Hamid Cana?"

"Never come across that either."

"This is who the security officers called. The man who was sitting in an office on the second floor of the house you tracked the call to. Who took over, or at least works with whoever took over King Zoltan's weapons smuggling."

"And we know that because?"

"Grens, you were the one who persuaded me to trust Latifi. And if we do—then yes, we know."

"It's just after nine."

"I'm aware of that."

"Just a little more than one day left, Hoffmann, to find out who the man in that picture is working with in Sweden. The person who left three murders in their wake, that's *my* job to solve, and whoever is threatening your family, which is *your* job to solve. One day—then I have to let Zaravic out, and he might just come into possession of some papers and figure out who put him behind bars for six years and made him miss his son's funeral. If he gets that information, you and Zofia and the children will have every criminal in Stockholm after you—when it comes to things like that, they hunt in a pack. My search warrant didn't really pan out as planned, and I have nothing for a prosecutor to hold him in detention longer than planned."

"I'll do what I can."

"Wrong—you do whatever the hell it takes, okay? I don't want to know how, but make sure you get that fucking name."

Late night in Shkodër.

Piet Hoffmann looked around at the desolate bar.

Even here there was a clock on the wall that seemed to be counting down.

The crumpled napkin he kept at the bottom of his knife holster now lay in front of him on the bar counter, between a bottle of local beer and the phone that had just carried Grens's stressed voice. He ran a finger over the crosswords from one edge of the napkin to the other, chains of squares that became a plan, which had to be filled in and crossed out. He'd had two rows left, two words to solve, and now he crossed one more out.

Survive, eleven letters

P O S I T I O N I N G

But he left the very last one untouched.

Survive, fourteen letters

E—N—C—R—Y—P—T—I—O—N—C—O—D—E

The crossword's final boxes. In order to strike
through those, he'd have to force a man with hawk eyes
and an overgrown birthmark to talk. He was prepared
to go a long way, just as Grens had insinuated, without
going *too* far—a dead man could reveal no codes. He
would have to enter a house surrounded by armed
guards, get into a secured tower room, and then break
a man who had probably endured torture in the past,
but now had to be broken in just a few hours.

Because that man was the key to the person in charge
in Sweden.

Because time was ticking.

7:06 AM

(14 hours and 52 minutes remaining)

Cheese. Marmalade. Vanilla yogurt. Crispbread. Orange juice. And a cup of coffee for herself.

They'd woken up early. Not because they needed to,
sleeping made being here easier to stand, but Luiza
started crying at six thirty, inconsolably, and woke up
both Rasmus and Hugo, too. Now they were all
squeezed close together on the sofa, which until a few
days ago had belonged to someone else. Breakfast was
set on the ugly glass coffee table and the morning news
program was on the TV, which the boys had so far

mostly used for video games that all seemed to be in one way or another about shooting each other. She closed her eyes. For a moment, she was somewhere else. Home. Normal morning, normal breakfast. The spoons clinking against the yogurt bowls, the crackers crunching as everyone chewed at the same time. Until she couldn't help but look around at this apartment, which was so alien, and out through its window at a neighborhood she had never wandered.

But the news in the morning studio was the same. The morning host was presenting images from violent demonstrations ahead of a Paris summit, the US president was promising to lower taxes from the White House pressroom, and UN troops had been attacked while guarding a food transport in West Africa. The Swedish news was also a repetition of last week, and the week before that—an explosion at a police station in Malmö, a twenty-year-old man killed in Norsborg, two schoolchildren severely injured after a knife attack in Bergsjön. She had turned to Luiza to adjust her bib and entice her with the last few bits of oatmeal and the last spoonful of mashed bananas, when Rasmus screamed.

"Mamma! Look!"

His voice was as surprised as it was confused.

"That's our house!"

She didn't really understand what he said at first, just calmly wiped food off Luiza's cheeks and chin.

"Mom! Look now!"

So she did what Rasmus wanted.

The flashing images of a rapidly changing Sweden

were replaced by another picture. A war zone. That's what it looked like. Like when missiles accidentally hit civilian targets far from the heart of the battle. The house that filled the TV screen was in a Stockholm suburb, and it had been attacked, destroyed, a powerful explosion turned it into smoking ruins and left blast marks on the surrounding houses. The bomb, the TV reporter said in her neutral news reporter voice, had detonated less than an hour earlier, and the neighborhood had been partially evacuated.

Ice cold. Inside.

She froze in a way she never had before.

"Our house, Mom. It doesn't exist anymore. Do you see?"

Rasmus didn't seem to know if he should be afraid or excited that their house, their whole block, was on TV. But he saw how Mom reacted, how Hugo—his big brother, who knew so much more than him—reacted, so he stopped talking. They didn't want to hear what he had to say, he could see that they were sad.

Then the image changed to a report from the Swedish Parliament and politicians debating the annual budget. Normal again. The world goes on.

"Keep eating. I'm just going to the bathroom."

The cell phone was still behind the ventilation cover in the corner above the towel hanger, and she pressed the button for the only number that was preprogrammed into it.

"Piet, it's me."

She didn't know where he was. His voice was as clear as if they were standing next to each other.

"You were only going to call in case of emergency."

"This is an emergency."

"Zo?"

"We were just now eating breakfast in front of the TV. Me and the kids. And there was a news report about a house being blown up. Our house."

"What . . ."

"Someone blew up our house, Piet."

He hesitated a moment. Maybe it was the connection. If he was far away, that is.

"Piet—what's going on?"

"I still can't tell you that."

"Didn't you hear what I said? Our house has been bombed! It doesn't exist anymore! Everything is gone! Everything!"

She screamed.

"Now you tell me what's going on! Or I hang up and call the police! You decide, Piet!"

He hesitated again. It wasn't just the connection. She knew it.

"You can't call the police."

"So talk!"

"The more you know, Zofia, the more dangerous it is for you and the children. We've talked about that. Before. That people like me, who do what I did, we just know how much a person should or shouldn't know. And if you land in a situation, if you or Rasmus or Hugo or . . ."

"Piet? Tell me now."

She heard his breathing. The worry. That he couldn't control, and which therefore made him even more worried.

"Someone's leaking information at the police station, a dirty cop."

"A . . . ?"

"A cop. Who's working for criminals—and has access to all my records. Every secret meeting and every organization I informed on. Information they're using to make me do something I don't intend to do. That's why I found a live hand grenade in Rasmus's backpack. That's why I've masked my identity and hidden all of you. And Zofia, now I've broken off contact with those who threaten us—and that's why they blew up our house."

She held the phone tight long after they hung up, crumpled onto the floor, weeping. Sometimes that's the only thing left for a person who can't go forward and can't go back, even though it hurts so much to be still.

Then she opened the door and all her loves were waiting for her in the hall.

Rasmus at the front, weeping like her, then Hugo a step behind with Luiza in his arms.

"Mom, I . . . I want to be with you."

And Rasmus grabbed hold of her with no intention of letting go.

"Then you'll have to come in here with me. We have to change Luiza."

Rasmus slipped past her into the toilet as she spoke, worried Mom would change her mind, and she stared quietly at Hugo—her eldest, her wise son—as he handed over his little sister. She kissed his forehead, and then he was alone. Without any clue where he should go. The only thing he was sure of was that he wasn't going to wait in some strange hall for Luiza's diaper change or maybe bath when their house had just been blown up. After a while, he pushed the toilet door closed without Mom noticing. Now was his chance to figure out what he hadn't been able to last time. The floor inside the closet in the bedroom. The one that moved when he jumped on it, and that had a little black knob in the back corner. If he was quick and had some luck, he could sit outside with the closet door open and not block whatever was in the floor with his own weight.

It was nine quick steps from the bathroom to the bedroom.

He didn't walk, no, he ran.

To the closet. Squatted down. Pulled on the small knob.

And the whole floor . . . opened up.

The square of wood just disappeared and when he lit his phone's flashlight he was met by a large, round hole.

He leaned in and searched with his arm without reaching any stop. So he braced his legs against the low empty shelf, and lowered his top half into the hole. Then he reached it. A thin board. And when he knocked on it, he could hear there was nothing on the other side, it echoed.

The hole under the wardrobe floor led somewhere else.

Now he was sure.

This *was* what Dad meant when he said there was an escape route.

7:25 AM
(14 hours and 37 minutes remaining)

Keep going.

Keep going without feeling.

He was there again. At one of those moments that was always lurking, pulling at him. His longing to think about the only thing he couldn't think about, which was also the only thing he wanted to think about.

She'd said that their home had been destroyed, the center of their lives and their safety had been taken from them.

There was only one way to interpret that.

The people who threatened him were showing him they were prepared to take the next step if he didn't obey—and the next step was people, not a house of wood and stone.

So just like during the last moment, and the moment before that and before that, which wanted to fill him with doubt and longing, he now had to shield himself, avoid all emotion, never let that other reality in.

There wasn't much time left.

But it could work.

It had to.

"Bad news, Larsson?"

Latifi had chosen a café that opened early but rarely had guests until a few hours later. That's why they were alone, other than the owner, who was at the stove behind the counter warming up sugar and water that he proudly announced would turn into the world's best baklava.

"You could say that."

"Well here comes a little something to balance it out. My news is good."

He laid a large envelope next to Hoffmann's coffee cup.

"Don't open it yet. Wait until we part ways. The drawings you got when we were on the roof were from the general archive—these come from a much more classified vault. Highest confidentiality. I'm owed a few favors by a few officials. Last night I cashed a couple of them."

Piet Hoffmann knew what the Albanian police officer was actually saying. That he'd exposed himself to enormous risk in order to help a man he didn't know from a country he'd never visited.

"You already understand where all the rooms lie in relation to each other. The number of guards, surveillance cameras. Now you'll have access to all of the less official paths in."

"In?"

"When those houses were built for political commissars, they made sure to add a few secret entrances and exits. That was just the culture of one-party rule, that's how you did it, but the nouveau riche who own them these days don't know that."

Hoffmann had no idea what to say. "Thank you" wasn't even close to enough. But that's what he said anyway.

"Thank you."

Latifi nodded briefly. Embarrassed. Not used to handling appreciation.

"I also found out a little more about our man with the hawk eyes and the birthmark."

On top of the envelope he put down a photograph.

"Hamid Cana splits his time between two places. Most of the time he's in the house we were watching. But he also regularly travels a few miles up into the mountains to another house. To her."

A passport photo. A middle-aged woman with a slender face framed by long, dark hair. Few wrinkles though she seemed to lack makeup, a forced smile that exposed white, even teeth. She looked uncomfortable, but that meant nothing, very few are comfortable being photographed.

"A relationship?"

"Not by law. But a man who visits a woman his own age several times a week, sleeps over—well, what do you think?"

Hoffmann nodded. Relationship. But it didn't really matter. What Latifi was saying, what mattered, was that Hawk Eye left the two-story house regularly, he even spent some nights away. And that was when, with only a few guards left behind, an uninvited visitor might take the opportunity to enter through a secret tunnel few knew about, and avoid the extortion, violence, and perhaps even deaths that might otherwise be required to obtain the information he sought.

"How about a piece for you; coffee?"

The café owner had slipped over to the table and handed each of them a golden brown square that smelled like home and far away at the same time.

"The layers of sugar might be a little on the warm side—but I think you can still have a taste."

They each took a piece, both because it smelled like

heaven and to be polite, tried it, and thanked the café owner who was convinced he'd kept his promise and served them the world's best baklava.

"Well then, Larsson."

Latifi dried off his sticky fingers with a napkin.

"Do you have all the information you need?"

"If what you claim is actually in that envelope, then I have it."

"I still don't know what you're up to. Maybe that's for the best. But I've made sure I can be at your disposal all day. If you need assistance."

"Can you do that? Without exposing yourself to risk?"

"Listen, the fewer crackdowns I do, the happier my bosses are."

The café was still empty when Piet Hoffmann stood up, grabbed the envelope from the table, folded it, and slid it into his pocket. Keep going. Keep going. That's all he could think about, had to think about. Keep going to a secret entrance, an encryption code, a name for a Swedish contact that Grens could focus his search on.

8:36 AM
(13 hours and 26 minutes remaining)

A concrete foundation. Dressed in rubble. Only half of the brick walls still stood, a few metal cabinets stacked up, the rest was just black smoke coming from the corners the firefighters' water jets hadn't yet reached.

Ewert Grens asked the head of the rescue service just

one question when he first arrived. Now he asked it again.

"No bodies?"

"Still no bodies, Superintendent."

He walked down the closed-off residential street.

It didn't feel one bit better from a distance.

A violent explosion was always followed by a violent shock wave, and the hammock he knew Zofia liked to sit in with her youngest in her arms, singing her to sleep, had been thrown against the fence. The swing set on the backside of the house had been blown away, the hedge to the neighbors' that the boys crawled through lay in tatters.

Contact had been broken, and this was the result.

Grens hoped Piet Hoffmann was right, that his family was hidden somewhere else. In safety.

The sun's heat was combined with the heat of the smoldering ruins, air colored by soot. He saw Hermansson talking to the forensic technicians as they crawled around with plastic gloves and cameras, and the two cadets gathering witness statements from neighbors who had yet to be evacuated—their training periods had, in a very short time, included virtually every serious form of crime.

Sven walked over to him, looking tired, too many early mornings.

"We have to talk, Ewert. In private."

"Okay. Talk."

"First, this is—was—Piet Hoffmann's house, wasn't it?"

"Yes."

"And if I were to guess that this was related to every-thing that's been going on recently? The executions? The documents that disappeared from Wilson's safe? You asking me to follow Hermansson? No bullshit now, just answer me, Ewert."

"It's related."

"Then it's Hoffmann you've been collaborating with in a parallel investigation without telling me about it?"

"It is."

"And this—a bomb in a suburban neighborhood?"

"A warning."

"That's all you're going to say?"

"For now."

Sven Sundkvist had something else to discuss. An excerpt from a recent analysis of the blood traces they'd secured on a kitchen window during the search of Dusko Zaravic's apartment.

"No matches."

Sven held out his phone and the enlarged text of an email from the National Forensic Centre.

"You see? The blood isn't in any of our criminal da-tabases. And—it also doesn't match any employee of the homicide unit."

Ewert Grens tried his best to make out the letters that were still too small no matter how much Sven had enlarged them. But what he heard was good news, even though a match, a nearly one hundred percent identifi-cation, would of course have been better. This meant that no colleague of theirs had broken in. It didn't rule out that someone had changed sides, had sold out their own world, but no one could be linked to the possible burglary meant to cover tracks.

Sven Sundkvist had said what he came to say and had started to head back to a house that was no longer there. Grens joined him.

"Sven?"

"Yes?"

"I want you to inform Hermansson and the cadets to wrap up their work here and head to my home."

"Your home, Ewert?"

"For a meeting that we can only have there."

9:58 AM
(12 hours and 4 minutes remaining)

They'd all squeezed in, five people was one too many according to the small metal plate in the elevator, but since the two cadets and Mariana Hermansson were quite slim, and Sven was hardly what you'd call overweight, only Grens really contributed much toward reaching the maximum weight limit. EWERT AND ANNI GRENS. Both names stood above the mail slot. Despite all the years that had gone by. The detective superintendent thought he caught a few pitying looks, but didn't react to them. He could have any damn names he wanted to on his own door.

"Before you step in."

He unlocked, but didn't open it completely, hesitated with his hand on the handle.

"Mariana, you dropped in unexpectedly a few days ago—so you know a little more about what we'll be talking about in there. Sven, you've also been here once before, but that was a long time ago and not particularly pleasant, I think we can both agree. And for you, Lucas and Amelia, this will be your first opportunity and the fact that this is happening during your training period is as odd for me as it is for you. But everything about this investigation has been odd."

He looked at them, one by one.

"Because this is it—whether you've known me for many years or just a few weeks, the following rules apply: when you cross this threshold and enter my hall, you're entering into silence. Into an alternative police world. Are you okay with that?"

They nodded. All of them. And at about the same time.

"Good. Then you're welcome inside. Continue straight as far as you can, then turn right into the kitchen."

While Grens grabbed some extra chairs from the living room, his four guests stood in front of a whiteboard with documents pinned to it and arrows pointing in various directions. It certainly looked like a police investigation. And the longer they looked at it, the more it turned into a police investigation.

"You guys have made some progress since the last time I was here."

Mariana Hermansson was close to the board, reading the reports, examining the pictures.

Sven Sundkvist showed up at her side.

"Ewert . . . what is all this? Investigation results and forensic analyses that I've never seen. And when Mariana says *you guys* have come a long way—she sure as hell isn't referring to you and me."

The detective superintendent asked them to sit down, put the coffee-maker on, and brought out five cups and a fresh roll of Marie biscuits. He poured a cup for each of them, then turned to the two cadets.

"You heard Hermansson's voice? She tried to hide it, but she didn't manage at all. And you heard Sven? He almost never swears. What you hear from both of them is annoyance. Since I know them well it's quite obvious to me. And do you know why they're annoyed? Because they've never been through this before. Even though they've worked in the homicide unit for twenty and ten years, respectively. And as for me—I've worked there twice as long as either of them, and I've never been through this. So what I'm doing now, what I've been doing, is in no way based on experience, it's just how I think this will work out best. And therefore, Lucas and Amelia, I think it's time for them to stop being annoyed and instead focus on solving a crime. What do you say, sounds reasonable, right?"

He didn't look at either Sven or Mariana. He didn't need to. They could stay annoyed at him for shutting them out. They understood why. Their boss had considered both of them suspects.

"But here's the thing, Lucas and Amelia, I haven't had any other option, but to work from here. And now that I've invited you all in because I need your help, you, too, have no alternative. The kitchen table you're sitting at is as close to the police station this investigation will get."

He tapped his finger on a red cross in the middle of the whiteboard, which had four green lines leading out from it to four pictures of hit men involved in the arms trade. Three dead, on their backs, and one sitting in a jail cell for his third and final day.

"I trust no one, and you trust no one. Because what we're looking for in our little side investigation is—a police leaker. One of your colleagues thinks it's more fun and profitable to work with whoever's face should be sitting there on that red cross. It's because of a police leak that we have three murders on our hands. And it's because of a police leaker . . ."

The detective superintendent opened the biscuits and offered them to the group, but found no takers. So he grabbed a couple for himself.

". . . that Zaravic was locked up on such vague grounds. Because I, too, have someone in place—a man who needs to be left to his own devices while he works his way closer to that face we don't yet know."

"In place?"

Sven was really annoyed. At having been suspected of betrayal, confused for a quisling. In his world, which was based on loyalty, nothing was worse. He knew that trust took a long time to build, and could be destroyed in an instant.

"Ewert—in place? What the hell does that mean?"

"I'm sure you've all started to figure this out. You saw what was written on the mailbox, which somehow managed to survive the blast. *The Koslow Hoffmann family lives here.* Our very best infiltrator. Piet Hoffmann has traveled to northern Albania and a city called Shkodër on my behalf. We believe that the top man of this arms smuggling operation is based there—and that he will connect us to the man who's shooting people in Sweden."

"The top man? Who?"

"We don't really know yet. I thought at first that it might be someone I'd arrested before who was connected with the dead like Zaravic—but he's been executed, too, in the same way. We now have a new name that Hoffmann was able to track down with local help. But whether that's the top man, or just someone who's working close to him, we don't really know yet."

Grens looked for the first time directly at Mariana and Sven. They were sitting here because he invited them in. Needed them. He'd counted on the cadets' reactions, they'd responded almost solemnly, proud to be part of something so real, and ready for anything. But for this to succeed, he was dependent on his closest colleagues. What he was going to have them do, he couldn't really say yet. That depended on Hoffmann. But he must, as their supervisor, know that they, too— even though he'd insulted them with his lack of confidence—were prepared to invest themselves totally in an investigation that wasn't even close to officially sanctioned.

He watched them. Until they finally nodded.

They were with him.

"Thank you. Then it's like this. I can . . ."

Grens glanced around for his phone, there was a small clock on it.

"What are you looking for, Ewert?"

"My phone."

His guests started to help him search. But found nothing more than their own cell phones.

"Okay, Sven, can you check yours? What time is it?"

Sven Sundkvist turned over the phone that lay in front of him.

"Quarter past ten."

"Thank you. So here's how it is: I can keep Dusko Zaravic locked up for twelve more hours. That's how long we have to prevent a fourth murder—either Zaravic's or Hoffmann's."

"Hoffmann?"

"I can't tell you more, not yet. But the whole Hoffmann family is in danger."

"But if you won't explain, how are we going to . . ."

"Twelve hours, Sven. That's how long we have to find the police leak. Piet Hoffmann from where he's located, and us from here. Okay?"

12:03 PM
(9 hours and 59 minutes remaining)

The house that Piet Hoffmann had broken into lay opposite the white two-story house, and according to Latifi it, too, was built for one of the Communist Party's political commissars. Today, it was owned just like the two-story house, by a member of the nouveau riche, but it had neither armed guards nor a forest of antennas on its roof. After a couple of hours watching the house from his car, he was certain the owners weren't at home, and he could break a window on the backside and move freely inside as he followed the path on the drawings that led down the stairs to the basement and then to the boiler room at its far end, which was warm, narrow, and whose air smelled like old oil, but he didn't notice. He focused on the brick wall behind the big furnace, trying to read it, running his hand over it, letting his fingers wander across each seam. That wall—according to the secret documents that his new Albanian cop friend had dug up—was the key. He checked the right half, from floor to ceiling, and he was approaching the middle of the brick wall when his phone rang. A phone that only four people had the number to. Zofia—who knew not to call for the next few hours. Grens—who had agreed to wait until Hoffmann contacted him. Latifi—who was going to call only when the two-story house was empty, which could take a while. And Andy—who sat in a studio apartment with its blinds drawn watching images of people who needed protection, and who was only supposed to call about one of the families he was guarding—the one that had seven cameras pointed toward them, who were hidden in a ground-floor apartment in Gamla Sickla.

Hoffmann's family.

"One of the kids just disappeared."

"What?"

"Camera 6, on the apartment's front door. One of

the kids, the older boy I think, went out into the stairwell. And didn't come back."

"Andy—went where?"

"I don't know. He didn't go out the front door. And he's not visible in the stairwell."

"My boy."

Hoffmann had whispered that, and it was difficult to make out over a long-distance line.

"What did you say?"

"I said we have to take care of it."

"What do you want me to do? Drive over there? If so, no one will be guarding the others. Or should I call Carlos, who's probably asleep before tonight? Boss, this is what I warned you about, a protective target that's so far away from the others, I . . ."

"You sit tight. I'm glad you called me. I got this."

The floor had opened up, and he had stared down into a hole. A secret exit. Hugo had just managed to put it back down and closed the closet door, when Mom and Rasmus and Luiza came out of the bathroom after the diaper change. Then he had waited. And waited. Until the right moment, when Mom was busy with the others.

Now.

She didn't see when he turned the lock and snuck out into the stairwell.

She didn't see when he continued on toward the basement.

That's where he had to go.

To find out what was down there.

Their escape route.

Zofia?"

"We weren't supposed to . . ."

"Where are you?"

"In the kitchen. Lunchtime. I'm making . . . what is it, Piet?"

"Hugo? Do you see him?"

"He's playing video games."

"Do you see him?"

"He was just on the sofa. And I hear the sound."

"Go there."

"Wait."

"Are you there?"

"Soon."

"Zofia, I . . ."

"Piet?"

"Yes?"

"He's not there."

It really smelled like basement. And it was creepily dark with just his cell phone flashlight to light the way. But he was close. There. Behind the thick door with round metal wheels he had to turn to open. If he got in there he would be standing right under the apartment and the closet. Hugo pulled and dragged at the sluggish wheels on the heavy door. Until it glided up. And he could step into a space he thought was called an air-raid shelter. They didn't have one at home—well, they didn't have anything at home anymore, because it didn't exist—but he'd been in shelters before, at Willy and Jari's, classmates of his who lived in one of the high-rises in Farsta. It was even darker in here. Pitch black. No windows. He pointed his flashlight to the ceiling. Searching with the light beam. Until he discovered a bit where the white paint seemed a little whiter. If he pushed over the big metal rack that stood in one corner—he had no clue what it was for—he could climb up and reach the ceiling. And when he knocked on the surface with the slightly different shade, the sound was just like when he knocked on the hole in the closet—empty, echoing.

Zofia? Listen to me. Hugo isn't on the sofa. He left the apartment. And you have to follow him! Even though you weren't supposed to leave. None of you should!"

"How do you know that? How do you know he left?"

"I just know it. Hurry."

"Are you watching us?"

"Not me."

"Are you having us watched?"

"Hurry, Zofia!"

"I'm on my way."

"He can't be seen!"

"I'm soon . . . Piet, the front door. You're right."

"What?"

"It's unlocked."

"He hasn't gone far, so if you . . ."

"Hugo? Where . . . where did you come from?"

"What exactly is happening, Zofia?"

"Just when I was about to run out into the stairwell, he was standing here."

"Ask him where he's been!"

"Hugo, you can't leave. You know that."

"Where has he been!"

"Where have you been?"

"What did he say?"

"That he wanted air. But changed his mind."

"Air?"

"That's what he says."

"Lock the door. And have a serious talk with him. You promise me, Zofia?"

Piet Hoffmann had tried to call Andy three times to tell him that everything was fine, the boy was back. No answer. That wasn't like his most reliable guard. Didn't he hear the phone—was he on his way anyway? In that case, he'd soon realize that the family he was guarding was actually Hoffmann's own. It shouldn't matter that Andy knew. But it felt wrong now, after he chose not to tell him, even lied to him.

His hand, fingers, searching every inch of the brick wall. There wasn't much wall space left, and he still hadn't found what he was looking for, and it was at that point that the heat and stink of the boiler room started to penetrate his consciousness.

The brick at the bottom left.

The seam between the bricks was a little rougher there, his fingertip's journey not as smooth and even.

He pressed the stone, very hard. And the whole wall started to move. From that seam, an awkward door slid up.

Houses built for high-ranking politicians, linked with secret tunnels.

That was what Latifi's papers had shown. Tunnels created for escape, or unofficial meetings, or maybe it was just the dictatorship's way of reinforcing the feeling of inaccessibility. A solution reminiscent of the one he'd used in a house that—according to Zofia—no longer existed, brick walls were forgiving because seams were rarely symmetrical and therefore tricked the eye that didn't know where to look.

He turned on his flashlight and stepped into the tunnel. He pushed the same brick to shut the hidden door behind him. Seventy-five meters, a little hunched over, with everything he needed on his back. Then, according to the drawings, the next brick wall would be waiting for him.

12:52 PM
(9 hours and 10 minutes remaining)

The sun reflected off the waxed floor of the Kronoberg jail as Ewert Grens exited it. Dusko Zaravic was still sitting in the fourth cell on the left, and just as unwilling to talk as the first time—he'd stared at the floor while the detective superintendent questioned him about his role in the Swedish weapons trade, mumbling *no comment* to all the questions about his relationship to Albania, and told the detective to go to hell when the conversation turned to his three dead colleagues. They were both professionals, and they knew how it worked. Grens needed something concrete that would constitute evidence or suspicion enough to extend the arrest warrant, Zaravic knew the less he talked, the less likely they'd be able to keep him.

Elevator down, a new corridor, elevator up.

Erik Wilson was waiting as promised at his desk, and also as promised, he hadn't changed his mind.

"I'm not contacting the prosecutor. I'm not negotiating the arrest. I did that last time, Ewert, after your subtle threat, but not again."

"In that case, the bastard will be released tonight."

"You got your chance. But you haven't shown me anything to hold him."

"If he's released—you know what that means. The papers stolen from your safe, Wilson. You know what's in them, about Hoffmann, what he used to do for us, for you, and you know what will happen if Zaravic finds out."

"We can't just lock up someone who's not suspected of committing a crime."

Grens looked at his boss. There was nothing else to say right now. Wilson was technically right—and Grens wasn't showing all of his cards.

"And Ewert, I understand why this is so important for Piet Hoffmann. But why is it important to you? We both know what Hoffmann is good at and that you're helping him—so what's he doing for you that I should know about?"

That was a question the detective superintendent wasn't ready to answer. Not as long as someone was leaking information from this unit. He stood up to leave, but Wilson stopped him.

"By the way, Ewert, this is yours, right?"

There were two cell phones on Wilson's desk. One of them was extremely similar to Grens's own.

"I was looking for you earlier. The explosion, Hoffmann's house, I wanted to know more and . . . when I called you, a phone started ringing outside in the corridor. Your phone, Ewert. It was on the copier. Guess you must have taken off in a hurry this morning?"

The phone he and his small team had searched for in vain at their meeting on Svea Road.

"On the copier?"

"Yes. Please keep it with you now. This goddamn investigation . . . I want to be able to reach you at any time, Ewert. Put it in your pocket and leave it there."

Grens thanked him and for once did as he was told, slipped it into his inner pocket, and left the room. On to the coffee machine for two cups, black.

He'd had three days. He didn't anymore.

Time was running out.

1:29 PM
(8 hours and 33 minutes remaining)

One hundred and four steps. Between the wall at the beginning of the tunnel and the wall at its end. Here, according to the paperwork, another brick would open the door. Now he had to wait. Until Latifi texted that Hawk Eye and his guards had left the house.

2:14 PM
(7 hours and 48 minutes remaining)

Piet Hoffmann couldn't wait any longer. On the other side of this brick wall there was a phone or a computer or a safe that contained information that would lead him to a distorted voice and the organization that threatened him. He was so close, but time was ticking and Latifi's signal never seemed to arrive. He had to be sure that the passage worked. So he pressed the brick, which this time sat at the top in the center, and heard that same metallic click as at the other end of the tunnel. A piece of the wall slid up. A door with uneven edges. And he was hit with the smell of oil, the sound of a dripping tap—another boiler room, but in the basement of that white two-story house with a tower.

2:50 PM
(7 hours and 12 minutes remaining)

He rested, stretched out on the concrete floor beneath a jumble of pipes of various sizes that ran back and forth between modern heat pumps and very old oil boilers. Now and then he thought he heard voices, but knew that was impossible; the boiler-room door was closed, and according to the drawings it was far from the basement entrance. It was easy to imagine life when your own life didn't feel real. Just a few days ago, he'd set the kitchen table in his family's home, opened the window, and called out to two boys to come inside and eat their snacks. Now that home no longer existed, the boys were hidden with their mother and little sister, and he was in a disguise, armed, lying in a basement in northern Albania.

3:15 PM
(6 hours and 47 minutes remaining)

He jumped a little when the text arrived. The phone buzzing in his palm. It was time. Latifi, who was watching from the roof of the warehouse, wrote that Hamid Cana had just driven away from the house, accompanied by his personal bodyguards, which usually meant an overnight trip to the woman in the mountains. Two guards remained outside, and inside, a man cleaning upstairs. Piet Hoffmann left the boiler room and headed for the stairs, then up to the ground floor. New message from Latifi. The guards were facing the gate and the cleaner was in one of the bedrooms. Hoffmann hurried through the kitchen and living room to the next staircase, toward the upper floor, and could now see the guards' backs, hear the vacuum cleaner.

Quick steps to the tower room, he pushed the handle down.

Locked.

He continued into the next room, probably the mas-

ter bedroom, careful to close the door behind him. He
stabbed the plaster ceiling with his knife, and then slid
a small battery-operated jigsaw, not much larger than a
screwdriver, in where it could now grab hold. He
pushed a chair over, and lifted himself up through the
hole. The attic space between the roof and the ceiling
was smaller than he expected, but large enough to be
able to crawl. When he estimated he was in the middle
of the tower room, he sawed open a new hole, dropped
his backpack, and then jumped down himself, landing
on a handmade rug.

3:45 PM
(6 hours and 17 minutes remaining)

Piet Hoffmann snuck over to the window, carefully
peeking out—the guards' attention was still directed
toward the iron gate and the surrounding wall. Attacks
from outside, not in.

He'd turned the tower room upside down and still
couldn't find what he was looking for.

What he needed to survive.

Nowhere in the Albanian arms dealer's office were
there any documents that revealed the Swedish members of the organization.

Nor did the phone, which he found in a now broken-
open desk drawer, lead him any further—all communication had been encrypted.

The computer, which he had seen the hawk-eyed
man working on via Latifi's telephoto lens, was also

protected—encrypted information that couldn't be accessed without the code.

There was only one more option. He had to find the encryption key.

It had to be here, somewhere. He was sure of it. No one who regularly changed his RSA code—a combination of fifteen or maybe even twenty numbers and letters and question marks and dashes—could keep that in his head. That kind of asymmetric encryption code had to be written down.

If he found that key, he could decrypt the contents of the computer. See where the track led him. He'd infiltrated every kind of criminal organization and knew that whether they were selling drugs or humans or weapons, they all had one thing in common—they kept good books. Not because they were proud. Or because they weren't aware of the risk of preserving evidence. It was about preventing unnecessary violence. Making sure that everyone involved could see that the money was being distributed fairly. It minimized the risk of these constitutionally suspicious individuals suspecting they were getting screwed and starting to war against their own instead of rival gangs and the police.

He looked around the room he'd already searched.

Looked at everything he could see. And everything he couldn't.

"Latifi?"

He'd called the Albanian policeman who was watching the house from the roof, who probably caught a glimpse of him now and then.

Maybe he even saw him right now.

"Yes?"

He had a feeling how this might play out.

"The drawings. You got them handy?"

"Yes."

"The tower room. How big is it?"

"Wait."

Hoffmann heard a rustle, heard the click of Latifi's glasses case.

"Six meters and thirty-five centimeters long, five meters and twenty centimeters wide."

"Just a second."

He chose the wall on the opposite side of the window, where he was least visible, walked across the room, one foot in front of the other from wall to wall. He knew that his feet were twenty-eight centimeters long, and after two rounds he had an answer he felt was correct.

"I thought so."

"What, Larsson?"

"The room is smaller than I remembered the drawing. More square. I got five meters and fifteen on one side and five and twenty on the other."

"One meter and twenty centimeters shorter in one direction."

"Yep. And I think I know why."

A dark oak built-in bookshelf covered most of the far wall. He'd run across brick walls that turned into doors only a few times, but hidden rooms were more common. They were also usually easier to detect. He had completely missed this one. Cleverly constructed—even now, when he concentrated on every corner, edge, and strip of wood, nothing revealed itself. He knocked, listened, grabbed hold of shelves, pressed and wiggled various curved ornaments. Until he, more or less by mistake, leaned against the glass door of an illuminated cabinet with a hodgepodge of trinkets inside, and just like the brick wall—there was an almost inaudible click. The glass door just followed his hand back, and before he knew it, the entire shelf wall was gone.

A hidden room.

One meter deep, a few meters wide. With a single object inside. A safe.

Here.

The encryption key *had to be* inside that heavy steel structure.

4:01 PM
(5 hours and 59 minutes remaining)

He'd blown safes before, most recently in northern Africa. But this time, a regular, fast explosion wouldn't work. The whole neighborhood would be able to hear that, and he didn't want them to find out he was here before time was up. It would attract the guards, and if people were to die, there was a law-abiding police officer not far away who would be forced to act—and Hoffmann wanted that police officer on his side, not against him. Above all—it was too risky for the contents, the encryption key.

He would have to open it in another way. A slower,

more cumbersome way, one he rarely used and that would eat up time he didn't have.

He took a small drill, detcord and a detonator, a plastic pipe and a tightly rolled hose out of his backpack. He drilled a hole through the safe—the outer layer of steel, the middle section of concrete, the interior of steel—and poked through the thin pipe connected to the hose. Now he needed water. Latifi's latest message had said that the room next door was being dusted now, and the cleaner never even noticed Hoffmann until two hands were around his chest, and soon he was bound to a pipe inside the bathroom. With one end of the hose on the faucet, the time-consuming work of filling the safe with water began. Piet Hoffmann checked to make sure the first liter had reached its destination and sat down on the floor. Now all he had to do was wait, and check now and then to make sure the guards were still in their places, with their attention turned in the wrong direction, ready to meet any external enemy.

5:43 PM
(4 hours and 19 minutes remaining)

Filling a safe with a few hundred liters of water via a very small drilled hole no more than eighteen millimeters in diameter was like filling a bathtub through a McDonald's straw. It took even longer than feared.

He was looking at the time, estimating about fifteen minutes more, when the safe should be full and the detcord could be poked in and ignited.

When the phone started to vibrate in his hand. A text message. From a number he didn't recognize.

Not one of the four he'd given his number to. Neither Zofia, Grens, Latifi, or Andy.

A text with a link to a voice message. That was it. No instructions, no greeting. He pressed the link and was thrown straight into a recorded phone call between two unknown voices.

> *"It took you a while to answer."*
>
> *"Who the hell are you?"*
>
> *"Aren't you at all curious how a phone ended up in the mattress in your cell?"*
>
> *"I don't give a shit."*

The same distorted voice that threatened him, and which he'd broken off contact with.

Hoffmann had no doubt. That was the voice that spoke first.

> *"You got a phone, now a gift. Look at the stool next to the bed, the one anchored to the floor. You're not supposed to be able to unscrew the seat—but you'll be able to. And when it comes off you'll be looking down into a hollow pole."*

And the second voice, the man who had been called, had a slight accent.

> *"Just tell me who the hell you are and what the fuck you want then hang up."*

He recognized the man's voice. But couldn't place it. However, the situation was slowly becoming clear. The man being called was in a prison or in a jail.

Who was he?

And why did someone want Piet Hoffmann to listen to this?

"I'm not hanging up. You'll be grateful for that fact. Also, when we're done, you'll have a phone inside the Kronoberg jail that you can use however you want. How many of your neighbors have that?"

Kronoberg jail?

Now he knew. That voice.

Zaravic.

"I don't get what you're talking about."
"Have you unscrewed the seat?"
"No."
"Do it. And tell me what you see."

There was a bump. Then Zaravic sounded like he was farther from the phone. And a scraping, rustling sound as paper was unfolded and smoothed out.

"You found it?"
"If it's a bundle of papers you're talking about, I did."
"Good. But let's start with you. You're sitting in a jail cell even though there's no reasonable evidence."
"Not the first time."

"But do you know why?"

*"Because the idiots think I killed my friends. Or
that I'm next."*

*"They probably thought that was the case. And
that's the official explanation. But that was never the
main reason. Okay? The main reason was there's a
cowardly little shit who instead of doing what he's
supposed to do decided to work off the record for
Grens and follow a trail to Albania. And that
cowardly little shit was a little worried some
documents that have gone missing might reach you
and mess up his pretend police work."*

"Still don't know what you're talking about."

Piet Hoffmann had clicked on the link sent from an
unknown number.

Now he realized why. The distorted voice wasn't
just talking about him indirectly—he was speaking to
him.

He shouldn't listen anymore.

He had to focus on the safe, which would soon be
filled with water.

But he let the sound roll on.

Trying to understand what was happening.

"Zaravic? Are you still there?"

"I'm here."

*"If you look at the first paper, which has a red 'I'
in the right corner. If you read the fifth line, you'll
see a name. Paula. A code name that belonged to a
successful infiltrator. On the next row you'll see the*

initials EW. Stands for Erik Wilson, who was a
handler in the homicide unit at the time, and is now
its chief. You're reading from a report written
during the police's secret and illegal criminal
infiltrator project."

"And?"

"Go a little farther down. Rows eighteen to
twenty-three, I underlined them. There you'll see
another name. Yours. Because right there, this
infiltrator, Paula, is the one who gathered the
evidence that sentenced one Dusko Zaravic to prison
for assault and kidnapping, and made him miss his
son's funeral. And isn't it true, Dusko, that you've
been searching for a long time for the person who
ratted you out? Now you'll know. If you look at the
next paper. There's a copy of what was kept sealed in
an envelope, Paula's real name. Do you see?"

"No."

"Ah, you don't see. Because I've crossed it out."

"What the fuck . . ."

"But I promise: you'll get it—along with the
address where his family is hiding—when you're
released in a few hours. Yes, unless that cowardly
little shit stops what he's doing and heads home to
complete the mission I gave him. He really should
do that. Because he has children, too. Just like you
used to."

That was the end of the recording. And Piet Hoffmann understood exactly what it meant. If Dusko
Zaravic got that last document.

But he didn't understand the rest. Like how a phone and classified documents had been placed in a closed jail cell. Or how the distorted voice could know he was in Albania tracking down a dead weapons dealer. And, what he understood least of all—was how this number, which he gave to only four people he trusted, had ended up in the wrong hands.

5:59 PM
(4 hours and 3 minutes remaining)

A few more liters.

The safe was completely full now.

He poked in the detcord, then detonated it.

It made a dampened bang inside that left the contents mostly whole. But when the safe door came loose, it hit the wall hard and the metallic sound was sharp and loud. *That could have penetrated through the window of the tower room.* He stood still. Listening. Had the guards heard anything? Did they turn their attention to the house instead of the gate? Were they on their way—here?

No voices. No sound.

After waiting ten minutes, he decided to examine the interior of the safe.

The banknotes packed on the upper shelves were soaking wet, but would retain their value when they dried. He wasn't interested in them. He got down on his knees in the water that flowed out over the floor and searched the lower shelves for anything that might contain the encryption key. He soon found, beneath a jewelry box and a couple of smaller gold bars, a little notebook with a black cover. He knew of course that documents could be damaged by water, by the blast and gas expansion, but also the notes in a closed notebook would probably still be intact as long as they weren't written down with the wrong kind of pen.

6:12 PM
(3 hours and 50 minutes remaining)

He had flipped to the last page of the notebook and cried out.

From joy, from relief.

Everything was possible again.

There they were—row after row.

Written down and crossed out RSA codes.

Neither pencil nor marker—Hamid Cana had used an ordinary ballpoint pen, and its ink wasn't affected by the water. And at the very bottom, on a line that began with yesterday's date, stood twenty letters and numbers and characters in no particular order at all, which had *not yet been crossed out*.

The current code. With this he would be able to decrypt the contents of that computer and find whoever was trying to take over the Swedish weapons market by threatening his family and murdering their competitors. He could tell Grens, who would then have enough time to act.

Piet Hoffmann didn't laugh, he was too busy, but his elation felt almost tangible, softened his whole body as he left the safe and pushed the secret entrance back into place. He'd packed Cana's computer and phone into his backpack and was climbing up to the hole in the ceiling, when his phone buzzed again. The same number. But no link this time—just a picture. At first Hoffmann couldn't make out what he saw. Then he magnified it. Now he could see—but he didn't want to.

The picture was of Andy.

A dead Andy.

Slumped over at his usual place, his head had those unmistakable double bullet wounds.

The rest of the studio apartment was visible in the background—the drawn blinds, the monitors with their various surveillance images. And when Hoffmann enlarged a little more, he saw something else he wished he hadn't.

On one of the TV monitors, obviously intended to be centered in the composition, just as much as Andy's slumped-over body, you could see that the surveillance cameras had caught two faces looking out a window.

Zofia. And Hugo.

6:23 PM
(3 hours and 39 minutes remaining)

Piet Hoffmann stood in the middle of the tower room's drenched floor and stared at his phone. He knew it was going to ring now.

"Good evening, Hoffmann. You thought you could break an agreement. That has a cost."

The distorted voice.

"You just received some information. First a link to a telephone conversation. Then an interesting picture. Just so we're clear on where we stand with each other. Okay?"

He was shaking.

An absurd picture.

Andy, staring at him, appealing to him, with extinguished eyes. Zofia and Hugo looking out through a window without knowing they were no longer protected.

He had never understood that fear could hurt so much.

"Good. Then I need you to listen to me. We know now where your family is hiding. But, unfortunately, we heard you're running around in northern Albania and won't be able to do what you're supposed to in time."

They had tracked down his position even though no one knew where he was.

They had access to his new, secret number.

Hoffmann could see only one explanation—the police leak wasn't just located in the police station and the homicide unit. Grens had been right the whole time. The leak was in the detective's inner circle.

"We don't like executing families. Hit men are no problem, a Piet Hoffmann now and then is fine, you've chosen to be part of this twisted world of your own free will. But a wife? Three young children? They never had a choice. So I think there might be a way. We can postpone their deaths for a short time. Because we happen to have another little job that you can do right where you are. You

have three and a half hours, if I count correctly, and if you can finish in time, we won't execute your family. Yet."

An electronic, distorted voice with no gender, no identity, who seemed so distant and monotone. But for a moment they almost sounded personal. As if they felt something, were more than just arms dealers.

"It's like this: You went to Albania to look for Zaravic's former employer. Realized he was dead, and started to seek out his successor. We know that much. And we want you to continue that. You find him, kill him. If you send us proof, a picture, we won't give Zaravic that last document when he's released tonight. The one with your name on it."

A new mission? With just a few hours left?

The voice that for a moment became almost personal, revealing for the very first time a glimpse of something that wasn't just programmed confidence and inaccessibility. A tiny, tiny crack in their invulnerability. And Hoffmann thought he knew why. The insight the organization's Swedish branch had been given into Grens's private investigation hadn't just revealed that the detective superintendent—via Piet Hoffmann—was on his way to the other end of the smuggling route, where everything began. It had also revealed that *if* the Albanian leader was located, and *if* he were forced to speak, the Swedish members' identities would be revealed, too. That would be the end for them. So they'd rather sacrifice one of their own, because a dead man can't talk. But they had no idea that Hoffmann already had access to all that information. A computer and a decryption key that were already in his backpack.

"Fail, Hoffmann—and you'll be alone by tonight. Carry out the mission, and we'll talk again, while your children and your beautiful wife will have at least a little longer—we are far from done with each other."

Then the moment was over.

The monotonous, distanced, genderless voice was back.

"Oh and by the way. Avoid alerting the police. If we see even one cop at the apartment building where your family is hiding, we'll blow up the whole damn place, regardless of our agreement. We're pretty good at that, as you know."

6:29 PM

(3 hours and 33 minutes remaining)

"Can we talk?"

"Talk."

"You were right, Grens."

"Yes?"

"The police leak is very close to you."

"I used to think so. Now I've changed my mind. No one I trust has betrayed me."

"You saw I destroyed the phone. Broke contact. You even warned me about it. Only you and Zofia and Latifi and Andy, one of my employees, got my new number. Andy was just murdered, but would never reveal anything. Zofia is the only one *I* trust, and Latifi also never talks, I've seen that for myself. So that leaves you, Grens. And if it's not you, I don't think it is, it's someone who has been close to you in the last twenty-four hours."

"What did you say? *Just murdered*? What do you mean by that?"

"I feel sick about it. But I don't have time. Not yet. I'll send you the address when I hang up. Take care of him."

"If you . . ."

"Grens—they murdered my employee and called my new number to tell me about it! *Someone knows that I'm involved and that I'm here!* How many people are aware that I'm working with you? That cop lady who met me in the kitchen, she's one—who else? Are there more, Grens!"

"Calm down."

"My time is running out while we . . . I can't afford to calm down when your dirty fucking cop finds out about everything I do, or while they wait outside the house where Zofia and the kids are hiding! They even smuggled a phone and documents into Zaravic's cell! He knows now that an infiltrator got him locked up for six years—and when you let him out tonight, Grens, he'll know it was me."

6:34 PM
(3 hours and 28 minutes remaining)

First, the sound of heavy steps.

Then a loud voice.

Ujë.

He didn't know very many Albanian words, but he'd picked up that one. That's why he'd stopped at the gas station on his way to Shkodër. Two bottles, lukewarm. And that was what he'd been buying and carrying around in a city plagued by Mediterranean heat.

Ujë. Water.

That was what someone was shouting outside the door.

He hurried to the window. The yard was deserted.

The safe door was thrown against the wall, and that sharp ringing leaked out.

Two phone calls had distracted him while the sound had attracted the guards to the house. Now they had discovered the water running across the floor and seeping through the gap under the door.

They'd soon force the lock.

Piet Hoffmann looked around, searching four walls that had turned into a death trap.

6:36 PM
(3 hours and 26 minutes remaining)

Good training.

That's what he thought when the armed guards broke down the door and made their way across the wet floor. Perfect pattern and in complete control while they quickly secured the area.

Good training—but they made *one* mistake.

Even though they were looking for an intruder in a locked room, where the window was closed and intact, they never looked up.

And when they reached the bookshelf that covered

the far wall—where the leak seemed to originate—
without understanding how or why shelves of trinkets
would drip large amounts of water, they stopped in exactly the position Piet Hoffmann had hoped. He just
needed to lie on his stomach on the attic floor and
lower his gun slightly through the hole and press the
trigger.

6:43 PM
(3 hours and 19 minutes remaining)

"Sven? Hermansson? Put your cups down and come
with me."

Ewert Grens, after a short search, had found them in
the kitchenette at the end of the corridor, each with a
fresh cup of coffee in hand, surrounded by stacks of
papers spread across the table and chairs, a few documents even sat on the dishwasher and fridge. Any other
evening he would have taken a seat, relieved not to have
to go home, grateful to be in the company of his closest
coworkers.

"Now!"

This time, he didn't even slow down, just kept walking toward the other end of the corridor, expecting
them to follow his shouts. Soon he heard those familiar
steps—Mariana's had a determined bound, Sven's were
smoothly compliant. If it was true that the movement
of our feet is an extension of our personalities, he wondered sometimes how he must sound.

"What's this all about, Ewert?"

"Life and death."

He pressed the elevator button, and Mariana and Sven caught up to him, stood on either side.

"Isn't that always the case around here?"

"Right now the difference is just a matter of a few hours."

"What are you talking about?"

"That Zaravic, in a locked and well-guarded cell, has learned the one thing I *didn't* want him to know."

Two elevators and three corridors later, the detective superintendent stormed into the eighth floor of the Kronoberg jail and could barely contain himself while the guard searched for the key in his rattling bundle. Dusko Zaravic was lying on his bunk, no longer in his tuxedo, just the shapeless uniform of the correctional facility. He didn't seem especially surprised when three police officers barged into his tiny cell.

"Well, well, you're a little early."

"Stand up."

"And here I thought you were gonna hold me until ten. But of course, I'd be happy to head home now. How about a beer this evening, Superintendent?"

"Get up so we can search your cell!"

Sneered. That's what Zaravic did. While Grens and Mariana and Sven turned over what little there was to turn in that cell.

"Did you lose something, Detectives?"

"Undress."

"Mmm . . . *that* I did not see coming. You and me, Detective?"

"The sweater, pants, underwear, socks, slippers. You

shake them while I watch, then drop them into a nice little pile on the floor."

The sneering smile turned into a sneering laugh as Zaravic exposed his pale, naked body, and posed with exaggerated coyness for his three visitors.

"Do you like it? What about you, beautiful police lady? And you, my silent stranger? Or maybe the old cop, maybe you . . ."

"Grab your fucking buttocks, bend forward, and spread until I'm satisfied. Okay?"

Zaravic had been detained and imprisoned before. He shrugged, turned around, and did as he was asked.

"Like this?"

"Get dressed."

"You seem disappointed, Superintendent. Were you looking for something? Because if there were anything, I mean, like a phone or maybe some paper, you know, the kind of thing you could end up with in a cell, well, if that were the case then I guess I would have pretended I needed to go to the bathroom not that long ago, and flushed all that shit. I mean, if I were to have it."

Grens didn't say a word as he pushed Sven and Mariana aside, threw open the cell door, and rushed across the hallway toward the toilets. He pulled on the plastic gloves he always kept in the inner pocket of his jacket and knelt down with aching legs and hips in front of one toilet bowl at a time. But no matter how far he dug or how far he pushed his hand into the pipe, he met only water. The phone was gone. And with it the possibility of tracing where the call came from.

He was furious.

But he'd never let that smiling bastard see it.

He commanded Sven and Mariana to leave the cell and slammed the door without so much as a glance at the still-naked Zaravic, then hurried to the guards' glass cage.

"Do you have a spare cell?"

"What?"

"A cell. Unoccupied."

The young guard seemed to think he hadn't heard right.

"An empty cell?"

"Yes?"

"What are you gonna do with that?"

"Is there one or not?"

The third cell on the opposite side of the hall from Zaravic was until just a few hours ago home to a suicidal junkie. It wasn't particularly clean. But Grens didn't notice that or the pungent odor as he ordered Sven and Mariana to come inside and close the door behind them.

"Which one of you?"

Sven and Mariana looked at their boss, then at each other.

"Which one what, Ewert?"

"*Goddamnit—who!* Who leaked the information about Hoffmann so fresh, so unique that it only could have come from one of very few I trust, someone close to me. Really. Fucking. Close. There's no other explanation. And I've had enough!"

Ewert Grens used to hit things when he couldn't keep this rage inside. Better than hitting people. The shiny rolling instrument carts at Forensic Medicine in

Solna made a quivering ring that corresponded to the anxiety he sometimes felt in the presence of the dissected dead, and his own coffee table in his office made a dull thud when it hit his corduroy sofa. Here there were no tables. So he used the white walls, an almost silent sound that barely registered even though his knuckles turned the white paint red.

"Please, Ewert, please calm down."

"Calm down, Hermansson? I've worked here for more than forty years! I'll be retiring soon! But I have never—*never*—been used like this!"

He and Hoffmann shared that. They didn't trust anyone. They talked about it, how now and then you have to *choose* to trust. But one thing that Grens realized was when a person chooses to trust, they also expose themselves to the risk of being betrayed.

"Answer me!"

And that was exactly what had happened.

"Which one!"

Mariana Hermansson had backed against one cell wall as he screamed at the top of his lungs. She stepped forward, stood close to him again; she simply didn't like when people tried to scare her.

"I warned you, Ewert, do not doubt me again. I even told you it would be the same as losing me, either you trust me or you don't. But you won't listen! You run around accusing me and Sven and Wilson, and then you do it again! I understand that this is stressful, that the whole investigation is personal for you—I'm even happy that you can feel anything at all. But now, Ewert, you've lost not only me, you've lost yourself."

"You've changed your pattern, Mariana."

"What?"

He was no longer screaming.

And yet, his statements were sharper, more aggressive—they cut deeper.

"I've had you followed. You lie about canceled meetings, spend time in places you have no connection to."

"What did you say? *You had me followed*? Who . . ."

She stopped short. She'd seen a movement on Sven. Some discomfort on his face.

Shame.

That was the expression. She was sure of it.

"You . . . ?"

And now he looked down at the cell floor.

"*You*, Sven? Have *you* . . ."

"Yes. Ewert asked me."

A cell is a tight space. Too tight for two people's rage.

And now Mariana Hermansson's fury crashed into that of Ewert Grens.

"Ewert?"

"Yes?"

"When we're done with this, when this investigation is over—you and I are over, too."

"Excuse me?"

"After ten years? Everything we've gone through? And you still don't know if you can trust me!"

"People will do anything if they're forced to, Hermansson. Is someone threatening you? Like Hoffmann? I would understand if that were the case, and if so, we can turn it back on them, if you just let me . . ."

"Ewert, it's *me*."

"What?"

"I admit it."

Now Sven lifted his gaze from the floor.

Now Grens punched the wall with his other fist.

"You, Mariana?"

"Yes, it's me. I'm Wilson's secret relationship."

It was so quiet.

Still.

Despite three people breathing in so little space.

"Now I'm getting a little . . . Wilson?"

"Yes."

"So you and he . . . ?"

"Yes."

There was a small stool next to the bunk, just like in all the other cells. Grens sank down onto it, sank into himself.

"So . . . so . . . *that* was what your small lies and canceled meetings and strange walks were all about?"

"Yes."

It was no longer just his hands and knuckles . . . it was as if he'd run his whole body straight into that cell wall. He'd been going in the wrong direction and someone had stopped him.

Dizzy.

That's how he felt.

"Well, that's, well . . . very nice. That you found someone, I mean. And that Wilson found someone. That you no longer, well, need to live alone, I mean. But still—he's your commanding officer, Mariana. You work in the same unit. One of you is going to have to transfer. That's what the regulations say. Don't you know that?"

"And why do you think we didn't want to talk about it?"

The stool was hard, lacked any back support, and it was difficult for him to sit without pain. But he couldn't stand up, not yet. He asked Sven and Mariana to leave the cell and wait for him at the guard's box. He had heard what she said. He knew her so well, her serious ways that he'd come to depend on so much. *Lost me. You and I are over, too.* Unlike him, she'd never say that and not mean it.

He had nobody other than those two. His closest colleagues were also his closest friends.

And he already knew how it would feel, once he had time to feel. When the last few hours of this race against time were over, and he could do no more for Hoffmann. Despair. That was what awaited him if she really did leave him, and he hated that goddamn terrible feeling, he'd tried his best to bear it after Anni disappeared.

7:15 PM
(2 hours and 47 minutes remaining)

The brick at the center and top, a light press. Then that metallic click. And a wall slid open.

Piet Hoffmann left the boiler room's oily odor for the smell of mold and moisture in a seventy-five-meter long tunnel. He had reopened the hidden space behind

the bookshelf and dragged the two bodies inside it—
they'd lie there until their stench seeped out like a dead
animal stuck in the wall. He'd made his way through
the house and down to the basement, worried with every
step that the gunshots might have attracted more notice.
Halfway into the tunnel, he relaxed somewhat, he was
on his way. Out. Away. Toward somebody he thought
he'd seen for the last time. Because when Latifi gave him
the message that Hamid Cana had left his house with his
hawk eyes and his bodyguards, Piet Hoffmann assumed
he would never have to think about where that Albanian
arms dealer was again. When he came across the decryption key in a watery safe, he was convinced. Their paths
would never cross. Then everything changed. Again.
The organization's Swedish branch realized they were at
risk and sacrificed their boss to protect themselves. And
to ensure that, they renewed and intensified their threats
to a hidden family. They now had access to their address
and their executioner.

The other end of the secret tunnel, the exit that was
his entrance a few hours earlier. He pressed the brick at
the bottom left and the built-in door became visible as
if out of nowhere. According to the text message he'd
just received from Latifi, this house was still empty, the
owners still gone. Hoffmann hurried through the basement and up the stairs to the kitchen and hall and the
broken window. He checked his watch. He needed to
squeeze out every minute, hold on to the seconds as
long as he could, so he could locate Cana and determine how their limited time would end.

7:33 PM
(2 hours and 29 minutes remaining)

Latifi could have heard the gunshots. If he had, then he would have been forced to act, regardless of who was shot or why. The murder of Albanian citizens, even if they were in the employ of the mafia, couldn't be ignored, even by a cop working on the good side. But he didn't say anything and asked no follow-up questions when Hoffmann climbed into his car, stating that he'd found the information he'd come for. As if they had an unspoken agreement. As long as the Albanian policeman didn't know, he didn't have to act.

"And where to now? The airport?"

However, he could see the obvious. Piet Hoffmann was stressed. When he should have been relieved.

"That is if you really *are* finished now."

As if the Swedish visitor were hunting for something. Maybe even *someone*.

"I have one more thing I have to do."

"Yes?"

"A question I have to ask Cana."

"I thought you said you had all the information you need?"

"About something else. That's not in his computer."

"And it's about . . . what?"

"I can't tell you. It's between me and him."

Latifi hesitated, looked at Hoffmann, judging him.

"So what you're saying is that you don't want to go to the airport?"

"What I'm saying is that I need you to give me the address of the house where he's staying."

Latifi stretched his big body, unconsciously running his hand over his square face. He seemed to weigh what he knew against what he suspected.

"I can't give you the address."

"Latifi, goddamn."

"But I can drive you there."

Hoffmann nodded. Thankful. And, of course, realized this clever police officer's motive—by following along, being on-site, he hoped to prevent or at least mitigate the consequences of any possible confrontation.

Latifi started the car, and they rolled out of the neighborhood.

"Hamid Cana is one of the criminals I keep track of. Because I think it's my job. Even though I, as you already know, can't arrest him. Or, I can always arrest him but I've learned it's pointless, he's released before I even finish the paperwork."

It was still light, but the first signs of twilight were approaching as they left the city on a large highway headed east.

"I don't just know that he makes his living selling off the Albania arms surplus—I can prove it, and in another country that would mean his conviction. I also know that the woman he's with right now, where we are headed, is the same person who owns the house you were just inside."

"Same woman?"

"The same."

"Mistress and *also* technically the owner of their headquarters?"

"Mistress—yes, but she's involved as more than just a legal technicality. I'm pretty sure they run the guns together. Vesa Lilaj. Forty-seven years old, and nothing more serious on her record than a few parking tickets. But she's related to this on another, higher level—she's the sister of the man who was once in charge of the gun smuggling network to northern Europe. And then he was murdered. Power struggle, if our information is correct. A clear execution in . . . Sweden, I think, your homeland, Larsson. His wife and children were shot, too. At least that's the info we got. That will be— twenty years soon? The murder of a whole family that you, as a Swedish police officer, would of course know well?"

"What was his name? The brother?"

"Mirza. Mirza Lilaj."

Piet Hoffmann wasn't familiar with the names Mirza or Vesa Lilaj. But then again he wasn't a police officer either. He wondered if Ewert Grens might have heard of them. Or the murders Latifi was referring to. He had to remember to ask him about it, later, when this was over.

"No, sorry, twenty years ago was before my time."

"Mirza Lilaj was—and this comes from verified surveillance information, there *were* a few good cops before me—one of the network's clearest leaders until his death. And he was replaced by King Zoltan, who was one of the only clear leaders until *his* death. That murder we talked about the first time we met, I'd guess there was another power struggle, even if I can't confirm it. But when Zoltan was replaced four years ago, the leadership was again divided into two. If my info is correct, and it usually is. Hamid Cana and Vesa Lilaj. He's the front, the outward face. She makes the big decisions, works behinds the scenes."

Now twilight arrived. The dark gently pushing away the light. The car's headlights became two searching eyes on a road that was getting more narrow, winding, and rough.

"There's a map in the glove compartment. If you take it out, Larsson, you'll see on page seven the property we're heading to. I've circled it."

Hoffmann flipped through a well-used atlas that Latifi had probably had since his first day on the job. His personal guide through Albanian crime. Each page contained little arrows in different colors pointing to streets and buildings and a lot of scribbled notes that were impossible to read.

The circled property on page seven sat by itself at the end of a road that led straight up into the mountains, and its nearest neighbor seemed to sit two kilometers earlier.

And that was where he had to make his way—alone.

Hoffmann glanced at the Albanian policeman. Renegotiating so that he could drive the last bit by himself was pointless. Latifi had made up his mind—if there was going to be a confrontation it was best if the authorities were there to act as an airbag. But overpowering him in the car, or trying to anyway, and then continuing on by himself, did not feel good—this was a decent man, and besides, even if he succeeded it would cost Piet time he didn't have.

"Can you stop over there?"

With the map on his knee, he suddenly had a better option. He knew where they were heading.

"At the gas station."

"Now?"

"I need the bathroom."

Latifi glanced at him without slowing down, a look that was used to searching for alternative agendas, and it wasn't entirely convinced.

"You seemed to be in such a hurry."

"I didn't really have time to take a piss in either of the houses I broke into. I was busy."

As they passed by the gas station, Latifi was still glancing at his passenger. A couple of hundred meters later, he slowed down, made a U-turn, and drove back. He parked wedged in between two other cars, windshield facing one of the big windows.

"I'll grab a coffee while I wait. You want one, too, Larsson?"

On either side of the gas station there sat a half-full cafeteria and a small packed arcade. A place to meet in what was otherwise deserted terrain, maybe the only place in this area where you could go for company on a weekday evening.

A lot of people and lots of cars—it was perfect.

"Would love a coffee. Thank you."

Hoffmann smiled at Latifi. That always made it easier to hide uneasiness at one's own lies.

"And when I get back from the john I'll finally be ready to drink one again."

Because he wouldn't be. Coming back.

He followed the robust metal signs that led the way to the public toilets on the back of the building, opened the door to the men's room, and was met by the stench of urine. On the right, a urinal that hadn't been scrubbed in a while, on the left, three stalls with shitty toilets. He checked to make sure he was alone, and acted quickly.

He removed his stomach. He waved two fingers on his right hand until the vacuum released and the prostheses slid off.

He poked away the hanging eyelids, the crooked nose, the enlarged nose wings, and the large silicone piece that constituted his fluffy cheeks and chin.

He tore off the mustache, ruffled his well-combed hair, unbuttoned the shirt, and used the knife to cut the pants above the knee.

Then he threw everything except the prostheses into the trash.

The man who walked out of that toilet in shorts and a T-shirt a few minutes later was much younger, much more fit than the man who walked in. Though maybe not as well dressed. And he walked in the opposite direction, toward the back door of the cafeteria, and settled down on a vacant chair while looking for Latifi. There. On the other side of the window. The Albanian policeman was already in the car with a plastic cup of coffee, waiting for his Swedish colleague. Piet Hoffmann put a hand over the cigarette lighter that lay on the table, grabbed it as he rose to his feet, and used the cafeteria's back door again. Now he headed along the back of the building toward a small auto repair shop and car wash, which only had room for one car at a time. He slipped inside and over to a long workbench, looking at the tools that were hanging in perfect order on hooks on the wall. He grabbed a screwdriver, a wrench, and a thin sheet of metal that resembled a blade gauge. And then he walked in a wide circle around the gas station area before using the cover of a small grove of trees to enter the parking lot for guests who were planning to stay longer than just a trip to the toilet.

Stealing a car in Albania took him back many years. Down here it was still common to drive those old Mercedes models that were once his favorite. Dusty, often with more than two hundred thousand kilometers on them, and no modern technology that got in a car thief's way. He looked around, made sure no one was watching, and lay down on his back on uneven gravel, sliding in under one of the four possible cars. He cut the cable that connected to the horn, crawled out, and pushed a screwdriver into the tank lid lock, twisted until the air pressure dropped and all the doors were unlocked. He sat down in the driver's seat and warmed the thin piece of metal with the lighter until it was hot enough to insert into the ignition. He turned and rooted around with it, pulled it out again, warmed it, turned again, warmed, turned. Melting the pins on the inside of the lock a little more each time. He then chose one of the keys from his own keychain: now that there were no pins inside the ignition, just about any of his keys would work.

Piet Hoffmann switched on the headlights, so as not to attract attention, and just as he turned out onto the highway, he caught a glimpse of Latifi, still sitting in the car with an extra cup of coffee that was getting cold.

8:36 PM
(1 hour and 26 minutes remaining)

The last persistent rays of sun seeped out where the mountains touched the sky. Soon the landscape would be as black as it was deserted. Piet Hoffmann drove the stolen Mercedes as fast as he dared; his map was only in his mind, and he didn't want to risk missing a crossing and losing more time by having to double back. Seventh exit on the right. Then the third exit on the left, still paved. Then the last five kilometers on winding gravel roads and an even denser darkness.

And just as he passed the last neighboring house and turned off his headlights, his phone started ringing. Latifi. Hoffmann didn't answer.

It rang again, he let it.

Then an angry text.

Where the hell are you?

He stopped and turned off the engine with just a few hundred meters left. A slow walk along the fence of the property, and he was sure there was no external security. In the city the two houses he broke into had been protected by straggling rolls of barbed wire, here the visitor was met by an elegant iron gate framed by white pillars and green plants. He climbed up and jumped over.

The ground was dry, and with no flashlight his steps landed in cracked soil occasionally, a couple of times he stumbled over low, sunburnt bushes. If he turned, he could make out a few lights scattered in the valley, large farms with beautiful groves of grapes and olives.

He checked his watch.

Just an hour. Until death.

Zofia's death, Hugo's death, Rasmus's death, Luiza's death.

Or the death of Hamid Cana, someone he had never met, never talked to—an Albanian gunrunner who had been sentenced by his own colleagues just an hour ago.

9:08 PM
(54 minutes remaining)

He'd snuck in, step by step, hunched over as low as he could get.

The last stretch, from the three-car garage to the rippling fountain, he slithered.

Now he lay in a grove of five thin, newly planted orange trees, fifteen meters from the house and with a full view into the illuminated rooms.

Four people.

He was starting to feel sure there weren't more.

Hamid Cana he recognized, his jacket hanging on a chair, shirtsleeves rolled up, comfortably leaning back in a leather armchair with a glass of wine in his hand in what seemed to be the living room. Opposite him, also with a wineglass, sat the woman who, according to Latifi, owned both this house and the two-story house in the city, who together with Cana led this gun-smuggling organization. Vesa Lilaj. A beautiful name for a beautiful middle-aged woman, who laughed and gestured and filled up more wine, perhaps in love, maybe even happy. In the kitchen, two bodyguards stood leaning against a long row of cabinets, both in suits that were more elegant than what you usually see in the Balkan area.

Piet Hoffmann waited.

Not sure for what.

Some movement—a visit to the bathroom, a walk down to the wine cellar—whatever got Cana alone, or those bodyguards at a distance from their protective target. Twenty minutes. That was as long as he could wait. Then he had to act, no matter the risk.

9:31 PM
(31 minutes remaining)

No movement. No change. Other than time ticking by.

He had to make a decision.

Taking shots from here was possible. Cana constituted a perfectly lit target, his head exposed, his chest exposed. But since the bodyguards had all the knowledge of the surrounding terrain, which he himself lacked, he wanted to get closer, maybe even inside the house, to be sure he succeeded.

One slow step at a time.

Wrapped in darkness.

He'd reached the small fence that marked the beginning of the entrance, where the gravel path turned to granite squares, when protective darkness suddenly turned to naked, angry light. When all of the outdoor lighting switched on simultaneously. Without realizing it he'd passed by some sensor, and the movement he'd waited for in vain came as Cana and Lilaj put down their wineglasses and turned and tried their best to see outside.

It all happened very fast.

Piet Hoffmann took his first shots through the hall window at the bodyguards who weren't expecting a confrontation, and didn't have their weapons up, and then hurried toward the front door. The next shot penetrated the window of the living room, then Hamid Cana's white shirt. Vesa Lilaj sank to the floor, unarmed, seeking cover while the shooter ran into the house.

9:40 PM
(22 minutes remaining)

When Piet Hoffmann screamed *don't fucking move* to the woman on the floor and then took a picture of the man lying beside her and whose heart had been pierced, it was the kind of moment Grens sometimes talked about, a moment that seemed so arranged, bizarre, and awful that the viewer had to take a few steps back to make the surreal turn real again. He took more pictures, got close to those lifeless eyes, pulled up the dead man's shirt and zoomed in on the bullet hole, then one more, one last shot of the blood still oozing out of him. And then he sent them to the phone number that belonged to that distorted voice. He'd made it—Zaravic would soon be released, but he wouldn't be told where his own family was hiding.

Piet Hoffmann felt his legs getting heavy and his arms hanging without any will of their own. Thirsty, dizzy. He'd hunted as far as he needed to, and when he was done there was nothing left.

He just wanted to lie down, between the dead man and the weeping woman. Curl up. Fall asleep and wake up in bed with Zofia at his side, the sound of the children's gentle snoring in the house that was their home, even though it no longer existed.

Then the phone buzzed again—confirmation that the pictures had been received.

But no, that wasn't it.

That buzzing. It told him his text was never sent.

Fuck.

Fuck.

His phone had no reception. The signal was gone.

He hurried into the bedroom, the office, the kitchen, the hall, the guest bedroom. No signal there. Just the house's Wi-Fi, asking for a password.

He returned to the woman who was lying as quietly as he'd told her to.

"The password. To your network."

She looked at him. But said nothing.

"Answer me—the password for your network! I know you understand English!"

She stayed silent. So he shot her. The lower leg, as little damage as possible.

"Answer me!"

She shook her head defiantly. He shot again. Left arm.

"You can . . ."

She was in pain, it showed on her face, and she spoke haltingly a few words at a time.

". . . keep shooting. But you'll get no help from me."

She looked at him, challenged him. She meant what she said.

He would have to find another solution.

He ran through every room of the house again. Emptied closets and turned drawers over. Until he opened a cabinet that looked like a broom closet. There it stood, on the shelf at the top. A router.

He remembered now. Passwords often sat on the bottom of the router, a factory code with small and large letters and numbers.

He lifted up the square black device and turned it over.

And there—there it was.

zfqbgs3dwv

He looked for the local network, entered the code.

Waiting.

Waiting.

And . . . yes.

Yes!

He was connected again, sent the pictures of the dead man again.

The only thing left was enduring the wait—for a signal to reach where it was going, out there, up there.

He counted seconds until that became too much, instead he started to pace uneasily back and forth in the house—stacked firewood in the fireplace, ran his hand over the sofa's fabric, which reminded him of a pair of armchairs his grandparents once had, crouched under the glittering chandeliers and stood in front of a bookshelf with few books, but many photographs in golden frames. He looked at the one that was closest to him. The woman who owned the house, whose name was Vesa Lilaj, she was just a child in this picture, he was sure of it, dressed up in fine clothes at a photographer's studio. In the next, she sat with a tiara in her hair at a fancy restaurant, probably together with her big brother, mother, and father, a glass of juice in her hand, toasting a life that seemed so obvious.

Now she was lying on the floor, shot in one arm and one leg, holding onto a life partner who had stopped breathing.

Piet Hoffmann put down the picture of the past doing its best inside a gold frame, walked from room to room, was about to give up, stop his meaningless search and send the message again, when he finally heard a weak buzz. He hurried to the table where he'd put the phone, picked it up, but suddenly hesitated, unable to push the message symbol.

If the photographs of a dead man hadn't made it. If they hadn't arrived in a telephone in Stockholm.

It would be too late.

9:56 PM
(6 minutes remaining)

He wept.

Not like the woman on the floor who had lost her love.

This was the same pitiful little cry as the first time he balanced Rasmus's new toy in his hand and realized he was holding a lethal weapon, the kind that stuck fast somewhere at the bottom of the throat before it finally decided to ooze down into the gut.

But this time it was a cry of relief. The photos had made it. The proof that his mission was completed, and that Zofia and the children were still hidden in safety.

Felt so easy to run across the dry earth and climb over the iron gate and drive away in a stolen car. Back. For one night in Shkodër, then a flight home in the morning. After a few kilometers, just at the start of the valley where the houses were denser and the people about to go to bed more numerous, a pair of headlights pierced the darkness. A car heading in the opposite direction. And when both drivers slowed down in order not to crash in that narrow passage, they briefly caught sight of each other through their rolled-down windows. Hoffmann and Latifi. The Albanian police officer, after a toilet visit that never ended, realized his Swedish colleague had deceived him and continued the journey alone. And soon, when Latifi reached the property at the end of the road, he'd also realize there was no longer any confrontation to prevent.

Piet Hoffmann sped up without ever noticing how the potholes made the car sway and hit his body like little knives, or how the gravel let go in those sharp curves and the deep ditches came rushing closer. If running and climbing had felt easy, this felt like flying, he was done, he was free. Absolutely free! And he wanted to hear it. That's why, for the very first time, he called that distorted voice for answers.

"*Yes?*"

"You didn't get back to me."

"*Back to you about what?*"

"The photographs you requested, the evidence that my mission was completed."

"*We got your little illustrations. But too late.*"

He froze.

A sharp icicle fell through his body.

From his mind down to his chest.

"I sent it at 9:56, six minutes to spare. *My* phone confirms *that.*"

A short, unpleasant silence.

That was what Hoffmann heard as this icicle began burying itself inside him.

Finally the distorted voice answered.

"*10:07—five minutes too late—the pictures were received. My phone confirms it. So when Zaravic was released he was met not only by his lawyer, but also by the address where your family is hiding. And, as you can probably understand, he's already on his way.*"

rive, for fuck's sake!"

Piet Hoffmann screamed into his phone.

"Zaravic is on his way! You have to go there, now!"

But Ewert Grens didn't really understand.

"Lower your voice. This damn phone, I don't know, it doesn't seem . . ."

"Atlas Road 41. Gamla Sickla. First floor on left side. Zofia and the boys and . . . *now, Grens, now!*"

Last year when a boy who had come to trust him was found dead in a refugee foster home, Ewert Grens had run for the first time in a couple of decades. The detective superintendent, whose hip was shattered once and never moved the same again, for a moment chased shadows without pain and without limping.

Now, not only did he feel like he was running, he was.

With Sven and Mariana just a few steps ahead, through corridors and down stairs, toward his car on Kungsholms Street.

nother long day trapped in an apartment that wasn't theirs. Because they had to hide. Because Dad disappearing and guns hidden under the sink and Mom destroying SIM cards in acetone were all things that meant something dangerous was going on. But it didn't feel dangerous. Sitting on the edge of the kitchen table in front of the window looking out on a boring street where nothing happened. He'd being staring for a half hour into the darkness and only counted four cars looking for a place to park, nine people walking home, two dogs who peed on the same exact lamppost. Still, it was more than yesterday at this time; then only seven people had walked by and one dog, a little tiny one.

Four cars and nine people.

If he didn't count the people sitting in the big black car. The people who parked on the other side of the street and then didn't do anything else, didn't get out. If they did, his count would be higher. Two more, it looked like anyway, unless someone was sitting in the back seat.

"What are you up to?"

Mom. He hadn't even noticed her. She was also good at sneaking. And it was so nice when she ran her hand through his hair.

"Nothing. Looking outside."

"Time to sleep, Hugo."

"Why? We're not doing anything tomorrow."

"Because . . . people need routines. *We* need them. So things can feel at least a little normal."

He lingered on the kitchen table. If they got out of the car, at least for a little while. Then that would be eleven people. A record.

"Some people are sitting out there, Mom. You see them? In the black BMW."

"Where?"

"There."

He pointed. And she saw them.

"I think, they look like . . . like your dad. Security guys. Sometimes Dad makes sure we're guarded. Because he wants to know we're okay."

She caressed his cheek, Mom had kind hands.

"Five more minutes, Hugo. Then you brush your teeth, okay?"

"Okay."

Over there. At the tree, where the road turned.

What luck.

A new dog, that wasn't here yesterday. That meant three dogs. And a tenth person, the old lady holding the leash, who looked kind of like how he remembered his grandma.

It was completely still again. Not so much as a bird or a cat to count. Then he noticed something strange.

The two men Mom thought Dad had sent. They were putting something on. Stocking caps, now? In the middle of summer? And finally they climbed out of the car, making his count twelve, another new record, he thought, just as the men pulled their stocking caps over their faces. Black masks. They were heading straight toward their front door, their apartment.

Toward him.

Mom. Mom!"

Hugo screamed as loudly as he dared. But Mom was slow, she didn't understand.

"Mom! Hurry!"

Then she came. And he didn't need to say more. She saw what he saw, realized what he realized. The two men in black masks were on their way here. They weren't guards—they were the danger.

"Away from the window!"

Mom grabbed him so hard it would probably leave a bruise on his arm, she never did that. But it didn't matter, he understood why. He ran after her, in to Rasmus who was lying in bed playing a football game with the hand control on his stomach, and Luiza who was sleeping next to him and whimpering anxiously, as if she knew what was about to happen.

"The extra security door!"

"Hugo—there's no time."

"We have to close it, Mom!"

"Stay here, I said! With me, with us. And be completely silent."

There was just a short staircase up to the entrance.

Seven steps, he'd counted them. That's why it was possible to hear when people came and went. He didn't understand how the others who lived here could stand it. But now it was a good thing. They could hear when the door to the building opened and closed. They could hear two sets of feet with hard soles walk then stop. Outside their door.

Mom pulled them all close on the big bed, holding them at the same time. They sat there very, very close to each other, and it felt very serious, even Rasmus didn't ask any questions or move a muscle the whole time—Hugo couldn't even remember his little brother ever being that silent and still at the same time.

Then he heard something much louder than footsteps. Someone was trying to tear into their door. Hard metal pressed against the door, pressed, pressed, until it started to give.

They had a minute, maybe less.

And Hugo knew something that Mom didn't know, that the black masks didn't know either.

"There's an escape route."

"Lie still, Hugo. Quiet. In my arms."

"A secret path. The kind Dad likes. Hurry up, Mom!"

He got up and opened the closet just a few steps away.

"Hugo, listen now, I . . ."

"Look here, Mom."

He lay on his knees outside the closet with the door open and searching with his hand for the little knob that would open up the floor—found it, just where he remembered.

"The whole bottom, Mom, like a hatch."

He pulled it. The unsteady floor that had rocked when he first jumped on it, now followed his hand up. He moved so Mom could see. A round hole. That became a doorway to the basement and the air-raid shelter, as he hung down with his upper body and pulled away the plasterboard.

A powerful crash in the hall.

An even larger part of the front door had broken.

The black masks would soon be inside.

"Mom, I'm jumping down. It's not that far. And then I'll catch Rasmus. And then . . ."

"Jump, Hugo. Jump!"

She looked sad when she said it. But determined.

He crawled into the hole, braced his hands against the wood of the basement ceiling, hanging there with his feet down, straightening out as far as possible. And let go. It was a pretty good landing. When he looked up, Rasmus, younger and smaller, but more agile, always had been, his little brother landed softly, Hugo hardly needed to help him.

"Mom, listen. There's an iron stand here, I'll push it over and you can hand Luiza to me. Bend down into the hole. Do it, Mom!"

Her little boy. Who was so big, so wise.

With Luiza tight between her hands, she leaned over and down into the hole in the floor of the closet, stretching every joint in her body, and when Hugo reached his little sister's foot, Zofia loosened her grip. Luiza seemed unaware that she had changed hands, that Hugo, balancing on the iron stand, had ever for one moment not been holding her.

"And now, Mom, now you can . . ."

When the front door couldn't withstand longer, it fell heavily backward, into the hall, and the bang was as loud as a gunshot. Zofia barely had time to close the hatch, close the closet door, and turn around. That was it. Then they were in front of her.

We heard children's voices."

They cut off the escape route between an unmade bed and a closed closet. They were taller and wider than Piet, intense and at the same time in command, and they were carrying guns she'd never seen before. Their black masks made their eyes animal-like, staring and aggressive.

"Little boys. *Your* boys."

Zofia had often imagined this. Not because she wanted to experience pain or anxiety or because she was trying to understand what Piet had experienced so many times. It was to prepare herself. As if she'd known for a long time that life would bring her to this moment.

"I used to know your husband a bit back in the day. And I happen to know he has not one, but two boys— the ones I just heard."

But now that it was happening, she didn't feel the way she'd always expected to. She wasn't shaking. It wasn't hard to breathe. She wasn't afraid.

"You don't wanna talk? No problem. We've searched

for children before, found them under beds and behind shelves, dragged them out against the protests of their hysterical parents and done what we came to do. But that was just a job. Pay the rent, put bread on the table."

Because fear came from being lost, filled with doubt—and she had no doubts. She knew exactly what she was going to do. What she had already done. Protect her children. Her only task. Every thought and every tense muscle revolved around Hugo, Rasmus, Luiza. If she didn't sink to the floor even though her legs didn't want to carry her, didn't scream even though this weight on her chest wanted out, didn't cry and beg and give the bastards something of her own. If she just held on to this and never, never, never let go, there was nothing to fear.

"But this time, Mrs. Hoffmann, this isn't about bread. This is personal. I once had a little boy, too. Who died. And I never got to say goodbye—your husband made sure of that."

The man who was talking stood in front of her with his predator eyes, while his assistant walked from room to room. Opened cupboards and turned over furniture. When he came back, he politely asked her to move, he was going to examine the bedroom closet.

She didn't move.

Until he hit the butt of his gun against her forehead. The metal dug deep and no matter how much she focused, she couldn't stand it, she fell back and the two masked men were able to open the closet. Look into it. See that it was empty.

"I know your boys are here."

His voice was still controlled, just as unnaturally and unpleasantly calm.

"So where did you hide them?"

The blood ran from her forehead over her cheeks, and when she shook her head in response to his question, it changed direction, perhaps bled even more as it broke into three smaller rivers down her throat and onto her breast and quite a bit onto the floor.

"You get one more try. Before I shoot."

He cocked his gun, looked at her with his predator's gaze. He didn't know she'd made up her mind.

She wasn't going to say a word.

And she wasn't going to close her eyes when he pulled the trigger.

Luiza lay in Rasmus's arms. She was sleeping, her breath deep and even. He had to remember to tell his little brother later how proud he was of him, it's easy to forget if you don't make a point of it.

He was still standing on top of the iron stand. From there it was possible to hear what they were saying on the other side of the floor. They weren't screaming. They barely sounded threatening. But there *was* a threat.

He could see Mom in front of him. That expression that just drove a person crazy. When she'd really made up her mind.

"So where did you hide them?"

The man's voice was angrier now. And it was hard to make out what was happening, a dull blow like when you hit your leg, and a heavy thump like when you fall on the floor. But even though he couldn't see, he just knew somehow anyway. And it didn't feel good.

"You get one more try. Before I shoot."

That deep, strange voice.

Hugo felt it stabbing in his stomach and chest.

He understood—this was real. They weren't just threatening Mom, they were going to kill her. And he didn't think, he just did it. He shouted at the hole in the ceiling that was also the hole in the floor.

"We're here!"

As loud as he could.

"Don't shoot our mom!"

Silence. They'd heard him. They'd been listening. They weren't going to shoot.

Until it wasn't quiet anymore.

He jerked at the first shot. He lost his balance and fell down from the iron stand on the second shot. Then he screamed, and Luiza screamed, awake now.

Zofia had kept her promise to herself. She had protected her children. And she didn't close her eyes when the shots went off.

In the midst of everything she imagined Hugo's voice. Imagined he was screaming, revealing where they hid.

As if death were playing a joke on her.

It took a while for her to realize it wasn't the man with the predator eyes who was shooting. Because he was the one who fell. And after him, the other man landed on top of him, his equally masked colleague.

They were the ones death was playing with.

Blood was still flowing from her forehead as she raised herself up. She wasn't the only person here. Not the only one alive. There was someone else in the room, she sensed someone breathing, just behind her.

A woman. Young. She held her weapon so confidently, a gun that looked like the ones the Swedish police used.

"Where are your children?"

The woman's voice was just as confident. Warm and safe. As if she hadn't just shot two people.

"In the closet. Are you with the police?"

The young woman looked into the empty closet, then at Zofia, then back at the closet.

"Yes. I'm with the police. But I think . . . you must be in shock. Surely you see they're not in here. But I can hear a small child crying, somewhere. Please try to remember where you saw them last?"

"If you lift the floor of the closet. Underneath it. In the basement. An air-raid shelter."

The young policewoman kneeled down as she searched across the square board, while Zofia stayed on the bedroom floor, her legs didn't really want to follow her up.

"What's your name?"

"*Under* it, you said?"

"Who do you work with?"

She was beautiful, Zofia hadn't noticed at first glance, but she turned to the side in the closet and her profile emerged. Her face was finely drawn, her hair dark and shiny, and her eyes seemed intelligent, full of experience even though she was so young.

"Sorry, I just wanted to know if your kids were okay. My name is Amelia, and I'm doing my training period for six months with a detective superintendent named Ewert Grens, and being supervised by another police officer named Mariana Hermansson. Answer me now— this bottom part, does it lift as well? Are you sure about that?"

"I just saw it. My son pulled it up from the top right corner."

The policewoman whose name was Amelia found

what she was looking for. She pulled on the knob and the hatch went straight up. She stared down into a hole and caught a glimpse of three children.

"Hello . . . everything is okay up here. There's no danger anymore. I'm a police officer, and I'm helping your mom. Do you know how I can get down to you? Is there any other way besides through the hole?"

A boy who looked to be about nine, ten years old answered.

"I'm Hugo. You can go out into the stairwell and down to the basement and all the way until you reach a metal door with two wheels that you have to spin. We're in there. I'm here and my little brother Rasmus and my little sister Luiza. And now I want to know . . . is Mom okay?"

"I'm fine, honey!"

Zofia had heard his question, and it felt so good to shout out an answer, as if she were following her own voice all the way to her three wonderful children.

"Good. Then I'll come down to you while your mom waits up here."

Amelia winked at Hugo as she left the closet, and Hugo winked back. She went out into the stairwell as he told her to, but didn't go directly to the basement. She had another errand first, which involved two cars.

In her own car—still unlocked, she'd only had seconds—a folder lay on the passenger seat. She grabbed it and headed over to a black BMW parked across the street. The car of the masked men. She opened it with the key she took from Zaravic's jacket, while Zofia Hoffmann was still lying there unaware of what happened. Now she placed the folder on the passenger seat of his car. As she headed back toward the building and the basement where the children were, she wondered how long it would take before Ewert Grens, Mariana Hermansson, and Sven Sundkvist arrived in one of their police cars with sirens blaring and lights flashing. And which version of events she would give them—because the truth was the only story that couldn't be told.

PART

8

The truth is that I was supposed to die.

Die for real this time—I had no cupboard to hide in.

I even heard the gun fire.

We'd been driving to the airport through the densest darkness, along the most winding roads, and our car was stopped by the brightest headlights, and a dark silhouette had approached us.

Why are you calling yourself Lilaj?

Lorik pointed a gun through the car window and used a voice I didn't recognize.

Answer me—why!

I tried to hide myself and for the first time wished I was just Hannah Ohlsson.

Because he . . .

My aunt was trembling with fear, for my sake, I saw the gun was pointed at me and knew he was going to shoot.

. . . was my father.

And then.

Then the same thing happened that just happened here.

It wasn't Zofia Hoffmann who was shot—it was Zaravic who fell onto the bedroom floor. It wasn't me who was shot—it was Lorik who fell into the window and hung there with his upper body halfway inside the car, looking at me, surprised.

Aunt Vesa shook even more afterward.

She'd shot straight through the car's metal body. My aunt, who had never killed before, didn't even like guns, but still had one with her that night that her brother had given her, my father, and she had the presence of mind to pull it out of her left jacket pocket and angle it upward while Lorik was screaming at me.

I didn't know it then, but that was surely when all of this really started.

Aunt Vesa's shot was like my starting shot.

All those feelings and thoughts. Those tiny fragments of memory that would never fuse together suddenly did.

My aunt's gunshot connected me to those very first gunshots, which up until that moment I'd lived alone with every day. The nightmares of a little girl. Who became a teenager who realized those were no nightmares, they might have happened, they might be real—there might have been a mother, a father, a big brother, a big sister, and the sound of gunshots as they disappeared.

But I never went totally under. That's how love works. Those who took care of me, Thomas and Anette, they loved me, gave me security.

Until even that wasn't enough.

When he fell down from the balcony.

I hadn't planned it. I was fourteen years old, and my

boyfriend took it too far, and neither he nor I could understand where my rage, strength, and brutality came from. And since I didn't know myself, I couldn't explain it when the police asked me their questions.

Other things had happened before. Not like that, like on the balcony, but now and then I did hit back. A little harder. If someone hurt or threatened me or got too close. Friends and classmates knew it. But I never understood why that spontaneous rage would come to life or where it went afterward.

I remember that feeling as he lay three floors below and the party kept going as if nothing had happened. One moment there's a person with thoughts and a life, then nothing. For the first time, the nightmares and fragments started to make sense. I started to sense why my sister had stopped crying. What happened after Mom spat in the man's face. That it was connected to all of my questions, all my images and Albanian words that had suddenly just arrived.

After Zaravic's car, she headed back to the apartment building, took the stairs down to the basement and a dim hallway, which she followed to its end. This should be it—right around here, one floor up, was the apartment with a hole in the closet floor. And exactly like the boy named Hugo had told her, there was a heavy metal door with two large wheels you had to turn to open. First she stepped into a smaller passage, as if the air-raid shelter had a hall, then into its heart. They were sitting there. Together. Hugo, the eldest, holding a little girl in his arms, and his little brother next to him, leaning close.

We three. Against the world.

"Hello, nice to see you again. But this time no ceiling between us."

The two boys responded simultaneously.

"Hello."

And then the younger one continued.

"Are you sure?"

"What?"

"That Mom is really okay. We heard gunshots."

"I promise—your mother is completely fine."

She was so happy. She'd made it. They were alive. They were still three siblings on their way.

"And she's waiting for you."

The youngest boy glanced up at the hole in the ceiling.

"Did you save her?"

"I don't know if . . ."

"They weren't the ones who were shooting—it was you. Right?"

She nodded. Barely, but enough.

"Then you did save Mom."

He got up from his brother's side, walked over to her, his arms high in the air. His hug was long and tight.

"My name is Rasmus. One time another police officer saved us. Ewert. Do you know him?"

Aunt Vesa's gunshot and Lorik's lifeless eyes were the beginning of the answers I'd been seeking all my life.

But also new questions.

Aunt Vesa, why did we have to drive on this road? Why were we in such a hurry? Why were you so scared?

Why did he want to kill me?

We pulled Lorik's body out of the car and pushed it down into the ditch. There was no time to bury him or cover his body with branches. We couldn't go back to my aunt's house. Or to Shkodër. Or the airport. Not even Tirana felt safe. We circled aimlessly on tiny mountain roads, while she made up her mind. We'd go to Pristina, Kosovo, to a man my father knew.

Aunt Vesa seemed relieved, even hopeful.

And promised to answer all my questions before we got there.

Your father, she said as we drove straight into the night with our headlights off, smuggled weapons during the Kosovo War. For him that terrible, violent conflict was positive, even meaningful—unlike for the rest of us, who hated it. It gave him status, he became somebody, he built up his profile in the criminal underworld. Then the war ended—and with it his business and his income.

My aunt stared straight ahead as she spoke, of course she had to concentrate on the narrow and harrowing roads, whose edges were invisible in the dark. But it wasn't just that. It was as if it were easier for her to get it all out, if she didn't meet my eyes, everything she'd held so tightly inside her that she never thought she'd share with anyone. And I was thankful for it, because I didn't want her to see what I was thinking and feeling now that the story I was searching for was finally being told, the one that belonged to me.

Your dad had a few years that weren't so great. Violence became his new tool when the smuggling business bottomed. Never turned inward, toward me or the family, but outward. Until one day. I remember it so well. He found a golden egg. How I don't know, he never said. Or where. But he told me about the contents—and that he was the only one who knew. Somewhere along the northern shore of Lake Shkodër, where there are kilometers of almost untouched nature, there was an abandoned rock shelter. Where a completely new and unknown machine gun was stored. Ten thousand of them. Much more powerful than any other machine gun on the market. One side in the civil war, I never knew which, had ordered those weapons, and they were manufactured and delivered—but just as the war ended! A product no one needed, and a customer that didn't want to take them or pay for them.

My aunt slowed down, two wild rabbits were sitting in the middle of the road, and as we got closer they started running in front of the car. After a while, at such a low speed, it started to feel awkward to stare straight ahead, so we looked at each other and it felt almost good. She was speaking of a beloved brother, and I was hearing the story of a longed-for father.

Mirza, she said as the rabbits ran out into the dark meadow and we were able to speed up again, he was impatient—status in the criminal world is an addictive drug—and he decided to use his golden egg. The key to making big money in new markets. In Sweden at that time, there was another criminal we grew up with in Shkodër, a man who called himself King Zoltan, who ran all the micro-smuggling routes from here to there. Your father had an idea—his secret weapons stash and Zoltan's established Balkan route could be merged, together they'd expand and take over even bigger markets when the time was right. I tried to warn him, begged, but your father wasn't always very good at listening. He moved there, to Sweden—*all of you* moved there. And I had no idea that a person could feel so lonely. My god, little darling, how I missed you!

My aunt stopped the car and stepped out into the darkness, jumped over the ditch and continued down a small hill. A small river ran there, I could hear it murmuring. She knelt down and rinsed off her face. She must have been tired. Or maybe it was the tension draining out of her. And that's what continued when she came back, talking, handing over everything to me.

Your father started working for King Zoltan in Sweden; in fact it was Mirza who handled the micro-smuggling, the whole Balkan route. Not big money, five or ten weapons at a time, buy for a hundred dollars each, sell for a thousand dollars, but it was a comfortable, well-to-do living. After a few years, the time was finally right—perfect for taking over the arms trade in several countries using his golden egg. But they were no longer in complete agreement. Zoltan demanded that your father give him all the information about the secret weapons stash, the exact coordinates, before their contract was written as equal partners—he wanted to go there, investigate the place. But Mirza refused to give him more than a few samples, a couple of machine guns every now and then, until everything had been agreed on—the gun stash was his insurance policy. That's why one day they came to your home and you saw and heard your mother and father and sister and brother be executed. When they left the apartment with your father's computer, you were still in the closet, and they had what they came for. Or so they thought. False information. Your father had made sure that the directions on his computer weren't the real ones—he sent them on a wild-goose chase after his death. The real directions were hidden elsewhere. *Still* lie hidden elsewhere.

Aunt Vesa turned to me. Looked at me. It was as if she was trying to crawl into the closet toward me, take my hand, comfort me.

Then you came here, Zana. Showed up out of nowhere. Eleven years later. You started asking questions about the name Lilaj, and the ones who shouldn't know soon found out—one daughter had survived. A witness. She also had to be killed.

It didn't turn out that way. I killed your would-be murderer instead.

And so that's why we're sitting here, in my car, in the darkness, driving down back roads, fleeing.

She held one hand of each boy as they walked out of the air raid shelter and through the dark basement. Rasmus was on one side, Hugo on the other, still with his little sister in his arms, he refused to let go of her.

"Amelia, is that your name?"

"Yes."

"And you're really a police officer?"

"Almost. I'm still learning, but I will be soon."

"And how could you . . . how did you know we . . . ?"

"You have a lot of questions, Rasmus."

"Yes. And I want to . . ."

"First let's go see your mom. Then you can ask me more questions."

Zofia Hoffmann met them in the hall, her arms held wide for a hug as they stepped inside. She'd done her best to wash away the blood on her forehead and face. Don't worry the kids. When all four were united in a giant hug, they made a vision of love and security, and the person watching felt happy to see it, but also a little sad that she couldn't share in it.

But after a while Zofia looked up at her and smiled with heartfelt warmth.

"Thank you."

We drove all night, and as morning came we rolled into the streets of Pristina. Aunt Vesa had managed to get ahold of one of my father's former smuggling partners, and we were able to hide out in his house temporarily. A good man around the age my father would have been. He had small, sharp eyes that reminded me of a bird, thin gold rings in his ears, and a substantial birthmark on his neck. He spoke so kindly about us, showed pictures of me as an infant on his knee, and one of him and Dad standing in front of a truck while making some weapons delivery, their arms slung proudly around each other's shoulders.

A temporary hiding place with a temporary friend—but within a year we had created a future together. I changed. Or, maybe I didn't at all? Maybe it was more that once I was with my aunt and my father's old friend I finally understood who I was, where I came from, and maybe it was difficult or even impossible to escape something you want to get closer to? That kind of fear that turns into strength and determination when it's paired with trust. Because we made up our minds. *I* made them make up their minds. We would take back what belonged to us, finish what Dad had started, and we'd do it with the help of Hamid's and Dad's old contacts. We hired professionals to take out Zoltan's men one by one. Always Ulcinj execution. The same method used to kill my own family while I watched. We saved King Zoltan for last, and I took care of him myself—it was the third time gunshots changed the meaning and direction of my life.

Now we had taken back the Balkan route.

And we'd do what Dad had been preparing to do—use the secret stash of the world's most advanced machine gun to take over bigger markets.

That's why we split up. Hamid and Aunt Vesa led the organization from Shkodër, while I, with my newly acquired knowledge of explosives and ammunition—becoming Hamid's student had felt like getting closer to Dad—would travel to Sweden and solve the mystery of the hidden weapons. I changed my name, again—Zana Lilaj became Hannah Ohlsson became Amelia Schmidt—and with my new name, I applied to the police academy. That seemed like the best way to complete my three objectives. First, I needed to get access to the police investigation into the murders of my family, specifically the address of an apartment with a small square hole in its floor. Secondly, to get the names of the men who were arrested and interrogated at the time, but never locked up. And finally, so I'd get the best cover in the world—someone in a police uniform running the Swedish illegal arms trade.

She asked Zofia and the boys to take Luiza to the sofa in the living room and wait there until Superintendent Grens arrived, while she went and got them some water and a bag of buns that was sitting on the kitchen counter. A few minutes to herself before the apartment filled up with voices and energy. And then it just happened. It wasn't anything she was planning, but her legs carried her to the two men in the bedroom, and she did the same thing she'd done in Albania when they were lying on the floor after a professional hit: she kicked them. Hard. Again, again. Kicked them even though she knew they couldn't feel it.

Hamid and Aunt Vesa rebuilt the Balkan route and made it even better. More weapons than ever were smuggled to northern Europe and, above all, to Sweden where gang activity had increased the most. Meanwhile, the police academy was just a long wait for that fifth semester—my training period and the access I'd come here for. To be able, from the inside, to find the key to the weapons stash and then finally destroy those who had destroyed my world.

The first burglary in the police station was also the easiest.

Already during the introductory tour Mariana Hermansson showed us, her two cadets, the archive, those shelves in the dark rooms of the police station's basement where the files from every criminal investigation were kept, she even gave us the task of looking up a couple of old cases and rewarded us afterward with the code—*here you go, you'll have to go down there sometimes, just part of the job.* Here were the traces I was looking for. Those who had been erased in reality, but who lingered on in stacks of paper in brown cardboard boxes. Early the next morning I made my first visit. Alone in that absurd collection of assaults and crime victims, I found at the top of a shelf at the end of one of the halls, the preliminary investigation.

REPORT REGARDING DALA STREET 74.

One page. In order to access the full case files—with complete crime scene investigation and list of suspects—reference was made to the restricted archive. But at that point a single page was enough. I got the address, the floor, and I could go to the apartment. I broke the lock just the way I'd learned to and stepped into a hallway that transported me back in time. The furniture was different and the smell, but the rooms were the ones I remembered so well. Perhaps I should have wept, broken down. But I didn't. I was there for a reason. And those bastards would never force me into a cupboard again.

Somehow I just knew about that little square hole in the floor of Julia's room. It seemed so obvious. Dad must have let us see it. Maybe he guessed that one day one of his children might have to finish what he started, what someone tried to take away from him.

And there it was, in the hole in the floor, a USB drive. The information that would lead to a stash of weapons worth one billion kronor—coordinates of its exact position, detailed descriptions of how to get there, pictures from inside the rock room with pallet after pallet of heavy machine guns that no one had ever seen before.

Getting into the restricted archive was more difficult.

Late one night I got my chance—via a webcam I placed in a small crack in the wall, I was able to record the archivist inputting his long code. And via an equally small directional antenna, I copied the frequencies on the archivist's access card. The next night I went in, found the investigation and sat down in the kitchenette of the homicide unit and started to read about the murder of a family. The report from the forensic technicians was as horrific as the medical examiner's. Details that not only brought me closer to my parents and siblings, they brought me *inside* of them. The descriptions of myself, on the other hand, from the perspective of the police, I couldn't take inside—it was as if I were looking at a photo of someone else. That was also when, sitting there late one night reading those files, I realized that the policeman who had carried me out of the apartment, who took care of me those first few weeks, who I'd thought about so many times without having a face or a name, that he was sitting in an office just a few doors away! Ewert Grens was the one who came to the apartment that day. I remembered him as so old, so I was sure he wasn't working there anymore.

I wanted to know more about him.

The man I had trusted, who made sure I got a new home, a new world.

I went back down to the archive, searched for his name, and read all about his career. That was how I stumbled across Piet Hoffmann, in three very remarkable investigations during which Grens's and Hoffmann's paths crossed—and I realized this was exactly the person I needed. So I carried out a third burglary. I used the same already successful method, webcam and directional antenna, and I captured—just like in the restricted archive—Erik Wilson's personal eight-digit code and the electronic information on his access card.

As expected, I found exactly what I needed in the safe.

All of the information about the criminal infiltrator project—the logbooks, intelligence reports, code names.

I spent another late night in the homicide unit's kitchenette and read until I arrived at Wilson's notes about Hoffmann's plan to knock out a heavily armed MC gang all by himself—and I didn't need to read more.

My name was Amelia, I left Hannah behind long ago, but that was when I really became myself again, Zana, completely.

• • •

She kicked the two bodies until she didn't need to anymore, then went in to the Hoffmann family and sank onto the sofa in an empty spot between the boys. They were shaken, but more composed than she'd expected. They had their mother, they had each other.

She never even noticed her phone ringing—it was the youngest one, Rasmus, who poked her thigh gently and pointed to her jacket pocket. She answered. Grens. Stressed.

"I just wanted to tell you we'll soon be there and that we . . . is that Amelia?"

"Yes."

"Are *you* the one who's already there?"

"Yes."

"The alarm, did you . . ."

"It was me. I called in the alarm. Everything is under control."

"I'm not sure I understand . . ."

"We'll discuss that later. When you get here. Where are you now?"

I had accomplished two of my three tasks. I had the best cover imaginable for an arms dealer—a police uniform. I found the USB stick and through it located the hidden weapons stash. Now I was going to take the lives of those who took my life. In the investigation Grens led seventeen years earlier, it was clear he suspected four people who had carried out the murders on behalf of a fifth—King Zoltan, who I dealt with in Shkodër. Five men who Grens interrogated and arrested but had to release.

Now you can't have any more kids.

Voices, fragments.

But you can still meet a new woman, think about that.

I tracked them down—police records are handy for many things—and executed them. Dejan Pejović. Branko Stojanović. Ermir Shala. In the same way they carried out their executions. I didn't feel much. I expected happiness, elation, even a sense of closure. But it felt more like this was my right. I had one left. Dusko Zaravic. When Hermansson commanded me to follow Grens to Söderköping. Home. To Thomas and Anette. The place Hannah Ohlsson had left behind. Of course I had an excuse ready, an escape plan, if we ended up going to that brick house that once gave me a sense of security. I never needed to use the excuse. We met the social worker who gave us a name and a place, but from there, Grens chose to go on alone to meet my adoptive parents, while Lucas and I went to dig up my childhood at the local police station. What I didn't foresee was that Hermansson would arrest Zaravic in the meantime. That they would lock him up, put him away, for three days. Beyond my reach. And when the detective decided to search his apartment to try to find something that they could hold him for, I was forced to break in and clean out a computer, a few illegally obtained guns, and even a few suits I was sure might connect him to a big hit on a wholesaler. It was a surreal moment afterward to stand in the hall of the homicide unit and watch Grens furiously accuse Wilson of having leaked the plan to search Zaravic's apartment—and a great relief to realize the blood from the window where I cut myself wouldn't be linked to me, because cadets weren't expected to contribute to the DNA bank.

We were five, I was the only one left.

They were five, Zaravic was the only one left.

But our two sides wouldn't remain mirror images much longer.

"Amelia?"

"Yes?"

"You said Uncle Ewert was coming."

"He's coming."

"When?"

"If you press your ear against the window on the balcony door, Rasmus, you'll soon hear the sirens. Really loud."

"Like this?"

"Your whole cheek and ear against the glass."

"I don't hear anything."

"Soon. Several police cars. First, Ewert, then others."

"You promise?"

"I promise soon everything will be okay again."

Three days delay. That was that. But if I waited all this time, I could wait until Zaravic was released. I'd confirmed in my family's autopsy records exactly what the distance should be between the holes in the forehead and the temple—he'd be shot in the same way as the rest.

Then came the moment when I had to change my plan.

I'd blown up Hoffmann's house to force him to make contact, and for some respect, then Grens had invited us home for an unofficial meeting because he knew there was a dirty cop. He couldn't know that it was me—that bringing us there wasn't going to help him. It was in his kitchen that the detective superintendent told us about his secret collaborator. *Piet Hoffmann has traveled to northern Albania—we believe that the top man of this arms smuggling operation is based there—and that he will connect us to the man who's shooting people in Sweden.* That bastard Hoffmann wasn't doing what he was supposed to! The opposite! He was working with Grens to expose us! I had no choice. Hamid was a good man, I had became very fond of him, but he wasn't nearly so strong as Mom or Dad, and he might break down under pressure—with a man like Hoffmann the risk was great, too great, that he would unmask me and Aunt Vesa.

I stole Grens's phone and got Hoffmann's new number.

I offered money, a hefty sum, to a newly hired guard at the Kronoberg jail to hide another phone and some documents inside Zaravic's cell.

And I shot Hoffmann's employee and exposed his family's hiding place on the TV screen so the bastard would understand the consequences if he did not carry out his new assignment in Albania.

Now Amelia! I hear them!"

"Yes, they're driving really fast."

"The police sirens! Uncle Ewert is coming!"

"I told you, Rasmus."

She laid a gentle hand on his tousled hair. He was so happy, so open, as only a child can be. She looked at his sibling, at Hugo sitting on the sofa and guarding his mother uneasily, taking on a responsibility that was too much for one his age, and Luiza lying between them, unaware of the drama surrounding her.

They had each other. Like siblings should.

Everything's connected. So what began with Aunt Vesa killing for my sake ended when she called and said Hamid had died, but the shooter had spared her. I hadn't realized that what I had changed in my haste would reach all the way to my beloved aunt, the only one I have left. And something happened. Inside me. I broke down. I was thrown back. Except even harder. To those days and nights with dead people. To the place where the police officer I'm waiting for now, found me, gave me back my life—the man who's been trying to save these children over these last few days, saved me, too. I know, better than anyone, what it means for siblings to pay with their lives as a threat to their parents, to be used in that way. And when our plan right now couldn't be carried out to the end, I changed my mind. It was too late to stop Zaravic from getting ahold of the documents, but there was still time to stop his revenge—and complete mine.

I think I'll sit down again.

And just wait for Grens and Hermansson and Sund-kvist to arrive.

With the children and Zofia.

It feels good, and I'm tired.

Howling, screaming sirens.

Flashing, rotating lights.

The whole world was angry noise and urgent lights until the car stopped in front of the apartment building and it became silence and stillness. When Ewert Grens, Mariana Hermansson, and Sven Sundkvist entered the apartment on the first floor they encountered a scene that also encompassed the same extremes. In one room, death and chaos, in the other, life and nascent calm. Two dead men and a shaken but unharmed family—and one police cadet who was a hero without even seeming to realize it. Grens rarely arrived at a crime scene so soon after the crime had occurred. His job as a detective superintendent usually meant showing up long after, searching for details that became the puzzle of circumstances and facts that made up the evidence. Perhaps that's why he walked around feeling so uneasy even though everything had ended well. He didn't understand what he was seeing because the acute threat had been averted.

But he understood the hatch and the hole in the closet floor that Hugo showed him, a very Hoffmann touch. *Always alone, trust only yourself.* He also understood Dusko Zaravic's motives, that's why he'd wanted to lock him up for three days, and why Hermansson in the middle of all that wreckage looked so proud as she spoke of her young protégé.

"What Amelia did must be absolutely unique. A cadet, Ewert—who read this investigation so much better than her superiors did. Who was in the right place. With just seconds to spare, she took the shots that saved four lives."

Grens offered his hand to the young woman, shook it long and hard. He couldn't even think about what would have happened if she hadn't arrived. If Zofia, if Rasmus and Hugo, if . . . now he felt it again. Not the uneasiness of not understanding what he saw. This was more like the despair he sometimes still felt when he thought about Anni. To lose someone who was a part of you.

"Thank you. What you . . . It's invaluable. Irreplaceable. I can't find any better words."

She nodded, almost shyly. The detective superintendent continued.

"But how could you—how did you know? How did you manage to get here, in time?"

He looked into her intelligent eyes, and she seemed almost embarrassed. He liked that a lot. Someone who wasn't chasing after confirmation, thirsty for attention like so many others.

"I . . . don't really know why. At the police academy, our lecturers talked a lot about gut feeling, said it can be dangerous, things can go very wrong if a police officer lets themselves be led by that. But that *was* what I felt, a—gut feeling. When Zaravic was released. And when I saw him, how he . . . I had already parked my car on Bergs Street and followed him. It took them a few minutes to break in with the crowbar, break down the door. That's why I was able to get here in time."

Grens's inner pocket buzzed. Piet Hoffmann's current number. The detective superintendent apologized and headed toward the kitchen and the balcony, pulled the door shut behind him. A strong wind was blowing, he hadn't noticed before.

"Yes?"

"What the hell is going on, Grens? I called Zofia and got no answer, and I called you and you didn't answer and . . ."

"It turned out fine."

There are different kinds of silence in a conversation. This one was longer than the usual, and more powerful than most Grens had experienced.

"And . . . what does that mean?"

"That your wife and your children are safe—right now they're sitting on the sofa drinking water and eating biscuits with my colleagues. And Dusko Zaravic and his associates are dead in the room next door."

"How, Grens . . . if they're dead, and if you were so late . . . who shot? Zofia? Was she the one . . . ?"

"A very brave police cadet. The best officers are always the ones who ignore their bosses. And this young woman, she . . . without her, things would have ended differently."

"And without her, Paula wouldn't be back either."

Grens spun around. Hermansson stood behind him, had come out on the balcony without him noticing it.

"What?"

"Sorry, Ewert, I didn't mean to disturb you—but Paula, the secret documents about Hoffmann. All the original documents were in Zaravic's car."

She handed him the folder.

"Here. Take care of them. I mean, it might be a good thing if we look into these ourselves—so it doesn't end up in the general evidence folder?"

Ewert Grens didn't like being interrupted. But this time he smiled warmly at Hermansson before returning to the phone.

"You heard that, Hoffmann?"

"I heard."

"For me, two mysteries remain to be solved—who executed three hit men in the inner city of Stockholm, and who leaked that information to the arms dealers in the first place. But for you this is over. They're no longer going after your family."

"Are you sure?"

"Zaravic is dead and the original documents back. Don't you trust me?"

"I'm working on it, Grens, I promise. And in that case—I need to stay here for one more day."

"Why?"

"It's better if you don't know."

"If you say so."

"In the meantime—can you keep your eyes on Zofia and my kids?"

"I'll keep an eye on them. Since you trust me."

Before Grens could leave the balcony, Hermansson returned, and now she was the one who made sure the door was closed behind them.

"I have something I need to talk to you about."

He knew her so well. That seriousness, it was real.

"That sounds alarming."

He tried to smile. It didn't go so well.

"Ewert—I've made a decision."

She took a deep breath.

"I was going to wait a little to tell you. But . . . well, it feels like this investigation is reaching a wrapping-up point, so now might be a good time."

She did it again. Took a deep breath. Then another.

"I'm going to request a transfer."

"What?"

"I'm not staying at City Police. I'm going to apply at another district."

That emptiness, or was it despair, that he'd just now felt flapping inside his chest when he thought of Anni or of Hoffmann's children or losing people you care about and need, came back with full force. It ached right there where his breastbone covered his heart.

"Is it because I—I'll never question you again, Mariana! You know that!"

"I know. That's not why."

"For over ten years! I was the one who cleared your path through the bureaucracy so you could hop over people with more years under their belt because I knew how good you were, how important to us you would become. Mariana . . ."

The big body. With a small detective superintendent inside.

". . . you can't quit! Don't you understand that? You . . . You!"

He embraced her. He had never done that before, never wanted her to misunderstand what he felt. Now it didn't matter.

"You've been like my—I've never put it into words for you, but . . . I've thought of you as a daughter. The daughter I never had. And . . ."

"I know, Ewert. You didn't have to say it. But either Erik or I *have* to quit. It's not about who's the boss or not, man or woman—I'm going to transfer because he was here first, has been employed longer than me. Because it's the right thing to do. That's the only reason. And, of course, because I love him."

She managed to smile. It was lovely.

"Don't transfer! Don't go to another department. Do you hear me? I've only got six months left—and I want you here, at my side!"

Then she smiled again, more widely.

"You have more than that, Ewert."

"Sixty-four and a half, today. Six months. Then I have to . . ."

"I've been looking into what's worrying you so much, and I was going to talk to you about it later, but feels like now might be a good time. Ewert—you can keep your job up to age sixty-seven. That's how it works these days. Flexible upper limit. I've confirmed there are police officers who served up until sixty-nine and even seventy. The kind of knowledge you have doesn't age just because you do."

He looked at her. The same silence as with Hoffmann earlier on the phone.

What she'd just given him was the most beautiful gift in the world—he didn't have to fall into that black fucking hole, not yet at least. The abyss would have to manage without him for a few more years. But it didn't matter. One of the few people he cared about more than himself was telling him she was leaving him.

"I can keep a secret, Mariana. I'm good at it. No one needs to know about your relationship with Wilson. Please—stay with me!"

She put her hand on his cheek and he flinched, because he was so unused to it, but he didn't pull away.

"It doesn't matter if you stay quiet, Ewert. We've decided—we don't want to sneak around anymore. I requested the transfer yesterday. And you and I, just as I warned you if you continued to doubt and accuse me, will never see each other again."

She remained with him for a while on the windy balcony.

Neither of them said anything.

There was no more to say.

As Gezim Latifi walked toward his office in the Shkodër police station, he met a man standing in the corridor waiting for him. On the younger side of middle age, sharp blue eyes in a slightly angular face, in good shape and with a close shave, wearing a T-shirt and cargo pants. Two fingers were missing on one hand, his only visible defect, and when he stood up, it was with smooth movements.

"Latifi?"

"That's me."

"I would like to talk to you."

English. Strange days with so many foreign visitors.

"About what?"

"About what happened yesterday."

Latifi looked at his guest in confusion.

"Yesterday?"

"When you and I stopped at the gas station."

Another couple of seconds of feeling lost. And then—anger.

"It was . . . you?"

"Yes."

"You! *Larsson!*"

"I look a little different and that's not my name—and I'm not a police officer. If we're starting over. But I *am* here on behalf of a Swedish police officer."

The large, honest man hesitated—studied Hoffmann for a long time, so deep in his own thoughts that he seemed unaware he'd taken off the police cap he always wore low on his forehead and exposed his large scar.

"Go inside."

He nodded toward Hoffmann and the simple visitor's chair, the only thing in that tiny office besides the desk itself.

"As you may be aware, I'm pretty busy right now looking for whoever shot Hamid Cana in the chest and injured Vesa Lilaj."

Piet Hoffmann sat down, looking for a place to stretch his legs. There wasn't one.

"You never got the whole truth."

"I was on your side. But I can't sanction murder."

"And maybe I won't be able to give you the whole truth now. But enough for you to understand why I chose to come back here."

"On the contrary, I lock up murderers, no matter their reasons. And I just decided—to call for reinforcements. You're going to be arrested and put away."

Latifi reached toward the black, clumsy, old-fashioned Bakelite phone on his desk, lifting the handset and starting to dial some internal number on the round disc.

"No."

Hoffmann put his hand over the telephone cradle and broke the connection.

"You're *not* gonna arrest me."

Gezim Latifi's gun had been in one of the desk drawers. Now he pointed it at Piet Hoffmann's head.

"Please put your hands on my desk so I can cuff them."

Hoffmann kept his hand over the phone.

"If I'd wanted to disappear I would have, and you never would have seen me again. You know after last night that I'm pretty good at it. But I came here voluntarily. And, unlike you, I'm unarmed."

Latifi looked at his visitor while moving the muzzle of his gun from head to chest, from chest to head.

"If you arrest me now, Latifi, you'll never know why I'm here. And why what I have to say might be crucial to you."

From head to chest.

From the chest to the head.

While the Albanian policeman silently tried to make up his mind.

"*If* I choose to lower this gun. *If* I choose to wait to arrest you. What exactly is it that you want?"

"Come with me on a little excursion."

"We did that yesterday. It didn't end so well."

"And we're going to use this."

Piet Hoffmann had a small backpack with him. Now he pulled out a laptop and held it up toward the gun.

"There you go."

"And what am I supposed to do with this?"

"I grabbed it while you were sitting on the roof of a warehouse keeping watch for me. It belonged to Hamid Cana, and its information is only accessible with a twenty-character decryption code. But no one can keep track of that many letters and numbers, so it has to be written down and hidden. The code for this computer was in a safe behind a secret wall, and in order to get ahold of it I had to waste a hell of a lot of water. As you can see, the paper ended up a little wrinkled."

Hoffmann handed the Albanian policeman a folded sheet.

"But the code is intact—we were lucky, he'd written it down with a regular ballpoint pen, waterproof. When you and I split up, you use this code and read all the text in its original form. This is my first repayment for your help. You'll get the solution not only to what happened yesterday, you'll have proof of several years of extensive organized weapons smuggling. The names of employees here in Shkodër and Tirana and Pristina. Their colleagues all along the entire Balkan route. My Swedish employer is content with just the Swedish names—you'll have the honor of arresting the rest of them."

Latifi just sat there, without any hint of movement.

"If what you have with you contains what you say it does, that's good. But it changes nothing—you're a murderer and murderers have to be arrested."

Hoffmann turned the computer screen toward the policeman, then unfolded the wrinkled piece of paper.

"Latifi, take some time to look at this. Once you've done that, you'll see that what I have to say is true. My *small* thanks to you. Then we'll get up and head to your car parked behind the police station. And go on our excursion. We'll drive to Lake Shkodër, and at a jetty quite far from the nearest house, we'll find a simple motorboat. That will take us to repayment number two—and my *much bigger* thanks. You can take your gun with you, I'll remain unarmed like now. Once we're there you can decide if you want to arrest me or let me go."

E wert Grens had no idea how long he lingered out there on the balcony. Long enough to make his legs feel much stiffer than usual. When he came back inside again, Sven was with the two patrol cars and Mariana was with the medical examiner and forensic technicians, while Amelia still sat with Zofia and the Hoffmann kids, speaking to them in her pleasant voice. He walked closer, listening. It felt so good to see them all safe and sound.

"Ewert!"

Rasmus had caught sight of him and patted the space next to him on the sofa.

"Come and sit with me!"

"It looks a little crowded."

"There's room. If I squeeze closer to Hugo, and if Hugo gets closer to Mom, and if Mom . . . just sit down. Right here."

Rasmus's eight-year-old voice was determined. Grens had no choice. He sank down between the Hoffmann boys, and it felt as natural as it did comfortable.

"You saved us once, Ewert . . ."

That determined eight-year-old voice was accompanied by a serious eight-year-old look.

"Now Amelia did, too."

They sat there, together. Without saying another word. Maybe they were all doing like Grens—letting what Rasmus had said sink in. What it means to save someone. Or be saved by someone. How it forever changes a relationship.

Until the detective superintendent cleared his throat and turned to Zofia.

"I've been thinking. And I don't believe you can stay here any longer. This is a crime scene now. Just like your real home."

And then he turned to Hugo and Rasmus.

"So . . . well . . . if you want to that is. Would you like to come stay with me? And live there. Until, well, things get figured out a little better."

"With you, Ewert?"

Now it was Hugo who spoke, taking over for his little brother. That's what it meant to be a big brother, taking responsibility for stuff.

"Don't you want to?"

"Yes. A lot a lot a lot. But—is there room? For our whole family?"

Grens smiled again.

"Yes, Hugo. There's room. I promise."

Zofia and the two boys seemed happy, relieved, and started to pack up what little they'd brought from home. While Grens and Amelia remained on the sofa, just the two of them. For a moment it felt a little strained, as they didn't know each other, weren't part of each other's lives, but because standing up and leaving felt blunt and impolite, for the first time they were forced to meet without Hermansson or Lucas or anyone else to act as a bridge. Grens was older, so maybe that's why he was the one to finally break that embarrassing silence.

"I'd . . . just like to say once more. That I'm so grateful both as your temporary boss and on a personal level for what you did, Amelia. How you did it. You're gonna make one hell of a police officer."

She looked down, almost seemed shy.

"Thank you."

Then it became strained again. Small talk had never been Detective Superintendent Grens's strong suit. They both smiled in embarrassment until he continued.

"You said you had a gut feeling."

"Yes."

"And that's what made you act?"

"Yes. I think so."

"But, there must have been something more? There always is. You must have seen something we missed? Put together some information? I'm old, but I still like to improve."

It felt easier now. When they were talking police work.

"So tell me. I'm curious! For real."

But the young cadet was just as reticent.

"I'm afraid I don't have a better explanation. I knew Zaravic's past from your briefing, and I knew Hoffmann must have been in the same world, and I knew his family was being threatened . . . it just added up. I was there. In the right place. And I got lucky."

"You didn't get lucky, Amelia. You were clever. Cleverer than any young officer I've ever encountered. You had presence of mind. You were able to shoot under pressure. You weren't just in the right place, you made the right decisions under immense stress—not many people can do that."

Then they sat there again, wrestling with the silence, an old police officer on his way out and a young one on her way in. But just as the silence was becoming too awkward, Rasmus came running in with his red backpack and loudly proclaimed that they were ready to go now. Grens made sure that Mariana Hermansson and Sven Sundkvist had an overview and all the resources they needed, then left the apartment with two dead men in the bedroom and headed for his car, followed by a big brother, a little brother, and their little sister in her mother's arms. Twenty minutes later, when they parked in front of his turn-of-the-century building on Svea Road, the whole family was now asleep. After several days of constant worry, they'd finally relaxed. The detective superintendent considered letting them rest, didn't really have the heart to interrupt their deep breaths and loud snores, but finally he cautiously woke them up one by one. And just as they stepped out of the elevator and into his enormous apartment, the boys seemed to regain their energy and started running from room to room to room, and then said they were super-super-hungry and checkered pancakes—the kind they'd made together that first evening Grens had been their babysitter—were exactly what they needed in order to go to sleep. That's why for the first time ever there was a search of Grens's apartment for the ingredients to make pancake batter that would then be cooked in a waffle iron and not in the frying pan so as to get the right pattern. And maybe that's also why all the children fell asleep so deeply in various sofas—a feeling of security, even in the shape of checkered pancakes, makes it easier to rest.

"So . . . this is where Piet hid out? This was where he went?"

It had been dark for a long time when Grens and Zofia sat down at the kitchen table, each with a glass of wine in their hands, far too sweet for this late hour, but the only alcohol he had at home. And Zofia couldn't say exactly how she knew, but she just felt that this was where her husband went when he was in need. To the detective superintendent who had once been his greatest enemy.

"Yes. He did. And you should know how much he missed you and the kids."

"And this?"

Zofia turned over the whiteboard, looking at the police investigation held there by magnets.

"It's not over, is it, no matter how much you pretend it is?"

"Not for me. But for you, I promise."

She absently looked at the forensic reports from Nils Krantz, followed Grens's lines and arrows, trying to interpret photos whose faces were crossed out.

"She . . . never hesitated."

"Who?"

"The young police officer who saved our lives. She

didn't hesitate. She acted in the way I've only ever seen one other person act, like Piet. That determination. Presence of mind."

Zofia Hoffmann was an intelligent, warm person. It was nice to sit with her in this unexpected calm. Even if it was under unfortunate circumstances. Her husband had been his first guest in years, but she was the first woman who had sat at this table since Anni. Laura, the autopsy technician who had been his first relationship in three decades, he'd always met at her home. Soon. Soon he'd be strong enough to meet someone again, trust someone again.

"Ewert—this is lovely. Being able to stay with you for a while. Thank you. From me and the children and Piet. But now I think I have to sleep."

"I put sheets and towels on the bed in the guest room."

"Finally I'll be able to fall asleep—without worry."

"And tomorrow morning when I head off to Kronoberg, you can sleep in. I've got officers guarding both the entrance on Svea Road and the inner courtyard."

She hugged him, and it felt as natural as it was simple. He filled a glass with ice-cold water and walked out to the balcony to look out over Stockholm on a summer night. Too many thoughts, too much buzzing inside him, and he needed to find some calm before he went to bed. So many nights he'd spent out here, leaning against the railing and listening to the wind over the rooftops.

But the calm did not come. His thoughts wouldn't stop spinning.

No matter how hard he tried to share in the silence, be in the stillness.

Gut feeling. She'd talked about it. Repeated it. It wasn't enough. That's why he couldn't rest. A young, fresh police officer just doesn't act like that. Even if she is uniquely present, shoots without hesitation, and is better than everyone else.

It didn't make sense. She didn't make sense.

The time was approaching two. It didn't matter. He found his phone and called the same contact he'd called at the beginning of this investigation. The administrator at the Swedish Tax Agency, who he sometimes traded favors with. And it was obvious when he picked up the phone he had been deeply asleep.

"Yes . . . Hello?"

"It's me. I need your help."

"Not now."

"Yes now."

"I'm hanging up."

"If you do, we will never work together again. And you know that next time you might be the one who needs my help."

The man whose name he never said out loud on the phone because that's what they'd agreed on didn't hang up. He asked Grens to wait, and it was possible to hear him getting out of bed and trudging out into his home.

"What's this about?"

And now he pulled out a chair and turned on a computer, the sound was easy to recognize.

"I want help with a name."

"Yes?"

"Amelia Schmidt. Spelled with a s-c-h at the beginning and d-t at the end."

The administrator tapped on the computer's keys, hard, smashing them like an old typewriter. A few seconds, he returned.

"One hit—only one person by that name in the whole country. Registered in Stockholm. Twenty-two years old."

"That's correct. That's her."

"And what do you want to know?"

"I'm not sure exactly. See if you can find anything else connected to the name. Anything at all. You and I have worked together before, I know you'll know it when you see it."

"Give me a few minutes."

Grens returned to the warm wind over the rooftops of the capital, which was resting up for the day to come. There was a time when he used to come out here to see if he dared to jump. Over the balcony railing, toward the street, away from everything. When what he'd feared for so long finally happened. When Anni left him. What he didn't realize then is that once the thing you've feared finally happens, it can't happen again. And that once you know that, make peace with that, you can rebuild. Come back. Not the same as before, not the same life—but something that's different and sometimes a little different in the most beautiful way.

"I think I have what you're looking for."

The administrator at the Tax Agency sounded almost excited, his voice clear despite his tiredness and unwillingness to get out of bed.

"When I went through her history."

"Yes?"

"I found an application for a name change—three years ago."

"Yes?"

"Hannah Ohlsson."

"Excuse me?"

"Hannah Ohlsson. That was her name. The same social security number, but both the first and last name were changed. I never approved of that new law for name changes, makes it so easy, I mean . . ."

"And if you follow the social security number?"

Ewert Grens felt like he was freezing. In the middle of a warm summer night.

"Then I end up . . ."

Those hard clacking sounds. The tax officer really slammed his fingertips when he typed.

". . . nowhere. Hannah Ohlsson is nowhere to be found in the records. Has no history."

"Yes. She does. But only in paper form."

"There's nothing here about it when I . . ."

"Because that was the name you helped me find last time. Zana Lilaj. She was the one who became Hannah Ohlsson."

He never said the last part aloud.

Who then became Amelia Schmidt.

But he thought it.

Just before she applied to the police academy.

So magnificent. The pristine shores of Lake Shkodër looked like something out of a glossy travel magazine—the dark green vegetation, the soaring rocks, sky and water in that same intense shade of blue. Like stepping into a fairy tale.

The simple motorboat huffed and puffed its way along surrounded by bird cries. It had been a while since they'd glided over the border to Montenegro, and according to the coordinates in Hamid Cana's computer, which were now loaded in Piet Hoffmann's telephone, they were getting close to their destination. Latifi had asked him many times what this was about and where they were going, but he never received an answer. He would, soon.

Piet Hoffmann turned off the engine and the boat floated that last bit into a crevice that formed the narrow entrance to a beach. He jumped out, then up onto a stone with a rope in his hand, then to the next stone and a tree branch hanging there, which met him like an outstretched arm. He tied the boat to a knotty tree trunk and asked Latifi—who was still keeping his distance with his gun easily accessible—to follow him toward the mountain through dense, impenetrable bushes. Not even wild animals moved through here.

The coordinates were no longer helpful, not precise enough. To reach their final destination, he would have to follow the instructions stored in the same document on Cana's computer.

Seventy-four steps north from the stone shaped like a head until you reach the split tree.

Thirty-nine steps southwest from the split tree to the cliff's edge.

Fifteen steps south from the cliff's edge along the foot of the mountain, stop at the protrusion of rock.

There it is. The entrance.

They were in front of a cracked-up mountain wall. Grooves, irregularities, sharp edges. And, as he got close, he saw the outlines of a door. Impossible to make out if you weren't looking for it.

Run your hand along the ground until you find two orange-size bulges.

Turn them clockwise.

What looked like two natural formations were not that at all.

When Piet Hoffmann grabbed hold of them, twisting them at the same time, it was as if the whole rock wall started to shake. Then out of the cracks and uneven surfaces a door slid to the side.

"Go in, Latifi."

"No."

"Inside you'll find my second repayment. I think you'll be satisfied."

"I still don't understand this. And I don't take part in things I don't understand."

They stared at each other, as quiet as their surroundings. Not even the constantly screaming birds seemed to want to disturb them right now.

"You go first, Larsson. Or whatever your name is."

Their eyes met and Latifi pointed to the doorway. Piet Hoffmann slowly started to walk into the darkness.

Steps echoed in the stone room.

He lit the flashlight he was carrying, and Latifi stopped abruptly.

"Is that . . . what the hell, Larsson . . . is that what I think it is?"

"Yes."

Side by side they tried to take in this uncanny vision.

"Of course, I've—*my god!*—heard of them, everyone who lives around here has, but I've always considered it a tall tale. That they . . . *they're real!* . . . I never even considered it."

They stood in front of pallet after pallet after pallet of weapons that didn't exist.

And they didn't even have to count them.

Ten thousand copies of the world's most powerful machine gun—the key to taking over foreign markets. The weapons cache that led to the death of a family, and then many years later to even more deaths.

E wert Grens had left the balcony and the view of the city he'd spent his whole life in.

He'd never ventured elsewhere. Never longed to. This was his place, his life, and he'd made peace with that. It was good enough.

His car was still parked outside his apartment building on Svea Road. He nodded to a colleague in uniform as he headed out, and then sank down in the front seat. He'd visited most addresses in this town by now, but Gärdet, where he was headed now, was still a surprisingly rare destination. There just weren't many criminals living in that part. Life could be unfair like that.

He started driving while making a new call. A new person pulled out of comfortable sleep. Life could also be unfair in that way.

"Nils? It's Grens."

Nils Krantz, the forensic technician, sounded like everyone else Ewert Grens had ever woken up in the night. Confused, slow. It took him a minute to grab the phone, get it right side up, catch his breath. While Krantz was doing that, Grens considered the fact that they were the same age. He wondered if Krantz knew you could stay on nowadays for a couple more years. Or if he even wanted to. Maybe he was counting the days that couldn't end soon enough. Strange—they'd known each other well as colleagues for many years. And yet not at all.

"Yes. I'm here. What do you want?"

"The blood sample. From the window in Zaravic's apartment."

"Yes?"

"I want you to widen the search."

Krantz fumbled with the phone again. It sounded like he dropped it, looked for it. Found it.

"I widened it as far as I could. With the help of my contact at NFC, I ran it against all four DNA banks. Trace samples, open case files, general registry, and the elimination database from our personnel. I even searched—above and beyond your request, Ewert— quite a few of the other EU databases as well. Without success."

"And now I want you to search in one more."

"There aren't any."

"The police academy. I want you to compare the samples they take from students during their DNA tracking class."

"That's only used as a teaching exercise, it's not an official database."

"No—but it exists. And compare our sample to all of theirs. Especially those taken in the last three years. And I want you to do it now, Nils. Immediately."

A long, deep sigh straight into the phone.

"That means I'll have to wake up other people who are sound asleep."

"Welcome to my world, Nils."

Ewert Grens, during the conversation, had driven from Svea Road toward Gärdet. It wasn't far, just a few kilometers, with almost no traffic at all. When he arrived at the right address on the right street and turned his eyes to the top floor, one window was lit despite the late hour. She was awake.

N either of them spoke for a long time. They were standing next to each other inside an illuminated mountain room, breathing dry air, surrounded by the smell of cellar and gun oil. It was that real surreal moment, again. Because what they were looking at didn't exist.

"Infiltrator."

When Piet Hoffmann finally began to speak, and Latifi allowed himself to listen, Hoffmann had to go back in order to go forward.

"That's what I was."

"Infiltrator?"

"Yes."

Latifi rocked on the soles of his feet while his eyes drowned in the pallets of thousands of unused machine guns. He seemed to consider it, then nodded.

"Then I think I get it. Get you."

"For many years, I was the Swedish police's most important tool for taking down organized crime. I exposed criminals who were convinced I was their best friend. My work led to many arrests and aborted robberies. But this, Latifi, is by far the most significant thing I have ever done. Giving this to you. Knowing you'll make sure these weapons are destroyed. And that no one else will have to die for this bizarre fucking scene we're standing in the middle of, it will almost give these hellish weeks meaning."

Latifi was still rocking. But not as visibly.

"And now you expect me to say thank you and let you go?"

"Basically."

"Even though you killed at least three people? I have colleagues who wouldn't ask a single question about three lives if they got ten thousand machine guns on their CVs. But I'm not one of them. I see a murderer. No matter the reason."

"I exchanged their lives for others. *It's you or me and I care more about me than you, so I choose me.* Right? And I'd do it again."

The huge mountain room seemed like its own version of reality.

The sound carried like nowhere else, bounced silently and freely then rapidly ebbed away, the light was intense and intrusive, even the air pressure seemed different. How could that be?

Standing close like they were, shoulder to shoulder and staring into each other's future, was a very strange feeling.

As if nothing mattered.

"So do what you think you have to do, Latifi."

As if everything did.

"Arrest me—or let me go."

A melia Schmidt. That's what stood on the door. A handwritten note taped over a more permanent name—she must be subletting. He knocked on the door, and it reminded him of another knock on another door in another time, strangely muted, strangely hollow. Ewert Grens waited in the sleeping stairwell, knocked again. And again. And again. Until hesitant steps crossed a creaking wood floor and the lock whined as it was turned.

"Superintendent?"

She cracked the door. He glimpsed an eye, half a mouth.

"Yes. It's me. I saw the light was on."

"Yes?"

"I came here because I want to talk to you."

She said nothing, did nothing.

"Did you understand what I said, Amelia?"

"Give me five minutes. I have to get dressed."

She pulled the door closed again, and Grens was left in a stairwell where every sound echoed: the scrape of a foot became a dull rumble; clearing one's throat, an angry roar. And when the beep arrived inside his inner pocket, an incoming text message, it sounded like an ominous emergency alarm. Grens took out his phone and opened a text message from Nils Krantz.

> MATCH.
> POLICE ACADEMY STUDENT.
> ACCORDING TO STUDENT REGISTRY
> A CADET IN YOUR UNIT.
> AMELIA SCHMIDT.

Maybe deep down he had still been hoping that he was wrong. That he could knock on the door one last time, shout through the letterbox that this conversation could wait for tomorrow, then wish her a good night and leave. That was no longer possible. So he sent a text message to Hermansson and Sundkvist.

> SANDHAMNS STREET 25.
> IMMEDIATE REINFORCEMENTS.
> WATCH MY SIGNAL.

He'd just finished when the lock was turned again, and now Amelia's face, though more than an eye and half a mouth, was still obscured by an only partially open door. They observed each other silently, just as they had when they'd sat on the sofa at the Hoffmann family's hideout. And just like earlier, it started to feel awkward.

"Can I come in?"

And didn't get any better when she wouldn't open the door wide enough for him.

"Amelia? I have to come inside. We need to talk. About things that aren't appropriate for a stairwell chat."

Another moment of hesitation.

Then it was as if she suddenly made up her mind, no longer stared at him, and allowed the door to swing wide. Ewert Grens stepped into a young person's apartment, brighter colors than at his home, furniture that didn't take as much energy as his own. A living space that seemed easy and simple to enjoy. In one corner there was a small workplace with a computer connected to three huge screens. Was it from there that she had observed Piet Hoffmann's home, his office, and the apartment where one of his employees was killed?

"So, Ameila . . . you're still awake?"

"I couldn't sleep."

He pointed to an armchair with a dozen colorful cushions on it; his leg and hip hurt, like always, and she gestured for him to sit.

"You shot two people. Saved the lives of twice as many. It's natural not to be able to relax, let alone sleep."

"Is that why I'm receiving this visit—in the middle of the night? Debriefing? If so, Superintendent, you can leave here with a clear conscience. They offered someone for me to talk to a couple of hours ago. A psychologist. But I told them no thanks."

After their first few meetings, she'd reminded him of a modern version of Anni. Or a younger Hermansson. Someone who was a little smarter and braver than everyone else. And what she just said should have added to that impression.

"No. That's not why I'm here. And I'm pretty sure you know that."

But now he saw someone else. So much younger.

"Please sit down, Amelia."

With stains on her dress and a cake with five candles waiting for her, singing Happy Birthday as if it were the most important task in the whole world.

"Opposite me, please."

She shook her head.

"I'd rather stand."

"You don't need to be afraid. I came unarmed. I want to find a solution."

"A solution?"

"Just you and me. We can take my car to Kronoberg jail. No big arrest, just you and me because we choose to trust each other."

She had hidden her gun behind her back, stuffed it into her waistband. That's how she got dressed while he was waiting in the stairwell.

"We're not going anywhere."

"You're not gonna shoot me. I know that. Because we mean something to each other."

She'd heard what he said. For a moment it lay there between them. Like a possibility. Until she shook his words off.

"I don't want to shoot you. But I'll do it if you force me to."

"You won't shoot me just like you couldn't let the Hoffmann family die. Because after everything that's happened, you know the difference. Between right and wrong."

She laughed. Not scornfully or heartily. Emptily.

"Superintendent, there's no such thing as right or wrong. All of that ended in an apartment seventeen years ago."

Ewert Grens looked at the young woman.

And she looked at him.

And for the first time it didn't feel strained or awkward.

"Now and then, Amelia . . . I've let people go. Despite being guilty of a crime. Because in some cases justice and the law are two different things. I considered doing that for you. But those I've allowed to go were victims who made the wrong decision at the last minute. You're also a victim, my God, *I* know that. But you made your choice. You decided quite consciously to do what you did. To take other people's lives. I can't let you go. But if you put down the gun and come with me peacefully and quietly to the station, I will do everything in my power to make sure your crimes are seen in the only possible light. In light of what happened back then, long ago, when we first met."

S he paused in the hall, leaning against the door of the living room, listening to her three children breathe. They were sleeping. Safely. She'd been walking around Ewert's large apartment since he left it in the middle of the night without explaining where he was going or why he looked so upset. Nor had she asked, it wasn't her place, and she knew from those times when she'd seen a look like that on Piet's face that it was useless.

She had stood on the balcony just as Grens usually did, and she understood why; there was a special kind of peace out there. She'd sat in his worn leather armchair in the small library, saw the portraits on the wall of two young police officers in their brand-new uniforms, Ewert and the woman who must have been Anni. But she couldn't rest. And it didn't matter. It was enough that the children were. As she headed into the kitchen to fill a kettle with water and make herself a cup of tea, her phone rang. The only voice she wanted to hear.

"Hello, my beloved wife."

"Hello, my beloved husband."

They could have hung up after that. It was enough, no more explanation was needed.

But while they both held their phones they started to weep. First Piet, then Zofia. Not violently—just a slow, shared crying.

They were alive. They were uninjured.

"Tomorrow, we'll be together again, Zofia, we can hold each other."

"Tomorrow?"

"I found a solution. With a very wise man down here. He got something from me, and I got my freedom from him. We promised each other we would never meet again. Never have to see each other again. Sometimes it's that simple."

They wept no more.

Peace, that's what they felt.

A calm that a body truly allows inside.

don't have any children."

"Why?"

"Never worked out."

Ewert Grens sat in an armchair surrounded by pillows with a gun pointed at his chest. And the only thing he could come up with to talk about was the daughter or son he never had, because that was the only thing that seemed natural.

"But there is one child I've thought about, who's followed me, and who I've wondered about over the years—where she ended up, how she was doing."

They looked at each other again. He'd been so sure she wouldn't shoot. He wasn't anymore. Her intense gaze was single-minded and defeated at the same time, though that was impossible, and somehow she stared straight through him in a way he'd never experienced before. No matter how long you live, no matter how many people you meet, there's always something new.

"A little girl who hopped around her siblings' bedrooms on one leg at a time. And who leaned her head on my shoulder when I carried her out."

Her hand was just as steady, her gaze as sharp. She'd

heard him, maybe even listened and understood, but she wasn't letting it get close to her, not losing control for even a second.

"Until I was a teenager, I had no real memories of my father. I couldn't reach him. But you, Superintendent Grens, I could remember. Not your name or who you were, but just that you existed—I could always call to mind how you lifted me up, held me, protected me. Sometimes I wondered if you were real or just something I dreamed up. Maybe I was remembering wrong."

So far she'd stood with her back to her small kitchen, now she moved toward the window, glanced out quickly and then back at Grens again.

"I see your reinforcements have arrived."

"It doesn't matter. What I said still applies—if you let me arrest you, here, just you and I will go to Kronoberg. No one gets hurt, no drama. And you won't get the book thrown at you. Trust me just like you trusted me back then. You're still young, Amelia, you have a long life ahead of you, when you're released and all this is finally over, forever."

"You know my name isn't Amelia. You also know, Superintendent Grens, that this will never be over for me."

Amelia who had once been Hannah who had once been Zana, was now just herself. It was as if he was meeting every version of her at the same time. A little girl who was reinventing herself. She'd been as clever as she was patient. Applying to the police academy, positioning herself in the right place to seek the answers she needed, then participating in the investigation of her own revenge and using every available scrap of information to stay ahead of them, whether it was stolen cell phones or technically advanced equipment hidden in the unit's corridor.

"Seventy-two hours, Superintendent. That's how long you could hold him without proof, and that's how long you could stop me from finishing this. The same amount of time I—according to the autopsy records I've now read—lived with my dead family."

A few days and a few nights.

He couldn't even begin to imagine how that would have affected a child who had lost everything she knew.

"Amelia, I . . . or do you want me to call you Zana? Like back then? I can . . ."

"You were right at the time, Superintendent. The man you once arrested and were forced to release—that *was* the man who ordered the murders of my family and who took over my father's business. He moved back to Albania and a town called Shkodër, close to the border of Montenegro, but you probably know that already. I tracked him down there. I did what you did, interrogated him, but I was better—there were no rules to restrain me. And I remember every word he said. *Listen, little girl, this is how you do it. If you wanna go on like this, you have to learn. You go in and shoot the kids first. Then you tell the person you want answers from that they can make a new family. And then, whether you get your answers or not, you shoot them afterward.* I remember how he looked at me while I held a gun to his head, his eyes were so alive while he tried to provoke me. *That's what you do—you don't shoot from the top, you shoot from the bottom up. Like we did to your family.* He knew he was going to die. So he described their deaths to me in graphic detail. It was like if he was taking my family away from me again, do you understand, Superintendent Grens?"

She glanced out the window again. And the whole time she kept her gun pointed at him. She opened the blinds even farther, pulled them up completely, the summer night would soon turn to dawn, the darkness to timid light. Grens tried to meet her eyes, to reach her, share something with her, it's harder to kill someone once they've done that.

"If I'd solved the case then. Found the evidence I was missing. We wouldn't have to be here today. You wouldn't be standing there with a loaded weapon pointed at me, you wouldn't have had to avenge your family's murders."

"He wanted me to shoot him. Quickly. For the same reason my mother spit in his face—she'd already figured out what he told me long after, she was going to die, no matter what."

"Zana, I . . ."

"You're right. You didn't catch him then. But I never would have found him unless you, Superintendent, had found him first."

She leaned back, pushing her back against the window. Then she cocked the gun with a slow, obvious movement.

And suddenly Grens understood.

She was doing the same thing.

Right now.

She was trying to provoke her own death.

"No!"

He was just about to stand up, run toward her, stand between her and the window, but she put her index finger on the trigger and started to squeeze.

"Sit down if you want to survive!"

She meant it.

He was sure of it now.

"Zana—I know what you're doing."

"Good. Then I want you to shoot me from the front, afterward. Two times. You know what the distance should be between forehead and temple. I want it to look exactly like my parents and siblings."

"I won't accept being forced to shoot you, please, listen, let me . . ."

"If you try to stop me then I'll take your life first and then let them take mine."

"I won't allow you to die!"

"You should have thought of that before you prevented me from using Hoffmann to take over the Swedish arms market. Or from taking out Zaravic, the only one left besides me who was in my home that day. Being the only survivor is hell, Grens! And I'm finally going to finish what they probably should have finished back then—because I'll never let you put me in a fucking prison or a fucking institution."

Then she raised the gun.

With the same exaggerated slowness she'd used to cock it.

And fired.

Above him. Beside him. Ewert Grens saw that—but his reinforcements outside couldn't. Even though he was rushing toward her. So they did what they were supposed to do—shot the perpetrator who was exposed in the window.

She fell forward, into his arms.

E wert Grens held her lifeless body, gently stroked her still warm cheek.

Soon he would carry her out one more time.

And she would lean her heavy head against his shoulder.